"Crosby's plot is taut and her dialogue crisp. A touch of history and a wealth of suspense make this novel a journey not to be missed."
—*Mystery News*

"Filled with an insider's knowledge of wines and the wine industry. . . . Crosby has concocted a rare vintage that offers many subtle flavors of romance, scandal, passion, and violence."
—*Alfred Hitchcock Mystery Magazine*

THE CHARDONNAY CHARADE

"An engaging mystery with likeable characters. . . . a quick and fun read."
—Associated Press

"Complex, likeable Lucie's suspenseful second is another hit."
—*Kirkus Reviews*

"A wine lover who delighted in history class and kicks back with mysteries couldn't ask for much more."
—Washingtonian.com

"Nicely plotted and paced. . . . A particular treat for oenophiles."
—*Booklist*

"Deft use of setting . . . and pleasingly drawn characters."
—*Chicago Sun-Times*

"Plot twists and romantic tension add body, developing into a smooth finish."
—*Publishers Weekly*

THE MERLOT MURDERS

Also by Ellen Crosby

Moscow Nights
The Merlot Murders
The Chardonnay Charade
The Bordeaux Betrayal

THE
RIESLING
RETRIBUTION

⚬⚬⚬

A Wine Country Mystery

ELLEN CROSBY

POCKET BOOKS

New York   London   Toronto   Sydney

Pocket Books
A Division of Simon & Schuster, Inc.
1230 Avenue of the Americas
New York, NY 10020

First Pocket Books paperback edition August 2010

POCKET and colophon are registered trademarks of Simon & Schuster, Inc.

For information about special discounts for bulk purchases, please contact Simon & Schuster Special Sales at 1-800-506-1949 or business@simonandschuster.com.

The Simon & Schuster Speakers Bureau can bring authors to your live event. For more information or to book an event contact the Simon & Schuster Speakers Bureau at 1-866-248-3049 or visit our website at www.simonspeakers.com.

Cover design by John Vairo Jr.

Manufactured in the United States of America

10 9 8 7 6 5 4 3 2 1

ISBN 978-1-4391-3764-2
ISBN 978-1-4391-6599-7 (ebook)

For my sons, Peter, Matt, and Tim

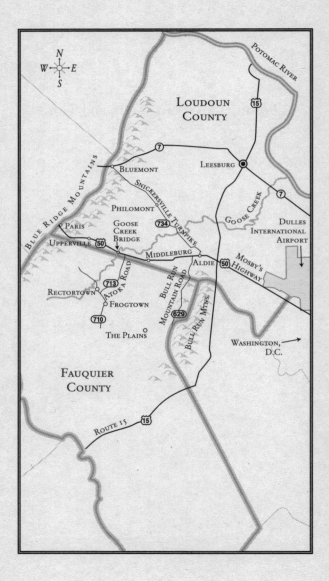

MONTGOMERY ESTATE VINEYARD

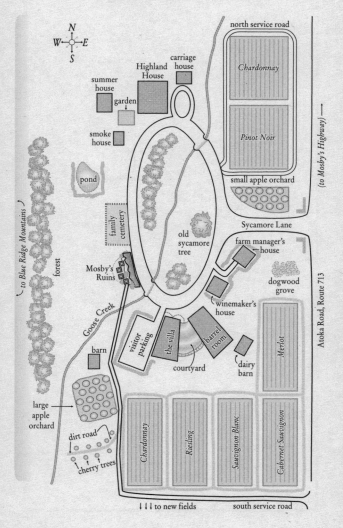

Something of vengeance I had tasted for the first time; as aromatic wine it seemed, on swallowing, warm and racy: its after-flavor, metallic and corroding, gave me a sensation as if I had been poisoned.

—Charlotte Brontë

Be awfully nice to 'em goin' up because you're gonna meet 'em all comin' down.

—Jimmy Durante

Chapter 1

⸺◦◦◦⸺

We all have a right to our private lives; it's living a secret life that gets us in trouble. At least, that's been my experience. Either the house of cards comes crashing down when the lies and deceit finally catch up with us, or we die with our secrets and someone uncovers them after we're gone. Either way, we break the heart of a loved one, and that's our legacy.

I own a vineyard at the foothills of the Blue Ridge Mountains in Virginia on a five-hundred-acre farm that has been in my family almost as long as this country has existed. Every Montgomery who lived here for the last two centuries is buried in a brick-enclosed cemetery that sits atop a hill near my home and commands a particularly breathtaking view of the mountains. My parents lie in the two newest graves.

Every few weeks I make a point of stopping by the place and always find peace and tranquility there. I spend most of the time at my mother's grave, leaning against her headstone and talking to her as the clouds drift across the Blue Ridge in a pretty tableau of chiaroscuro. I do right by Leland, too—my father preferred his children to call him by his first name—although I don't stay long with him or talk much.

They say God gives us families so we don't have to fight with strangers. My father somehow managed to be both family and stranger to my brother and sister and me. Each time I stare at his polished granite tombstone with its chiseled epitaph—"The acts of this life are the destiny of the next"—an Eastern proverb that seemed more warning than prophecy in Leland's case—I wonder about the man he was and the layered life he hid from us. Leland had done a good job of keeping secrets about some of the acts of his life, but in the two years since he passed away, so far nothing he had done had altered my destiny, or that of my siblings.

Though that was about to change.

Today's visit to the cemetery on a sultry late July afternoon was brief. I had picked my mother some fragrant pale pink Renaissance roses from her garden. She planted the bush shortly before she died eight years ago, a few months before my twenty-first birthday, and never saw it bloom. If she had, I know it would have been one of her favorites.

When I had finished, I got back in the two-seater Gator and drove to a remote part of the farm where I'd agreed to let a group of men spend a weekend shooting at one another. That probably sounds sinister, but it's not. A person can't tread on a patch of land around here that hasn't somehow been part of the Civil War, a fact that still eats at plenty of folks. Of all the states that fought in the war, none suffered like we did in Virginia. Gettysburg lasted four horrific days. We had four years of misery.

So when B. J. Hunt, who owned Hunt & Sons Funeral Home, approached me last year and asked if I'd allow Company G of the 8th Virginia, his reenactment unit, to stage the 1861 Battle of Ball's Bluff on my land, how could I say no?

Especially when B.J. said the local battle wasn't often reenacted, meaning we'd not only draw spectators and participants from all over the country but the vineyard would also get a healthy shot of national publicity.

I am not martial in my interests, nor do I hunt and shoot, unlike my father who was an expert marksman, but I do honor my forebears and our history. The real Ball's Bluff, now preserved as a national battlefield and a park, is a few miles down the Old Carolina Road at the edge of the Potomac River, and is the site of the third-smallest military cemetery in the United States.

B.J. and his reenactors did not want to fight on hallowed ground, but they did want to stage their event as close to the battlefield as possible, preferably someplace near water. On October 21, 1861, Union soldiers had taken a few small boats across the Potomac from Maryland to Virginia, expecting to find a deserted Confederate camp near the town of Leesburg. What happened instead was a day-long series of skirmishes that ended with the panicked retreat of Federals down the cliffs of Ball's Bluff into the fast-moving Potomac. The sight of dozens of bloated bodies in blue floating downriver to Washington, as far away as Mount Vernon, so horrified President Lincoln and his Congress that a commission was established to oversee the conduct of the war from then on, forcing Union commanders to answer to a bunch of nonmilitary lawmakers.

Goose Creek, one of the Potomac's tributaries, runs through the middle of my farm. Though it meanders mostly through woods, the creek also skirts a large field beyond the vines that B.J. said would be an ideal place to hold the reenactment, now scheduled to take place in less than two weeks.

I was a few dozen yards from the field when the Gator, anemic sounding ever since I'd left the cemetery, stalled and died. I turned the key in the ignition and pumped the gas, hearing nothing but dead-sounding clicks. I was about to climb down for a closer look at the engine—though to be honest, I wouldn't know what I was looking for if it hit me in the face—when the ominous sound of wind rushing through the treetops made me look up. The birds suddenly had gone silent. We were in for a storm. A fast-moving one, too.

The weather forecast hadn't said anything about a tornado, but there was no mistaking the ropy-looking gray funnel that had materialized out of nowhere on the horizon, spewing debris like dirty smoke. The dust cloud swelling at its base was shaped like an old-fashioned oil lamp, and the twister, rising in the middle, had the furious torque and spin of an angry genie.

As though its appearance was a cue for what came next, a lead-colored wall of clouds descended from the sky like a curtain slamming down on a stage. The wind picked up, twisting tree branches unnaturally until all I could see were the undersides of leaves flashing like millions of silvered coins.

I fished my cell phone out of my pocket and started to call Quinn Santori, my winemaker, until I remembered that he was twenty miles away at a meeting of the winemakers' roundtable in Delaplane. Instead I hit the speed-dial number for Chance Miller, our new field manager, and heard him say, "Hello, Lucie," before the display flashed "call lost . . . searching for service" and went blank. The storm must have knocked out reception from the tower.

Across the field lightning arced the sky like God was throwing down pitchforks. I tossed the phone, now a lightning-magnet, in the Gator's open glove compartment and started counting. One-Mississippi. I got only to four when the crack of thunder came, sounding like it had split open the earth.

A hard, slanting rain moved in, slapping my shoulder-length hair in my eyes and tearing at my clothes. In my head I heard the litany of warnings television weather reporters shout as they are lashed by rain and wind in some perilous edge-of-the-world location, moments before they bolt for safety when the camera is turned off. Seek shelter immediately! The safest place is the basement of a house! If you do not have a basement, find an interior room and barricade yourself inside! Cover yourself with a mattress or hide behind a piece of furniture! Abandon all cars and mobile homes! They will not protect you! Seek shelter immediately!

The warnings never provided for the foolhardy soul who wasn't about to be whisked out of the path of destruction by a waiting car. The tornado danced closer, teetering and swaying like a drunkard. If I didn't get out of here soon, I was doomed. I fought against the panic crawling through my mind and tried to focus on my options. How fast did tornados travel? How much time did I have?

The surrounding woods were no safer than the field. The vineyard, where wooden posts could be uprooted and trellis wire become as sharp as a razor, was a worse idea. Get to a low place, that's what they always said.

On my way here I had driven across a stone bridge my great-great-great-grandfather built across Goose Creek shortly after the Civil War. Calling it a bridge was a stretch, since it was really more of a culvert. But it was nearer than the winery or my house, both at least two miles away. Another flash of lightning looked like it struck something in the woods. My skin tingled as I heard the crack of timber splitting.

I grabbed my cane from the Gator and began moving toward the bridge. Four years ago an automobile accident left me with a crippled left foot and a devastating pronouncement from my doctor that I would spend the rest of my life in a wheelchair. I changed doctors until I found one who saw things differently. It took surgery and months of therapy and swimming until I finally managed to get around with the help of a walker. Later I graduated to a cane, which I still need for balance and support. But I can no longer run—and I never will—other than managing an awkward lope like I'm half of a shackled team in a three-legged race.

The wind shifted and I glanced over my shoulder. The darkening wall of clouds obliterated the sky and it sounded as though a jet or an out-of-control freight train was bearing down on me. I dragged my bad foot like a reluctant child. The dirt road dissolved into a muddy, rutted stream and my right work boot made a sucking sound with each step.

How much longer until I reached the bridge? What would happen if the tornado overtook me before I got there? Would it pick me up, like Dorothy in *The Wizard of Oz*, and spin me around, depositing me safely somewhere else? At least Dorothy had been inside a house. What really happened to people who got caught in a tornado's vortex? Were they hurled through the air like human javelins? Or was the drop in barometric pressure so intense it literally tore them apart?

The outline of the bridge, blurred and softer looking in the downpour, loomed ahead. I slid down the embankment, grabbing a branch to keep from landing on my rear or tumbling into the creek. Underneath the air smelled of cobwebs and decomposing vegetation. I threw my cane into the darkness, coughing and swallowing what tasted like dirt, as I felt around for a dry spot that wasn't some animal's lair. The rising creek rushed past me in a torrent, but the noise could not drown out the apocalyptic sound of what was happening outside.

The bridge was too low and shallow to stand. Instead I knelt as though I were praying and dug my fingernails into the crumbling mortar between the old stones. The rain changed to hail, dancing like hot grease in a frying pan as it crackled on the ground and hissed on the water. Wind buffeted the bridge, sending debris hurtling at me with such force it seemed to penetrate my skin.

Only one other time in my life did I wonder with the same desperation if these were my last minutes on earth. For months after my crippling accident, I woke from sweat-drenched dreams where I'd relived the slow-motion moment I knew the car driven by a now ex-boyfriend would not make the turn and instead slam with a killing force into the stone wall at the entrance to the vineyard. Now the storm slammed into me with that same violence, inhabiting my body and crowding my mind like a demon that would need exorcising.

The bridge shuddered as the tornado passed by—how close I couldn't tell—but so much debris and dirt rained down that I was sure it would collapse and bury me alive. Gradually the throbbing diminished and the roaring grew dimmer. My arc-shaped view of the world changed from black to gray. Then the rain stopped as suddenly as someone shutting off a faucet.

I found my cane and crawled back outside. My muddy clothes stuck to me like skin and my hair felt like seaweed when I pushed it off my face. To the west the sky was still death colored, but to the east the tornado seemed to have sucked the storm clouds with it, leaving behind blue skies and improbable sunshine.

The hail had transformed the summer landscape to a

winter scene that dazzled and glittered. In the distance, the yellow-and-green Gator—exactly where I'd left it—was a bright blotch of color against a frozen carpet.

The tornado's wide swath stretched from the edge of B.J.'s battlefield through the woods. I squinted at the low-slung Catoctin Mountains to my south, and the Blue Ridge, which filled the skyline to the west, and made some calculations. The twister had traveled from southwest to northeast. On that trajectory it probably sliced right through the vines in the south vineyard, which meant it might have destroyed more than half of our grapes. I closed my eyes and contemplated the loss of a few million dollars' worth of vines and thousands of cases of wine. But my life had been spared, and if the tornado missed my home and the winery—and God was merciful—then everyone who worked here had survived as well.

I retrieved my phone. Still no service. Unless someone came looking for me, I had a two-mile hike back to the vineyard. Before I left, though, I wanted to see up close the gash the tornado had cut through the field.

At the edge of the trench a dome-shaped object gleamed in the late afternoon sunlight. I knelt and brushed away dirt to get a better look at it. The first thing I saw were empty eye sockets staring into space. There was a perfect triangular orifice where the nose had been. The mandible with its lower row of teeth was missing, but the maxilla and top teeth were intact. Distant thunder rumbled like a drumroll near the vineyard.

It was a hell of a way to announce that the tornado had unearthed a human skull.

Chapter 2

❧

Those dead eyes seemed to bore through me, and the mouth, or what remained of it, looked like it might have been formed as a scream. Or did I imagine it? I stumbled back from the trench as though whoever it was might rise out of the ground like a Halloween apparition and say "boo!"

What was a human skull doing out here, in the middle of nowhere? Everyone in my family—at least as far as I knew—was buried in our cemetery. Who was this?

We had seen our share of Civil War conflicts since this region had been the territory of the Gray Ghost—the nickname for Colonel John Singleton Mosby, legendary commander of the Confederacy's most famous guerrilla brigade. Known for daring expeditions and midnight raids on Union supplies and horses, Mosby and his Rangers tormented the enemy with their ability to escape into the countryside and elude capture, hiding behind the miles of stacked stone walls that checkerboarded fields and lined roadsides, or taking shelter in barns and outbuildings offered by the locals. One of those buildings was a tenant house on our land, which

Union soldiers burned during their search for Mosby. Maybe these remains belonged to a Union soldier who'd been part of that expedition? A Confederate in these parts would have been given a proper burial.

But the grave was shallow, an unmarked site in a deserted field. No casket, not even a shroud. Besides, the skull hadn't decomposed enough to have been here for more than a century and a half. Whoever this was had been left in an obscure spot on purpose. A grave like this said nobody had given up a prayer as they shoveled dirt over the body.

The sound of an engine broke the silence and I stood up to see who it was. Chancellor Miller, driving the Mule, another ATV, like he stole it, raced across the field toward the Gator. I raised my arms above my head and waved. He waved back as he caught sight of me, changing course in my direction. Bruja, his black Labrador retriever, barked from the passenger seat like a parent scolding a child who got lost at the shopping mall. Chance pulled up and cut the ignition, vaulting out of the Mule. The dog followed.

"You all right, Lucie?" He pulled me to him in an unexpected, fierce bear hug. "You're soaking wet. Shivering, too. Let's get you out of here."

He rubbed my arms briskly, trying to warm me up. Chance's eyes were the same dusky blue as the Blue Ridge, his hair the color of sunshine, and he had a scar underneath his left eye that he said he got when he went after a stranger who was beating a stray dog with a broken whiskey bottle.

In the few months since he'd started working for us, our relationship had never been anything other than strictly professional, though I'd occasionally felt a glimmer of something from him and wondered if he wanted there to be more.

"I'm okay. Nothing broken. I'm fine." I eased out of his

arms, aware of his touch and the surprising odor of alcohol on his breath this early in the day. "What about the others? Was anyone hurt?"

He dialed right down through the false bravado. "You don't look too okay to me. Why don't you let me take you to the emergency room? You ought to get checked out. No offense, but you look pretty banged up."

"As bad as that?" I tried to smile, but my voice wavered. "It's dirt, not bruises. And thanks, but I don't need to go to any hospital."

"Come on, just to check—"

"No. No hospital, thanks." I shook my head. "What about everyone else? You haven't said—"

He brushed my arm with his fingers. "All accounted for. No one hurt. Power's out, so the villa's dark, but the generator's working in the barrel room. Everyone in the crew sat on the courtyard wall and watched it. One of the guys had a bottle of Scotch so we all took turns. Jesus, God. I've never seen anything like that in my life."

"So the buildings are okay, then? Do you know anything about my house, or—?"

"The winery's fine. I haven't seen your house but I'm sure it's okay, too. The tornado wasn't moving in that direction." He spoke as if he were soothing a child. "What happened to you? We were afraid you were . . . I mean, we didn't see how anyone could survive out here when that twister came through. Where'd you go? What did you do?"

"I managed to get to the bridge and hide underneath. The tornado went down the middle of the field and missed me. I was lucky."

I nodded toward the creek as Bruja shoved her wet nose under my hand, seeking attention. She wagged her tail as I bent and scratched her muzzle, grateful for the distraction. I didn't want Chance to read anything more in my eyes or he'd know I'd expected to die out here, too.

"Damn right you were lucky. What were you doing here anyway?"

I straightened up. "I stopped by the cemetery, then decided to check out the reenactment site one more time. Probably would have made it back to the vineyard before the tornado came through if the Gator hadn't died on me."

We were back to being boss and employee. He knew what I meant. The equipment and crew were his responsibility. Just this morning Quinn complained that we seemed to be jinxed because every time he turned around something else had broken down or gone missing. His way of reminding me that he hadn't been in favor of hiring Chance, even though we'd been desperate for a new manager after Chance's predecessor took a job at a Charlottesville vineyard to be near his fiancée.

It still irked Quinn that Chance's easy smile and obvious charm had seduced me into ignoring the thinness of the experience on his résumé. But even Quinn had to admit that when Chance helped out in the tasting room on weekends—not in his job description—he could have sold bottled dishwater and people would have bought cases of it.

The Gator breaking down was another matter. The dusky blue eyes grew cloudy and his pupils became black pinpricks. Quinn would have given him hell for something like this.

He folded his arms across his chest. "I don't know how that could have happened, but I'll get it towed and have a look at it right away. Thank God you're all right. I'm really sorry about this."

I didn't want to say it was okay, because it wasn't. "Be sure and let me know what you find."

He nodded, eyes still narrowed at the chill in my voice, but he accepted the rebuke without further protest. "Of course. As soon as I drive you home I'll get on it. I—hey, girl! What have you got there?"

I whirled around. While we'd been talking, Bruja had wandered away. Now she was gnawing on what looked like a large stick less than five feet from where I'd found the skull.

Another bone. This one was about eighteen inches long.

"Oh, God, Bruja, no! Chance, I think that's a human bone. When the tornado plowed through the field it unearthed a grave. The skull's over there." I pointed at the site. "What Bruja's got could be . . . more of it."

He looked from me to the dog, happily chewing on her find. "Bruja! Drop it!"

Bruja looked up with implicit trust in her liquid brown eyes and opened her mouth. The bone fell to the ground and Chance ran to her. The dog's tail thumped happily against the ground.

"Good girl, good girl." Chance knelt and examined the bone.

It had absorbed the color of the soil, and both ends had been chewed long before Bruja got to it. I wondered how scattered the rest of the remains were.

I joined him, scratching the dog behind her ears. "Do you think it's human? It's big enough to be part of an arm or a leg. Unless it's from a deer."

"I don't know. If it was found this close to your skull, my guess is it's human."

He went over and examined the skull. The sun had warmed up the afternoon, melting the hail. Somewhere in the woods a woodpecker rat-a-tat-tatted against a tree.

"Any idea who it is?" he asked.

"None. At first I wondered if it was a Civil War soldier, but now I think the grave's too new."

He nodded. "It's definitely not Civil War. There hasn't been enough decomposition."

"You sound like you know what you're talking about."

"A few years ago I worked at a retirement home." He shrugged. "People died. I used to help out when the funeral directors came around. They told me all kinds of stuff about dead bodies and preserving them. How long it takes bone to decay, tissue decomposition, stuff like that. Looks like there might still be some hair attached to this skull, but it's hard to tell unless we dig some more. I could find a stick and just—"

"Oh, God, please don't! We really shouldn't touch anything. In fact, I need to call the sheriff and report it."

Chance had service on his phone, but when I got through to 911 the woman who took my call sounded harassed and overwhelmed.

"A skeleton?" she said. "I'll send someone over to check it out, but look, hon, we just had a tornado come through here and my deputies are backed up from hell to breakfast dealing with it. We'll get to you, but probably not for a while. If the guy's not bleeding and he's been buried for a decade or two, another few hours won't kill him, if you know what I mean."

"I know what you mean," I said, and hung up.

"What did they say?" Chance asked as I handed back his phone.

"The dispatcher said it'll take some time before they send someone on account of the tornado."

"In that case, let's get you back to your house so you can clean up and change."

He traced his finger from just under my left eye along my cheekbone and showed me the smudge of dirt. My face grew hot at his touch.

"Ready?" he asked.

I pointed in the direction of the south vines, hoping he hadn't noticed that I was blushing. "Not before I see the tornado damage to the vines. If the power's out at the villa, then it's out at my house, too. Which means I don't have any water since the well pump won't be working. I'm in no rush to get home."

He shrugged. "Okay. Let's go."

He drove me by the broken-down Gator so I could retrieve my phone, which still showed no service.

"Where's Quinn?" I asked. "Has anybody heard from him lately?"

"He called the barrel room just before I left to find you, wondering where you were. Said he was on his way back from that winemakers' meeting. They didn't even know there was a tornado over in Delaplane."

"I'd better call him," I said, "and let him know what happened."

I borrowed Chance's phone again and dialed in for my messages. Four, all from Quinn, exhorting me to call him right away and keeping me posted on his current whereabouts as he drove back to Atoka. By the third message he was shouting. The fourth was a long moment of silence followed by a groan and a curse before he hung up.

I dialed his number. He answered in the middle of the first ring, sounding mad. "Where the hell is she?"

He thought I was Chance. "Right here."

"Lucie? Where have you been? How come you're calling on Chance's phone? How come it took you so long to call back?"

"Because we had a little situation with weather here, that's why. I got kind of tied up."

"I know, I know. The tornado. I was worried sick about

you when I found out about it. Tyler told me you were gone
and no one knew where you were. I think he's been drinking."

Tyler Jordan was one of our cellar rats and the son of a
couple who owned a nearby bed-and-breakfast. We'd hired
him to help out with the chores around the winery as a favor
to his parents while he tried to figure out where someone
who'd double-majored in classical studies and kinesiology in
college might get a real job.

"Apparently the crew passed around a bottle of Scotch
when the tornado came through. It was unbelievable, Quinn.
Like a preview for the end of the world." I glanced over
at Chance. "I'm going over to look at the new fields with
Chance. Looks like it probably passed through there."

"The new fields?" His dismay was tinged with an extra
measure of regret, more so, I thought, than if we'd lost some
of our oldest—and most valuable—vines.

I knew why.

The vines in those fields were his, planted shortly after he
signed on as our winemaker, the foundation of an ambitious
expansion and gamble we hoped would catapult us from
small boutique winery onto a national stage. Though Quinn
would never admit it, those vines also represented his opportunity to emerge from the oversized shadow of Jacques
Gilbert, his predecessor. Schooled in France in Old World
ways of winemaking and production, Jacques' stamp was still
evident in our wines, our production, and in the field. Even
now, we were still selling some of his wines.

The fact that I revered Jacques and my mother with near-
to-saintly devotion had been at the root of most of the passionate debates between Quinn and me.

The loss of the new vines, though they were still a year
away from their first harvest, meant it would take even

longer before Quinn finally put his imprimatur on Montgomery Estate Vineyard.

"How bad is it?" he asked me now.

"I'll call you as soon as I know."

"Hang on, will you? I'm almost there."

"Where are you?"

"Marshall. Almost to Maidstone Lane."

"Marshall? Maidstone Lane? It'll take you at least twenty, twenty-five minutes to get here."

"No way. See you in ten."

"Serve you right if you get a speeding ticket," I said. "Nothing's going to change if you get here faster."

He groaned again and disconnected.

The tornado had mowed a sweeping path through the Syrah, Malbec, and the edge of the Seyval block. The devastation took my breath away. A few hours ago this had been a lush canopy of green, the vines aligned in neat rows like soldiers, representing promise and optimism and prosperity. Now there was nothing, nothing at all, just a tangled twisted mess of debris and ruin plowed back into the earth. The only thing missing was the salt.

I heard Chance suck in his breath next to me. "Wow."

"We'll have to get a Bobcat in here to clear this out." My voice sounded like it was coming from inside a drum. "Start from scratch with new posts and trellises. New vines."

"I'm sorry, Lucie."

"Yeah. Me, too." I'd never seen tornado damage up close like this, but it was true what they said: A few yards on either side of the path it had taken, the vines were comparatively unscathed, almost like nothing had happened. "At least we can tie up the vines that were blown down by the wind." It still sounded as if someone else were talking.

"Sure. I'll get the guys on it right away. Now let's get you home since you've seen what you wanted to see. You don't need to deal with it this minute—"

"No." I cut him off. "I need to do something. Get the crew out here. I want to start cleaning up today. And get someone to tow the Gator. We need all the equipment we've got."

"I'll take care of it," he said, "if that's what you want. There's a box of trellis ties on the backseat. My pruning shears are there, too."

"Good."

He made the calls as I began tying vines to their trellis wires. Most of the work at a vineyard is tedious and mind-numbingly boring. Anyone who says any different—that we live in some kind of Dionysian paradise, spending our days wandering among rows of vines sipping a glass of wine as we survey God's handiwork—is out of his mind. Quinn downs ibuprofen like candy for his aches and pains, as do I when I've been working in the fields. Some days a song gets stuck in my head and plays over and over like a loop, just to pass the time. Right now I couldn't get the lyrics to "What a Wonderful World" out of my mind. Talk about irony.

Quinn showed up in the other Mule—we owned two of them, one red and one green, like Christmas—about twenty minutes later. Benny, Jesús, and Javier, three of our regular crew, came with him. I didn't understand the rapid-fire Spanish they spoke as they climbed out of their seats, but I didn't need a translation to understand shock and grief.

The look on Quinn's face probably mirrored mine, as if he showed up at a funeral for someone no one expected to die. He was still dressed for the winemakers' roundtable, pressed khakis and one of his favorite Hawaiian print shirts—the silver one with dancing pink martini glasses on it. He wore a thick gold chain around his neck with a cross hanging from it, a stamped silver cuff that was a gift from a Navajo friend on one wrist, and something with leather and steel on the other. Lately he'd started wearing reading glasses and those, too, hung around his neck on a leather cord. He'd probably forgotten to take them off after the meeting.

Most men couldn't pull off that shirt and the jewelry without looking like they were overly in touch with their feminine side. Quinn, as near as I could tell, not only didn't have a feminine side, his masculine side generally ran on overdrive. He was a strictly macho guy with a disciplined toughness that could come across as sexist if you happened to be a woman and he worked for you. Since I was, and he did, I was in a good position to know.

He came straight over to me, worry lines making small canyons in his forehead, his eyes dark as obsidian.

"There's not a traffic light working from Haymarket to Atoka. Flooding, roads closed. It's a mess. The tornado completely missed Delaplane." He stopped and assessed me. "Nobody told me you were out in this. I thought you were at the house or something. My God, you look like you just crawled out of a cave."

"Thanks. It was a bridge."

"Are you out of your mind? Outside in a tornado away from any kind of real shelter? What in the hell were you doing, anyway?"

"I went out to see the reenactment site. The Gator died on me. And I don't need a lecture, okay?"

His eyes automatically went to Chance, who was tightening a trellis wire while Benny propped up the wooden post. Chance seemed to know Quinn was watching him because he raised his head and they stared at each other.

Quinn swung back to me. "Died? We just had it completely overhauled in the spring. Dammit, it *shouldn't* have died."

I'd lost count of how many nails were in the coffin Quinn was building for Chance, but right now I didn't want to deal with it. I rubbed my forehead as a dull ache began to pulse between my eyes.

"We'll find out what happened," I said. "Tyler's going to tow it back to the barn with the pickup."

"Okay, but I'm going over it myself. Jesus, Lucie. You could have been killed out there because of someone's carelessness."

"Or maybe something just wore out."

"Come on. I'll drive you home. You should take it easy." He saw the hesitant look on my face. "Don't tell me you want to stick around here?"

"There's something else."

"You mean, besides the tornado?"

"Because of the tornado. It unearthed a grave near the stone bridge at the edge of the reenactment field," I said. "I found a skull."

He looked stunned. "What's a grave doing in the middle of nowhere?"

"I don't know. But Bruja found another bone a few feet away. Chance and I guessed it was human, too. We thought it might be part of an arm or a leg."

His hand went to his cross and he fingered it. "The dog was chewing on a human bone?"

I nodded.

"That means whoever it is, the remains are scattered around."

"Maybe." I hesitated. "There's another possibility."

"What?" he asked.

"Maybe there's more than one grave."

Chapter 3

⬥⬥⬥

Quinn turned right on Sycamore Lane after we passed through the south vineyard. It was the longer way to my house.

"I want to look at the Pinot and the Chardonnay in the north fields," he said. "Let's see how much cleanup we've got over there. That wind did a lot of damage."

Though the tornado had not passed through here, it had taken its toll in downed leaves, limbs, and small branches. The private gravel road that wound through the vineyard in a lazy ellipse was littered with debris. Wherever I looked, fresh green leaves carpeted the ground.

"Have you checked on your house yet?" I asked as we passed the private cul-de-sac where his cottage and the now-empty farm manager's house sat on the edge of the woods.

"Nope."

He swerved to avoid a large limb and stopped the Mule with a lurch that made me grab the dashboard. I was about to ask what he was doing when I saw that he'd leaned forward so his elbows rested on the steering wheel and his fingertips covered his mouth. He was staring at the old sycamore—or what was left of it—with an expression of shocked disbelief.

The tree that had given the road its name had stood here as long as my family owned this farm. Something—wind or, more likely, lightning—had cleaved it down the middle. The right side had fallen across the road, creating an impenetrable barrier that seemed to reach the sky. What remained upright, a jagged spear of new-looking wood, made me think of a wound so deep it exposed bone.

My eyes filled and I looked away so Quinn wouldn't see the tears. Losing that tree was like a death in the family.

"I'm sorry, Lucie," he said.

"I wish it had been any tree but this one. I even wish it had been my house. That could be rebuilt."

"I know."

It was pointless, but I asked anyway. "Do you think an arborist can save it?"

He started the Mule and shifted into reverse. "I wish I did, but honestly I think it's too far gone."

I nodded and wiped my eyes with the back of my grimy hand.

"We'll still try," he said.

"Must have been an incredible lightning strike to bring it down like this."

"I'll get some of the guys over here with chain saws to clear the road. Let's hope nothing else came down between here and your house."

"Can you let me know when they do that?" I asked. "I can't bear to watch. I need to be sure I'm somewhere else."

"Of course." His voice was gentle. "I promise, I'll take care of it. We'll do our best to save it."

We drove through more storm-wrought debris but

encountered nothing as devastating as the sycamore. I hadn't realized I was holding my breath until he pulled into the circular driveway to my home. Built more than two hundred years ago by my ancestor, Hamish Montgomery, and named in honor of the 77th Highlanders, his regiment that had fought in the French and Indian War, Highland House was a graceful blend of Federal and Georgian architecture made of stone quarried from our land. Hamish had carved the Montgomery clan motto—*"Garde bien"*—in the lintel over the door like a talisman. "Watch well. Take good care." Except for more small branches scattered on the lower-pitched roofs of the two wings, the house looked exactly as it had when I left this morning.

I closed my eyes and said a silent prayer of thanks.

"At least it spared the buildings," Quinn said, pulling up at the front door.

"I know." I let out a long breath. "We're lucky. It could have been so much worse."

"Wonder how long we'll be without power," he said.

"A couple of days, I imagine."

"How are you going to manage a shower with no water?" he asked.

"The water tank will be full, so at least I can get cleaned up even if it's tepid water."

"I think I'll just go—what's your French expression?—au naturel until we get power restored."

"You mean miss the weekly bath on Saturday night?"

He grinned. "Listen, princess, I bathe and shave every day. I change my underwear."

"I'm not touching that." I climbed out of the Mule, glad to be back to our usual exchange of banter. "And I'd better get ready before the sheriff's people get here."

"Any idea who that body is?" he asked. "Maybe it's some black sheep relative who didn't make it inside the family burial ground."

"I thought of that. But there's no coffin and it looks like he was just dumped there in a shallow grave."

"What makes you so sure it's a he? Maybe it's a she."

I shuddered. "I guess we'll find out, won't we?"

"Guess so," he said.

Inside, the house was still and airless. Already I could feel the weight of the outdoor heat filtering into the two-story foyer as it reclaimed the dry air-conditioned coolness. Upstairs, my bedroom would probably soon be unbearable. At least I could sleep in the hammock on the veranda, as I'd done when the air-conditioning system died two years ago. I found camping lanterns, candles, and flashlights in the front hall closet and put them next to Leland's favorite bust of Thomas Jefferson in the foyer alcove. Then I climbed Hamish's grand spiral staircase, watching dust motes swirl around the Waterford chandelier in the dying daylight.

I'd nearly lost the house once in a fire, but I'd rebuilt what had been destroyed. Thank God this time I'd been damn lucky.

I took a sponge bath instead of a shower to save water and didn't bother to dry off. The landline on my bedside table rang as I was in the bathroom pulling my wet hair into a ponytail. The answering machine would be knocked out, but at least the phone worked.

"Two deputies are waiting at the villa for you, and you'll be happy to hear the Gator is back in business," Quinn said when I answered.

"I'll be right there. What was wrong with the Gator?"

He snorted. "Someone put the gas-and-oil mixture we

use for the weed whacker in the tank. I figured it might be some dumbass stunt like that. I drained the tank. Caught it before it fouled the plugs and we had a real mess on our hands."

"So it was an accident."

"Accident my ass. Those gas cans are labeled in English and Spanish plain as the nose on your face. The only way you could have screwed up is if you had your eyes closed while you were filling the damn gas tank," he said. "If I find out who did this, he'll be cleaning wine barrels from now to harvest."

"I'll talk to the guys and say something about paying attention and being more careful."

"That would include your boy Chance."

"He's not 'my boy.' Plus he knows better. It might have been Tyler. He can be sort of scatterbrained."

"You mean the Tyler who caused a volcano this morning when Chance let him top off one of the barrels of Pinot?"

I closed my eyes and rubbed a spot on my forehead. A volcano was our term for filling something too full. If the wine was still fermenting and someone overfilled the barrel, it caused the kind of explosion that resulted from shaking a bottle of beer and opening it, or popping a champagne cork too quickly. Not something anyone wanted to happen to a five-thousand-dollar barrel of wine.

"Yes, okay, *that* Tyler. Maybe he shouldn't be topping off barrels anymore."

"Maybe he shouldn't be working here."

"I promised Jordy and Grace—"

"Yeah, yeah. That we'd babysit him until he finds a real job. Wherever he goes next, he shouldn't be allowed to operate heavy equipment or be around sharp objects." I heard him sigh. "You're the boss, so if you want him to stay, he stays. But wait 'til he forgets to take the valve off one of the tanks and it blows up. Or runs the forklift through it. I do plan to say 'I told you so.'"

"You know, I was sort of dreading the meeting with those deputies," I said. "But after all that cheery news, I think I'm kind of looking forward to it."

"That's good," he said. "Because they can't wait to talk to you."

Though I knew a few of the deputies who worked for the Loudoun County Sheriff's Office, I didn't recognize either of the men who waited by their cruisers when I pulled up in the winery parking lot five minutes later. Their name tags said Mathis and Fontana. Mathis was a gray-haired African American built like a football linebacker, with eyes that looked like they could pin me to a wall, metaphorically speaking. Fontana was small and muscular, dark haired and dark eyed. His uniform stretched taut across his chest, showing off the physique of someone who hit the gym regularly.

After we got through the introductions, Mathis said, "How do we get to where you found the body?"

"It's probably best if I take you there in one of our ATVs," I said. "Some of the terrain is pretty rough on a car, especially if you don't have four-wheel drive."

Mathis sat next to me on the drive over to the grave site and flipped open a spiral notebook. He asked the usual questions.

"Has anyone else been to the site besides you and Mr. Miller?" His voice reminded me of melted butterscotch.

I knew the two of them were going to hate my answer.

"Chance's dog, unfortunately. I'm sorry. It was an accident. She found a bone near the skull and started playing with it."

"You let a dog dig around a grave site?" Fontana said.

"We stopped her as soon as we realized what she was doing. But she wasn't the first animal to get hold of that bone. The ends had already been chewed."

I pulled up a few feet from where I'd found the skull and they got out. Mathis must have had a sixth sense for locating dead bodies because he walked straight over to the place before I could tell him where it was. For a heavy man, he moved gracefully. He knelt and pulled on a pair of latex gloves he got from his back pocket. Fontana photographed the scene. I stayed out of the way and waited.

"Vic," Mathis said, "you'd better call it in. Have them get hold of Noland. And bring a search warrant."

I'd known Bobby Noland, one of my brother Eli's close friends, since we were kids. By the time Bobby was in high school, he'd gone from the honor roll to the detention hall, hanging out with a tough crowd who spent nights getting wasted on booze and drugs at the fields near the old Goose Creek Bridge. At least, that's what I heard. After he graduated I figured Bobby'd leave town, but he surprised everyone by saying he wanted to fight for his country and signing up for the army. Two years later he came home from Afghanistan with a Purple Heart and a Silver Star he didn't want to talk about and joined the sheriff's office. By the time he made detective and got assigned to Narcotics, he'd picked up another award for bravery. A year ago he moved to Homicide.

"You won't need a search warrant," I said to Mathis. "You're welcome to do whatever you need to do."

Fontana joined us. "Noland and the ME are coming. Also a crime scene guy, but that's it for now. Everyone else is busy handling tornado stuff," he told Mathis. To me he said, "Thanks, but Biggie, here, likes to do things by the book, so we'll be getting that search warrant just the same. Saves a lot of headaches down the line, especially if we have to go to court."

Biggie. I'd bet money that's not what his mother named him. But I wasn't going to object if Mathis wanted to dot his i's and cross his t's by getting a search warrant, so I nodded in agreement.

"Do you have any idea how long he's been here?" I asked.

"Long enough to change the terrain," Fontana said. "See how much greener the grass is around here? And that indentation where the ground has collapsed? You'd see it pretty good if you looked down from above—if you knew what you were looking for."

He did an air sketch with his finger indicating where the earth seemed to have settled. "If that other bone belongs to this body, the remains could be pretty scattered. A grave needs to be at least six feet deep so an animal won't dig it up. This one looks like it's no more than two feet."

Mathis stood up and I heard the joints in his knees crack. "You're quite sure you have no idea who this might be, Ms. Montgomery? An old family feud, maybe? Ever hear anyone talk about something like that? How about any skeletons in the closet?" He smiled with his eyes as he peeled off his gloves, but if there had been a wall, I would have been pinned to it. "No pun intended."

I tried to meet his gaze. "We wouldn't be normal if we didn't have our share of problems and a few family secrets, but I can tell you for sure that there are no skeletons in the closet that would lead anyone to kill someone, if that's what you mean."

Mathis kept that laser vision trained on me and I did my best to project self-assured confidence.

"We own five hundred acres, Deputy Mathis. It's a lot

of land. Whoever did this, a complete stranger, could have come and gone without anyone ever seeing him or her."

Mathis nodded, but the expression on his face said he'd heard that one a million times before.

"We're certainly going to check that out," he said. "And I appreciate your cooperation."

"We need to rope off the crime scene," Fontana said. "That means you and any of your employees, and that dog, have to stay away from the area until our investigation is finished."

"Do you have any idea how long that might take?" I asked.

Mathis tucked his gloves in his pocket. "As long as it takes. Two, three days. Maybe longer. Depends what we find."

"After all this time what could you possibly find?" I asked. "Surely it's been too long?"

"You'd be surprised," Mathis said. "Locard's principle doesn't usually let me down."

I took the bait. "What's that?"

"A killer always leaves something at the scene of a crime or else takes something away with him."

"Always?"

He nodded. "Always. That's why it's Locard's *principle*. Make no mistake, Ms. Montgomery. There's no statute of limitations on murder, if this turns out to be a homicide. So if there's anything else you want to tell us, now would be a good time."

Chapter 4

———❦———

"Do I need a lawyer?" I asked.

When had the dynamics shifted, transforming me from a helpful public citizen to someone trying to spin what Mathis seemed to imply was an improbable tale: that I really had no idea how a dead body ended up on my farm?

Now that the storm had passed, the woods were again filled with the pleasantly discordant symphony of birdsong and the cicadas' gentle whirring. A breeze like a warm caress rustled the leaves, carrying the unmistakable baked-earth smells of summer. The tornado seemed like it had happened a lifetime ago.

Mathis and Fontana stood there and watched me.

"You tell us," Fontana said finally. "Do you need a lawyer?"

"I . . . no. I don't."

Mathis shot Fontana a look that seemed to tell him to back off.

"You're not being charged with anything," he said, warming up that rich voice a little. "But if you know something and we find out about it later, you could find yourself in real hot water. Understand?"

"There's nothing you're going to find out because I don't know anything."

Fontana's cell phone chirped.

"It's Noland," he said. To me he added, "Can you give him directions to this place?" I nodded and he handed me the phone.

Bobby Noland knew the layout of my farm almost as well as I did since he'd spent so much time here when we were growing up. He and the medical examiner showed up in a Jeep with the sheriff's department logo on the door a few minutes later. Unlike the deputies who were in uniform, Bobby wore khakis and a black polo shirt with "LCSD, Homicide Division" on it. His badge was clipped to his belt. Though he was only two years older than I, his face had settled into the heavyset demeanor of someone who has seen too much evil and cruelty in his work and understands the burden of keeping that knowledge locked away from the rest of us.

The medical examiner, deeply tanned, fiftyish, and lanky, wore a broad-brimmed leather hat trimmed with what looked like a crocodile band and carried a black leather bag. Up close I could see the result of years in the sun in the age spots on his face and exposed forearms, but there was a youthful spark of animation and interest in his eyes as he looked us over.

Bobby pulled a pack of gum out of his pocket and offered it all around. Only Fontana accepted.

"Hey, Biggie. Hey, Vic. Friedman's coming from the CSU but she'll be awhile. Junie, you know these guys." Bobby stuffed gum into his mouth and said to me, "Lucie, this is Junius St. Pierre. The county medical examiner. "

We shook hands. "Nice to meet you."

"Same here." He drawled "heah" with a Down Under accent—either Australia or New Zealand, I couldn't tell. Like Mathis, he pulled a pair of gloves out of his pocket and went over to examine the skull.

"I guess this is what they mean when they say 'his jaw dropped.'" Junie grinned at Bobby, whose mouth turned up in a small ironic smile. "Poor chap. Wonder what happened to the mandible."

Mathis and Fontana smiled as Junie winked at me.

"No disrespect intended to this fella, you understand," he said.

I nodded, used to morgue humor after listening to Bobby talk about his work. "You can tell it's male? I mean, that he's male?"

"I can't be a hundred percent certain until I see the pelvis, but based on the skull I'd say it was an adult male. Probably Caucasian."

"How do you know all that so fast?" I asked.

"Come here." I obeyed and squatted next to him. So did Bobby. Junie moved his gloved index finger along the forehead, hovering just above the bone. "In general, males have a heavier browridge over the eyes. It's called the supraorbital ridge. And the orbits, or eye sockets, tend to be smaller and more square than a female's, with rounded edges. Males also have more pronounced markings where the muscle used to be attached to the bone, like this one here." He indicated a rough-looking bump that ran down the forehead above one of the eye sockets.

"How long do you think he's been here?" Bobby asked.

"Roughly . . . I'd say less than forty years. Maybe only thirty."

"Will it take you long to find out who this is?" I asked.

Junie glanced at Bobby. "Could be easy, could be tough. Depends."

"On what?"

"Whether anyone ever reported him missing or not," Bobby said. He stood up and brushed imaginary dirt off his khakis. "People vanish for all kinds of reasons. Sometimes nobody says anything because maybe they wanted the person to disappear." He blew a bubble and popped it. "If that's what happened to this guy, we got our work cut out for us."

It was just after seven when I drove back to the winery parking lot. Bobby told me they'd probably start excavating tonight and would return in the morning. He also said I should expect a cruiser at the vineyard with someone babysitting the grave site.

"Why do you need to do that?" I asked. "It's completely isolated. No one's going to go there."

"Chain of custody," he said. "You get screwed if you can't account for evidence every single second from the moment you bag it until you go to trial. Since we're not recovering all of it tonight, I need someone to make sure nothing happens to that crime scene."

I climbed the flagstone steps to the porticoed courtyard, which connected the ivy-covered brick building where we sold wine to the semi-underground barrel room where we made it. The whine of a car engine coming down the road broke the evening stillness. A van with "Mobile Crime Scene" stenciled on it barreled toward the south service road. Probably Friedman, the crime scene investigator Bobby mentioned earlier. She seemed to know where she was going as her lights fishtailed and disappeared from view.

After so many years, could they really find some shred of evidence that tied the killer to the victim? Mathis seemed to think so, but I wondered.

First, though, they had to identify the man with the missing jaw. I wondered about that, too. How long would it take? Who had died out there on my land?

The fan-shaped gravel courtyard was littered with bright blotches of color. Geraniums and pansies, which had overflowed cut-down wine barrels, were crushed and broken on the ground wherever I looked. The hanging baskets had been stripped of the impatiens and fuchsia that had filled them this morning. Their blossoms glowed like jewels in the fading daylight, some clinging to the white portico columns like starfish, others carpeting the ground. By tomorrow we'd have a sodden mess of bruised brown petals to sweep up.

A terra-cotta pot of red geraniums and variegated ivy lay on its side next to an old winepress. I knelt and tried to brush the dirt into the pot with my hands.

"Need some help?"

I looked up at Quinn. "Thanks."

He took care of the dirt while I untangled the ivy and reset the plants. When we were done, he handed me a broken geranium.

I stared at it. "I could do with a drink."

"Me, too. Why don't I grab a growler and we can taste the Sauvignon Blanc?"

A growler is a bottle of wine we filled directly from one of the stainless-steel tanks or oak barrels. Though a lot of science and chemistry go into growing grapes and winemaking, there's no substitute for drinking it at regular intervals to see how it's coming along. We need to know how it tastes.

I nodded. "Everything still okay in the barrel room?"

"Yup. Generator's working fine," he said. "The villa's okay, too, except there's no power. Frankie got all the tables and chairs and umbrellas from the terrace moved inside in time, so no casualties there. But we're going to have to stay closed until we clean up. Frankie said she'd be in early tomorrow to get started."

Francesca Merchant ran our tasting room and had begun handling all our special events like concerts and festivals.

"If they ever figure out how to clone anything besides animals, Frankie would be my candidate for first human." I tossed the geranium over the stone wall to the garden below. "How did we manage before we hired her?"

"We had you."

I made a face. "Why can't I decide whether that's a compliment or an insult?"

He grinned. "I'll get the wine. Let's sit on the wall and drink here. The sunset's going to be pretty tonight after that tornado."

We sat on the low wall with its view of distant rows of vines and ridges of pines and deciduous trees. Framing the scene was the softly contoured Blue Ridge. The sun had turned the ribbon strips of clouds blood colored and the mountains had darkened from heathery blue to violet.

"I heard on the car radio that forty thousand households are without power in Loudoun County." Quinn poured wine into two glasses and handed one to me. "Another twenty thousand in Fauquier." He touched his wineglass to mine. "Here's to not losing everything today."

"To the glass half full. Did you get a chance to talk to anyone else who was at the roundtable?" I asked. "Anybody take a hit like we did?"

"When Harry Dye got back to his place he found he'd lost half of his crop," Quinn said. "I can't get hold of John Chappell at Mountainview so maybe he lost phone service. No idea how bad it was there."

I drank some wine. "Half the crop? Poor Harry. That's going to kill him. Maybe we can sell him some grapes."

Quinn pulled a cigar out of his shirt pocket and fished in his trousers for a lighter. "That's going to be tough with what we lost."

"Have you done the math?"

He bent his head and lit the cigar, puffing on it until the tip glowed. "It's gonna be a big number. Buying and planting new vines, then all that revenue lost waiting three years until the first harvest. Throw in the expense of buying grapes from somebody else while we're waiting for our vines to produce, if you want to go that route."

Though it was common for vineyards to buy fruit from other sources, he knew I didn't like doing it. Our wines came from our own soil, our own *terroir*, and I was proud of it.

"I don't know. I can't even think straight right now."

Quinn rubbed his thumb across his chin, the way he always did when he was thinking.

"We lost about two acres, so about twenty grand for vines and labor. As for the production loss, with three tons an acre that's six tons of fruit times three years of no wine. Nine hundred gallons, all red fruit. Probably ninety thousand dollars, give or take. Buying more fruit, if we decide to do that. About twelve thousand per harvest, so times three. That's—"

"Thirty-six thousand plus ninety plus twenty." I tipped my head and swallowed a lot of wine. "Damn. If we don't buy fruit we've lost a hundred and ten thousand. If we replace it, it's almost a hundred and fifty."

"Guess we won't be buying another tractor for a while," he said.

"Guess not."

"Let's talk about replacing the fruit another time." I stared into my wineglass. "I really can't wrap my mind around it tonight."

For a vineyard to be profitable—or at least, self-sustaining—it was necessary to make a certain amount of wine. Make too little and you go broke. The break-even number, as we'd figured it, was about ten thousand cases. Today's loss meant we'd be teetering on the precipice.

He refilled our glasses. "How'd it go with those deputies?"

I shrugged as a pair of barn swallows swooped over our heads and flew into the eaves of the arcade.

"They asked a bunch of questions, then tried the good cop/bad cop thing to see if they could scare me into admitting I had some idea who it is out there."

"And did it work?"

"It spooked me, yes. But I have no idea who he is."

"He?"

"Bobby showed up with the medical examiner. I think he's Australian. Junius St. Pierre. He said it was an adult male. Caucasian. He'd probably been buried there for thirty or forty years."

Quinn tapped his cigar with his thumb and ash dropped onto the wall. He brushed it off.

"So it happened while your parents were living here?"

"I guess so."

"You guess so?"

"Okay, what if it did?"

He shrugged. "Maybe they knew something. Your father—"

I cut him off. "I knew you were going to bring up Leland. My father didn't murder anyone."

He pretended to duck. "Whoa, sweetheart. I never said that. You're being awful defensive."

He was right. I was.

Leland had hired Quinn shortly before he died, but Quinn had spent enough time with my father to take his measure. A lousy judge of character, a sap for every crummy business deal that came down the pike, and a womanizer. Everyone in Atoka knew it, too. As my godfather, Fitz, used to say about him, when you lie down with dogs, you get up with fleas. Leland had been a man with a chronic itch from all the fleas.

"The minute word gets out about this everyone in town is going to try my father, convict him, and say something like, 'What'd you expect from Leland Montgomery, anyway?'" I said. "Though they'll do it behind my back."

"People are always going to talk. You can't stop that."

"What you mean is, I can't stop Thelma or the Romeos."

They say three people can keep a secret if two of them are dead. The exception to that rule would be if the one person still living was either Thelma Johnson, who owned the General Store, or one of the Romeos, a cantankerous group of senior citizens whose name stood for "Retired Old Men Eating Out." Tomorrow morning the number-one topic of conversation around the coffeepot in the General Store would be the body on my farm. Maybe I should just give up and sell tickets.

"What's the matter, Lucie?" Quinn said, when I remained silent. "You're worried there might be something to it, aren't you?"

The clouds were now dark against a bright sky and the layered lines of the Blue Ridge had blended into a single silhouette, reminding me of a negative from a print photograph. It was too early for the fireflies to begin their balletic performance, but as the birds quieted down, the cicadas' comforting serenade became more audible. Usually I liked this time of evening, especially in summer, when everything seemed so peaceful.

Tonight, though, I felt restless and jumpy.

"Of course I'm not."

"You're a lousy liar, you know that?"

I played with the stem of my wineglass. "I just don't want Leland to be judged before we have any facts."

"You know the folks who gossip will say their piece, regardless. Your friends will wait and see what happens. And they'll stick up for you." Quinn picked up the bottle and poured the last of the wine into my glass. "Doesn't the Bible say something about giving wine to those that be of heavy hearts? Come on, drink up."

I drank, but my heart was no less heavy. The tornado had left its visible mark on the vineyard and it would take a long time for us to recover. But I also feared that by uncovering that grave we hadn't seen the last of the maelstrom. If I were right, then what was in store would be worse than anything that had happened today.

Chapter 5

⸺◦◦◦⸺

I fell asleep in the hammock on the veranda. When I woke the next morning I was still in my clothes and the power was still out. The airless house felt like a sealed tomb. Out of habit I headed for the kitchen before remembering no electricity meant no refrigerator and no running water. At least I had a gas stove so I could heat water for instant coffee. The orange juice was nearly room temperature, which meant it wouldn't be long before everything in the refrigerator went bad. I poured a glass of tepid juice, found a baguette in the bread box, and drank a cup of boiled-tasting coffee.

Upstairs I splashed bottled water on my face and rubbed a damp washcloth over the rest of my body. As I was on my way out the door, Quinn called on the landline to say he'd be in the field with the crew working on cleanup. I promised to join him after checking on Frankie in the villa.

The weather report on my car radio said the temperature would hit the upper nineties but promised low humidity and no rain. A newscaster reported that "only" thirty thousand homes were without power in Loudoun and another ten thousand were in the dark in Fauquier. They were working around the clock but it might take days to get everyone back online. No specifics whether that meant two or ten.

I switched off the radio. A lot of people still didn't have electricity. Maybe we needed to plan for the long haul. At least the weather was good news. It had been a hot, dry summer so far, which was terrific for the vines. If we could get past yesterday's setback, we might still have a good harvest with the grapes we had left. Maybe even a great one.

When I arrived at the villa just after eight, Frankie Merchant had already opened the four sets of French doors onto the terrace and was busy moving the wicker patio furniture back outside. Early morning sunshine made pale stripes on the Persian carpets and quarry tile floor. A light breeze ruffled the floor-to-ceiling curtains and the reproduction tapestry from the Musée de Cluny in Paris that showed winemaking and coopering in the Middle Ages. Half a dozen copies of the tasting notes for our wines blew off the tiled bar and sailed to the floor.

I retrieved the papers and put them back, weighing them down with a corkscrew. Most of the patio tables and the chairs with their green-and-white-striped cushions were still inside, stacked everywhere.

"I'll help you with these," I said. "Where's Gina?"

"Late." Frankie brushed tendrils of strawberry blond hair off her face. Her cheeks were pink and she was perspiring.

"You look like you didn't get much sleep," she said. "Want coffee?"

"Real coffee? I'd kill for it. Where'd you get it? The General Store?"

"You think I'd let myself get grilled by Thelma about what's been going on around here? Please. I'd rather climb into a tank of piranhas." She headed for the kitchen and called over her shoulder. "We got our power back at home. Came on around three a.m. I brought in a thermos."

She returned, handing me a mug. We sank into patio chairs.

"I got here early and brought all the crews' coolers home so I could fill them with ice water since it's going to be a scorcher."

"You're an angel. I don't know what we'd do without you."

She smiled a serene, knowing smile and crossed her legs, swinging a sandaled foot that showed off a perfect pedicure and stylish neon pink polish on her toes.

"Oh, don't you worry," she said. "There will be payback."

I burst out laughing. "Whatever you want."

She cocked an eyebrow as she sipped her coffee. "You think I'm kidding."

I didn't know much about Frankie's past but I did know her children were grown and her husband worked for a D.C. law firm with hours so long he often slept at work. She'd taken this job to keep from going stir-crazy at home. I'd bet money when her kids were growing up she probably ran the PTA and never missed a sports game, concert, bake sale, or field trip. She was probably one of the stalwarts at school fund-raisers, the kind of person everyone counted on because she never let anyone down. Like now.

"I think we should have a backup plan for the weekend," I said. "In case we don't get our electricity back."

"I thought I'd work on that today," she said. "After I get this place cleaned up."

Twenty years ago this weekend my parents had sold their first bottle of wine. We'd been planning our anniversary celebration for months.

"You going to talk to Dominique?" I asked.

My cousin Dominique Gosselin owned the Goose Creek

Inn, a small auberge founded by my godfather forty years ago that had become one of the region's most popular and well-loved restaurants. Over the years it increasingly attracted Washington's high and mighty who liked its cuisine, romantic charm, and distance from the nation's capital. Dominique probably knew more secrets than the CIA about off-the-radar trysts and furtive romances. Many nights when I dined there the Secret Service hung around being visibly invisible, keeping an eye on some guest and his or her "friend."

"I thought I'd go over to the Inn for lunch, if that's all right with you. Get things sorted out." She grinned. "Your treat."

The Inn's waiters and waitresses often helped us out on weekends serving wine in the tasting room or working at our dinners. Goose Creek Catering, which Dominique also ran as part of the Inn's expanding franchise, handled all our big events.

"You meant it about the payback, huh?"

The landline phone on the bar rang and I stood up.

"Let me," she said. "You don't want to take that."

I heard her end of the conversation. "Sorry, no comment . . . no, she's not available. We sustained a lot of damage from that tornado yesterday and she's got her hands . . . no, we're closed for the foreseeable future until our power is restored . . . the Loudoun County Sheriff's Department might be able to answer that . . . would you like the number? . . . no? . . . no problem . . . good-bye."

She came back and flopped down in her chair. "I've lost count how many of those we've gotten."

"Reporters?"

"You want to see the messages?"

I shook my head. "Who called from the *Trib*? I would have thought Kit would have tried to reach me directly."

Kit Eastman was my best friend since we'd played together in the sandbox and, for the past two years, she'd been Bobby Noland's girlfriend. A few months ago she'd been named Loudoun bureau chief for the *Washington Tribune*. A story like this would be a big deal for her paper. If it didn't make the A section, it would at least be above the fold in Metro.

"From the *Trib*?" Frankie wrinkled her forehead. "Some guy. I think he's new because I didn't recognize his name. He got the standard reply. Maybe Kit's going to drop by and ambush you here."

"Maybe Bobby already told her all there is to know, which is nothing."

Frankie stood up. "Speaking of Bobby," she said, "he's coming up the front walk. Looks like he's got some papers. What's that all about?"

I took a deep breath. "Search warrant."

"Oh."

Bobby looked like he'd slept better than I did, but he still looked tired. Frankie offered him coffee and he accepted. She left to get it and he handed me the paper.

"I'm sure you know what this is," he said, leaning against the bar.

"Yep. I've got nothing to hide, Bobby."

"I know. We're just doing it nice and legal, that's all."

"What are your plans for today?"

Frankie returned with Bobby's coffee, then busied herself sweeping the terrace.

"We've got guys out there with metal detectors right now looking for bullets or anything else like that." Bobby picked up his mug and drank. "Might clear out some of your brush, too, if we need to expand our search. We'll bag the remains and send them back to the lab. That's the first priority."

"You mean you're taking him apart?"

"What do you suggest? Levitate him? There's nothing to hold him together, no flesh."

"Then you put him back together again in your labora-tory?"

"Just like Humpty Dumpty."

"Funny. More like a human jigsaw puzzle."

There were 206 bones in an adult male. I'd found most of the skull and Bruja had unearthed one of the long bones—maybe a tibia or a femur. How many would Bobby and his crew find?

"It's the only way to find out who John Doe is and how he got there."

"So what happens next?" I asked.

Bobby squinted at me like he was weighing how much to reveal. "Take it easy, Lucie. I'm sure we'll be talking. This guy has probably been here since before you were born. It's someone else's story."

"But you and your deputies already think it has some-thing to do with my family."

He expelled a long breath and stared at the tapestry as though he might find the answer woven through the threads. "It isn't engraved in stone, but there are a few things that happen so often in cases like this that you can almost predict how it's gonna turn out."

"Such as?"

"Such as fifty percent of the time, the victim is found on property owned or controlled by the perpetrator."

"And the other fifty percent he's not."

"True." He laid a hand on my shoulder. "Look, you've got nothing to worry about. You're not in trouble."

"All the same, I'm betting it's the other fifty percent," I said.

"You could be right." He finished his coffee and set the mug on the bar. "Off the record, I hope you are."

After Bobby left I helped Frankie move the rest of the furniture outside and then drove over to help Quinn and the crew with the cleanup. Whether I was just plain tired or distracted—or both—within ten minutes I sliced up my index finger with my pruning shears like a rube picker.

Quinn saw me trying to stop the blood gushing out of the wound and came over with the first aid kit.

"What are you doing? You almost took your finger off. That cut might need stitches."

"It'll be all right. It's superficial."

"Give me your hand." He tore off a strip of gauze and tied it around my finger. "Hold that for a minute. Look, why don't you go do something else? We've got it covered here."

"There's so much to clean up—"

"Your head's not in it right now. Give yourself a break."

He took my hand and untied the tourniquet, putting antiseptic on the cut.

"I can put the bandage on myself," I said. "You don't have to fuss."

"If you get gangrene and die, you did leave the place to me, didn't you?"

"You sound so hopeful."

Did I imagine it or did he hold my hand longer than he needed to?

Early in our relationship we'd agreed to keep our personal and professional lives separate—a promise that hadn't been too hard to keep since we disagreed on just about everything. Add to that the fact we had nothing in common and didn't fit the other's profile of someone we'd like to go out with—he preferred good-looking sexy women young enough to be his daughter while I went for older men who broke my heart—and I knew if we ever got together it would be like the *Titanic* meeting the iceberg.

But lately, like now, there had been moments when our eyes held each other's and an electrical current that was new and a little dangerous seemed to pass between us.

I removed my hand from his. "Rumors of my possible demise are premature."

He grinned. "Go on. Get lost and clear your head."

"Maybe I'll go over to the cemetery and see what damage the storm did there."

He gave me a searching glance. "I hope you don't find anything."

I nodded. We both knew he wasn't talking about storm damage.

The cemetery looked as wind tossed and littered with debris as everywhere else on the farm. The pewter vase that held my mother's Renaissance roses had tipped over and was wedged between her headstone and Leland's. The flowers, which I'd picked only yesterday, were wilted and the petals had gone brown on the edges. Most of the miniature American flags I'd placed at each gravestone for the Fourth of July had either fallen over or were tilted at crazy angles like rows of bad teeth. Branches and leaves covered many of the graves and stuck to markers.

I was on my knees tidying the area around Hamish Montgomery's weathered stone marker when a car drove up the road and cut its engine. I looked over the wall in time to see my brother climb out of his dark blue Jaguar. Eli worked for a small architectural firm in Leesburg, about fifteen miles away. For him to show up at the vineyard in the middle of the day meant he either needed something or he was in trouble—or both.

"Hey, babe." He closed the wrought iron gate with a clank and threaded his way between the rows of headstones. "Took me awhile to find you. What are you doing here?"

I still hadn't gotten used to Eli calling me "babe." Or calling his wife "princess," though that was a little more fitting.

"Cleaning up." I moved to the grave of Thomas Montgomery, who had been one of Mosby's Rangers, and started picking up leaves and small branches.

Eli squatted next to me and clasped his hands together. I knew he was taking care not to get dirty. Today he had on beige trousers and a polo shirt. Probably linen and definitely some designer like Hugo Boss or Armani, since that's all he wore anymore. My sister-in-law, Brandi, saw to that since she chose his clothes. His shoes were soft-as-butter leather that looked Italian. Oakley sunglasses hung around his neck. It looked, also, like he'd had a manicure.

"What are you doing here?" I asked. "What's wrong?"

"You think I stop by only when something's wrong?" He smoothed his gelled hair like a preening rooster and looked offended. "I was in the neighborhood so I figured I'd see how my little sister was doing after that tornado went through her vineyard."

"Oh." I carried the leaves and branches over to the wall and dumped them on the other side. "That was thoughtful. We lost some grapes in the new fields. It could have been worse if it had damaged the winery or the house. Still it's a huge financial loss."

"Uh-huh." He sneezed and pulled a packet of tissues out of his pocket. "This is killing my allergies being out here. Tree pollen."

Checking on his little sister. Sure he was. "Did you hear what I said?"

He blew his nose. "You lost grapes in the new field. The winery and the ancestral pile are still standing."

I put my hands on my hips. "What's going on?"

He wadded up the tissue. "I learned a little something today. Apparently you found an old grave on our land after the tornado came through. Not in this cemetery."

"Well, yes—"

He folded his arms. "Thelma attached herself to me like she was superglued on when I stopped by the General Store just now. If Homeland Security ever hired that woman she'd be their top interrogator. She could wear anybody down in nothing flat."

"What'd you tell her?"

"What do you think I told her? Nada. For the simple reason that I didn't have a clue what she was talking about," he said. "You should have seen the look on her face when she figured that out." He did an uncanny imitation of Thelma's high-pitched voice. " 'Well, now Elliot, do tell. How odd your sister didn't tell you about that dead body. A person has to wonder if there's something conspirational going on, don't you think?' "

"Conspirational, huh? You sound just like Thelma."

An accomplished mangler of the English language, in addition to being a world-class gossip.

He tapped his fingers on his arms and glared at me. "I'm so flattered. How come you didn't call?"

"I'm sorry, Eli. Between the tornado damage and finding that grave, things were insane around here. Bobby came over this morning with a search warrant. They're out there right now excavating the remains."

"Jesus." He stopped tapping. "Who is it?"

"I don't know. The medical examiner said he reckoned the body had been there thirty or forty years. A Caucasian male." I righted a flag in front of a marker of another ancestor who had fought in the Civil War. "Can you help me fix a couple of these?"

Eli raised an eyebrow and indicated Leland's grave. "Wonder if Leland knew him?"

"Just because someone's buried on our land doesn't mean anyone in the family knew anything about it. We both know Leland didn't have the best judgment when it came to business deals, but he would never kill another person and you know it." I stood up and faced my brother.

He threw up his hands like he was putting on brakes. "I just asked if he could have known him and you bite my head off. How can you be so sure he didn't do it?"

"Because of Mom. She would have known and she couldn't have lived with it, that's how."

"Leland kept secrets." He walked over to our parents' graves and fixed Leland's flag.

I joined him. "Not that secret. Not murder. Whose side are you on, anyway?"

"Yours," he said. "Ours."

"I hope so."

He cleared his throat. "Hey, Luce?"

"What?"

"Got a little favor to ask you."

I knew it. "What favor?"

I also knew the favor. Money.

"I'm a little tight this month and I was wondering if you could—"

I cut him off. "I can loan you three hundred, maybe four, but I want to know when you're going to pay me back."

"Three or four hundred?" He looked startled. "You can't do more than that?"

"I can't really do three or four hundred since I just took a hit that's going to set us back well over a hundred thousand dollars. How deep in debt are you, Eli?"

He ran his thumb along the edge of our mother's marker. "It's not too good. I'm on the verge of bankruptcy."

He spoke lightly, but I saw his throat constrict. It was probably worse than "on the verge," but he wasn't saying. I knew him too well. Still, he'd caught me off guard.

"Bankruptcy? How could you let it get this far?" I stared at him. "You'll lose everything."

He cleared his throat again. "Right now I just need enough to cover my August mortgage payment since today's the first and it's due soon. That's all. I don't want to lose my home, Luce. Brandi loves that house."

Of course she did. He'd designed it for her, giving her everything she wanted. Now they lived in a nouveau riche palazzo that combined the most garish extravagances of Versailles with the Disney Castle, including a multitiered fountain in the front yard that looked like he'd borrowed it from Trafalgar Square in London.

"How much is your mortgage?"

"We refinanced a few times to consolidate our debt." He paused and said, without looking at me, "It's just under eight thousand."

"Eight thousand?"

He needed that just for his mortgage? What about everything else? Groceries, car loan—all of it? Could he cover those expenses, or were they down to eating the labels off cans?

"Why don't you sell something?" I said. "That antique

Sarouk carpet you just bought for the great room. The gold faucets in the master bath. Anything."

He looked pained. "I haven't got that kind of time. It's not the first payment I've missed, so they're already knocking on the door." He laughed, but it was the self-mocking laugh of someone pushed to the edge. "We're barely answering the phone because most of the calls are collection agencies. Besides, Brandi would just die if I started dismantling her dream house. You know I can't do that to her."

"Brandi needs to go to credit card rehab, and I'm not joking. Cut up her cards, take away the checkbook, and give her a cookie jar with money in it. Tell her that's it. You can't go on like this. She's as bad as Leland was, blowing money on junk she doesn't even care about the next day," I said. "That's why you're in so much debt."

"You are being unfair."

"I am being honest."

"Aw, jeez. Give me a break. I come to you for help and what do I get? A lecture." He started pacing in front of our parents' graves. "You're the one talking about family and being on the same side. You could help me out if you wanted to. I'm not asking for a handout. I'll pay you back once I get on my feet. I just need some time."

Sure. Like he'd paid his other creditors back. "You can't repay me and you know it."

He stopped pacing and looked at me with an odd glint in his eyes. "How can you turn your back on me when you've got a five-figure sum in the vineyard checking account right now?"

"How do you know that?" The hair prickled on the back of my neck.

"Aha! Knew I was right. You do, don't you?"

I'd fallen for the oldest trick in the book. "It's not my

personal piggy bank, Eli. It's a business account and that money is there to pay bills."

He spread his hands apart, palms up. "I'm tapped out, babe. Are you going to help me or are you going to throw your brother to the wolves?"

It was a low blow, and he knew it. I wasn't responsible for his problems. He was.

"Giving you more money without doing something about the way Brandi spends it isn't going to help anyone. You can't pay me back the eight grand any more than you can pay your creditors back. Take the four hundred as a gift, okay? You don't need to repay that."

He looked like I'd slapped him. "I don't need your charity. Forget it. I'll go elsewhere."

"Eli, wait!"

But he was already moving toward the gate, raising his hand in a backward salute, dismissing me.

"I gotta go. I'm late for something."

He slammed the gate, as I expected he would. I sank down by my mother's gravestone.

"Now what?" I asked her. "How did he do that? Why am I the one feeling bad?"

Giving my brother money would be like giving alcohol to a drunk. He didn't have his spending under control—and his wife was dragging him down to the depths I remembered from when Leland was alive. When we lurched from feast to famine, either flush with cash or nearly flat broke. Eli's story was just a downward spiral.

I paused at Leland's marker as I left the cemetery. Years ago my mother hid a fabulous diamond necklace given to one of her relatives by Marie Antoinette because she knew if my father got his hands on it he'd sell it, just like he'd sold all her other jewelry to fund his business ventures. I'd found the necklace two years ago, hidden in a barrel in the wine cellar. Eli got a third of the money from its sale and had blown his share. I used mine to pay for our expansion and putting in new vines.

Right after Leland died, a French live-in boyfriend had sweet-talked my bank in the south of France into letting him withdraw all my funds, claiming I needed the money because I was moving back to the States. As soon as I got home, I planned to call Blue Ridge Federal and check on my account.

Not that I thought Eli could pull off the same scam, but I knew he was desperate enough to try anything. Including cleaning me out.

Chapter 6

I called Seth Hannah, the president of Blue Ridge Federal and an old family friend, the moment I walked through the front door. Like Leland, Seth was one of the Romeos and he used to play poker and hunt with my father. I'd long suspected Seth had a crush on my mother, as did so many men who were captivated by her beauty and indefinable French sense of style and allure.

"What can I do for you, darlin'?" he asked.

"Just checking my balance. I wasn't sure if something cleared or not." Or got cleared out.

I heard some clicks of a computer keyboard and he quoted a figure that matched the one I had.

"Happy to oblige, but you can do all this online, you know."

"I know, but I wanted to ask you about something and I can't get that from a computer." I wondered if he heard the relief in my voice that we still had funds to talk about.

"What's on your mind?"

"I just want to make sure that no one besides me has access to that account," I said.

"Well, that's how it's set up, Lucie. Why're you asking about this?"

I hesitated and Seth waited.

After a moment he said, "This wouldn't be about your brother, would it?"

"Please don't say anything to anyone, Seth. He came to me for a loan just now and I turned him down. He knows I've got a lot of cash in that account."

There was a long pause. "It's no secret your brother's in a pretty deep financial hole, honey. You thinking he might try to cash a check of yours or something?"

"When we were growing up and Eli got a bad report card or a note about detention, he used to forge my parents' signatures. He could copy either one of them and you couldn't tell they weren't genuine."

"I see." Seth cleared his throat. "Counterfeiting a check's a serious crime, you know."

I was sitting in the foyer in one of my mother's toile-covered Queen Anne chairs staring at Leland's bust of Thomas Jefferson. I leaned back and pinched the bridge of my nose. The house was even warmer than it had been this morning. Although the windows were open, I felt like I was suffocating.

"I know."

"I will tell you this. We get our share of forged checks and I can't tell you how many times the forger was a relative or someone who had access to the individual's financial information," he said. "If you don't trust Eli, you'd do well to put things under lock and key."

"It's not that I don't trust him—"

"Honey, you don't have to beat around the bush with me.

I know Eli's a good man." Seth made a sound that wasn't quite a laugh. "But who said, 'I can resist anything but temptation'?"

"Everyone?"

This time he did laugh. "Look, I'll put a note here in your file that you're the only person authorized to handle transactions with this account. Will that settle you?"

"I guess so. I feel awful about this, you know. Eli didn't actually do anything."

"Better safe than sorry, Lucie. I've seen more people feuding over money than you can shake a stick at. You have no idea the stuff we've got here in folks' safe-deposit boxes because relatives couldn't come to an agreement over something. Hell, we even got an urn with someone's ashes in the vault."

"You're joking."

"No, ma'am. Whoever locks up for the night wishes him sweet dreams. Been doin' that for going on sixteen years. We've gotten kind of attached to him."

"I hope that never happens to us. Feuding, I mean."

"Then talk to your brother. Get it out in the open."

"I couldn't. He's already mad at me because I wouldn't loan him money for his mortgage payment."

"You want my opinion, honey?" I was going to get it, even if I didn't. "I've known you and Eli and Mia since you were born. Your pa wasn't always a straight shooter and it pains me to say that, but your mother was as rare and precious as a hothouse flower. She had more integrity in her little finger than most folks got in their whole body. If she were alive today, she'd be telling you to be square and honest with your brother."

The lump in my throat made it hard to talk. "I know. Thanks, Seth."

"You're welcome." He paused and I thought he was going to say good-bye or something else in parting. "By the way, any word on that body you found on your land?"

I sat up straight. He knew as well as I did it was too soon to know anything official. This was fishing to see what I'd tell him.

"Nope. Nothing."

"Well, I sure hope . . ." He left the sentence unfinished.

I waited as though I expected him to tell me what he sure hoped, which was that Leland had nothing to do with it.

"Thanks for the advice, Seth. I appreciate it."

"You all right, darlin'?"

"Don't you worry about me. I can handle this."

"Of course you can." He backed off. "Look, Lucie, I want you to know that I'm in your corner whatever happens. If you ever need to talk or you have any questions, all you need to do is pick up the phone. I owe that to you children and the memory of your mother."

He hung up and I wondered why he hadn't mentioned anything about what he owed to the memory of my father.

Bobby returned to the villa at the end of the day while I was in my office filling out the endless tax forms we sent the government so they'd grant us the privilege of selling wine. Frankie showed up in the doorway and told me he was waiting in the tasting room.

She kept her voice low. "I have a feeling they're done. The other cruisers and that crime scene van just left."

"It only took them one day?"

"Guess so. Maybe you can ask him."

"Don't worry. I will."

Bobby's shirt was soaked with perspiration and his hair was plastered to his head like he'd gone swimming.

"Can I get you something to drink?" I asked. "We've got bottled water and a few sodas in a cooler. They're still cold."

"Thanks, but I got my own cooler in the car." He wiped his forehead with the back of his hand, revealing a triangle of white skin at his hairline that contrasted with the rest of his sunburned face.

"I came by to let you know that we're finished," he said. "The crime scene tape will stay up for a few more days and we're coming back to clear out the underbrush that's nearby in case we missed something there."

"You've removed the remains?" I asked. "Completely?"

He nodded.

"Did you find anything else besides the skull and that bone Bruja dug up?"

His smile was weary. "Sorry. I can't say."

"Well, could you identify him from just the skull, if that's all you got?"

"That's Junie's department."

"You're not going to tell me anything."

"Right now there's nothing to tell."

I sighed and gave up. "You and Kit are coming this weekend for our twentieth?"

His face cracked into a small smile. "We're counting on it."

"I knew I'd get you to answer at least one question," I said.

"You always were like a dog with a bone," he said. "As long as I've known you."

"You could have picked a different analogy than dogs and bones. Or answered a different question."

He grinned. "I kind of liked that one. Be seeing you." He had his hand on the doorknob when he paused and turned around.

"I will tell you this. It seems like we're talking about only one person out there."

After he left I made so many mistakes on the tax report that I finally threw down my pencil and went outside on the terrace. Frankie found me there, staring at the fields and vines. She handed me a glass of wine that I hadn't asked for. Perfectly chilled Riesling.

"Where'd you get this?"

"I went over to the barrel room. Want to talk about it? Might make you feel better."

I drank some wine as she sat down in one of the wicker chairs and pulled it closer.

"I know I should be focusing on the tornado damage, but I just keep thinking about that skull. Wondering who he is and how he got there. Bobby thinks the odds are good whoever killed him had ties to the farm." I paused. "Even Eli wondered if Leland might be involved somehow."

"And you don't think he was?" Her voice was gentle, but there was a hint of reproach that I shouldn't kid myself.

I chose my words with care. "My father was a complicated man who didn't always show good judgment. He made lousy business decisions and he gambled. And he had his share of affairs, though through everything he loved my mother. Sometimes I think he didn't believe he was worthy of her and that's why he had the affairs."

"I wish I'd known your mother," Frankie said.

I raised an eyebrow. "You don't wish you'd known Leland, huh?"

"I didn't say that—"

"Never mind. I'm just giving you a hard time." I sipped my wine and touched the chilled glass to my cheek. It felt good. "It probably seems odd that I'm defending my father, but I know he's no murderer. He didn't kill that man and then cover it up for the rest of his life. It would have consumed him if he did."

Frankie put two fingers across her lips like she was thinking as her eyes roved over my face. I thought I saw pity in them.

"You don't believe me?" I asked. "You think I can't be objective."

"Of course I believe you," she said. "Maybe the best thing is to put this out of your mind until they identify the body. Then take it from there." She stood up. "Let me get that bottle of wine."

Plato said that wine fills the heart with courage. Frankie refilled my glass and poured a glass for herself.

My heart was not filled with courage as I drank. Instead it was filled with foreboding and a sickening feeling of apprehension. Until yesterday I thought all my family's sins and secrets lay buried in our graveyard.

What if I was wrong?

B. J. Hunt called at the end of the day. I'd been expecting to hear from him once word got out about the discovery of the body on land he planned to use for the reenactment.

"Wondering if I could drop by and check things out," he said. "Sounds like we might have to change our plans now that you got crime scene tape strung up in that field. I understand you had some tornado damage as well."

"Bad news travels fast," I said. "I suppose Thelma had her megaphone out this morning?"

"Word does get around, doesn't it?" He chuckled. "Well, it's not just me that's interested in coming by. Ray Vitale is in town. He wants to see the site, too, especially since he hasn't been here before."

"Who is Ray Vitale?"

"The Union commander. The guy's so hard-core he lives like it's still the 1860s. All my communication with him has been by mail. That's U.S. Postal Service mail, not e-mail. He's such a stitch Nazi that he won't do it any other way. Damn annoying at times."

"What's a 'stitch Nazi'?"

"A guy who says everything has to be absolutely authentic right down to the number of stitches it takes to sew a button-hole," he said. "Me, I don't care what a person's wearing for skivvies and I don't think you need to piss on your uniform buttons to make them look old. Stinks like hell when you do. As long as no one shows up wearing Nikes and a wristwatch, and carrying a cell phone, it's good enough for me."

"Your friend sounds like a zealot," I said, laughing.

"Nope. A zealot is someone altogether different. 'The South shall rise again.' That's a zealot. They haven't forgiven the Union for winning. Some of them never stopped fighting the war. And a Yankee zealot still wants to punish us."

"How'd you get involved with someone like Ray?"

"Oh, the usual. Business. He owns several assisted-living centers in Virginia and North Carolina. We've handled funerals for a number of his residents."

"How about if you come by first thing tomorrow morning?" I asked. "I'll take you over there myself."

"How about right now? Say, half an hour? Ray's heading back to Richmond this evening."

B.J.'s event had been attracting considerable media attention and that meant publicity for the winery. We had no idea how many people would show up, but it was possible that as many as a thousand visitors could pass through the vineyard that weekend, including both reenactors and spectators. For us, it was a big crowd.

I'd been hoping to close up the villa and head home, but if B.J. wanted to come by tonight, we'd do this tonight.

"Of course," I said. "Meet me in the parking lot at five thirty."

"I appreciate this, Lucie," he said. "Ray's awful anxious about your goings-on over there so it'll be good to calm him down."

My goings-on. Bad news really did travel fast.

I locked up and called Quinn on my cell phone, which finally had service restored. He sounded tired.

"We made some progress cleaning up, but it's slow," he said. "I'll probably rent a Bobcat in the next day or two once we finish pruning and tying up vines that can still be saved. And, uh, Benny took the chain saw over to where the sycamore came down. The road should be passable now if you're heading home."

He caught me off guard about the tree.

"Thanks, but I'm not going home yet," I said. "B.J. and some guy who's the Union commander want to see the site. They're worried about the reenactment. The Union guy heard about the body and he's really anxious. B.J. needs to calm him down."

"You don't think they'll cancel, do you?"

"Nope. They just want to know if they need to adjust their plans."

"Want me to come along?"

"I can handle it, but thanks anyway. Go home and get some rest. You sound beat."

"Yeah, guess I am." He paused. "All right. Wait a minute. Tyler wants to know if he can come, too. He wants to meet the Union guy."

B.J. once explained to me the three main reasons people got involved in Civil War reenacting. Either they were so fascinated by a period in history they wanted to experience it as fully as possible, something akin to time traveling, or they were like boys with toys—men who liked shooting guns and playacting war. The third reason fell somewhere between the first two and had to do with teaching the next generation about a time in our history when America had gone to war with itself. It also was a way of honoring those who had given their lives for what they believed was a worthy cause. Tyler got involved for reasons one and two. He became interested in the Ball's Bluff reenactment soon after he started working at the vineyard and signed up with B.J's home unit, Company G of the 8th Virginia Infantry.

"If you don't need Tyler—" I began.

"Oh, believe me," Quinn said, "he's done here."

I decided not to pursue that. "Tell him to meet me in the parking lot in fifteen minutes. I'm on my way to the equipment barn to get one of the Mules."

"I think Chance is over there," he said, "fixing a broken weed whacker. Do me a favor and tell him he needs to start answering his phone. I've been trying to reach him for the last hour."

"Maybe he doesn't get service there."

Quinn snorted. "We're missing the *dodine* and I want to do the *bâttonage* tomorrow on the Cab and Merlot. Tyler says he has no clue what happened to it. Maybe Chance stashed it somewhere."

A *dodine* was a stirring paddle used to move around the lees, or sediment, in wine barrels and looked like a long metal pole with a small propeller attached at the bottom. Once it was lowered inside the barrel it whirred away, stirring up everything much like shaking a carton of pulpy orange juice after it sat in the refrigerator for a while. Quinn believed in frequent *bâttonages*, or barrel stirrings, for both reds and whites. He said it yielded better results, softening the red tannins, deepening the aromas and flavors, and making a creamier, smoother wine.

A broken weed whacker and a missing *dodine*. Was Quinn right that we had more than our usual share of bad luck and trouble?

"I'll speak to Chance." I sighed. "How could something as big as the *dodine* go missing?"

"That's what I'd like to know." His words were clipped. It sounded like he blamed Chance again.

"Okay," I said, but he'd already disconnected.

The simmering headache behind my eyes began to throb. When I got nearer to the equipment barn, the thudding bass from a boom box turned up loud enough to make the ground pulse beneath my feet mirrored the pounding in my head. Chance didn't notice me until I tapped his arm. Bruja, improbably, was sound asleep but her front paws covered her ears.

"Can you turn that down?" I mouthed at him.

He went over and hit the power switch. The silence seemed to fill the space between us and Bruja raised her head, her tail thumping.

"Now I know why you didn't answer Quinn's phone calls. Next time, at least set your phone to vibrate."

He smiled his mesmerizing smile and pulled the phone out of his pocket. "Battery's run down. I forgot to recharge it last night. What does Quinn want?"

His eyes held mine, friendly, questioning, with a hint of suggestiveness in them. I needed to get the conversation directed back to business.

"The *dodine*'s missing. He's wondering if you know where it is."

I pawed through the key cabinet until I found the key to the red Mule. It wasn't on the hook where it belonged. Nor were most of the other keys. I began moving them to the correct hooks.

"That barrel stirrer? Sorry, no idea," he said. "I haven't seen it for a couple of days."

"What's wrong with the weed whacker? Whoever is using these keys needs to put them back properly. You can't find anything here. It's a mess."

"I'll talk to the guys. And the weed whacker needs a new string. I'm replacing it."

I finished sorting the keys. "You'd better see Quinn before you leave tonight."

"I'd just as soon avoid him when he gets like this."

"Like what?"

He was still smiling, but now his face showed genuine puzzlement. "Come on, Lucie. Don't tell me you don't know. I figured you've just been turning a blind eye to it all this time."

"What are you talking about?"

"The way he treats the crew. Me. How do you work with someone who's so . . ." He shrugged.

"So what?"

He stared at his feet for a while, then looked up. "Abusive. That's the only word I can think of to call it."

It stung like a slap. Quinn could be abrasive, even irritable and ornery. But I would never characterize him as abusive. That implied cruelty.

"Quinn's a good winemaker," I said. "Sometimes he can be curt and maybe he's short-tempered when the pressure's on during harvest. But he's harder on himself than he is on anyone else."

Chance shook his head like I didn't get it.

"Sorry. Not true. He's really tough with the crew when you're not around. You don't see or know everything that happens."

I ran my finger over the notched edge of the ignition key.

"I'm not blind to his faults. But in the two years he's worked for me, I've never had a single complaint."

"You really want to take his side over something like this? Come on, Lucie."

He sounded almost jocular, as though he were trying to cajole me into something as innocuous as joining him for a drink, instead of indicting Quinn for violent behavior toward the men.

"I just can't believe—"

"The guys won't speak up about it, either. They're scared of him."

My phone rang and "Hunt & Sons Funeral Home" flashed on the display. "Hang on, I've got to take this."

I opened my phone. "Hey, B.J. Yes, I'm on my way. Is Ray Vitale with you? He is? Give me two minutes . . . Right . . . 'Bye."

I closed the phone and said to Chance, "Look, this is a pretty serious accusation. I've got to go, but we need to finish this conversation another time."

He stood there, holding the new line for the weed whacker, a flat, unreadable expression in his eyes. Disappointment in me? Disgust?

Actually, it seemed like something else.

"Sure," he said. "We'll talk whenever you want."

"Chance," I pleaded with him. "I'm sorry but B.J. wants to calm down the guy in charge of the Union reenactors because he's all freaked out about that grave. I need to take them out to the site."

"You're the boss." He picked up a rag and wiped grease off his hands.

"You want me to tell Quinn you don't know where the *dodine* is?"

"That's okay. I'll talk to him. I'll be over in a few minutes."

"Don't worry. He won't bite your head off."

"Unlike the day laborers, I can handle myself with Quinn."

He was still wiping his hands with the rag, no longer looking at me. I wanted to say something to end this conversation on a better note, but for the life of me, I couldn't think of anything.

Instead I turned and left, clenching the key until the hard edges dug into the palm of my hand.

It was true that Quinn had become increasingly exasperated with the inexperienced day laborers who worked for us. Many had never worked in agriculture before and often didn't seem to know what they were doing out in the field when it came to some of the tedious but necessary chores like leaf pulling or dropping fruit. Had the never-ending series of accidents and mistakes along with an erratic and inept crew caused Quinn to cross the line into abuse as Chance suggested?

If the men were too terrified to complain, Chance had just put another problem on my overfull plate, in addition to the tornado damage and Bobby's investigation. Right now, this one crowded out the others.

Sooner or later, I would have to confront Quinn. I got in the Mule and drove over to the parking lot. It was a conversation I dreaded.

Chapter 7

—◦◦◦◦—

Tyler, B.J., and a third man, who had to be Ray Vitale, made an incongruous-looking trio waiting for me in the parking lot. B.J. and Vitale looked as though they were posing for a daguerreotype, each with one arm across his breast and a soldier's erect bearing. Both had longish hair—B.J.'s was the color of snow, Vitale's chestnut brown—along with beards and muttonchop sideburns. Put them in their uniforms and you'd swear you were looking at Lee and Grant in the flesh, with their somber bearing and unsmiling faces.

Tyler, by contrast, towered over the older men at six foot four, still possessing the gangly awkwardness of a kid newly adjusting to his height and long limbs. Unlike the others, he smiled and waved, his cherubic red-blond curls blowing in the light breeze as he pushed wire-rimmed glasses up the bridge of his nose with an index finger. His pale skin, which refused to tan, had turned strawberry colored from so much time working with the vines.

I pulled up and idled the engine. Tyler waited for Vitale to climb into the backseat before hopping in behind him with a well-worn copy of Marcus Aurelius's *Meditations*. B.J. got in front and introduced Vitale to me.

I reached over the seat and held out my hand. Vitale pumped it once and released it. "How do you do, ma'am?"

His voice was high-pitched and querulous. He gave me a cursory glance before settling back in his seat and focusing his attention on the scenery, ignoring me as though I were no longer of any consequence.

I turned back to B.J. sitting next to me. He wore an I-told-you-he's-eccentric expression and waggled his eyebrows, so I had to stifle a laugh.

On the drive out to the field, B.J. kept up a one-sided explanation of the vineyard for Vitale's benefit, talking about how successful we were as a small family business now run by the next generation. To hear B.J. tell it, I was on a par with the top women in the California wine dynasties. But by the time we reached the reenactment campsite, Ray Vitale's monosyllabic comments had deflated B.J.'s well-intentioned patter and we all fell silent.

I reached for my cane as the others climbed out of the Mule.

"I don't imbibe spirits, myself," Vitale said in that reedy voice as I stepped down. "You know what the Bible says. 'For the drunkard and the glutton will come to poverty.' I'm glad to see that this site is well removed from your vineyard, Miss Montgomery. It's not good to have temptation too near our young people. We do not allow any alcohol on the campground premises during the reenactment, you understand. I presume you will not be serving anything to those who come to watch, nor encouraging folks to visit your winery. We cannot have drunkenness marring these events."

His prissy choice of words was right out of another

century, uncharitable and stinging. I was about to make a sharp retort when B.J. intervened.

"What Ray means," he said, in the soothing voice he used to comfort the bereaved, "is that it's just common sense not to allow anyone to bring alcohol to the camp around guns and bayonets and the like."

"I certainly appreciate that," I said. "But I'd just like to say, Mr. Vitale, that there's a difference between drinking and drunkenness. As we all know, Jesus turned water into wine and even imbibed himself, since you bring up the Bible. I'm sure the adults who attend the reenactment can make their own decisions about whether they'd like to visit my vineyard or not."

B.J. placed a hand on my shoulder. "How about if Ray and I take a little walk so I can show him the campsite?" Under his breath he said in my ear, "Let me handle this."

He caught up with Vitale, who was striding over to take a look at the tornado damage. B.J. pulled a couple of cigars out of his breast pocket and offered one to Ray Vitale. They bent their heads and went through the ritual of slowly rotating the match flame until the tips glowed like early evening fireflies.

Tyler showed up at my elbow as I watched the silhouettes of the two men, backlit by the setting sun, talking through a haze of smoke.

"Where were you?" I asked.

"Checking out that grave."

"You didn't go inside the crime scene tape, did you?"

He shrugged. "I didn't touch anything."

"Tyler! What were you thinking? It's not there for decoration. Bobby Noland will give me hell if he finds out you were there."

"Don't tell him."

"You mean lie if he asks?" I shook my head. "Just stay away from it, okay? I don't want to catch you there again."

"All right. Sorry." He bowed his head, repentant. After a moment he said, "I guess you told that Vitale guy, huh, Lucie."

"Trying to sweet talk me now, are you?" I said, as he reddened. "I didn't tell him anything. You can't persuade people who stand on the moral authority of the Bible to change their mind. They're too self-righteous."

Tyler waved his book. "Read this and people like him won't bug you so much."

"He doesn't bug me."

He looked at me over the top of his glasses.

"Okay," I said. "A little."

"Then stop letting him. Deny your emotions and you can free yourself from the pain and pleasure of the material world."

"Where'd you get that? You sound like a television evangelist."

"It's Stoicism. Marcus Aurelius was a Stoic. They were into all kinds of denial not to feel things."

"Sorry, a painless world would be nice, but not one without pleasure. Besides, what's the point of living if you don't feel anything?"

Tyler tapped the book's cover with its hollow-eyed bust of the philosopher set against a stark black background. "Vitale got under your skin not because of what he did, but because of how you reacted to him. Same with you getting mad at me just now. What I did was no big deal."

"I don't agree it was no big deal, but what's your point?"

"Aw, come on. I'm just a harmless kid." Tyler grinned a rogue's grin and indicated the crime scene tape. "I've heard things, Lucie. I know it's none of my business but you need to stop letting everything that's going on get to you. Don't worry about what other people say. It doesn't matter."

I wanted to ask him what other people were saying, but perhaps it was better that I didn't know. Instead I said, "Maybe I'll have to borrow that book."

He pushed his glasses up his nose. "Anytime. Too bad I can't talk Quinn into reading it. He's the one who could really use it."

"What's that supposed to mean?"

"It means Quinn isn't someone who stifles his emotions. Especially when he's mad."

"Quinn's got a lot on his mind right now." I studied Tyler. "Are you trying to tell me things aren't good between the two of you?"

He shrugged. "I guess they're okay."

"You guess they're okay?"

Tyler bent his book back and forth into a U-shape. "He got mad at me when we were topping off the barrels and I overfilled one of them."

"How mad?"

"He yelled a lot. Plus he thinks Chance or I lost that stirring paddle. The *dodine*."

Was it my imagination or did Tyler seem uneasy discussing Quinn? Funny thing was, I would have pegged Quinn as a Stoic like Marcus Aurelius, someone good at keeping his emotions bottled up. What had changed? Was he losing his temper at Tyler and the other men because those pent-up feelings finally were boiling over?

"Hey, Lucie." Tyler kept his voice low. "Here come B.J. and Vitale."

"I don't think we'll have any trouble working around that tornado damage, Lucie," B.J. was saying. "We'll have to move some of the campgrounds into the woods, but that shouldn't be a problem. Depends, of course, on how many people show up."

"How many do you expect?" I asked.

Vitale puffed on his cigar. "We cut registration off last weekend. Four hundred total." He gave me a stern look. "How much longer will that area be a crime scene?"

"I'm sure the tape will be down by next week," I said. "The remains that were found there were removed today."

I saw one of B.J.'s eyebrows go up, but all he said was, "Why don't we head over to the battlefield? I'd like Ray to see it before it gets too dark."

"It'll be faster if I drive you," I said.

"No one's going to drive us on the day. I'd like to get an idea of the terrain," Vitale said. "We'll walk."

"Be my guest," I said, and caught Tyler's eye. "Whatever suits you."

Vitale exhaled a cloud of smoke and Tyler coughed.

"Confederate bug spray," Vitale said. "Better get used to it, son. The whole camp'll be smoking cigars all weekend to keep down the mosquitoes."

"Except the ladies," B.J. said. "They use lavender."

"Lavender doesn't work for beans," Vitale said.

By the time they climbed into the Mule, after checking the battlefield, I had to turn the headlights on. All that was left of the sun was a bright line of light illuminating the undulating curves of the Blue Ridge. A few stars glittered in the blue-black sky, but everything else—bushes, trees, rocks— was now absorbed into the velvety dusk of a warm summer evening. A few tree frogs sang, accompanied by the usual serenade of the cicadas.

"Pity we're not really going to take full advantage of that creek," Vitale said from the backseat as I drove down the south service road. "I hope this doesn't turn out to be a farby event, B.J. If we were doing it hard-core, you can bet a lot of soldiers would get wet."

"What's farby?" I asked.

B.J. swallowed and I could see his Adam's apple bob. "It's reenactor jargon. Stands for 'far be it from me,' and it refers to reenactors who do or wear something that isn't correct or isn't period. 'Far be it from me to criticize that inauthentic whatever—jacket, trousers, shoes, even eyeglasses—since they didn't wear that in the early 1860s.'"

"It's amateur." Vitale's voice rose like it was a punishable crime. "I personally don't participate in farby events."

"This one's going to be unique, Ray, and you know it," B.J. said over his shoulder. "It's never been done as a water-based reenactment around here before. We'll attract hundreds of spectators."

"What are you going to do about the creek?" I asked. "Are you going to have Union soldiers swimming downstream after the battle?"

"Too dangerous, plus it's hell on everyone's uniform and equipment," B.J. said. "Though we will be demonstrating the Union panic as their soldiers retreated down the bluffs to the river."

"And we will be using boats," Vitale said. "Three canoes."

"Why only three?" I asked.

"That, Miss Montgomery, is historically accurate," Vitale said. "Two eight-man wooden skiffs and a sixteen-man metal lifeboat."

"That's why so many died or drowned," B.J. said. "It's why the Union lost Ball's Bluff. Not enough boats."

My headlights caught Ray Vitale's car in their wash as I turned into the winery parking lot, illuminating a pair of bumper stickers: "You can have my gun when you pry it from my cold dead fingers" and "Gun control is using two hands."

No mistaking the man's politics.

After everyone climbed out of the Mule, Ray Vitale shook hands with B.J. and Tyler, then bowed to me.

"I'll be back in a week to finalize those battle plans, B.J.," he said.

"That'd be fine."

Vitale saluted B.J. "The Union forever."

"The South shall rise again."

"They don't call it the 'Lost Cause' for nothing. Be seeing you."

After he drove off, I said, "Do you always say things like that to each other?"

"Aw, there's plenty of back-and-forth that goes on. Besides, the Union guys are jealous of us."

"Why?"

He looked surprised at the question. "Because everyone wants to be a Confederate, that's why. We're gentlemen. The whole 'romance of the South' thing. Who wants to play the role of a Yankee? That's why there's always more of us at these events."

"Seriously?"

B.J. nodded. "Thanks for being a good sport. I know Ray's a little tough to take."

"Far be it from me to criticize."

B.J. grinned and then turned solemn. "When we were out there talking alone, he told me a few things. Both his wife and daughter were alcoholics. Wife died awhile back and he doesn't know where his daughter is."

"I'm so sorry," I said. "I had no idea."

"Then a couple of years ago he nearly lost his business and almost had to declare bankruptcy. Says he trusted someone he shouldn't have. He's still dealing with it." He shook his head. "That's why he probably seemed bitter."

"At least now I know why."

B.J. pulled his key ring out of his pocket. It looked like he had enough keys on it to open every store in a major shopping mall. "Need a ride home, Tyler?"

"I've got my car. Thanks, anyway."

"I guess I'll get going, then. Emma will have dinner waiting. I'll be in touch to go over the logistics, once we sort out the tactical matters," he said. "I almost forgot. The Virginia Fiddlers are coming."

"The who?"

"You don't know the Fiddlers?" He searched the ring and plucked out what was presumably his car key. "Lordy, child. They're probably the best Civil War camp string band around. Made a couple of CDs. Been in a movie or two. They're famous. They'll be a huge draw for the spectators, plus they'll be playing for the camp dance Saturday night."

"You have a dance?"

He smiled. "Highlight of the weekend for all the women and the young people. Right, Tyler?"

Tyler reddened. "Yes, sir."

"You ought to plan to stop by, Lucie. Bring that wine-maker of yours. I'm afraid we've got our rules about not par-ticipating unless you're dressed in period clothes, but seeing as you're hosting us we'd love to have you come along and see what it's all about," B.J. said.

Now it was my turn to blush. The last place in the world I could imagine bringing Quinn was an old-fashioned dance where a Civil War string band provided the music.

"Sure. Yes. Thanks."

B.J. studied me. "I mean it. You bring him now, hear? By the way, I know you didn't want to talk about this in front of Ray, but I ran into Junie St. Pierre over at the hospital this afternoon."

"Oh?"

"Sounds like they're going great guns trying to identify those remains. Must have been a huge surprise for you to find that unmarked grave out there after all these years. Some unknown person buried on your land."

"Like Ball's Bluff," Tyler said.

"What are you talking about?" I asked.

"The cemetery at Ball's Bluff. Twenty-five graves. No one knows who's buried in twenty-four of them."

"That was different, son," B.J. said. "People knew the bodies were there. They just didn't get to them for a while."

He saw me staring. "You don't know the story, Lucie?"

I shook my head, glad to divert the conversation from the body on my land. "Nope."

"It took some time before the Union bodies were buried after the battle. The original graves were shallow, so eventually rain and the other elements exposed them again. It was only a matter of time before the animals who used the place as a grazing field found the remains. Chewing on bones and the like."

Like Bruja had done. "How gruesome," I said.

"If you've never been to Ball's Bluff, you ought to see it before the reenactment," Tyler said.

"I know I should. I'm embarrassed I haven't ever visited it."

"You and lots of other folks," B.J. said. "Plenty of people living around here don't know anything about the battle or have any idea the cemetery's right there at the edge of the Potomac. It's a pretty little park now. Real peaceful."

"Come on, B.J., it's haunted," Tyler said. "It's not peaceful at all."

"Rubbish." He waved an arm at Tyler and kissed me on the cheek. "Don't believe him. But go see it."

After B.J. left, I said to Tyler, "What are you talking about?"

"All those scattered bones," he said. "When the army finally built a proper cemetery after the war, they filled the twenty-five coffins with the body parts of fifty-four soldiers, since no one was still . . . intact."

"You mean, random body parts in the same coffin?"

"Yup." He sounded cheerful. "Except for one guy. James Allen. But based on the number of casualties, it's a known fact that there were more soldiers out there whose remains never made it inside the cemetery. Their ghosts still haunt the place."

"Hogwash."

He pushed his glasses up his nose. "I swear to God. People see lights, like candles, in the woods after dark. And tree branches shake when there's no breeze. Some of the sheriff's deputies who get assigned to patrol the area don't like it because they've seen things, too."

A light breeze blew up. I found myself glancing at the villa to see if there were unexplained lights shining in the windows.

Tyler followed my gaze. "I'm not making this up."

"There's got to be a rational explanation," I said. "I agree with B.J."

Though I, too, had heard stories about Mosby sightings. Folks who swore they'd seen the Gray Ghost on moonless nights returning to look for Union soldiers. Some even said he haunted our ruins, and Eli had teased me about it when I was a kid.

"Suit yourself." Tyler grinned. "Want to visit the place at dusk? We could see who's right."

"Are you trying to spook me?"

"Maybe."

He walked me over to my car, which I'd left in the lot, and I slid into the front seat.

"I wonder if the spirit of whoever was buried out by the vineyard is still wandering around," he said. "No one knows who it is, and whoever killed him got away with it. That would be reason enough to still roam the earth, don't you think?"

"You really are trying to spook me."

He smiled again and got in his car. "Nah. It's a good ghost story, though, isn't it?"

Tyler pulled out first and I followed him down Sycamore Lane. At the split in the road, he went right and I went left. I watched his brake lights in my rearview mirror until they disappeared around a turn. The road felt odd and exposed without the sheltering branches of the old sycamore. My headlights caught stacked piles of wood moved off to one side.

Tyler was right. Whoever had lain out there in that field was an unknown soul. If he had been murdered, his killer had never been brought to justice.

I drove back to my still-dark, quiet house. That thought alone was enough to haunt me.

Chapter 8

⸺❦⸺

That night I slept in my own bed, instead of in the hammock on the veranda. The last time I remembered looking at my alarm clock was just after three. When sleep finally came, I dreamed about the cemetery at Ball's Bluff and the grave on my land. I woke when a fox began crying in the middle of the night. It sounded like someone was strangling a baby. I sat up, seeing figures in the shadows that I could not persuade myself were imagined.

At five o'clock I quit pretending I'd sleep if I kept my eyes closed long enough, and got out of bed. The now-familiar absence of sound, like the house had stopped breathing, was a letdown. Another day without power. If we didn't have electricity, and especially air-conditioning, restored by to-morrow, we needed to think about implementing Plan B for the weekend and our anniversary celebration.

I went downstairs and threw out the contents of my re-frigerator and freezer, unplugged it, and propped the doors open. I found a box of baking soda in the pantry and put it on one of the refrigerator shelves, hoping it would absorb the sour odors of spoiled food.

The pantry search had also turned up a box of strawberry Pop-Tarts left over from the last time Eli's daughter, my two-year-old niece, Hope, had visited. The sell-by date had passed, which wasn't a surprise. Brandi once called my house a living mausoleum and made no bones about how much she disliked coming here. If I wanted to see Hope, the mountain went to Mohammed. But then, Brandi didn't much care for me, either, since she knew I disapproved of her profligate ways. Mostly I saw my niece when her mother went on a shopping spree up to New York or spent the weekend in Washington with one of her girlfriends.

I brought a foil-wrapped packet of Pop-Tarts back upstairs and started my post-tornado routine for getting ready for work. Another cold sponge bath from a bottle of water followed by rooting through the laundry basket to find my least dirty pair of jeans. Too bad I hadn't washed my clothes before the tornado, but the previous weekend at the winery had been hectic and I'd never gotten around to it. At least I still had clean T-shirts. We'd be back out in the fields today removing debris, so whatever I wore would be filthy by tonight.

Quinn called from the barrel room as I was trying to decide what to do with my hair. The last time I washed it had been Sunday, four days ago.

"I figured you'd be up," he said.

"I couldn't sleep. Tossed everything in my fridge. The cupboard is officially bare. I'll be over in a few minutes. I just need to braid my hair. It's getting disgusting."

"You could wash it here," he said. "There's hot water in the barrel room."

I picked up a strand of light brown hair that looked and felt dirty. "Maybe I will."

"Come on over now and you can have the other half of my breakfast while it's still hot. I picked up two fried biscuit sandwiches at the convenience store off Route 17. Egg, ham, and cheese. And an extralarge coffee."

I was in the middle of opening the package of Pop-Tarts with my teeth. "I can't eat your breakfast."

"You just said the cupboard was bare. I bet you're down to eating whatever old stuff is still in your cabinets, aren't you?"

"Of course not."

"Ha! Knew I was right. Come and get it before the grease congeals. The biscuits are great, but if they get cold they sit in your stomach like cannonballs."

"Give me five minutes."

I threw the pastry in the wastebasket and got my shampoo and a towel from the bathroom. If Quinn had any unclogged arteries before he reached his fiftieth birthday, someone should write about him in a medical journal.

He was sitting on the courtyard wall drinking coffee when I arrived. I set my cane down and joined him. The early morning sky was the color of a robin's egg and sun-gilded wisps of clouds dotted the sky. A breeze riffed the flowers in the hanging baskets and the halved wine barrels and the air was fragrant with wild honeysuckle. From here the vineyard looked serene and pastoral. Who would guess that just out of view a bulldozer sat amid enormous piles of rotting fruit, splintered posts, and trellis wire lethal as razors?

"Gonna be nice today." Quinn handed me a white paper bag with stains on it.

"Looks like it." I pulled out the sandwich, which was

wrapped in more stained white paper, and opened it up. "Someone took a bite already."

"That would be me. It's only one bite."

"You're still hungry." I tried to give it back to him. "I can't take this."

He waved me off. "Sure you can. Trust me, I'm full. It may look small, but one of those things will keep you going all day."

The sandwich, I had to admit, tasted terrific. "You ever find the *dodine*?"

"On the floor next to some barrels in one of the bays. I almost stepped on it. If I find out who did it, heads will roll. How'd your evening go with B.J. and the other guy?"

" 'The other guy' is a teetotaler and one of those hard-core types who want everything to be authentic Civil War era right down to your eyeglasses. Ray Vitale. He also wants to put the winery off-limits to all the reenactors."

"What'd you say?"

"No way. B.J. talked to him, too."

"Can't wait to meet him."

"Mmpfh."

"Good sandwich, huh?"

He passed me the extralarge coffee in a Styrofoam cup. I nodded and took a sip. Quinn liked his coffee brewed so road crews could use it to fill potholes if they ran out of tar.

"I know you don't mean 'heads will roll' literally," I said.

"It was careless and I spent a goddamn hour looking for the thing. You bet I do. Ever see anyone do *sabrage*?"

The art of beheading a champagne bottle with a saber. I'd seen it done once, years ago. I knew he was joking, but after what Chance had claimed last night, I wish Quinn had said straight out that it was a figure of speech.

"Maybe you shouldn't be so hard on the men." I crumpled the sandwich bag.

He drew his head back in surprise. "What are you talking about? Hard on the men? It's screwup city every day now. You ought to be as upset as I am about it."

"I am. I mean, not *as* upset as you are. But maybe you could just . . . go a little easier on them."

The truth, it seemed to me, had to lie somewhere between Chance's accusations of bullying and abuse and Quinn's feeling that he was justified in being angry at sloppy work and holding the crew accountable. Hell, it was my vineyard. Of course I didn't like all the careless mistakes and incompetent fieldwork. But if I tipped my hand to Quinn at what Chance said last night, would it be like pulling the pin from a grenade?

"Sometimes I don't understand you." He took the sandwich bag from me and crumpled it into a tighter ball. "Don't you care that all these mistakes are setting us back? Costing us money? Having an impact on the kind of wine we're able to make?"

"Sure I do, but—"

"But what?"

I closed my eyes and breathed in and out. When I opened them, he was staring at me with that dark, brooding look he sometimes wore. It usually meant we were headed for a showdown.

"What if . . . well, maybe you could be a little less demanding of the guys. Maybe we'd get better results. You know, encourage them rather than intimidate them."

It sounded, even to me, like I was pleading with him. His mouth hung open.

"Let me get this straight. The reason we have so many problems in the field and the barrel room is that I scare the crew? It would have nothing to do with the fact that they're so inexperienced they don't know what the hell they're doing. And in some cases, they don't even seem to care."

"Please," I said. "I know you've been under a lot of pressure lately. But please, try to take it easy on yourself and the men."

"Sure," he said. "Next time someone leaves off a bunghole cap and ruins a barrel of wine worth five grand, I'll smile and ask if he'll please pay more attention so it doesn't happen again. God forbid I should hurt someone's feelings. Is that what you want?"

"Yes. No. I don't know."

"Well, I'm glad you can at least give me a straight answer."

I held his coffee cup with both hands and stared unhappily into it.

"Look," he said. "Maybe my fuse is a little short because of so many things going wrong. But I just don't get it. It's like we're cursed all the time. Ever since Chance came."

"You can't blame it on him."

"Watch me."

"It isn't all his fault. Maybe we tried to expand too fast, too soon," I said. "A couple of years ago we were able to handle things with just you, me, and Hector. Plus we usually had the same crew of day laborers. Now I don't recognize anybody since we started competing for workers with all the new vineyards springing up like weeds after rain. They need help, just like we do. We're all looking for a few good men. The same good men."

"The 'few good men' are working for someone else. We get the bottom of the wine barrel as regular as clockwork." He held up a hand as if to physically stave off my response. "Okay, I've said my piece. And now if we're done here, you want to wash your greasy hair before the guys show up?"

I ran my fingers along my braid, feeling self-conscious. "You think it looks greasy?"

"You're the one who said it was. Okay, don't wash it. It looks fine."

"Now you're patronizing me."

"Believe me, I would never be that stupid."

"So you think it looks fine, then. Not greasy."

"Oh, for God's sake. You know, someone once told me that when a woman asks a man what he thinks, all she really wants is to hear her own opinion in a deeper voice. After two years of working with you, I now realize the wisdom of those words."

"You're impossible, you know that?"

He held out his hand and I let him pull me up. Together we walked over to the barrel room and he held the door. As I walked past him, he leaned close to my ear. "You look great, sweetheart, just great."

"Oh, shut up," I said, and he laughed.

I undid my braid and went over to the deep sink we used to wash out equipment. "Guess I'll get this over with."

I waited for the water to warm up, then ducked my head under the goosenecked faucet.

"What are you doing?" Quinn asked.

I brought my head up to reply and banged it against the lip of the faucet.

"Ow! I'm trying to see if I can knock myself unconscious if I hit my head hard enough."

"Don't move."

"Where am I going to go?"

He came back with one of the chairs we used for wine-maker's dinners and set it down facing away from the sink.

"Have a seat."

"I can't wash my hair sitting down like that."

"That's why I'm going to wash it. Sit."

I sat.

His hands were strong and gentle. Almost against my will I could feel myself begin to relax as he massaged my temples and my forehead. His gaze roamed over my face and my body until finally I had to close my eyes so he wouldn't guess how erotic I found his touch.

It had been nearly one year since we'd each been involved with other people. My relationship had been a torrid, stormy affair with Mick Dunne, an Englishman who lived next door. Quinn had fallen hard for Bonita, the daughter of our previous farm manager, and she had lived up to her name as a stunning beauty. They drifted apart, as Mick and I had done, until finally Bonita moved to California with her mother after Hector died.

But if he had any clue about my feelings as he wrapped the towel around my head and helped me up, he gave no indication.

"How was that?"

"You give great massages." I unwrapped the towel and began drying my hair, aware that his eyes were fixed on what I was doing. "Thank you. That felt terrific."

"You, ah, wouldn't consider . . . ?" He paused. "Never mind."

My heart began pounding against my ribs. I wouldn't consider what? Maybe he *had* read my thoughts after all?

"What is it?" I asked.

"Do you think I could borrow your shampoo?"

My shampoo.

"Be my guest. It promotes shine and brings out highlights."

He grinned and picked it up, tossing it in the air. "Guess I'll have to switch brands. Mine doesn't do that."

"Sit," I said.

"Oh, come on." But he sat. Then he said, "Wait a minute."

He got up and stripped off his shirt, keeping his eyes on mine as he did it. I didn't often see him bare chested. He looked good.

To be honest, he looked terrific.

He wrapped his fingers around my wrists as I shampooed his hair and massaged his temples, as he had done with me. But this time there were no romantic overtones and we were back to our usual banter.

"You look good from this angle," he said.

"Upside down?"

"For some people, it's their best side."

"Watch it. I control the water and you're in a vulnerable place. By the way, you do a good job of covering that bald spot."

He jerked upright, splattering water down the front of my T-shirt and jeans. "What bald spot?"

I laughed and eased him back in the chair. "Calm down. You've got more hair than a Chia Pet."

He chuckled and let me finish rinsing the shampoo out of his hair. When I was done, he sat up and I handed him my towel.

"Sorry it's so wet. I only brought one."

"It's okay." His eyes held mine. "I don't mind at all."

At the far end of the barrel room, the outside door opened and closed. A woman's voice said, "Knock-knock? Hello?"

"Sorry, we're closed," Quinn said. He threw the towel on the workbench and headed toward the front door, trying to pull on his shirt, which had gotten tangled up in itself. I shoved the shampoo under the towel and followed him.

A waiflike blonde with a boyish haircut, jet-black eyebrows, and exotic cheekbones waited by the door, hands in the back pockets of jeans that looked like she'd painted them on. Red high-top sneakers and a bright yellow tank top that didn't meet the waistline of her jeans. She looked about sixteen. Her gaze traveled from Quinn to me, taking stock of our wet hair and water-stained clothes.

Quinn still hadn't managed to get his shirt completely untangled. I reached over and tugged on it as our visitor watched, an amused smile creeping into her eyes.

"We're, ah, definitely closed," I said.

"I apologize for . . . interrupting," she said. "But a blond woman in the other building told me I could find the owner here. And I didn't come to buy wine." She zeroed in on me. "Lucie Montgomery?"

"Yes?"

She held out her hand. "Savannah Hayden. I work for the medical examiner. I need access to the site where those remains were recovered. Thought I'd stop by and let you know I'll be out there for a while."

I froze, with my hand half outstretched toward hers. "Is something wrong? Detective Noland told me last night they were finished."

Her voice was cool. "Maybe Detective Noland was finished, but I'm not. I need to take another look around and resurvey the area." She clasped my hand and shook it. "I trust there'll be no problem with that."

"Are you a doctor, Savannah . . . Miss Hayden?"

"Not an MD," she said. "But it is Dr. Hayden. I have a PhD in forensic anthropology." She looked over at Quinn, who had not taken his eyes off her since she'd introduced herself.

"What did they miss?" he asked. "It must be important or the medical examiner would be doing this. They wouldn't have sent a forensic anthropologist."

Savannah's smile was tolerant, but it looked like she appreciated the shrewdness of Quinn's remark. "I'm sorry, Mr. . . . ?"

"Quinn Santori."

"Mr. Santori. I can't discuss an ongoing investigation. But I need to see the site so I can put things in context."

"I'm not sure how much context you're going to get," I said. "The bones were already scattered when I discovered the grave the other day. That was before Bobby Noland and his deputies spent all day yesterday digging the place up."

She folded her thin arms across her chest. "I understand. Still, it's possible to learn a lot from visiting the site." She shrugged. "Maybe I'm looking for different things than they were."

"Like what?" I asked. "Generally speaking, that is."

"Generally speaking, you'd be surprised what can be determined by knowing the orientation of a body in the surroundings where it's found. Was it on a hill or in the woods? Facing which way? How deep was the grave? You look for clues that help you determine whether he or she had been killed somewhere else."

"So why didn't you come out here with the others to begin with?" Quinn asked. "Since you're asking all the good questions."

Another smile, this one revealing dimples in both cheeks. She was cute in a tomboyish way.

"Money. I'm a luxury. I get brought in only when they can't find everything they need and they hope I'll uncover something new."

"Need a ride out there?" Quinn asked. "I can take you in one of our ATVs."

"Thanks. I've got a map and a Jeep." She rocked back

and forth on the outsides of her red high-tops, a sweet, self-conscious trait that reminded me of my younger sister, Mia. "I'd better get going."

On her way out the door, she looked over her shoulder. "See you around."

She was talking to Quinn. He cleared his throat as the door closed behind her. "Interesting kid," he said.

"She may look like a teenager, but she's no kid."

"You all right?"

"Fine."

He patted me on the back. A brotherly gesture. "Don't worry about her, Lucie. They're just covering their asses sending her back to check the place out. Nothing's going to happen."

The prototype for every girlfriend he'd had since I knew him had just walked through the door and she was here to find something at that grave site that Bobby had missed. Savannah Hayden seemed to have her eye on Quinn and she also seemed sure she wasn't going out to the grave site on a wild-goose chase.

Plenty was going to happen.

Chapter 9

Frankie reached me on my cell phone, which I'd charged in the barrel room, while I was pulling leaves in the Seyval block just before noon.

"Praise the Lord and pass the ammunition," she said. "Power's back on."

"Hooray," I said. "When?"

I stripped off my gardening gloves and sat down in the shade of a large, leafy vine. A yellow jacket buzzed near a grape cluster that oozed sugary juice. I swiped at the wasp with my gloves and it flew off.

"Fifteen minutes ago."

"Great. Now we won't have to change our plans for the weekend."

"I called your cousin and told her. Thanked her for offering to bail us out with generators and anything else we needed."

"Thanks. What'd she say?"

"Her exact words?" Frankie said. "That it's been her experience in catering that ninety-eight percent of the time you never need to go through with your backup plans. But it's always good to be prepared for the other ten percent when things fall through."

I smiled. "Sounds like Dominique. She did save our bacon, though."

"She mentioned that. Told me that when it came to family she was always ready to stick her neck out on a limb."

Though she'd been in the country for more than a decade, Dominique still found American idioms challenging. Her interpretations could be baffling, but we always understood her perfectly.

"She means it," I said.

Frankie chuckled. "I know."

I stood up. "I am going home to enjoy a long, hot shower. I'll be by the office later to check e-mail and catch up on what went on in the world during the past few days now that my computer's back online."

"Do you want to tell Quinn we've got power since he's out there with you?"

"Sure. He's working in the Malbec block. I'll stop by and let him know."

But when I pulled up in the Gator to where Benny, Javier, and Jesús were making a bonfire-sized pile out of what had once been thriving Malbec vines, Quinn wasn't around. We hadn't planted much of that grape, but it had been a particular favorite of his because of its deep plummy color, rich tannins, and the complexity it would add to our Cabernet Sauvignon blend. We'd taken the biggest hit here and I knew he was upset about losing nearly almost all of those vines.

"Where's Quinn?" I asked.

The three men all wore baseball caps under which they'd draped towels to protect the back of their necks against sunburn. The effect always reminded me of something out of *Lawrence of Arabia*. Benny took off his cap and wiped his perspiring face with his towel. He had a thick black mustache and luxuriant black hair. Of the three, his English was the strongest.

"Queen went to see the señorita," he said. "Left a little while ago."

"Which señorita?" I asked. But I knew which one.

"*La rubia.*" He gestured in the general direction of the creek and the reenactment site. "The blonde."

"I see." I fiddled with the Gator key, nearly dropping it. "Thanks."

Benny's lively eyes rested on me. His expression was respectful, but his face softened with understanding. "Can I tell him something for you, Lucie?" His voice was kind.

"No, that's okay. You don't even need to mention that I stopped by. I was heading back to the house so I just thought I'd see how it's going."

Benny glanced over his shoulder at the growing pile of debris. "Going good. We're getting there. Maybe we can start replanting soon."

He pulled a flattened pack of Marlboros out of the pocket of his mud-stained jeans and lit up.

"I hope so," I said. "One more thing."

He exhaled smoke. "What?"

"Is Quinn . . . is everything okay with you and Quinn? I mean, with all the men and Quinn?"

Benny's eyebrows came together and he seemed surprised by the question.

"Okay?" he asked. "How do you mean, 'okay'?"

"Are you getting along?"

"Sure. We get along real good."

"Has he been . . . well, impatient lately?"

"*¿Cómo?*"

"Mad?"

"Sure, mad. When things break or we can't find something." He shook his head and made a clicking sound with his teeth. "And we got some new guys coming to work. They don't know nothing. He gets mad at that."

"Is he too hard on those men, do you think? Does he get very mad?"

Benny took a drag on his cigarette and blew out a long stream of smoke. He stared at the horizon while he seemed to consider my question.

"I think he's more mad at himself, sometimes. You know how Queen can be."

"Look, Benny, if there are any problems, you come tell me. You hear?"

"*Sí, sí.* I'll tell you."

"How about Chance? Everything okay with him?"

"Chance?" He expelled smoke. "Sure. Everybody likes Chance. He laughs. Jokes a lot. Doesn't yell at anyone." He shrugged. "Queen doesn't like him much."

"I know."

He finished his cigarette and dropped it to the ground. I watched him pulverize it under the toe of his heavy work boot. "Can I ask something, Lucie?"

"Sure."

"Something going on between you and Queen?" His eyes searched my face. "You two okay?"

We both knew what he was asking and that it had to do with a blond señorita. I didn't want to talk about it, so I put on my best poker face.

"I'm not sure what you mean," I said, "but everything's fine."

When I called Quinn's cell phone after I finished talking with Benny, it went straight to voice mail. I left a succinct message about the power being restored. On my way home, I took a different route so I didn't have to pass the grave site.

After showering and doing a load of laundry, I drove over to the villa. Frankie was on the phone at the tasting room bar, so I waved and headed to my office without stopping to talk. Quinn and I had adjoining offices off a corridor that could be reached through the small wine library that was just off the tasting room. Besides our offices, there was a back entrance to the galley kitchen we used when we had parties and dinners in the villa.

He was at his desk, staring at his computer monitor when I stopped in the doorway. His office, like his house, was half monastic cell, half locker room.

"I got five hundred and fourteen e-mails in the past four days."

He propped a foot on his trash can and leaned back in his chair, hands clasped behind his head. Like me, he looked like he'd also gone home, since he'd changed his clothes and shaved.

"Are you serious?"

He sat forward and frowned at his monitor. "I bet I could delete about four hundred of 'em. You know how many people want me to buy prescription drugs in Canada? And, uh, take advantage of other life-enhancing opportunities?"

"Try setting your spam filter on something more restrictive and you won't get so much garbage."

He glanced up. "You all right? You seem kind of touchy."

"I'm fine."

He picked up a corkscrew on his desk and began spinning it around with his index finger. "We ought to be done cleaning up the tornado damage by next week. I think we're at the point where we can split up the crew so some are back on canopy management. And I'm considering picking the Riesling early."

"How come?" I folded my arms and leaned against the doorjamb.

"After what we lost in the tornado, I don't want to take any chances. Hurricane season's gearing up. Did you see that new one over the Atlantic? 'Bill.'" He grinned. "Who picks these names?"

I didn't feel like grinning back and I was annoyed with myself—and him—for being irked because he'd gone off to see Savannah Hayden this morning.

"The National Weather Service. They use a six-year rotating list from the World Meteorological Organization and retire the devastating ones." It came out sharp.

"Oh." He rubbed his chin. "You are touchy."

"Look, they have no idea whether that storm is going to turn into a hurricane, stall out at sea, or what it's going to do. We've never picked the Riesling this early before. The more hang time those grapes have, the better," I said. "Why don't we see what Bill has in mind before we jump the gun? No offense, but our weather's a little different in Virginia. When's the last time California had a hurricane? I grew up here."

"California has fires and earthquakes."

"Then you get to call the shots first time we're dealing with either of those. Okay?"

He made a face. "I'm willing to wait twenty-four hours, but I don't want to be out on a limb with a saw because it's too late to get a crew in." He set the corkscrew down and leaned back in the desk chair again. "By the way, I stopped by the grave site. I think Savannah might come by tonight for a beer after she's done out there."

I kept my expression bland. "You invited her?"

He cocked his head and squinted at me. "Sure. Why not? Don't you want to know if she found anything new?"

"Of course I do. But she's as likely to talk as those bones are. You heard her this morning."

"A beer or two might loosen her up."

"Her? I doubt it."

"Okay, sorry. I'll call her and tell her it's off." He unclipped his cell phone from his belt.

So he had her phone number already. Probably even on speed dial. Maybe the real reason for getting Savannah to lose a few inhibitions had nothing to do with seeing if she'd talk about what she'd uncovered at the grave site today. Quinn sure hadn't wasted any time, but he'd also turned the tables so I looked churlish asking him to uninvite her.

"Don't call. It's fine you asked her. I just don't think anything's going to come of it, that's all."

"We'll see." He put his phone away and I thought I saw a glint of something in his eyes.

Maybe anticipating the possibility of a new romance? I went next door to my own office and closed the door. Quinn's personal life was his business and I'd been a damned fool for believing there'd been a change in our relationship and our feelings for each other.

Something could come of Savannah's happy hour visit this evening. But it wouldn't have anything to do with sharing information about whatever Bobby had missed finding out in that field. She was attracted to Quinn and now it seemed the feeling was mutual.

I turned on my computer and, with a heavy heart, began wading through my own clogged in-box. I was not looking forward to tonight.

*   *   *

Savannah showed up at the villa just after five. The knees of her jeans were stiff with mud and she had a smear of dirt across one cheek in the shape of a crescent moon. Her nose and the tops of her shoulders were bright pink with sunburn.

"Want to wash up?" I asked. "We might have some aloe for that burn."

"I forgot my sunscreen. Can you believe it?" She sounded rueful. "And I thought I had washed up. I've got hand sanitizer in my car."

"You missed a spot on your face."

Quinn arrived while she was still cleaning up in the bathroom. Since I'd seen him a few hours ago, he'd found time to change yet again. This time into one of his favorite Hawaiian print shirts, the blue one with fish swimming all over it. If at some time during the course of our drinks he mentioned to Savannah that it was a vintage shirt—and quite special—then he'd dressed to impress her.

"Savannah's here," I said.

"I know. She called and said she was on her way over. Want a beer?" His dark eyes met mine and I saw no spark of the affection or attraction I'd imagined I'd seen before. Just a friend, waiting for the reply to a question.

"Lucie? You all right?"

"Sorry. I'll have wine. I'll get it."

"I got it. White or red?"

"I don't care." Why hadn't I figured out some last-minute chore to do?

"I hate it when you say that. Go sit on the terrace and wait to be surprised."

I went outside and sat at one of the tables next to the railing, staring out at the mountains. Though it was only the beginning of August, already the shadows were less harsh than they'd been a few weeks ago. We still had nearly two more months of summer left—technically—but I always felt let down when the sunlight lost its sharp clarity, becoming milky and viscous as it was now. Nature sent better signals than the date on the calendar.

Savannah's laughter, bright and heedless, floated through the open French doors, followed by the sound of Quinn's deep voice murmuring something else that made her giggle. She came outside first, carrying a tray with a bottle of Riesling in an ice bucket and a wineglass. Quinn held two beers splayed between his fingers and a bag of chips. I'd gotten used to his preference for consuming his food in its most natural state. Beer from the bottle, chips from the bag.

"Great shirt," Savannah was saying.

"Thanks. It's vintage. See here? You can tell the quality of the print by how thin the fish lips are."

"No fooling?"

Too bad I hadn't bet somebody how fast he'd use that line. They sat down across from me. Savannah reached over and grabbed the bottle opener while Quinn poured my wine. She popped the cap with well-practiced ease and took a swig.

"Just what I needed." She leaned her head back against her chair and closed her eyes. "This is the life."

Quinn hoisted his beer. "To the life."

I raised my glass and we drank. His eyes met mine over his bottle before he turned to Savannah. "How'd it go today? Any luck?"

"It went all right." She cocked an eyebrow and for a second she reminded me of Peter Pan with her gamine boyishness and perky attitude. "I'm done."

"You finished everything?" I asked. "That was fast."

"You're not coming back?" Quinn asked.

She smiled, showing the dimples. "Not for work, at least."

I saw Quinn's self-conscious grin and set my glass down, sloshing wine on the table.

"You found what you were looking for, then?" I swiped the puddle with the side of my fist.

"I hope so," she said. "I'll know more after I get back to the lab and check things out."

"Any idea how long that will take?"

Savannah straightened up. "Look, I'm sorry I can't talk about this, but if I get called into court to testify, you think I'd like to risk being the one who leaked evidence and caused the case to be thrown out on a technicality? The judge would have my butt in a sling unless the sheriff got it first."

I met Quinn's eyes briefly with an I-told-you-so look.

"You must have been looking for something small," he said. "That small bone in the throat, maybe? The hyoid. You could tell if he was strangled if it was broken."

Savannah studied us like a teacher trying to figure out if we'd cheated by copying each other's exam papers. "Sure, just like on television. Look, guys, it's not that simple. Say I did find a broken hyoid. First of all there's a difference between a postmortem and an antemortem fracture. The crystalline structure in bone after death is different from injury to so-called living bone. Bone with no collagen in it will shatter like glass. Just because you find broken or fractured bones doesn't mean it has anything to do with the cause of death."

Quinn poured more wine into my glass and pointed a finger at Savannah's nearly empty bottle of beer. "Refill?"

"Sure. Why not?"

He left to get the beers.

"He's nice," she said to me.

"Yes."

"How'd you get interested in making wine?"

I suppose I couldn't blame her for wanting to change the

subject, which she'd just done with sledge-hammer subtlety. "Family business. How'd you get interested in skeletons?"

"I majored in archaeology as an undergrad," she said as Quinn returned with the beers, this time already opened. He handed her one of them and she nodded thanks. "My specialty was Egyptology."

"Mummies and pyramids?" Quinn asked.

"Mummies and pyramids are only part of it. The ancient Egyptians had an amazing funerary culture in their society," she said. "When you think of all the artifacts unearthed in roomlike tombs and the fabulous royal cemeteries, you realize how important death and preparing someone for the afterlife were to them."

"That's why it's true what they say about cemeteries. People are just dying to get in," Quinn said.

Savannah gave him a look that would wilt concrete. "Gee, did you make that up? I never heard it before."

"Ignore him," I said. "That's what I do."

Quinn smirked at both of us and drank his beer. "It's a long way from the Egyptians to the Loudoun County Sheriff's Department."

"Not as long as you'd think," Savannah said. "The Egyptians buried their dead in the desert where the preservation of bodies is exceptional. Finally it became sort of obvious that what I really enjoyed was looking at skeletons. Particularly trying to figure out how someone died. So I got a forensics degree in graduate school and then my doctorate."

"Guess you were dying to do it," he said.

"Will you shut up?" both of us said in unison.

He grinned some more and leered at us over his beer.

"So now you work full-time for the medical examiner?" I asked.

She shook her head. "They can't afford me full-time. I

only get called in on the cases where there's been so much decomp the medical examiner can't do a proper autopsy."

"What else do you do," Quinn asked, "when you're not working for the county?"

"Teach forensics in northern Virginia and D.C. Every so often I get to go back to Egypt to do research."

"That must be pretty cool." He eyed her.

"It is. The pyramids are incredible. If you've never been, you ought to visit them sometime."

Her unspoken invitation lingered in the air as a large bird flew out of the woods and sailed above us.

"A red-tailed hawk," Quinn said, filling the awkward moment of silence. "Look."

We watched as it turned west toward the mountains, a graceful silhouette against the peach-colored early evening sky. What remained of the sunlight bronzed the treetops as though they'd been burnished and the light breeze felt like a warm caress. Pockets of sunshine filtered through the branches like spotlights, shimmering on the leaves like moving water.

"I ought to be going," I said. "You two stay and drink your beers."

"You haven't finished your wine," Quinn said. "What's your rush?"

Savannah swung a leg over the arm of her chair and rocked it back and forth. The red high-tops were dirtier than they'd been this morning.

"Quinn says you're reenacting the Battle of Ball's Bluff here pretty soon."

"The weekend after next," I said.

"I'd like to see it," she said. "I know the cemetery quite well."

"I've heard it's haunted," I said. "That spirits of soldiers who were never properly buried come back to roam the battleground."

Quinn snorted. "That is such a load of crap."

"I've heard those stories. And I know people swear by them. They also claim they see Mosby's ghost." Savannah drank her beer. "Sorry, you two. When the spark of human life is gone, it's gone. A skeleton is nothing more than what's left after the really important stuff isn't there anymore."

"It's still part of who that person was," I said. "Isn't it?"

Savannah looked taken aback. "Of course. Don't get me wrong. I didn't mean to imply that it's nothing but a pile of bones. I always show respect for the remains I examine. In fact, when I'm at the museum in Cairo I give my skeletons names."

"That's kind of weird," Quinn said.

"Not really. The Egyptians believed the way to keep a person alive in the afterlife was by speaking his or her name, saying it out loud. That's why the enemies of the pharaohs tried to destroy their monuments, carving out or slashing the names. By doing that you erased the person in the afterlife."

"So you believe you're keeping someone alive, even though he's dead, because you say his name?" I asked.

"It's more like paying homage to the Egyptian belief that a person's name is an integral part of who he is."

"And you never sense that person is present—that he's there, somehow—when you're talking to him, saying his name?"

"Sorry, no." She shook her head. "Although I know plenty of people who do believe in that kind of stuff. I even know people who claim to be the reincarnation of Tutankhamen. Or one of the other pharaohs."

"You must have some interesting friends," Quinn said.

Savannah smiled. "I attend a lot of seminars, especially

ones that relate to ancient cultures. They show up there."

"Claiming to be Tutankhamen?" he asked.

"In the flesh. We, uh, call them 'pyramidiots.' I know that's not very nice, but some of these people . . ." She twirled her finger by her temple. "It can get pretty strange."

Quinn motioned to Savannah's empty beer bottle and my wineglass. "Another refill, anyone?"

"No, thanks," Savannah said. "Two's my limit. Besides, I ought to be going. Thanks for the beers and the hospitality. You've been very kind."

"Why don't I walk you to your car?" Quinn said.

"I'd like that." She stood and turned to me. "Thanks again, Lucie."

"It was nothing." I started to put the empty bottles and my glass on the tray.

"Leave that. I'll take care of it," Quinn said to me. "See you in the morning, okay?"

"Sure. Good night."

I reached for my cane and left without looking back. Quinn was already talking to Savannah about showing her the barrel room, persuading her not to leave just yet.

When I got home, I went directly outside to the veranda and watched the Blue Ridge disappear into the velvet blackness of the night sky. After a while I went inside and got another bottle of Riesling. Then I lit all the torches in the border garden and all the candles scattered on the tables until it felt like I was sitting in a gilded bath of fire. For a long time, I rocked back and forth in the glider, listening to the night sounds of the cicadas and frogs and the occasional owl, as I slowly drank glass after glass of wine.

Someone once said that if you wish to keep your affairs secret, you should drink no wine. But if there was no one around—and certainly no affair—then it didn't matter, did it?

* * *

Quinn woke me the next morning when the sun was already bright and hot in the sky. I was still in the glider wearing yesterday's clothes. My empty Riesling bottle lay on the floor and my wineglass sat on the glass coffee table among multiple sticky rings of sloshed wine.

"Now I know why you didn't show up for work." He picked up the bottle. "Been drinking up all our profits single-handedly, have we?"

I held my head between my hands. "Please don't. I feel dreadful."

"I'll make some coffee and get the aspirin. Don't move."

"Don't worry." I lay back down and closed my eyes.

He was back a short while later with two mugs and an aspirin bottle sticking out of the pocket of his jeans. "Here. Drink this."

He sat down next to me. As usual, he'd brewed coffee strong enough to strip paint.

"Thanks."

"Something you want to talk about?" he asked. "I knew you were upset last night when you left. I was going to call you, but things went kind of late with Savannah."

"It's okay." I felt numb, except for a headache the size of Pittsburgh. Did "kind of late" mean breakfast?

"I've got some good news. You'll like this." He blew on his coffee. "Savannah's teaching schedule is sort of erratic so she gets days off here and there. She agreed to help us out during harvest when she's free."

"She's going to work for us?"

"Yup. She's a real quick study. I took her over to the barrel room and showed her around after you left. Gave her a little education about winemaking. She's excited about doing this."

"That's nice."

I drank more coffee.

"That's all you've got to say? 'That's nice'? We could use the help, you know. People like her don't fall off trees."

He'd set the aspirin bottle on the coffee table. I shook out two tablets and swallowed them with a big gulp of coffee. He was right. We could use Savannah's help. I needed to pull myself together and get over any issues I had with how he felt about her. And jealousy. I needed to get over that, too.

"I'm sorry. I guess everything that's happened the past few days finally caught up with me last night. You're right. We could use her." I set down my mug. "Why don't I shower and change and meet you at the winery?"

"Sure. Come on over when you're up to it." He patted my knee like I was a child. "There's something I want to talk to you about."

"What?" My heart began thudding against my rib cage.

"It can wait."

"Maybe you'd better tell me now."

"If you say so." He cocked his head. "It's about the Riesling."

"The *Riesling*?"

"Yeah. I don't want to pick it all at harvest. I'm thinking about leaving about a third of the crop on the vines until the first frost so we can make ice wine."

Ice wine is a highly concentrated sweet dessert wine made from frozen grapes. No one in Virginia made it because it was such a risky and expensive venture. If the grapes stayed frozen, we could pick them at any time. But a hard frost at night, then warmer temperatures the next day meant the fruit would thaw and start to rot and we'd end up with nothing.

I massaged my forehead with my fingers. "It's an interesting idea except there's not a big market for dessert wines.

Certainly nowhere near the demand for our Riesling. You know that. Plus we're one of the very few vineyards in Virginia that make it. I think we'd be better off picking everything now. Look at what we lost already with the tornado damage."

"Why don't we have this conversation when you're not hung over?"

"I am not hung over."

He patted my knee again and stood up. "Sure you're not. Go take your shower and wake up, okay?"

I heard tires on gravel as a car pulled into the driveway and stopped in front of the house.

"Expecting someone?" he asked.

"Nope." Another car followed the first one.

"Sounds like a party. Shall I get it or do you want to?"

"I'll go. Can you, uh, clean—"

"Yeah, yeah. I'll get rid of the evidence. Drink more coffee. You got breath that would stop a charging elephant." He picked up my bottle and glass as the doorbell rang.

"Coming!" I called, then dropped my voice. "A charging elephant?"

"Better than a whole herd."

He disappeared down the back hall to the kitchen as I opened the door. Bobby Noland stood there with Biggie Mathis and Vic Fontana behind him. He held out a folded paper.

"Morning, Lucie. I got a search warrant here for your father's gun cabinet. I believe you still have his guns? All of them?"

I took the search warrant and nodded, not trusting my voice or my breath.

"We'd like to take a look, if you don't mind."

It didn't matter whether I minded or not. He was just

being polite, and that small courtesy, I figured, was because we had known each other for so long.

"What's this all about?" I asked finally. "Did you identify the body already? Savannah Hayden was out here yesterday looking for something. What did she do, work all night?"

Maybe that meant she hadn't been with Quinn very long, after all.

"We, ah, had a breakthrough," he said.

A breakthrough that brought them to Leland's gun cabinet.

"You know who it is, then?" I leaned against the door frame. My legs felt weak and my head was starting to spin again. "Did you identify the remains?"

"His name is Beauregard Kinkaid. Went by 'Beau.' Ever heard of him?"

"No. Should I?"

"According to his ex-wife, Beau had a falling-out with your father over some business deal they had going on. He told her he was going to pay your father a visit and straighten things out."

I did not like where this was going. "And did he?"

"She doesn't know. It was the last time she ever saw him."

Chapter 10

—⦾⦾⦾—

I opened the door wider and let Bobby inside. Fontana and Mathis followed, filing past me with their eyes averted as though they wanted to spare me any further embarrassment.

Bobby pointed across the foyer to the library, which had once been Leland's office. "The room over there, guys."

He knew our house probably as well as he knew his own. I half wished he'd been a stranger. Maybe I wouldn't have felt so betrayed and vulnerable.

"You want to get the key?" he asked me.

Leland always kept it above the doorjamb, which was out of my reach. I showed Bobby where to feel for it as Quinn arrived in the foyer.

"Morning, Bobby," he said. He leaned over and said in my ear, "What's going on?"

"They have a warrant to search Leland's gun cabinet." My eyes locked on his, beseeching him not to ask any more questions.

He put a hand on my shoulder and squeezed it. "It'll be okay."

I wondered if it would.

My father's gun cabinet was a large glass-fronted hutch that sat on top of a two-drawer base. As gun cabinets go, it was top-of-the-line. Cherry, rather than the customary oak or pine, so it matched the floor-to-ceiling bookshelves and all the other woodwork in the room. A deer standing atop a mountain had been etched into the glass, but even so, it was possible to see that the collection of firearms inside was equally impressive.

"His revolvers are in those drawers?" Bobby asked.

"Yes. The one on the left. Ammunition is on the right."

Biggie Mathis knelt, his joints cracking, and removed my father's Smith and Wesson .38. The room was silent as he placed it in a bag along with a couple rounds of ammunition.

When he was done, Bobby thanked him and asked if he'd wait outside with Fontana. This time both of them acknowledged me as they exited the room, as somber as if they were leaving a wake.

Bobby glanced at Quinn, but before he could speak, I said, "Quinn can stay, Bobby. I want him here."

"Okay." Bobby positioned himself in front of us, feet apart and hands clasped together, like a lawyer about to bring it home in his closing remarks to a jury. "I wanted to let you know that Annabel Chastain, Beau Kinkaid's ex-wife, is driving up from Charlottesville to talk to us. I'm sure you and I will be talking after that."

"How did you identify him so quickly?" I asked. "There must have been something obvious . . ."

Bobby looked like he was debating how much to tell me. Finally he said, "We caught a lucky break when we found that missing mandible. Kinkaid had some dental work done, a special kind of metal implant in his jaw that actually had a serial number on it. We traced him that way. His dentist also took care of the ex-wife. The guy was retired but he remembered that blade thing he put in. Apparently they were pretty rare thirty years ago."

Then why had they sent Savannah back? What else were they looking for?

Bobby saw the look in my eyes.

"I've said enough," he said. "The investigation's not finished."

"Can you at least tell me why Beau's ex-wife never reported the fact that he didn't come home after his meeting with Leland, not once in thirty years?"

"Because she wasn't sorry he didn't come home," Bobby said.

"What do you mean?"

"She said he abused her."

Until now, every time I pictured those bones out in the field I'd had only an out-of-focus image of a man in my head with no idea about his life or what kind of person he'd been. Now I knew he was married and someone who beat his wife.

"Doesn't that give his ex-wife a motive for killing him, too?"

"We're checking into that. Right now she's agreed to come in for questioning of her own free will," he said. "Look, try to take it easy and we'll go through this one step at a time. You're not in any trouble."

"Sure."

Bobby nodded at Quinn. "I'll see myself out."

After he left, Quinn pulled me into his arms. "It'll be all right," he said into my hair. "We'll get through this."

My voice was muffled on his shoulder. "I may not be in any trouble, but I sure as hell feel like I'm on trial."

Quinn urged me to take yet another day off and get lost somewhere, but as I told him, that only made it look like I had something to hide. It didn't help that Gina Leon, who worked in the tasting room with Frankie, was overly solicitous when I arrived at the villa, fussing over me while trying to pretend it was business as usual. It meant word had already gotten around about Beau Kinkaid and Bobby's visit to confiscate Leland's gun.

A lot of our customers wanted dark-haired, dark-eyed Gina to wait on them—especially the men, who liked the way she laughed and flirted, tossing her head and flashing her dazzling smile. Her personality was as effervescent as champagne fizz, but I learned to be careful what I said around her. I knew Gina was well-intentioned. She just leaked like a sieve.

Now she picked up a cream-colored vase filled with hydrangeas that had been sitting on an oak trestle table we used for additional wine tastings when the bar got too crowded.

"I made coffee and bought some croissants at the bakery in Middleburg. If you sit on the terrace, I'll bring you a tray as soon as I change the water for these flowers. The *Trib*'s on the bar."

"Why are you fussing over me?"

"Who's fussing? I'll pour coffee in a mug and slap a croissant on a plate."

"Gina—"

"Stop arguing. Go on out. I'll be right there."

I got the newspaper and went. The day was drenched in sunshine with a sky the limitless blue of a picture postcard. A soft breeze stirred the impatiens and pansies in the planters and hanging baskets and the air smelled of freshly cut grass. Most days it was the kind of glorious weather that made you glad to be alive. I unfolded the paper.

The short article about the body in our vineyard was at the bottom of the front page of the *Washington Tribune*. Kit

Eastman, my oldest and dearest friend in the world, had written it. The paper must have gone to bed before they identified Beau because he was still referred to as an "unidentified victim." I was in the middle of reading when Gina arrived with the coffee and croissant.

Her eyes darted back and forth between the newspaper and my impassive face.

I folded the paper and set it aside as though I'd been looking at something as innocuous as the weather report.

"Maybe I'll take this in my office," I said. "I've got bills that need paying."

She looked puzzled. "Whatever you want. Let me bring it in to you."

I didn't bother to insist that I could manage the tray, despite my cane. But as I left I saw her retrieve the newspaper and unfold it. Her hand went to her mouth and I knew she hadn't known about the article.

When she showed up in my office, I said, "Anyone who walks on eggshells around me is going to be fired. Got it?"

She nodded wide-eyed, then burst out laughing. "Okay. I'm sorry. We're all worried about you, Lucie."

"Forget it. I've got to deal with it. And no more hiding things from me, okay?"

Her eyes grew big. "Sure."

Gina couldn't lie any more than she could keep a secret.

"What else?" I asked. "You know I'm going to find out sooner or later."

"Chance called awhile ago. Apparently they've already had to chase a couple of reporters and a photographer away from the place where you found the grave."

I groaned. "I didn't know that. Someone should have told me."

"Don't say you heard it from me."

As soon as she left, I called Chance. "We had reporters on the property?"

"How'd you find out?"

"I tortured someone."

"Guess I'll lock up the sharp objects when you come over to the barrel room," he said.

"So it's true?"

"Yeah, unfortunately it's true."

"I hate to detail one of the guys to babysit, but maybe someone should be out there keeping an eye on things until this quiets down."

"We sent Tyler. He took his musket. Said he needs the practice before the reenactment."

I yelped. "Shooting at the press with a Civil War musket? My God, Chance, are you out of your mind? Whose idea was that?"

"Relax. He doesn't have live ammo. Says he needs to practice loading and reloading so it doesn't take him twenty minutes each time. He's not going to shoot at anyone, even if it's only blanks. Just scare 'em off."

"Call him and tell him absolutely no guns. You got that? I don't care if it's a water pistol. No guns."

He chuckled. "Yes, ma'am. I'll drop by and get it."

"Good. Do it now, please."

"Sure. But first any chance you might pay the crew this week? It's Friday and they have this thing about liking to get paid regularly."

"I wrote a check and left it in the barrel room yesterday. Didn't you find it? Just cash it as usual and pay them like you always do."

"I found it. But according to the folks at Blue Ridge Federal, you're the only person authorized to do anything on that account. That includes cashing checks, especially ones made out to cash."

"Who told you that?"

"One of the tellers. The lady with the blue hair and the mustache."

"It's not a mustache, it's . . . down. And I made some changes to my account about restricting the access. I guess they took it to an extreme. Let me call and straighten it out."

"Thanks. I'll pay Tyler a visit, then drive back to Middleburg and try to charm old blue-hair one more time."

"Don't take that musket to the bank. Drop it off somewhere."

"Probably have an easier time cashing the check if I did," he said, and hung up.

I paid the bills and waited until I cooled down before calling Kit Eastman.

"Hey, kiddo," she said. "I was expecting your call." She sounded tired.

"The front page of the *Washington Tribune*?" I said. "Aren't there more important things going on in the world? Wars? A mortgage crisis? Unemployment? The environ—"

"I'll make sure you get invited to the next editorial meeting so you can remind us about all those things. I guess we just forgot. We can also discuss the declining readership of newspapers in general, and the *Trib* in particular, and when our next round of buyouts will come down, how many of us will get offers we can't refuse. I mean that literally."

"So you put that article on the front page to sell newspapers?"

"It may surprise you, but that's our business. Or what's left of it. Do you have any idea how many people get their news beamed to their cell phones these days? And that's it, as far as what they read?"

"Okay," I said, "okay. Sorry about your lousy readership numbers. But that doesn't mean you had to put that story on the front page."

"*Au contraire*. It's exactly the kind of story that people are interested in," she said. "A skeleton lying in a shallow grave for nearly thirty years out in tony horse-and-hunt country. Unearthed by a tornado, no less. People are fascinated. They want to know who it is and how he got there."

"And you're going to turn it into a lurid tabloid scandal."

"Look, some poor schmo turns up dead in some godforsaken part of D.C., maybe somewhere in Anacostia, same circumstances, and what happens? People moan about the high crime rate in our nation's capital and turn the page. One news cycle, the guy's ancient history. You know as well as I do there's a prurient interest in what goes on behind closed doors in the lives of the rich and famous. Especially people who play polo and foxhunt and send their kids to boarding school and men have names like Bunny or Fluffy."

"I'm not rich or famous. As for that stereotype, you live here, too. You know better."

She sighed. "I gotta go to the nine-thirty staff meeting."

"It's ten o'clock."

"I know. And I'm holding the damn meeting. I know you're upset, Luce. Why don't you meet me at the Coach Stop at noon and we can talk about it? I've got an errand in Middleburg so I'll be over there anyway."

"I guess you know they identified him," I said.

She knew immediately which "him" I meant. "Beauregard Kinkaid."

"You know anything about the guy?"

"Not yet, but I will."

"I'm telling you up front that I never heard of him until Bobby mentioned his name. So I hope you weren't planning to ask me any questions over lunch."

"Of course not."

"You lie worse than I do. See you at noon."

Before I left for Middleburg, I did an Internet search for Beauregard Kinkaid, which turned up nothing. Same result when I looked for Beau Kinkaid. Annabel Chastain, on the other hand, was a gold mine. Her name appeared as one of the organizers or main contributors at almost every major Charlottesville charity fund-raiser. The hospital. The symphony. A homeless shelter. The library.

Chastain wasn't her maiden name, either. It looked like she'd remarried since her name kept popping up along with Sumner Chastain, CEO of a construction company bearing his name. According to the website, Chastain Construction was a multiaward-winning leader in the industry, advertising itself as "one-stop shopping" for any type of building project from retail to residential to commercial. Most of their work was on the East Coast. They even had a slogan: "Building Your World, Building by Building." Catchy.

I was about to close down the search when I saw a link that intrigued me. A polo website. With a photo. Annabel and Sumner at a match in Florida presenting a check to the director of a program that rescued pets abandoned during natural disasters like the hurricanes that plagued that state and the entire Gulf Coast. The photo was grainy but at least now I knew what she looked like. A pretty, willowy blonde in a white pantsuit and a double strand of Wilma Flintstone choker pearls around her neck. Either she'd been a teenager when she married Beau or she took good care of herself—maybe both. Sumner looked old enough to be her father. White-haired, black caterpillar eyebrows, heavy horn-rimmed glasses, and a movie-star tan.

I printed out the picture and studied it. They looked at ease and in their element, but who was I to judge after chiding Kit for her stereotyped generalizations? I folded the page in quarters, shoved it in my purse, and left for Middleburg.

I drove down Mosby's Highway as it narrowed to two lanes and became Washington Street inside the Middleburg town limits—which was only a few blocks. If I continued east for another forty miles or so, I'd be in Washington, D.C., and what was a winding country road out here would gradually widen to accommodate lanes of thundering traffic and the second-worst rush hour commute in the country.

But here in the western part of Loudoun County, we'd fought hard to keep our land open and green, and to preserve the charm and allure of villages like Middleburg, with its pretty main street of shops and restaurants owned and patronized by neighbors and friends. On weekends the town was always full of folks from D.C. who came to get away from the city's relentless pace and brutal politics, and metropolitan suburbanites looking to escape the sameness of strip malls, big-box stores, and fast-food restaurants. I saw them at the vineyard, as well. What they wanted, it seemed to me, was reassurance that small-town America, with all the nostalgia and conjured images of a sweet, simpler life, still existed as a place they could reclaim, even if only for a few hours.

The Coach Stop was one of those old-fashioned places, a fixture of Middleburg since the late 1950s that had retained its down-home atmosphere combined with family-style cooking. The restaurant was bustling with the usual lunchtime crowd and half a dozen people waved or called out hello, including all the waitresses, as I walked in. Kit waved from one of the booths. I slid into the semicircular banquette and we did the perfunctory air kiss.

"I ordered onion rings already," she said. "With ranch dressing."

She saw my face. "Oh, come on. Don't give me that what's-with-the-diet? look, will you? For the past month I've been totally stressed ever since I took over as bureau chief. Anyway, it's only an extra ten pounds. You know I can take it off like that." She snapped her fingers.

The "extra ten" had actually crept to an extra thirty, but that depended on when she began counting. And she'd been talking about the diet for years, long before she got her new job.

"You asked me to remind you," I said. "I'm only doing what I'm told."

"Well, don't do it today. I'll get back on track. But right now I'm still stressed."

Our onion rings arrived and we ordered. A chef's salad and iced tea for me, a bacon cheeseburger plus a strawberry milk shake for Kit.

She picked up an onion ring and dunked it in a blob of dressing she'd poured on her plate. "You're mad at me. I can tell."

I took an onion ring and skipped the dressing. "I hope the *Trib*'s not going to turn this into a soap opera involving my family."

"Luce, Bobby did pick up your dad's gun."

"You know about *that*, too?"

Kit had been going out with Bobby for the past two years, but he bent over backward to make sure the sheriff's department didn't cut the *Trib* any extra slack. Kit sometimes complained that not only did she not receive any special favors, she had to work harder than her colleagues for the same information. But Bobby was adamant about no proprietary information leaks. If Kit knew about Bobby confiscating the gun, word must be all over town.

"Someone saw the cruisers pulling out of the entrance to your vineyard this morning and went by the General Store afterward. My crime reporter happened to stop in for coffee and heard about it, so he called and pestered the life out of public affairs at the sheriff's department," she said.

Her crime reporter could probably do a bang-up job of reporting if he parked himself in one of the rocking chairs at the General Store and just sat there all day. Sooner or later he'd know everything about everyone.

"A lot of people own a Smith and Wesson thirty-eight," I said. "It doesn't mean Leland did anything."

"That's what it was? A thirty-eight?"

"You are trying to pump me for information, aren't you?" I slumped back against the banquette. "How can you be so disingenuous?"

The waitress showed up with our beverages. "Be right back with your food, ladies."

When she was out of earshot, Kit said in a low voice, "That's not fair. I'm not being disingenuous and I'm not trying to pry anything out of you. But I am worried about you."

"You don't need to be. I'm fine."

She picked up her milk shake and drank. When she set her glass down, she'd left a thick cerise lipstick kiss on the rim. Kit wore makeup like she was onstage at the Kennedy Center and needed to be seen in the balcony.

"I just don't want you to get hurt," she said.

"You think Leland killed him, don't you?"

"The evidence is stacking up—"

"What evidence? It's all circumstantial."

Our meals arrived, silencing us again.

Afterward, Kit said, "You know I'm on your side."

I picked at my salad. "I wasn't aware there were sides."

"Come on, Lucie."

"Can we talk about something else? How about Beau Kinkaid? Did you find out anything about him?"

She sighed and ate another dressing-drenched onion ring. "Not much. These days with the Internet all you have to do is be on some PTA committee and your name pops up on the school website. Unfortunately, Beau Kinkaid didn't do anything that made him show up anywhere on the Web. Believe me, I searched. What I found out the old-fashioned way was that he was born in Richmond, June 30, 1939. Went to high school same town, no college record anywhere. Married Anne Gresham, no kids. Parents and a brother all dead."

"That's it?"

"Some people leave a bigger footprint in the world than others." Kit shrugged. "The only one left who knows anything is his wife, Anne. Now married to—"

"Sumner Chastain. I checked, too. And she's 'Annabel' now."

"Well, the Chastain Construction machine is closing ranks around her. I called their house, and all calls are being forwarded to the company press office. The only thing I got was a two-sentence statement about Mrs. Chastain being distressed at the discovery of her ex-husband's body and that she's cooperating fully with the Loudoun County Sheriff's Department," she said.

"You going to talk to her when she comes to town?"

Kit finished chewing. "You bet."

"It's weird she didn't report that he was missing, don't you think?"

"You didn't hear? He abused her and she wasn't sorry he was gone."

"I heard. I still think it's odd not to report it at all."

She shrugged. "You know, she could have blackmailed your father, if she suspected him of murder. Had the best of both worlds. That would be a reason not to report it."

"That's an evil theory. She'd hardly be likely to admit something like that when she talks to Bobby, if that's what she did. Besides, she seems to have remarried well enough that she wouldn't need to blackmail anyone."

"Maybe. But after dating a cop for two years and hearing some of his stories, I'm less and less surprised at the stupid things people do that they believe they can get away with." She pushed her plate away. "You want dessert?"

"No, and neither do you. You could have drowned in that milk shake."

"Back to being my keeper, huh? Never mind, I've got to save room for dinner. Bobby's taking me to D.C. tonight." She raised an eyebrow so I could see all four colors of her Technicolor eye shadow as she signaled for our check. "He says he's got a surprise for me."

"What do you think it is?"

"With Bobby, who knows? Maybe a visit to the police memorial and then pizza and a beer somewhere. His idea of fancy is a restaurant where the paper napkins are rolled around the silverware instead of in one of those dispenser thingies."

I smiled and she picked up the check. "On me. You're feeding us this weekend. We're looking forward to your party."

"Me, too, now that we have our power back on."

She walked me outside.

"If you find out anything about Beau Kinkaid, will you let me know?" I asked.

"Sure," she said. "See you tomorrow at the anniversary party."

I drove home. Dead ahead of me were the mountains with their softly graded hues of blue. Solid and comforting. I usually never tired of the view, but today I couldn't concentrate on anything except scenarios of what Annabel Chastain might tell Bobby about Leland's role in her ex-husband's death. With Chastain Construction's press office stage-managing events, I had no doubt they would do whatever was necessary to protect Annabel Kinkaid Chastain.

That included throwing my father to the wolves.

Chapter 11

———◆◆◆———

I went back to the fields and spent the rest of the afternoon cleaning up storm debris. When I got home that evening, Eli's Jaguar was sitting in my driveway. I parked behind it and listened as piano music flooded through the open windows of the sunroom. It sounded like Chopin—something torrential and passionate played on my great-great-grandmother's Bösendorfer concert grand, a wedding present purchased by her husband on their Austrian honeymoon. I closed my eyes and let the music wash over me. Eli could have gone to Juilliard or studied with some top teacher and actually made a living as a concert pianist, he was that talented.

The piece crashed to an end with a dissonant chord Chopin hadn't written. I went inside, wondering what had happened to bring my brother here again. Maybe he was even more desperate for money than the last time we'd spoken.

He looked up from the keyboard when he heard me. Disheveled and unshaven, he had the look in his eyes of a dog that had been kicked repeatedly and had no idea why. In the cheery room filled with light pouring in through the banks of windows and reflecting off walls painted the color of liquid sunshine, he seemed dark, disturbed—and broken.

I crossed the room and wrapped my arms around his shoulders. "What happened? Where are Hope and Brandi? Are they all right?"

He shrugged and ran his finger across the top of the music stand as though checking for dust. "I suppose they're all right. They're probably at home."

"Why aren't you at home?"

"I'm not living there anymore. We're splitting. Trial separation."

I bent down so my cheek rested on top of his head. "I'm so sorry."

"Yup." His voice sounded strangled.

"You all right? Where'd you sleep last night?"

"My car. My office."

He hadn't answered the first question. "Since when?"

"Couple of nights."

"Why didn't you come here?"

"I couldn't."

I closed my eyes, not wanting to imagine what he'd done on those nights.

"You're staying here tonight," I said. "And as long as you need, until you get things sorted out."

"Thanks." He patted my arm, but he still sounded lost.

"You going to see a marriage counselor?"

"Don't think so. Right now she just wants her space."

"Where's your stuff?"

"I grabbed some clothes and threw them in the car. Everything else is still at the house."

"Well, get what you've brought and put it upstairs in your room. I'll go fix us drinks and dinner. I stopped at Safeway today and restocked my fridge after the power failure. You okay with grilled chicken and asparagus? If you want to take a shower, I'll start getting it ready."

"I'm not hungry. Thanks, anyway."

"You have to eat."

He got up and looked around the familiar room. "What am I going to do, Luce? What am I going to do?" His voice broke.

"First you're going to get your clothes out of the car. Then you're going to take a shower and change. After you eat something you're going to get a decent night's sleep in a bed. The rest will come." I shoved him gently toward the door. "Go on."

He showed up in the kitchen twenty minutes later wearing old jeans and a faded maroon-and-orange Virginia Tech T-shirt. His dark hair was still wet and he hadn't bothered with the usual gel, so it fell across his forehead the way it used to before Brandi began masterminding his clothes and appearance, turning him into her own personal dress-up doll.

"Where'd you get that T-shirt?" I uncovered a ceramic bowl of homemade topping for bruschetta.

"There's still a couple of things in my old dresser upstairs." He stuck a finger in the bowl and licked it. "Tomato salad?"

"It's for the bruschetta. Use a spoon if you want to taste it. It's gross when you use your finger."

"My finger is very clean. Don't worry." He rummaged in the silverware drawer and found a spoon, helping himself to another mouthful. "Tastes good."

"It ought to. Tomatoes and basil are from my garden." I pulled a baking pan with half a dozen slices of toasted baguette drizzled in olive oil out of the broiler and handed him a spoon. "Here. The tomatoes go on top of the baguette. Not too much or it gets messy. I'll finish the asparagus."

"Brandi orders from every restaurant in Leesburg. Otherwise, it's frozen." He heaped tomatoes on a piece of bread and ate it. "Where'd you learn to make this?"

"Dominique served it as an appetizer a couple of times at the Inn. It's her recipe. Are you planning on eating everything as you fix it, or will you leave some for our drinks?"

"Sorry." He unclipped his phone from his belt and checked it, setting it on the counter. "I stopped by the General Store. Heard they identified the guy you found. An old friend of Leland's."

"Business associate. Doesn't sound like they were friends," I said. "His name was Beau Kinkaid. Does it ring any bells?"

Eli picked up his phone and checked his messages again. "Nope. I was probably in diapers when it happened. I was precocious, but not that precocious."

"It seems it happened thirty years ago," I said. "So you would have been one."

"My memories that far back are kind of dim."

"Bobby said Beau Kinkaid's ex-wife is coming up here from Charlottesville to talk to him. She says the last time she saw her husband alive, he was mad at Leland and wanted to settle things."

Eli finished fixing the bruschetta and went over to the refrigerator. "What do you have to drink around here? I don't see any beer."

"I didn't know you were coming. There's a nice bottle of Crémant."

"Fizzy white. I guess I could drink that."

We brought the wine and hors d'oeuvres outside to the veranda. Eli took the glider and I sat in the love seat. He popped the Crémant cork and poured, but when we clinked glasses neither of us made a toast. I watched him check his phone yet again.

"Beau Kinkaid's ex-wife is now Mrs. Sumner Chastain," I said. "You ever run into Chastain Construction in any of your projects?"

"Chastain Construction has tentacles that reach every state in the southeastern United States. It's impossible not to run into them."

"Do they have a good reputation?"

He bit into a piece of bruschetta and thought while he chewed. "Let me put it this way. You know how Quinn talks about the homogenization of the wine world where everybody ultimately ends up making the same Chardonnay or the same Pinot? No distinguishing characteristics of *terroir*, nothing to reflect the land and soil it came from, or the personality of the winemaker?"

"They build the same buildings?"

"Over and over and over again. Churn 'em out, one homogeneous subdivision, shopping mall, and planned community after another."

"Nice."

"They're big and they get the job done." He shrugged. "You can't fight big."

"Their press people are in charge of managing Annabel Chastain. Kit tried to talk to her. They've erected a fortress," I said.

He glanced at his phone for a few seconds and did some scrolling, then set it on the coffee table.

"You keep doing that," I said.

"Habit."

"More like an addiction. Though I don't blame you for checking in case—"

He cut me off, looking pained. "I'm not just looking to see if she called. I gotta stay on top of stuff at work. This thing gets e-mail, you know."

"Which you read the millisecond it comes in."

"So sue me, I'm curious. Anyway, that last one was personal. Remember Zeke Lee? From high school?"

"Vaguely. Friend of yours."

"He's coming to that reenactment. Says he belongs to B.J.'s regiment. He asked if I'll be there."

"You *are* coming, I hope?"

"He means as a participant. He says he can loan me whatever clothes and gear I need, if I'm interested. It's too late to sign up, but I could be a walk-on."

"They didn't have cell phones during the Civil War. Or e-mail."

"What, you think I can't do without twenty-first-century gadgets for a weekend?"

"Not really. Do you?"

"Of course I can."

"Maybe you should try it. You mind lighting the grill? I'll get the chicken."

"Where's the electric fire starter?"

"I knew it," I said and left for the kitchen.

We ate dinner outside by candlelight. By tacit mutual agreement we avoided the subject of Brandi and his marriage. Finally, I brought up Annabel Chastain again.

"Beau's dead and Leland's dead. That leaves her," I said. "That means it's going to be her word against no one's. I think she's setting Leland up for this."

"If she's got the Chastain Construction public relations machine behind her, she's got no worries. They'll roll right over Leland and that'll be the end of it. That company's got more lawyers on their payroll than you got grapes in the vineyard."

"Well, we'll just have to fight back."

"Luce . . ." He leaned his elbows on the table and

massaged his temples. "How are we going to do that? They'll keep hammering at us until we quit. We haven't got the money or the resources to go up against them."

"So you're saying we should just give up?"

"Look, they must have found a thirty-eight slug if they came by and took Leland's thirty-eight. What if they find a match? The guy was buried on our land. The ex-wife says there was bad blood. So if I were a betting man I'd say it's not looking too good for our side."

"What if he didn't do it?"

"Then who did?"

"I don't know."

Eli clasped his hands behind his head as he stared out toward the mountains.

"I don't want to believe it, either, but there doesn't seem to be any evidence to refute that he didn't murder that guy and then cover it up for thirty years."

"There has to be something," I said.

Eli looked at me with something between resigned sadness and pity.

"If there is," he said, "it'll take a damn miracle to find it. And you can bet Chastain Construction will do their best to make sure you don't turn up anything. Be careful, Luce. You're playing with fire."

Chapter 12

—⟨⟨⟨⟨⟨—

The weekend celebration of the twentieth anniversary of Montgomery Estate Vineyard will be indelibly etched in my memory, but not for reasons I would have imagined. Though we started on a high note with an unexpected celebration, it didn't take long for things to head south.

Ironically, the weather for the entire weekend couldn't have been more perfect if we'd ordered it up ourselves. Sparkling sunshine, the vivid blue skies of a Van Gogh painting, scattered thin-ribbed clouds, a soft breeze, and none of the oppressive energy-sapping humidity that was our usual summer fare.

The first people to arrive showed up at the villa before we'd even opened the doors. Kit and Bobby, arms around each other, walked in looking like they'd just won the lottery.

"We wanted to tell you first. Well, second after my mother and Bobby's folks." Kit held out her left hand where a small diamond in a plain gold setting sparkled on her finger.

I had started to set a large tiered platter of grapes and assorted cheeses on the oak trestle table when she waved her ring under my nose. The tray tipped sideways as I bent to ex-amine it. Bobby grabbed one of the handles before anything could spill and we set it down together. Everyone laughed.

"Told you Lucie'd be surprised," Bobby said to Kit, who continued admiring her ring and grinning like a fool. "She thought I'd never do it."

"Darling, I thought you'd never do it." Kit arched an eye-brow as she ate a grape and looked seductively at him.

We laughed some more and I hugged Kit. "I'm so happy for you."

I hugged Bobby, too, but his eyes, though smiling like hers, turned grave as he patted me on the back. Something was wrong.

"We have to make a toast," I said. "To celebrate. The Mid-dleburg Business Association sent a bottle of champagne for our anniversary. It's chilling in the fridge. I'll get it."

"You should save it," Kit said.

"Nonsense. Just a small glass."

Kit glanced at Bobby. "I guess we could. Though my fi-ancé, here, would prefer a beer."

"Those bubbles give me gas," he said, "but I suppose I can make an exception."

I got the bottle and Bobby opened it on the terrace. The cork flew out and the fizzy liquid erupted. We laughed again as I held a champagne flute underneath and he filled it with champagne.

"So when did this happen?" I handed Kit her glass. "Tell me everything."

"Last night," Kit said. "We had dinner on that boat that goes down the Potomac to Mount Vernon."

"You think you were surprised." Bobby poured two more small glasses of champagne. "Kit nearly went over the railing when I got down on one knee. Got me all worried I might have to call the dive squad to find out if she accepted or not."

"He lies." Kit grinned at him and blew him a kiss. Their eyes met, exchanging a coded look.

Bobby set down his glass, from which he'd taken only a couple of sips. "Sorry we can't stay for your party, Lucie."

Kit looked like she was confessing a guilty secret. "We've both got to work. Things came up. But we wanted to make sure we told you about the engagement in person. That's why we came by." She also set down her glass.

I wanted to ask if the murder investigation of Beau Kinkaid had anything to do with the reason they both got called into work on a weekend, but the look in Kit's eyes asked me not to push it and spoil the moment. Still, a heaviness had settled over us like a shroud, so maybe I already had my answer.

"At least let me give you a bottle of wine for dinner," I said.

Kit twisted her engagement ring on her finger, glancing at Bobby.

"We'll take your wine, but I insist on paying," Bobby said.

"No, please—"

"Let us pay, kiddo," Kit said. To Bobby, she added, "I'll take care of it, honey. Why don't you talk to Lucie while I do that?" She opened her purse and pulled out her wallet.

"It's not a bribe," I said to Bobby. "You know me better."

"I know. But under the circumstances, it's just better if we pay."

I nodded, numb. "Have you talked to Annabel Chastain yet?"

"Sorry, but I can't say. Look, Lucie, I want to make sure you understand that this isn't about you. You're not being accused of anything."

"It's my family and our reputation that's at stake."

Kit came outside cradling a bag with a bottle of wine in it and holding a credit card receipt. "Chance tried to give me another bottle on the house once he found out the news. He says 'Congratulations.' " She winked at Bobby. "And he gave me a little kiss. He's sweet."

"Yeah, but I'm sweeter. And I better not catch him flirting with my fiancée." Bobby's smile was tolerant. "We should be going."

Kit kissed me good-bye and squeezed my arm. "Enjoy your big party and try not to worry about anything. It'll all work out, I promise."

Later I would wonder if that had been a Judas kiss or if she really didn't expect what would come next.

I didn't have much time to think about it, though, because after that, people began arriving in waves that never seemed to end. The villa and the terrace filled up and soon everyone spilled into the courtyard where we'd placed additional bistro tables and chairs. Frankie had hired a disc jockey to play songs that had been popular twenty years ago. We had him set up out there so folks could dance if they wanted to, along with eating and drinking. Besides our usual fare of crackers, cheese, and fruit, we served birthday cake and sold wine at a 20 percent discount.

By noon it was shaping up to be our best day in history with the girls so swamped pouring wine for the tastings that Eli, Quinn, Chance, and I pitched in, serving wine and ringing up sales instead of spending time with our guests. Quinn sent Tyler out to direct traffic and Benny and Javier ferried cases of wine from the barrel room to the tasting room when we ran out of supplies.

"I never expected anything like this," I said to Quinn

when he and I took a break to check on how things were going in the courtyard. "Wish we had more help."

"I wish the songs of the eighties were better," Quinn said, as a singer I didn't recognize sang about being addicted to love with a thudding bass backing him up. "How come your parents couldn't have founded this place in the sixties? Did you actually like this music?"

"I was in grade school," I said. "I don't remember."

"Why don't I call Savannah?" he said. "Maybe she can give us a hand. She had something to do this morning but she's probably free now."

"Sure." My heart gave an unwelcome lurch, but I kept my voice neutral. "Give her a call."

He pulled out his cell phone and turned away for some privacy. I leaned against a pillar in the shade of the arcade. Though the courtyard was overflowing with people, I felt a stab of loneliness that was becoming familiar. A light breeze blew, fluttering the red-and-white-striped umbrellas we'd placed to shade each of the tables. The music changed to a song by Madonna—"Holiday," with its bouncy dance-tune beat.

"Hey, Lucie." Seth Hannah, president of Blue Ridge Federal, held a bottle of Cabernet Sauvignon in one hand and two wineglasses between the fingers of the other. He was dressed for the occasion in a straw boater, seersucker jacket, pale blue shirt, and khakis. "I was hoping I'd run into you. Great party, sweetheart. Your momma'd be proud."

"Thanks, Seth. Glad you could come."

I wondered if he hadn't mentioned Leland on purpose once again. In the beginning, my father had been involved in the vineyard along with my mother. Later, she took over running it by herself while he went off on one of his many business ventures.

Seth smiled. "Wouldn't miss it for the world. I remember the day this vineyard opened. One of the first in Virginia back then. Saw that slide show you've put together in the library in the villa. What a lot of memories."

"I know. I wish my parents were here to see this."

"I'm sure you do." He paused. "I thought you should know. Bobby Noland stopped by the house yesterday wanting to know if I knew anything about that business associate of your father's."

"What did you say, if you don't mind my asking?"

"That I had no recollection of the fellow. Never met him as near as I can remember."

"That was it?"

"Well, we talked generally, of course. It's no secret that your father made some bad business decisions, honey. Lost a lot of money. His friends had to bail him out more than once."

"Is that a roundabout way of saying you think he might be guilty?"

"Now I never said that, Lucie." Seth adopted the tone of an adult who didn't expect to be second-guessed by a child. "Bobby's making the rounds, talking to the Romeos. I had drinks with some of the boys over at the Inn last night. Thought I'd help you out here by giving you a head's up."

"Do all the Romeos feel the way you do?"

"I think we agree that Lee had some questionable business associates." He'd hedged his answer, but his tone was still tough.

"He was your friend, Seth, and now that he's dead he isn't around to defend himself. If you're going to throw him under a bus—"

Seth straightened up and I could see the hardness travel to his eyes. "I resent that, Lucie. No one's turning against anyone and no one said a word about your father killing that man."

He walked away abruptly, weaving his way between the tables as the gaily striped umbrellas fluttered in the wind. A pretty tableau on a pretty day. I watched him sit down at his table and knew that I'd angered him. But I also knew something else.

He'd ducked my question about whether or not he believed Leland was a murderer.

Frankie came to me at the end of the day when Quinn and I were cleaning up in the little kitchen off the tasting room. The rest of the staff had gone, including Savannah, who had shown up to help for a few hours and promised to return on Sunday.

"What gives, Lucie? We got calls all afternoon from the Romeos. All of them who were coming to that private barrel tasting tomorrow afternoon canceled. You know anything about that?"

I stopped taking clean wineglasses out of the dishwasher. Quinn put down an empty cardboard box we used to store the glasses and regarded me warily.

"I might."

"What happened?" Quinn asked. "It's about Leland, isn't it?"

"I think I offended Seth Hannah."

"You think or you know?" he said.

I twisted my dish towel into a knot and Quinn threw up his hands. Frankie looked like she couldn't decide whether she wanted to wait around to hear what came next or drop through the floorboards.

"Why don't I call the people on the waiting list and let them know we've got space all of a sudden?" Her smile didn't make it all the way to her eyes.

"Thanks, Frankie," I said.

"Good idea," Quinn said. "You know how I hate doing tastings when there's nobody there."

"I'd better get right to it."

The door swung shut as she left. Quinn folded his arms across his chest. "What exactly did you say to Seth to royally piss him off?"

"I didn't royally piss him off."

"There's another expression for it?"

"You don't understand."

"You're right. I don't."

I ran a finger around and around the rim of a clean glass. "Bobby's been questioning all the Romeos about Leland and Beau Kinkaid. Seth said he told Bobby that he didn't know anything, but it didn't stop him from insinuating that Leland probably did it because of the kind of person he was."

"Bobby's a big boy. I'm sure he can separate facts from insinuation."

"You know what? If you repeat something often enough, regardless of whether or not it's true, after a while people start believing it."

Quinn set down my glass on the counter and put both hands on my shoulders. "People," he said, "are going to talk and there's nothing you can do about it."

"Yes, there is."

He looked at me like I'd already lost not only the battle but the whole damn war.

"No. Not this time."

"I can prove Leland's innocent. That'll stop the talk."

He let go of my shoulders. "There's no way you can do that. No evidence, nothing. You can't go up against Bobby."

"I can't let the Romeos imply that because Leland and Beau had a business deal that went bad, he's the obvious candidate to be the murderer. If that were true, I know a lot of people who'd qualify as potential killers. That includes me and a bunch of the Romeos themselves."

Quinn finished filling the wine box with clean glasses and closed it up.

"People who live in glass houses shouldn't throw stones?" he asked.

I folded the dish towel and slapped it on the counter.

"They shouldn't throw boomerangs."

Just like Saturday, Sunday's first crisis erupted right before we opened. Eli's wife, Brandi, walked through the front door of the villa and the room went quiet.

There are those who spread joy and sunshine because they've got such positive, upbeat personalities that people feel good just by being around them. My sister-in-law was not one of these people.

Beautiful, absolutely. Stunning, even a knockout. Unfortunately, although Brandi possessed the kind of classic dark-haired looks that made people think of kohl-eyed women who graced Grecian urns or inspired men to launch a thousand ships, it was paired with a personality as two-dimensional as a wine label.

My brother had fallen hard for her and every time she wanted him to hang the moon someplace different—which she often did—he never thought twice about dropping everything to fetch the ladder. I do believe he'd commit murder for her without hesitating.

At first I wondered if the two of them had set up this meeting and Eli had forgotten to mention she'd be dropping by. But the moment I saw the look of expectant hope in his eyes, replaced quickly by a mask of cool resignation, I knew it was unplanned and likely to be combustible.

"Hey, princess." Eli sounded wary. "You look pretty. New outfit? Where's Hope?"

Brandi wore an expensive-looking red sheath dress with a plunging neckline and a racy slit that exposed a tanned thigh. Black patent leather belt, black sling-back sandals. A ruby and diamond necklace and matching drop earrings. Eli could be in hock until the next millennium just from her jewelry purchases.

Her heels clacked on the quarry tile floor as she crossed the room, tossing her head like a runway model, well aware that all eyes were fixed on her. Frankie disappeared into the kitchen, dragging Gina. Quinn, who had been taking wine bottles out of boxes along with Eli, stopped and folded his arms like a spectator watching a sports event. I quit filling goblets with the small oyster crackers we served during tastings. The air crackled like she'd just laid down a live high-voltage line.

"Hope is with my mother. We need to talk, Eli. I'm broke and I need money. I can't go on like this." Her words came out in a torrent as she flung her Coach purse down on a bar stool. She seemed oblivious to her audience.

My brother came from behind the bar like he was about to step into the lion's cage without a chair or a whip.

"Look, sweetheart, let's go on outside and talk about it. I told you. I can't get you anything for a few days—"

"Don't give me that crap. I'm tired of it. What do you expect me to do in the meantime? Get it out of thin air?" She snapped her fingers in his face. "I don't even answer the phone anymore because it's always a collection agency. I'm on goddamn tranquilizers now to deal with the stress. I don't care if you have to rob a bank, but you'd better do something. Do you understand me?"

Her voice, like her nerves, seemed to fray as she spoke. Eli took her arm.

"Let's go home, babe." He sounded calm, despite the red rising on his cheeks. I wondered how often he'd placated her like this before. "We'll talk about it there. Have dinner tonight, work it all out—"

She wrenched her arm out of his grasp. "Don't touch me! What are you, insane? It's over, Eli. I told you already. The only reason you can come home is to get your stuff. What you haven't moved out by the end of the day tomorrow will be on the street to be picked up with the trash."

Her words landed like blows, except they were meant to humiliate as well as wound. I held my breath and waited to see what my brother would do. For a moment the only sound in the room was the rushing of the wind through the open French doors.

A muscle twitched in Quinn's jaw. He was biting his tongue like I was as Brandi faced Eli, her beautiful features twisted into the uncontrolled fury of a harpy.

"It's still my house." Eli maintained that surreal deadpan calm but now there was a steeliness in his voice. "And we're going to finish this conversation somewhere else."

He grabbed her purse and thrust it at her. "Get going."

"Don't you talk to me—"

"I said, move it."

Brandi looked as if he'd actually slapped her, but for once she didn't have a sharp-edged retort. Eli's eyes met mine as she tucked her bag under her arm and stalked across the room, head high in an attempt to salvage her dignity. Eli followed, hands in his pockets, eyes straight ahead.

I did not want to think about where the rest of that discussion would take them. Eli didn't slam the door, but he did close it with some force.

Quinn broke the silence first. "I'd give her a good spanking."

"I know you would. What do you bet Eli caves in and buys her something once he calms her down."

"A straitjacket?"

"Only if Versace makes them." I paused. "Look, I'm sorry about that scene—"

"Forget it. It wasn't your fault and no apology's necessary." He shoved an empty wine box under the bar. "I smell coffee in the kitchen. Frankie probably made a fresh pot. Let's get some."

I nodded, grateful he was trying to get things back on track again.

"I think we lost Eli for the day," I said. "We're going to be shorthanded again."

"We'll cope," he said. "Just like we always do."

The rest of the day was as busy as Saturday had been so it turned out not to be too difficult to banish Eli and his problems from my mind for a few hours and concentrate on taking care of customers and making sure things ran smoothly. The tasting room and terrace buzzed with the conversation of couples and groups of friends who laughed and talked and seemed happy to be with one another for an afternoon. Quinn caught me watching at one point and squeezed my shoulder.

"Don't go there. You can't solve Eli's problems. He has to work them out for himself."

"I'm not going anywhere. I know he does."

He patted me on the back like he knew I was fibbing and turned his attention to a good-looking young couple who just stepped up to the bar.

At noon my sister, Mia, called from New York to say congratulations on twenty years and ask how everything was going. I said everything was going great, just great, and that

Eli, with whom she also wanted to speak, couldn't come to the phone right now but he'd call her later. I also said nothing about Beau Kinkaid or Leland being a possible suspect in his murder investigation.

I hung up the phone feeling guilty for keeping so much from her, but my sister's obvious happiness at starting a new life in Manhattan after a rocky period following our mother's death had resonated in her voice. If I'd given off any vibes that anything was wrong she'd been too caught up in her own world to realize, so why spoil it? There would be enough time to tell her later—especially after the sheriff's department investigation finally wrapped up.

James Joyce was right. What the eye can't see the heart can't grieve for.

Besides, my heart was already grieving enough for both of us.

By five thirty the last guests had departed. Frankie, Gina, and I were in the courtyard clearing up wineglasses and dishes and wiping down tables when my cousin Dominique showed up. She hugged me and, without asking, pitched in with the cleanup.

When I was growing up my mother once remarked that it seemed apt that Dominique had been born on a Saturday since, like the old nursery rhyme, she truly was the child who worked hard for a living. Somewhere along the way, though, Dominique crossed over from hardworking to workaholic, becoming Saturday's child without an off switch. Thin and sinewy as rope, she had hazel eyes and spiky auburn hair that looked like she cut it with gardening shears—which on her somehow seemed fashionable and chic. Though my cousin hadn't lived in Paris for years, she still possessed that innate French sense of style that turned heads when she entered a room.

"Why didn't you come earlier for the party?" I asked. "Instead of for the drudgery?"

She lit a cigarette. "Something came up at the Inn."

Something always came up at the Inn and she was always the only one who could handle it.

"Looks like you had a good day." She waved the hand with the cigarette to encompass the courtyard. "You must have made money hand over foot."

I smiled. "We did well. How'd it go with you?"

She sucked on her cigarette and exhaled dragon smoke. "Eh, *bien*, the Romeos were in drinking at the bar," she said. "They were talking about your father and that skeleton you found."

"Seth Hannah told me Bobby's been questioning all of them about whether they knew him." I shrugged. "No one did."

Dominique picked up two wineglasses, which still had remnants of red wine in them, and dumped one into the other. "Do they know who he is?"

"Didn't you hear? A former business partner of Leland's. Beauregard Kinkaid. He went by 'Beau.'"

"Beauregard Kinkaid? Beau Kinkaid?"

She repeated the name as she flung the wine over the wall in a graceful arc of bloodlike drops.

She faced me, holding the empty glasses, a puzzled expression on her face. "I don't want to open a Pandora's box of worms here," she said, "but I met Beau Kinkaid. He came to visit your father at the house the summer you were born."

Chapter 13

⎯⎯❧⎯⎯

"You *met* Beau Kinkaid?" I asked. "You're sure?"

"I'm sure. He was not a nice man. I remember him."

I sat down in one of the patio chairs and stared at her. I'd just turned twenty-nine in July. Twenty-nine years ago Dominique would have been thirteen. Could she really be that certain she knew him?

"The summer you were born my mother came from France to help your mother. She brought me, too." Dominique expelled more cigarette smoke through her nostrils. "I remember Beau came to visit your father and they had a terrible argument. He was ugly and he scared me, but his name was Beau. It seemed odd."

Of course. In French, *beau* means "beautiful."

Still, I wondered how vivid—and accurate—her recollection could be. Even after spending the last few weeks looking through family photos for the vineyard slide show Frankie and I had put together, I'd been hard-pressed to recall long-ago events with any specificity. What memories remained had been as vague and impressionistic as the blurry, out-of-focus photos I'd discarded.

"Do you remember anything else?"

She ground out her cigarette on a plate that still had remnants of what looked like melted Brie on it.

"Sorry, I'm afraid not. You know I didn't speak English very well back then."

She kept grinding that cigarette and didn't look up.

"What is it you're not telling me?"

"I'm sorry, *chérie*. It's not very nice." Her smile was rueful. "Whatever happened during that conversation, it made your mother cry."

I closed my eyes as an image of my mother flashed in my head as clearly as if I'd been with her only yesterday. What Beau said to Leland must have devastated her. My mother didn't cry often. Children remember those moments—the unsettling discovery that adults aren't invincible and they can hurt enough to shed tears, too. My cousin's story was sounding increasingly plausible.

"You have no idea what they were talking about?"

Dominique shook her head. "No, but it upset my mother, too. All that shouting."

"Who was shouting?" I asked. "My parents?"

"*Non*, your father and Beau. We were sitting on the veranda when he showed up. Uncle Leland introduced us. Then he brought Beau into his office right away. After a few minutes, we could hear them hollering at each other." She sat down across from me and lit another cigarette. "After Beau left, things got sort of crazy."

"Crazy, how?"

"Because of you."

There was a half-open bottle of red sitting on one of the serving tables. I got it and found two clean glasses.

"I need a drink," I said.

Dominique took the glass I handed her. "*Tante* Chantal went into labor with you that afternoon so my mother and your father took her to the hospital. They left me at home to babysit Eli."

"You mean Beau came to see Leland the day I was born?"

Dominique nodded. "I was terrified he'd return when I was in the house all alone so I barricaded the doors with furniture and went to bed. When Uncle Leland and *Maman* came home from the hospital in the middle of the night, they had to break a windowpane so they could open a window to climb through. I was sleeping upstairs. I never heard them pounding on the front door."

If it hadn't been so important, I would have laughed.

"What happened after Leland and Beau's argument? Do you remember Beau leaving or if Leland went with him?"

Dominique drank her wine.

"I don't know what happened. When your mother went into your father's office after Beau left, I was sent to my room. That's when I heard her crying through the door to the office. By the time I was told I could come downstairs, my mother said *Tante* Chantal was lying down and that I needed to be quiet. Your father was gone."

"Where?"

She shrugged. "I don't know. But *Maman* was furious because she had to telephone his friends until she found him so he could drive your mother to the hospital."

I stared into my wineglass. What could Leland have done to make my mother cry over a business deal gone sour? Had he lost money? Gotten involved in some shady scam?

And where had he gone after Beau left the house?

If this was the argument Annabel Chastain had been talking about, at least I now knew for sure that Beau left our house alive. But where did my father disappear to for those few hours, leaving his wife who was distraught over the quarrel between him and his business partner and only hours away from giving birth? Did Leland track down Beau to finish the argument in private? Or did he end things between them for good?

I looked at my cousin. "You probably need to tell Bobby about this."

She swirled around the last of the wine in her glass, a somber expression on her face.

"Or I could just let dead dogs sleep," she said. "No one but you knows I met him."

In the silence that fell between us, I knew she wrestled, as I did, with the impact her news would have on my father's case if she spoke to Bobby versus saying nothing. A Hobson's choice that had already been made, ingrained in our psyches because of who our mothers raised us to be.

"It would probably go better for Leland if you kept quiet," I said. "Telling the truth corroborates what Annabel Chastain told Bobby, especially since no one knows where Leland went after Beau left, or what he did. Until now."

I shrugged and shook my head. Her smile was melancholy as she hugged me.

"Shall I call Bobby now or do you think it can wait until tomorrow?" she asked.

"Better get it over with. You wouldn't want to change your mind."

She pulled her phone out of her pocket. "There's no way to sweep the rug under the carpet on this one, is there?"

"Nope," I said, as she made her call.

The next article about the murder of Beau Kinkaid to appear in the *Washington Tribune* was not on the front page of the news section. Instead it showed up first thing Monday morning on the front page of Lifestyle. Lead story, this time above the fold. Pictures, too. The real kicker was the headline: "Sauterne Death: Who Killed the Victim in the Vineyard?"

I had never seen the photograph they used of Leland in his NRA cap. He'd probably been hunting and hadn't shaved for a few days so he looked particularly scruffy. A real gun-toting wacko. Chastain Construction's press machine had most likely provided the photo of Beau Kinkaid, who looked as all-American as a Boy Scout, sitting at a linen-covered table at some dinner event with a bank of American flags behind him. He was smiling, showing a lot of bad teeth, but even the smile didn't hide the fact that, as Dominique said, the man was as ugly as a roach.

I read the article with growing disgust. The obvious conclusion any fool would make—though it was never explicitly stated—was that Leland, a man of dubious business acumen, blurred-edge morals, and questionable relationships, killed one of his former partners and had gotten away with it. Until now.

Frankie was the first to arrive at the villa. She came straight to my office and the guilty look on her face, when she found me at my desk with the newspaper lying open, made it clear she'd hoped to do something outrageous, like burning every copy she could get her hands on before I saw it.

"Too late," I said. "But thanks."

"I'm really sorry, Lucie."

"Me, too. Anyone who still wondered whether Leland was innocent or guilty before reading this garbage won't have any doubts now."

She leaned against the doorjamb, her clear blue eyes filled with consternation. "They didn't say he did it."

"No, they just hinted, implied, insinuated, alluded, intimated . . . have I left any words out?"

"You're doing fine."

"I think I'll take a drive over to Leesburg." I stood up and reached for my cane.

"Do you think that's wise?"

"Do you think I should let them get away with this?" It came out sharper than I intended.

Her cheeks reddened and she pressed her lips together.

"I'm sorry," I said. "I shouldn't be taking my anger out on you."

"Maybe you could just ignore it. If you dignify it by reacting, it'll just keep the whole thing alive. Don't go over there and roll around in the mud."

"They're throwing it. Besides, how much more attention could we get than this?" I waved the paper. "We're going to be bombarded with press calls all day. Wait and see. Anyway, it's too late to ignore it."

She gave me a warning look. "That article didn't have Kit's byline on it. Be careful, Lucie."

The Loudoun bureau of the *Washington Tribune* was a small redbrick house on Harrison Street on the edge of Leesburg's historic district. I parked on Loudoun Street in front of the quaint log cabin that now housed part of the town's museum.

The last time I'd gone to see Kit when she'd been working in the D.C. office of the *Tribune*, I'd been required to pass through a metal detector, send my purse through an X-ray machine, and show my driver's license, which had been scanned—bad-hair photo and all—and became my stick-on badge for the day. Even then Kit had to show up at the front desk and escort me wherever I went. That included the ladies' room. But here in Leesburg, life was different. I opened the front door of the Loudoun bureau without knocking or being buzzed in and walked inside. The receptionist, whom I knew from experience was working on the *Times* sudoku puzzle in ink, looked up as the door closed. Normally we exchanged chitchat, but today I nodded without speaking and walked straight through the large open room where reporters and photographers sat at their computers, to Kit's office at the far end of the building.

Her door was open and she was leaning against the front of her desk, arms folded, one leg crossed over the other. Waiting for me. She'd been warned.

"I heard you left scorch marks on the ceiling on your way here," she said. "I'm sorry you're angry."

I leaned on my cane with both hands. "That story was straight out of the gutter. How come you didn't put it in the gossip column? Or maybe the comics, since it was such a joke?"

There were two pink spots on her cheeks. "I have nothing to do with Lifestyle. It's a completely different part of the paper. Different editors, different staff."

"Really? So where do they get their headline writers? Show up at the Comedy Club and recruit there? I'm sure that article sold a bunch of newspapers."

The flush now stained her face and neck. "The story was supposed to run on Saturday," she said. "I used up a lot of capital getting it delayed until today so it wouldn't ruin your weekend and your anniversary celebration."

We were going down a path of destruction, but now neither one of us was going to pull back.

"Too bad you didn't use your capital getting it—what's that journalism expression you use? Spiked?"

"There was no way they were going to kill that story."

"It belonged in a supermarket tabloid, not a serious news-paper in a major metropolitan area."

Kit uncrossed her legs and held on to the edge of her desk with both hands as she leaned toward me. "Believe me, I looked at that piece under a microscope when it showed up. Nothing in it is untrue, Lucie."

"You yourself said Chastain Construction is spinning the way this story plays out."

"I did not."

"I've got to go."

"Wait." Her voice was soft. "Let's not leave it like this be-tween us. Please, Luce. I wanted to come by after work today and ask you something. I was hoping . . . well, counting on, that you'd be my maid of honor."

I saw the smear of lipstick on her front teeth from where she'd bitten her lip as she waited for my reply. We stared at each other across a chasm that had opened up in the few feet between us that seemed as wide and deep as the Grand Canyon. Here was the one favor that symbolized what we'd meant to each other for so many years.

I struggled to control my voice. "Maybe this isn't the best time—"

"Of course," she said. "I understand."

I turned and walked blindly out of her office, no longer caring that tears were flowing down my cheeks. Kit's office door clicked shut, and a moment later I heard a muffled sound like a sob. I kept on walking, this time without even a nod to the receptionist, who said nothing as I passed her desk.

I stepped outside and closed the front door. From here, there was no turning back.

Chapter 14

———∞———

Quinn's salt-and-pepper head was bent over the record book in the lab when I showed up in the barrel room forty-five minutes later. I'd checked the rearview mirror in the Mini before getting out of the car. My eyes were no longer red-rimmed from crying. He'd never know.

I paused in the doorway as he closed the lab book and slid it over to a corner of the workbench. His eyes zeroed in on my face.

"You look like hell. I heard you paid Kit a visit. Guess it didn't go too well, huh?"

"I don't want to talk about it."

He pushed his bar stool back a few feet and studied me some more. "What do you want to talk about?"

I picked up a graduated beaker and examined it.

"How about the Riesling? Have you decided when you want to pick?"

He stuck his pencil behind an ear and folded his arms across his chest. Today he wore a gray athletic T-shirt and jeans with a hole in one knee. The usual chains around his neck and the leather and steel bracelet around one wrist.

"No later than Thursday," he said. "Before Edouard gets here."

"Who?" I set the beaker down.

"The newest hurricane. We're whipping right through the alphabet. This one may not hit us, either, but we're going to get slammed with rain." He wrinkled his forehead. "You haven't been following it, have you?"

"Of course I have."

"So where is it now, weather girl?"

"The Atlantic," I said. Hurricanes always started there.

He rolled his eyes. "I knew you didn't know. Look, I got a reefer truck coming in since we're going to have to move fast to get those grapes picked."

A reefer truck was short for refrigerated truck. We could keep the fruit chilled until we were ready to start processing it—putting it through the destemmer, pressing it, and moving it to the tanks to begin fermentation. It bought us time.

"Okay."

"I told Chance we'll need extra pickers that day."

"Okay."

Quinn stood and shoved me gently into the barrel room. "You aren't listening to a word I say." He walked me over to the long pine table and pulled out a chair. "Have a seat."

I sat.

"If you insist on talking about the Riesling," he said, leaning against the table, "I've been on the phone with Harry and John. They both think making a dessert wine is a terrific idea. I want to pick twice. Now and after the first hard freeze."

Harry Dye and John Chappell owned vineyards not far from ours. We helped one another all the time, sharing problems and successes with the types of grapes we could grow since our soil and climate were practically identical.

"Harry and John don't grow Riesling."

"That's why it would be unique to us."

I shook my head. "Too risky that late in the year because of the weather. And you know we're screwed if we don't get it picked in one night and the next day it warms up."

"I think we can do it."

We could probably put this argument on a loop and hit replay, we'd had it so often. As a winemaker, he wanted to experiment and push the boundaries of what he could do. As the one who paid the bills, I wanted to be able to pay the bills. Pick everything now and I'd sleep at night knowing we would have the cash to do it. Our Riesling was so good we generally sold out before we released our next harvest.

"Quinn—"

"Back me on this, Lucie. You're too distracted with everything else that's going on. Let me do it the way I want."

"I want to think about it," I said. "Give me one more day."

I expected him to balk when I said that, but instead he said, "All right. As long as you do something for me."

"What?"

"Take the rest of the day off. Go clear your head."

How many times had he said that to me lately?

"If I go home, I'll just—"

"Who said anything about going home? I gave Tyler some time off. He wants to take you to Ball's Bluff battlefield. It's a nice day. You'll learn some history."

I cocked my head. "Why did you give Tyler time off?"

"Someone left a bunghole cover open. We might have lost the entire barrel." He paused. "It was Pinot."

An entire barrel of wine. Five thousand dollars.

"Dammit. Are you saying Tyler did that?"

"Someone did it. My guess is he did. He was with Chance stirring the barrels yesterday."

"Did you talk to him?"

"You bet I did. I gave him hell but he claims he didn't do it. He can't be doing chores with his nose in a goddamn Latin book. I don't care how boring the work is and too damn bad if he thinks he's too smart to be doing manual labor. We lose enough with the angels' share as it is."

The angels' share was the name vintners give to the natural process of evaporation in the barrels. The story was that it went to the angels who liked drinking wine up in heaven. Depending on the humidity and temperature, the angels got as much as half a bottle a month per barrel. Not a bad share.

I wondered what kind of "hell" Quinn had given Tyler.

"That barrel is definitely spoiled?"

"I racked it over and I'm working on it," he said. "I'll let you know. After you come back from your field trip."

"How come I feel like I've been set up? You talked to Frankie about this, didn't you?"

His poker face was perfect. "Would I do something like that?"

I called Tyler, who agreed to meet me in the parking lot a few minutes later. He'd been primed, too, but he'd apparently gotten mixed signals from either Frankie or Quinn because he acted like the idea for the tour was a surprise to him.

He was wearing a T-shirt with something in Latin inscribed on it, baggy low-riding shorts like all the kids wore, and a UVA baseball cap.

"What does your shirt say?" I asked.

" 'If you can read this, you are an intelligent person.' "

"Oh." I smiled. "Well, it's all Greek to me."

He adjusted his baseball cap and gave me a tolerant smile. "Chance is meeting us at the battlefield," he said. "He had to pick something up at the hardware store in Leesburg so he's over there, anyway. Said he thought it would be interesting to see the place. He's never been there, either."

"Does Quinn know about this?"

Tyler shrugged. "I don't know. Probably. Why?"

"Because with you babysitting me for the day, he could use the help, that's why."

He looked guilty. "I'm not babysitting—"

"It's okay. Let's go. We'll meet Chance there and I'll have a word with him."

When we got in the Mini he said, "Chance isn't going to get in trouble for this, is he?"

"He reports to Quinn. If he's going to take off for a couple of hours, he should clear it with Quinn first." I looked over at Tyler as I pulled out of the parking lot. "You seem like you're pretty tight with Chance."

He pushed his glasses up his nose. "I like him. He's a cool guy. And he's nice to me."

Though he didn't say it, I understood the implicit message. *Unlike Quinn.*

Chance and Bruja were waiting when Tyler and I pulled into the gravel parking lot at Ball's Bluff Battlefield Regional Park in Leesburg half an hour later. Although two other cars were parked next to the vineyard's blue pickup, there was no sign of anyone except the three of us and the dog. I had just driven through a subdivision and passed a sprawling outlet shopping mall, but we could have been in the middle of nowhere it seemed so quiet and deserted.

"They've got leash laws in the park," Tyler said to Chance.

Chance opened the passenger door to the truck and got Bruja's leash, clipping it to the dog's collar.

"Does Quinn know you're here?" I asked him.

He gave me a roguish smile and winked at Tyler like a co-conspirator.

"I'm with the boss. Figured it would be okay for just a little while."

"You need to call him," I said.

"It's a dead zone for phone service." Tyler held up his cell phone. "I never get anything here."

I pulled my phone out of my pocket. "I don't have anything, either."

"Same here," Chance said. "We won't be long, Lucie. Besides, I had an errand in Leesburg, anyway. This is just a little detour."

I didn't like being an unwilling accomplice in deceiving Quinn about Chance playing hooky for part of an afternoon, but right now it seemed I had no choice in the matter.

"All right," I said. "Let's go."

We walked down a gravel path that cut through a heavily wooded area. The trees made a cathedral-like canopy above us, though enough sunlight filtered through in bright pockets to keep it from being gloomy. Still, it wasn't difficult to imagine why anyone who came here at dusk or at nighttime might believe this place was haunted. I'd never claimed to see Mosby's ghost near our ruins, but here, where so much blood had been spilled, something unsettling pervaded the air. Blue jays cawed from the trees and Chance had to restrain Bruja from chasing after the squirrels scurrying across tree limbs or diving into the vegetation. In the brooding silence, the rise and fall of the cicadas' metallic symphony seemed amplified.

"Which way?" Chance asked as we reached a fork in the path.

"The path on the left was made by the Corps of Engineers, which is why it's wider," Tyler said. "The one on the right is the old cart trail where the Union pulled a cannon and two howitzers up from the river. What you're looking at down there is where the Federals were." He waved at an expanse of woods at the bottom of a gently sloping hill. "Behind us in the parking lot is where the Confederates waited for them."

"I thought the battle took place in a field," I said.

"It did," he said. "In 1861 this place was a field. All these trees have grown up here since then."

"Let's go right." Chance pulled Bruja away from the stinging nettles that grew dense on either side of the path. "The way the troops came."

"You going to be okay, Lucie?" Tyler eyed my cane.

"I'll be fine."

The cart path was narrow but we still managed to walk three abreast with me in the middle. Chance's arm kept brushing against mine and once he looked over and gave me that heart-catching smile.

As we hiked downhill, the path meandered off to the right, deeper into the woods. There was no sign of whoever owned the other cars in the parking lot. It felt like we were all alone, and I was annoyed that it bothered me.

"Why did they pick this place to fight?" Chance asked. "The edge of a cliff with the Potomac below. There's no way to escape except the river."

"It was an important river crossing between Maryland and Virginia because it was so narrow," Tyler said. "Don't forget, all the bridges between Harpers Ferry and Washington had been burned. Neither army picked Ball's Bluff as a battle site. Both sides screwed up some things and they ended up fighting each other."

"Screwed up what things?" he asked.

Tyler took off his baseball cap and scratched his head. His

hair had been flattened by the cap except where the reddish curls stuck out around his ears. He reminded me of a clown.

"The area above and below Leesburg was important strategically because of the ferry crossings. Both armies were keeping an eye on it and placed troops in the region. But one of the Confederate commanders, Colonel Evans, got worried that his soldiers might be picked off by the Union troops. So without telling anyone, he decided to pull out of town and regroup somewhere else." We stopped walking as he bent down and picked up a stick.

"Here's Leesburg and here's the river with the two ferry crossings." He knelt and drew a map in the dirt with the point of his stick. "Evans pulls out of Leesburg and the Union troops over here watch him leave, figuring the town had been abandoned. What the Union didn't know was that Evans's commanders ordered him to return. Leesburg was too important to lose." He tapped the ground, indicating the Union soldiers. "These guys never saw Evans come back."

"Then what?" Chance asked, pulling Bruja's leash as she lunged for Tyler's stick. "No, girl. Leave it."

The dog obeyed and Tyler scratched behind her ears.

"After Evans left, a group of Union scouts crossed the Potomac from Harrison Island and climbed Ball's Bluff, figuring Leesburg had been evacuated. It was dark when they got here so they had to look around by moonlight. Unfortunately they saw a grove of trees"—Tyler paused to draw two stick trees—"and thought it was an abandoned Confederate camp, which is what they reported to their commander. The next day they came back with reinforcements to clear it out." He shrugged. "Evans's troops were waiting for them."

"It must have been a slaughter," Chance said.

"Not exactly. There were several skirmishes. Took all day. But in the end, the Confederates backed the Union soldiers up against the cliff. Over two hundred Federals died trying to escape or else drowned in the river."

He stood up and flung the stick into the woods as we continued down the path. Through a break in the trees I could see a chest-high stone wall and behind it an American flag hanging on a flagpole. The cemetery.

"You said only fifty were buried in that cemetery," I said.

"Fifty-four," he said. "Most of the others were lost and presumed drowned."

"I'd like to see that river crossing," Chance said. "How do we get to it?"

"There's another path." Tyler's gaze strayed to my cane. "It's pretty steep and it can be sort of treacherous."

"How did the Union soldiers get up here?" I asked.

"Same path," he said. "We could skip it and just check out the cemetery, if you want. Unfortunately there's no place to really see the river from up here because it's so overgrown with trees and bushes."

"I'd like to see the river, too," I said. "Let's take the path."

My shirt was already sticking to me and drops of perspiration trickled down my cheeks. Chance and Tyler mopped their faces with their shirts. Maybe we'd catch a stray breeze off the water to cool us off.

"If you guys are game," Tyler said. "We follow that sign over there."

"I'll spot Lucie in case it gets too difficult," Chance said. "Tyler, take Bruja's leash."

We weren't talking about bungee jumping off the bluffs, just walking down a hill. The first time I let my disability become more of an impediment than it already was, I knew it was the beginning of not fighting back and letting it dictate my life.

"Thanks, but I'm sure I can manage."

"We'll have to go single file," Tyler said. "It's the only way."

"Then Lucie should go in the middle." Chance took my hand. To me he said, "Tyler knows where we're going and I ought to bring up the rear."

The scent of his cologne mingled with perspiration filled my head. "All right."

The path, when we reached it, was narrower than I expected.

"Jesus," Chance said. "How many soldiers used this?"

"About fifteen hundred," Tyler said. "They got four horses and those cannons up here, too."

"How in the world did they do that?" I asked.

"The worst problem wasn't getting up here," Tyler said. "It was getting back down when the Confederates went after them. Some Federals ended up sliding down on their butts with their bayonets extended so they literally ran into their comrades and killed them."

He saw the expression on my face.

"Sorry. I know it's disgusting."

"How come so many drowned?" Chance asked.

"There were only three small boats to take them back to Harrison Island," Tyler said. "It wasn't enough. Some men tried to swim. Others just got caught on the floodplain, waiting. It was like shooting fish in a barrel for the Confederates."

Tyler waited while Chance and I took in the magnitude of what it must have been like for panicked Union soldiers under fire being forced to retreat down this funnel-like path, knowing they'd be sitting ducks for the Confederates if they even made it to the river.

"How many did the South lose?" I asked.

"Only about twenty-five." Bruja tugged on the leash in Tyler's hand. "Ready?"

The path, laid out as a series of switchbacks, was as

difficult to navigate as Tyler had warned. All three of us needed to put a hand out to steady ourselves on a fallen tree or a rock outcropping. No one spoke as we made our way down, but I could hear the breathing of the other two and the dog panting in the heat. Sweat stung my eyes and my clothes were as wet as if I'd gone swimming in them. Here and there blotches of sunlight penetrated the heavy canopy of trees, but the muggy air felt junglelike.

I tripped over a tree root and Chance grabbed my arm as I started to slide down the trail.

It took us nearly fifteen minutes to descend to the river. With each step I thought about what a protracted death this had been for the Union troops trapped at the edge of the cliff with too few boats to ferry them across the river. Once we saw the Potomac and Harrison Island, I wanted to get out of here.

The pea-green river was barely visible because of the many heavy, low tree branches that obscured our view. There was something flat and dead about this part of the Potomac. Nothing at all like the vibrant, swift-flowing river that was so entwined with the history and geography of Washington, D.C.

"Watch the mud and the tree roots," Tyler said.

Chance unclipped Bruja's leash and the dog waded into the river. He held out his hand to me. I took it as we walked around the Medusa-like root system of a copse of trees to get a better view of the river and Harrison Island.

I shaded my eyes against the light reflecting off the water. "Doesn't look too far to that island. I bet you could swim to it in under twenty minutes."

"Maybe now. Back in 1861, the river probably covered the entire floodplain," Tyler said. "Plus it had been raining hard for the past three weeks that October so it was higher than usual."

"Who owns it?" Chance indicated the island.

"It's private." Tyler pushed his glasses up his nose. His face gleamed with sweat and the glasses slid back down again. "They use it for hunting, but nobody lives there."

"We ought to think about starting back," I said.

Chance nodded and slapped his thigh, whistling for the dog.

"Stand back," he said as Bruja came ashore and shook herself off.

"When we get up top we'll take the path by the cemetery," Tyler said. "That way we'll make a complete loop."

The trip up the steep winding path didn't seem as arduous, but maybe it was because I was relieved to be leaving the riverbank. When we reached the clearing, though, everyone was again breathing hard.

"Whose grave is that?" Chance pointed to a solitary stone marker a few yards from the cemetery.

"It's where they think the Union commander fell. Colonel Edward Baker. He was also a U.S. senator at the time," Tyler said, as we walked toward it. "There are bunch of different stories about what happened and where he was actually killed. His death just about destroyed Abe Lincoln. One of his sons was named for Baker. They were really close."

Sunlight flickered on the small tombstone. Bruja, again on her leash, strained to examine it closer.

"It's not far from the cliffs," Chance said.

Tyler nodded. "That's how we're going to do it in the reenactment. Baker's going to drop dead near Goose Creek after he arrives by boat. Then everyone's going to rush him and fight over his body like they did in the real battle."

"I feel sorry for whoever plays Baker," I said. "That sounds dangerous."

"Nah, we've got it under control," Tyler said. "But it's Ray Vitale. Your favorite person."

"Who's he?" Chance asked.

"A guy Lucie and I met the other night," Tyler said. "Kind of hard-core. In charge of the Union reenactors."

"Let's check out the cemetery," I said. "Then we should head back to the vineyard."

Tyler unlatched the wrought-iron cemetery gate, giving it a shove so it creaked open. My eye fell on the raised lettering on the bronze plaque affixed to it. The bottom line read: "Interments—54. Known—1. Unknown—53."

Chance began counting the white markers arranged in a semicircle around the flagpole, pointing at each one.

"There aren't enough markers," he said.

"There's more than one person in each grave," Tyler said. "And nobody knows who's lying there, either, how many sets of remains are buried there."

I leaned against the sun-warmed wall of red river rock and felt the heat penetrate my clothing through to my skin, thinking about the mingled bones of Union soldiers moldering in this little cemetery.

"I still think that's ghoulish," I said.

"At least they're buried," Tyler said. "Parts of 'em, that is."

"The only one they could identify was James Allen?" Chance stood in front of the lone marker with a name on it.

Tyler nodded.

"We should go," I said.

Chance unlatched the gate. "You okay, Lucie?"

"I told her the place was haunted by the spirits of the soldiers who never got buried in the cemetery, but she didn't believe me," Tyler said.

"And I still don't," I said.

Tyler grinned. "Oh, yeah?"

"All right, I'll admit there's something disturbing about the place."

Tyler grinned. "Told you."

"Wonder where those people got to?" Chance said as we reached the parking lot and saw the same cars that had been there when we arrived. "Maybe they were watching us."

"Okay," I said, "enough with the scary stuff."

He unclipped Bruja's leash and smiled, climbing into the pickup. "See you home."

Tyler and I got into the Mini. "I think Chance likes you, Lucie."

"I think you have an overactive imagination."

We drove out of the park. "So what'd you think?" he asked. "Pretty interesting place, huh?"

"It is. Thanks for showing it to me."

"I know Quinn gave me time off today because he thinks I'm a screwup."

"No he doesn't. It's just that a lot of things have been going wrong lately."

"Yeah, and they always seem to be my fault." He sounded peevish.

"Is Quinn too hard on you?" I glanced at his profile. He'd taken off his baseball cap again. The wind blew his reddish-gold curls so they framed his face like a cherub in a Raphael painting.

"He's always asking me to do dirty jobs. Clean barrels. Clean tanks. Go out and pull leaves off vines one by one."

"Tyler, that *is* your job. That's what a cellar rat does. No one said it was easy work. Quinn and I do it, too."

"Chance would be a lot easier on me."

"Quinn runs the show. And if the work's too hard or too boring, no one's forcing you to stay, buddy." I kept my tone light. "If something's going on that I need to know about between you and Quinn, I expect you to tell me."

"Don't worry," he said. *"Ad utrumque paratus."*

"You want to translate?" I glanced at his innocent-looking profile and wondered whether he was keeping something from me.

" 'Ready for anything, prepared for the worst.' " He put his cap back on and adjusted it. "It means I can handle it."

As it turned out, he was wrong.

Chapter 15

⬦⬦⬦

Bobby showed up at the vineyard early Tuesday morning and found me in the courtyard deadheading flowers in the hanging baskets. Overnight the weather had shifted, bringing cooler temperatures and a tang in the air that smelled as though autumn would soon be here. The intense lapis hue of the summer sky had faded to steel blue, signaling that we were in for more changes including, possibly, an unwelcome visit from Hurricane Edouard.

I heard his shoes crunch on the gravel and looked up. He was dressed like a businessman in a sport jacket, dress shirt, and tie. His face wore the impassive expression of a cop, a stranger who was not my old childhood friend. I searched his eyes and wondered what went through his mind every time he had to deliver news that would crack open someone's universe, as he was about to do to mine.

"I'd like to talk to you," he said, helping me down from a stepladder next to one of the baskets. "I've got some news."

"Is here okay, or do we need to go someplace else?" I set my pruning shears on top of the ladder.

"Here's fine."

I reached for my cane. "Shall we sit on the wall, then?"

"Sure."

I looked out at the grape-heavy vines and the mountains. Thin clouds melted into the pale morning sky like a faded watercolor. I closed my eyes and wondered how bad his news was going to be.

"I'll get right to the point," he said. "Annabel Chastain came in yesterday to answer questions. After what she told us and based on some other evidence, we have reason to believe your father is responsible for the death of Beau Kinkaid."

He didn't sugarcoat it, I'll give him that.

"You can't really think—"

He held up his hand. "Wait. Let me finish. Leland Montgomery is dead and there's nothing to prosecute. If Mrs. Chastain wanted to file charges against your father's estate, it would go to civil court. The way it's looking, I don't think she plans to do that, meaning you're off the hook. It's over, Lucie, and we're going to wrap this up."

"Off the hook, except my father is a murderer?"

"Look, nobody knows how it went down. Maybe it was self-defense. Maybe not. But we have enough evidence concerning the feud between Beau and your father, plus a witness putting him at your home the day Annabel said Beau disappeared."

"Dominique."

"I appreciate her coming forward like that." He pulled a pack of gum out of his pocket and offered it to me.

"No, thanks."

He unwrapped a piece and stuck it in his mouth. "We've got a lot of active cases and you know how thin we're stretched with all the budget cuts hammering us. This one's pretty much open-and-shut. We caught a lot of breaks. Doesn't usually happen on a cold case, but this time it did."

"You said you had other evidence." I still felt numb. "Do you mean the bullet?"

"We haven't gotten final results back from the lab yet, but the bullet Junie found when he did the autopsy was pretty degraded," he said.

"So you won't know for sure if it was Leland's gun?"

He repeated like a mantra. "We have enough other evidence—"

I cut him off. "I don't understand why you believe Annabel Chastain. It's her word against nobody's. Dominique said Beau left our house alive. How come she couldn't have done it?"

He looked out at the horizon before answering. I knew then that the other evidence—whatever it was—had finally damned Leland. Something he knew and I didn't.

"Annabel and your father were having an affair. She has letters. Leland wanted Beau out of the way so he could be with her. It was more than a business feud, it was personal." He reached over and put a hand on my shoulder. "I'm sorry I had to tell you that."

My throat tightened. An affair. Bobby was satisfied this was a crime of passion. That put a whole new spin on everything. Leland had a reputation as a womanizer so it all fit together, didn't it?

"Dominique said Beau came to visit my father the day my mother went into labor with me. You're trying to tell me my father was carrying on a torrid affair with another woman when I was born? That he wanted to leave my mother with a two-year-old and a brand-new baby?"

"Wouldn't be the first time I'd seen it happen."

He pulled an envelope out of the breast pocket of his sport jacket. I didn't need to look at the contents to recognize

Leland's stationery. An engraved envelope with "Highland Farm" embossed on the back flap. Bobby handed it to me.

"Read it. I need you to confirm that it's your father's handwriting." When I hesitated he said, "Please."

I removed the letter and read it. Leland wanted Annabel to leave Beau. He also wanted her to meet him to talk about it. It wasn't Shakespeare, but Leland never had been one for poetry and roses.

"It's his handwriting."

"Thank you." He took the letter and refolded it.

"If Beau drove up here to see Leland and never returned, there must have been a car."

"We're looking on your property, in case it's still there," he said. "But even if it's not, he could have disposed of it elsewhere. He would have had plenty of time."

In the poignant silence that followed, I wondered if Bobby believed I had lied to him all along.

"I'm not hiding anything, Bobby."

"I never said you were. But it's over now."

"I still don't understand why Annabel isn't a suspect since she wanted Beau out of the way, too. And not to point out the obvious, but Leland didn't leave my mother for her, did he?"

"Annabel claims to have guessed what had happened and was so scared she'd get dragged into a murder as an accomplice that she ended the affair," he said. "Told your father it was over, left Richmond, and kept a low profile using her maiden name until she got a divorce on the grounds of abandonment and married Chastain."

"So she's off the hook, too, isn't she?"

He heard the scorn in my voice and his jaw tightened. "Let me tell you something. When I was at the academy, here's what I learned in Law Enforcement 101: The best approach to working a case is the simplest. Don't make it more complicated or convoluted than it is and don't read too much into anything. Most crimes are committed out of necessity or passion. Your father was motivated by both. He owed Beau money and he was messing around with his wife."

Then he delivered the coup de grâce. "Annabel agreed to take a polygraph test for us."

"And?" My mouth tasted like I'd swallowed nails.

"She passed."

Quinn found me sitting on the wall after Bobby left.

"I saw the cruiser," he said. "You want to talk about it?"

I took some deep breaths until I could steady my voice. "They're closing the investigation. Bobby says they have enough evidence to conclude Leland killed Beau."

He sat down and put his arm around me, pulling me to him. "I'm sorry."

I swallowed. "He says it may have been self-defense or not. But they're not going to look any further since they're satisfied he's guilty. Dominique put Beau at our house the day I was born, which corroborates Annabel's story. Plus Annabel produced a letter Leland wrote asking her to leave Beau. She and Leland were having an affair right before I was born."

His arm tightened. "This storm will pass. You're tough. You'll get through it."

"I don't believe he did it."

"I know, I know—"

"I'm serious. Leland did not kill Beau."

"It's probably hard to think straight right now. Give it some time." His voice was gentle. "It happened a long time ago. Who knows what the circumstances were?"

I lifted my head from his shoulders.

"That's a good question." I stood up.

"Where are you going?"

"To talk to someone who might know exactly what the circumstances were."

He stared at me for a long time. "Be careful."

In the sweet, nostalgic memories of everyone who pines for the bygone days of small-town America, there is always a General Store. An old-fashioned place that doesn't necessarily have what folks need, but it does have what they want—someone who remembers their brand of tobacco and the kind of motor oil they bought last time, and who asks to see pictures of the new baby or the wedding without being prompted. The inventory is never computerized because it's erratic and, besides, no one computerizes bloodworms or tomatoes fresh out of the garden of a local farmer. Our General Store had Thelma Johnson, who'd owned the place since God was a boy.

I parked outside the white clapboard building with its hipped tin roof and large picture window with the neon "Open" sign that now read "Ope." Thelma had tied sleigh bells that sounded like Christmas every time someone entered or left through the front door, and that was her version of security. As always, the place smelled of coffee, baked goods, and some pleasantly undefined essence that came from the patina of age rather than an atomizer of canned wildflowers or spring rain.

In the cramped back room where she did her paperwork, she also kept her soap opera magazines piled high around the recliner where she sat to watch her shows. Talk shows, game shows, reality shows—but her favorites were her soaps because she always fell in love with the good-looking young hunks on the screen.

The bells jangled as I opened the front door. From the other room a quavery voice called, "Coming!"

Thelma was the caricature of a sitcom grandmother with her overdone makeup and too-young clothes. Today she was dressed completely in Robin Hood green—sleeveless polyester sheath dress that fell two inches above her knobby knees, sequined stiletto slingbacks, and star-shaped faux emerald drop earrings. Her eye shadow, which I could see behind her thick trifocals, matched her dress. Her carrot-colored blush and lipstick were the same startling orange as her hair.

"Why, Lucille," she said. "What a treat! I haven't seen you in an age! Glad you stopped by. What can I do for you?"

"Just thought I'd come by and say hi. Get a cup of coffee and one of your muffins."

She placed her hands on her hips and considered me. "Child, my momma may have raised ugly babies but she sure didn't raise stupid ones. You came by for a lot more than just how-de-do. Why don't you just set a spell and tell me all about it? I presume you want the usual."

Thelma knew everyone's usual. Mine was a fifty-fifty blend of whatever coffee she was brewing in the pot labeled "Fancy" and what she called "Regular." Enough milk to turn it caramel colored, one sugar.

"Yes, ma'am."

"You'll be wanting a blueberry muffin. The berries are fresh from the farmers' market in Frogtown."

"Yes, ma'am."

"Help yourself. The Romeos were in this morning extra-hungry so you're lucky I got anything left other than the paper to wrap 'em in."

She tottered across the room in her stilettos and poured my coffee. I got my muffin from the glass cabinet that held all her fresh-baked pies, cakes, and breakfast items.

"What's the coffee of the day?" I asked.

She winked. "I couldn't decide between Jamaican Me Crazy and Sinful Delight, so I made both. How about Sinful Delight for you? A little sinning never hurt anybody every now and again, if you ask me."

At least we were on the same page. I wanted to talk about a big sin. We sat facing each other in her cream-colored spindle-back rocking chairs. Thelma's chair creaked comfortingly as she rocked and watched me drink my coffee.

I balanced the muffin in its white glazed paper wrapping on my knees. "These are great."

"Lucille, honey," she said, "you've been eating my muffins since before you knew how to walk, when Lee or your momma would bring you in here. You don't have to make small talk with me. You can just cut right to the chase. I can see you're dyin' to."

Thelma liked to boast that she had a mind like a steel trap—or, as she said, a steel trapdoor, which was probably more accurate. I was under no illusion that I would even make it home before everyone in two counties knew about our conversation. It would take either an elephant tranquilizer or direct threats to keep Thelma from reaching out all the way to the smallest roots of her thick grapevine and sharing what she knew—and I had neither.

"I came about my father," I said. "You probably guessed that."

"I do seem to have a special way of knowing what folks are thinking. A kind of extrasensible psychotic perception." She smiled and smoothed her dress. "And of course, my God-given ability to talk to folks' loved ones after they've passed."

I tried not to look nonplussed at her description of her special powers and nodded. Thelma did have moments where she became temporarily untethered from the real world, especially her conviction that she could get in touch with those who now resided in "the Great Beyond" as she called it, via her Ouija board. Would she really remember events from nearly thirty years ago, or was I grasping at straws?

"I don't want to talk to my father," I said. "Just about him."

"Now don't you give me a look like you think communicating with the spirits is a lot of hokeypokey." She wagged her finger at me. "I heard you were over to Ball's Bluff yesterday. If you didn't feel the presence of the spirits on those grounds—"

"You know I was at Ball's Bluff?"

"Course I do. That nice young man, Chancellor, was in yesterday evening. Buys a little something for his dinner on his way home from your vineyard at least once or twice a week. Good-lookin' fellow, if I do say so. Got a smile that lights up a room. He always has time for me, you know?" Thelma blushed like a teenager and I wondered what made Chance turn his considerable charms on her. "He's always asking questions about folks around here. I like a person who tries to fit in when he's new to a place."

"He's very personable."

"Yes, indeedy. You're lucky to have someone like that working for you." She leaned back in her chair and crossed her legs, surveying me. "Ask me about your poppa, honey. What is it you want to know?"

"You know everything about everyone, don't you, Thelma? You remember a lot of things."

She smiled, slyly pleased. "You don't need to butter me up, although I'm sure you've heard some people think of me as sort of a local Orifice of Delphi. The orifice was a special person in ancient Greece who talked a lot and answered everyone's questions. She was supposed to be quite the fountain of wisdom."

"Yes, I've heard of her . . . it." Just how clear *was* her memory? "Bobby Noland told me he has enough evidence to conclude that Leland murdered Beau Kinkaid."

It was news to Thelma. She stopped rocking and placed both hands on the arms of her rocking chair. "Where'd he get a damn-fool idea like that?"

"Dominique remembered Beau being at our house the day I was born, which fits with the information his ex-wife gave Bobby about the last time she saw him." I shrugged. "Plus Leland was having an affair with Annabel Chastain. Opportunity and motive."

"Phooey."

"What do you mean?"

"Gives *her* a motive, is more like it. I remember her. Annie Kinkaid in those days. Now she's"—Thelma waved a hand like she was mixing something in the air—"*Annabel* Chastain. All high and mighty. A real legend in her own minefield."

"You *know* her?"

"I never actually met her," she said. "But I know all about her. Chasing after your father when your poor mother was expecting you. It about broke your mother's heart."

I wrapped my half-eaten muffin back in the paper and set it down. "How do you know all this?"

"Your mother and I shared confidences in those days, Lucille. Especially because both of us were . . ."

She stopped and laid two fingers lightly on her lips. "Well, we talked a lot."

"So my mother told you that Annabel—Annie—was the one who was pursuing the affair with Leland?"

She nodded. "I told Bobby this the other day, but of

course he didn't believe me. Aside from it being secondhand information and no way to transubstantiate it. That's legal talk for proving it."

"Annabel passed a polygraph test and she had letters from Leland."

Thelma's eyebrows knitted together. "Isn't that interesting she kept hers all these years? Wonder what happened to the ones she wrote your father?"

"He had letters from her?"

"Oh, my yes. Your mother got hold of a couple of 'em." Thelma folded her hands in her lap. "I'm sure one of your parents burned them years ago if you haven't turned up anything by now."

I shook my head. "Unfortunately not. I've been through my mother's papers and you know Leland. He wrote down as little as possible. The fire destroyed what few things remained."

"Now you listen to me, Lucille." Thelma sounded stern. "Your father had his faults. We all knew that. He was a rogue and a rascal and he put your sainted mother through ten kinds of hell with some of the things he'd get up to. He may have had his secrets, but he was no murderer. Your mother . . . well, she would have known. And she couldn't have lived with it."

I wanted to kiss her. It was the vindication I'd been seeking somewhere . . . anywhere. If Thelma believed it, then I knew I was right that Leland hadn't killed Beau.

"I'm glad to hear you say that. Thank you."

"It's the truth." She regarded me and frowned. "Are you going to eat that muffin? I swear, child. You look like you're about to blow away in the next strong wind. Probably don't weigh more than a hundred and ten pounds soaking wet. Tiny just like your mother was. You look just like her, too, Lucille. Such a beauty she was. "

I opened the paper again, blushing. "You're very kind. I miss her so much sometimes."

"I know you do. So do I. My Lord, so do I."

"What was it that you started to say about the two of you . . . that you were both something. What was it?"

Thelma took off her heavy glasses and looked away. The silence that fell between us seemed to weigh her down. Her sharp shoulders rose and fell as she brushed a fingertip under one eye.

"I'm sorry," I said. "I didn't mean to pry—"

"Pregnant," she said. "We were both pregnant."

I had been reaching for my mug as she spoke. Coffee sloshed from the mug onto the little table.

"I'm so sorry. I had no idea—"

I sopped up the liquid with a napkin, embarrassed for both of us.

"No one does. The only person I trusted was Charlotte."

My mother's name was Chantal but Thelma always called her "Charlotte," just as I'd become "Lucille" and Eli was "Elliot." Thelma knew the history of almost everyone in Atoka, but who knew anything about her?

"Do you have a child . . . I mean, did you . . ."

Had she given the baby up for adoption? How had she hidden her secret all these years?

Her smile was full of sadness and remembrance. "I lost my baby before anyone ever realized I was in a family way. Your mother guessed, though. Came in one day and found me sick as a dog, throwin' up in the bathroom. She recognized right away that it was morning sickness. Knew I didn't want to see a local doctor because I was too scared that folks around here would find out. So she drove me all the way to Washington to see someone from out of town."

"Why didn't the baby's father help you?"

"Pfft!" She waved her hand. "Gone with the wind, darlin'. Back to his wife."

"Oh, Thelma."

"We've all chosen the wrong man at one time or another, haven't we?" Thelma put her glasses back on and fixed her gaze on me with the haunted eyes of a woman who has never known what it was like to wake up each morning with a man who loved her.

She knew my track record with men as well as I did. Maybe better. I wondered if, when I was her age, whether I, too, would have a string of broken relationships, and that would be it.

"It's the first time I've spoken about this since the miscarriage," she said. "But I thought you should know. You're exactly the same age my daughter would have been."

Her smile wavered. "Every time I see you I think of that. Wondering what color hair and eyes she would have had. If she would have been smart or musical or an athlete. Course I couldn't have kept her, so I wouldn't have known either way, now would I?"

My throat closed. I couldn't answer.

"I didn't mean to make you sad, child."

"I'm afraid I'm the one who made you sad."

She stood up and began cleaning imaginary fingerprints on the glass cabinet. "It's all right. I've learned to live with it."

I wanted to hug her but I was afraid she'd lose whatever shred of dignity she was hanging on to if I did.

"I hope you know I'll respect your confidence just like my mother did," I said.

"Of course I do," she said. "I trust you like I trusted Charlotte. And Lucille, what you told me today, that stays here, too. You have my word."

I nodded.

She finished cleaning the cabinet. "Well, now. At least you finished your coffee. How about another cup?"

"No, thanks. I'm fine. But could I get coffee and a donut to go for Quinn?"

"Sure you can. I know he likes those chocolate-filled donuts with chocolate icing. I got one left. Lordy, I wonder what that man's cholesterol is. How he manages to stay so fit and good-lookin' considering some of the stuff he eats."

I reddened. "I don't know. How about Jamaican Me Crazy for him? It kind of fits the way things are going between us at the moment."

She smiled. "I've been having a lot of those days lately myself."

The routine of fixing the coffee seemed to restore a kind of normalcy between us. But our relationship had nevertheless changed as though we'd shaken a kaleidoscope, rearranging familiar pieces of colored glass to make an entirely different picture.

"About your father." She waved away the money I tried to give her for the coffee and bakery goods. "If I think of anything else that might help, I'll let you know."

"I appreciate that."

"And don't you fret over what folks are saying, either. You know the truth about your daddy and that's what counts. Like I always tell myself, it's just a case of mindlessness over matter. You just can't mind because that kind of talk doesn't matter."

"Thanks for the advice."

She winked. "Just call me the Orifice."

This time I did give her a small hug and she patted my shoulder.

"You're a good girl, Lucille."

I drove home with a lump in my throat.

Now I knew for sure that Annabel Chastain—or Annie Kinkaid—was lying about her relationship with my father. Maybe that meant she was also lying about Beau's murder. Who killed him and how it happened. Too bad I didn't have any way to prove any of this.

At least not yet.

Chapter 16

⚬⚬⚬

Savannah Hayden's muddy Jeep was in the winery parking lot when I got back from the General Store fifteen minutes later. Quinn hadn't mentioned that she'd be dropping by. The last time I'd seen her was when she helped out at the anniversary celebration a few days ago. I wondered if he asked her to come over or whether it had been her own impulse.

I had hoped to talk over what Thelma had said about Annabel Chastain and her relationship with my father when I dropped off the coffee and donut. Now I regretted buying them. Maybe I could just quickly leave them and say I had business to take care of in my office.

It looked like Quinn had put Savannah to work cleaning the stainless-steel tanks we planned to use for the Riesling. I heard her laughter echoing inside one of the tanks, followed by Quinn's deep voice.

"It has to be completely clean before the wine goes in so there's no contamination," he was saying. "I'm using the smaller tanks because we're going to be working against the clock and the wine needs to cool down fast. But we gotta get all the schmutz out before any wine goes in."

More laughter from Savannah and muffled words.

He turned around as I stood there, feeling foolish clutching the Styrofoam coffee cup and the little white bag from Thelma's. One of his hands, I noticed, rested on Savannah's shoulder. Her head was still inside the enormous tank.

Something flickered in his eyes when he saw me, but he kept his hand where it was.

"I brought you breakfast. Payback for the other day. I'll just leave it on the table. Didn't realize you were busy. If I'd known, I would have bought two of everything."

"Thank you. So you went to Thelma's?"

I nodded.

"Did you get answers to your questions?"

"My questions?"

"When you left here you said you were going to talk to someone who could answer your questions."

"It's a long story," I said. "Why don't we save it for another time?"

Savannah's head popped out of the tank like a jack-in-the-box when the music stopped.

"Morning, Lucie." She rubbed the palms of her hands on the seat of her jean shorts like she was trying to clean them. Today she looked about Tyler's age in a faded University of Montana T-shirt over the shorts and no socks showing above her red high-tops.

"I had a few hours off so I thought I'd stop by. Quinn says you're pretty short-handed."

"I appreciate that. We could use the help."

"I can probably come back on Thursday when you pick the Riesling."

"Don't let us down, sweetheart," Quinn said. "We need you."

Savannah blushed. "I won't."

"I heard your investigation is all wrapped up," I said. "So I guess that's off your plate now that the sheriff's department is closing the case."

Her smile faded. "Once the final report's written. Look, I'm sorry about how it turned out."

"Why did you come back after Bobby finished recovering everything?"

"Why do you think? Because he *didn't* recover everything."

"He still moved from A to Z awfully fast the day after you were out here," I said. "Either you didn't find anything else or you found something really significant."

"Look," she said, "I can't even begin to imagine how difficult this must be for you. I'm not supposed to talk about the case, but there is one thing I'll tell you. Off the record."

It sounded ominous, whatever it was. "What?"

"Beau Kinkaid was killed somewhere else."

"Where? How do you know?"

She laced her fingers together and turned her arms inside out, splaying her feet so she was resting on the sides of the high-tops. With her white-blond hair and jet-black eyebrows she reminded me again of a pixielike Peter Pan.

"I don't know where." She paused. "But I found evidence the body had been wrapped in something, meaning odds are good it was transported from another place."

"So you'll be able to figure out where he was killed?" I asked.

"I doubt it. Anyway, it's a moot point since the case is closed."

"Meaning we'll never know."

"I'm sorry," she repeated. "Sometimes 'good enough' has to be 'enough' when you're trying to allocate resources and you're cash-strapped. Maybe not for the family who wants absolute certainty, but in this case the evidence is so lopsided . . ."

"It's okay."

I'd been through all that with Bobby. It was clear she was in lockstep with him. I knew a door slamming when I heard one. I set the coffee and the white bag on the winemaker's table.

"You don't have to explain," I added. "I know it wasn't your decision. I'll be in my office taking care of paperwork if you need me, Quinn. See you later."

"Sure." Quinn nodded. "You okay?"

"Fine."

If he didn't believe me, he didn't let on. "Look, after we're done here, I'm taking Savannah out to the field to teach her how to measure Brix. I'll call you with the numbers."

"Terrific."

They started talking again before I even got to the barrel room door. Outside in the courtyard, it seemed cooler than it had earlier in the day.

But maybe I was only imagining a chill in the air.

When I got to the villa a few moments later, Frankie was talking on the phone by the bar.

"I'm so sorry," I heard her say. "No problem. No, no, that's okay. It must have been awful when you found out . . . come on by and we'll take care of it. See you soon."

"What was that all about?" I asked after she hung up.

"One of our customers. Poor thing. She was in here this weekend with her boyfriend. They bought a case of Cab and a case of Chardonnay for an engagement party they're throwing for some friends. Over five hundred bucks. Charged it on her Visa, then the next day found out someone had gotten hold of her information and made purchases on that card so she canceled it. Our transaction was still pending. Apparently there was some kind of mix-up and it got canceled, too. She promised to come in and pay us for the wine," she said. "She's bringing cash."

"When's she coming?"

"Uh . . . soon."

"You think she's legit?"

Frankie looked unhappy. "It never occurred to me she wasn't. I trust everybody. Maybe I should have gotten her to secure those cases on another credit card until she showed up with the cash."

"I'm sure it will be fine," I said. "We've had our share of bad checks and people who try to charge things on credit cards that have hit their limit. It comes with the territory."

"She'll show up," Frankie said, pulling on her lip. "Or else I'll cover it."

"You will not. Forget it."

"Speaking of questionable credit, you had a couple of visitors awhile ago. Eli." She gave me a significant look. "And Brandi."

"Both of them?"

"He came first, then she showed up. They, uh, adjourned to your office. I didn't say anything since he's your brother and it's none of my business."

"What were they doing in my office?"

"Talking." She raised her eyebrows. "Fortunately we didn't have any customers at the time."

"You mean they were fighting?"

"Yup. Money again. I heard that part. I finally went out on the terrace so I don't know the rest of it." She shrugged. "When the front door slammed, I figured they might have left together, but then I saw her walking to her car by herself. The Jag was still in the parking lot."

"When did he leave?"

"About ten minutes later."

"He say anything?"

"Yup. 'Good-bye.'"

"I think I'll give him a call."

But Eli had either turned off his cell or he was ducking calls because he never answered mine. After leaving three messages, I gave up.

I had no better luck at his office. The receptionist at his architectural firm in Leesburg said he hadn't been in to work since last Friday. When I called his house as a last resort, I got the default message on his answering machine. Random words stitched together meant to imply that a genuine human being was asking me to leave my name and number and someone would get back to me. I hung up without saying anything.

Quinn called at the end of the day with the Brix numbers on the Riesling. A lot of people believe we pick our grapes when we think they're ready and that it's a somewhat subjective call based on upcoming weather along with a few other seat-of-the-pants assessments. It's true there's a certain crapshoot element in the decision-making process but there is also science, math—and the law.

Brix is the primary indicator in determining ripeness and when to pick because it measures the amount of sugar in the grapes. That measurement allows us to calculate the percentage of alcohol in the wine, which, by law, must range between 7 and 14 percent, depending on the wine varietal. Because Quinn and I liked our Riesling dry rather than sweet, we favored a low-alcohol wine that showcased the fruit—or as he said, a wine that wouldn't blow the top of your head off because of too much alcohol—so we picked at a lower Brix.

"We should be ready on Thursday," he said. "It'll be about twenty-one and a half or twenty-two Brix by then. We'll beat the rain, but just barely."

"All right," I said. "You'd better tell Chance to make sure we have enough pickers so we can wrap it up in a day."

"Don't you worry, I'll talk to him," Quinn said. "One more thing. When we drove back from the field I saw Eli's Jaguar parked over by the Ruins. Didn't see him, just the car. Everything all right?"

"I'm not sure," I said. "Thanks for letting me know. I've been trying to reach him all afternoon."

"Lucie?"

"Yes?"

"Are you okay? You seemed kind of distant this morning."

How could I answer him? My father had been accused of murder, my brother's life was falling apart as I watched, and Kit and I weren't speaking to each other. Despite what was going on between Quinn and Savannah, fundamentally I knew he was my friend, and that had to be good enough.

"I've got a lot on my mind right now, but I'm okay," I said. "By the way, Savannah's nice. I can see why you like her."

"What are you talking about?"

"Nothing. Just, she's nice."

"Sure. Yeah. Nice kid. Smart, too."

After he hung up I wondered why he sounded puzzled that I'd figured out he was interested in Savannah. He'd been anything but subtle about it.

It was dusk when I stopped at the Ruins on my way home. My brother's Jaguar was still there. I parked next to it and got out, calling his name.

The color had faded from the sky and the Blue Ridge was in silhouette against a bright white sky. The fields and stands of trees in the middle distance between the Ruins and the mountains already looked less substantial in the murky light. In a short while, it would be dark. The languid days of summer were already waning. On my way back from the General Store this morning I passed a Loudoun County school bus, the driver no doubt trying out a new fall route a few weeks early.

I found Eli on the far side of the Ruins, sitting where Quinn would not have been able to see him when he drove by. Eli had supervised the conversion of the burned-out tenant house into a stage for plays and concerts. He'd also added a dressing room and an equipment storage area. He knew the Ruins and its hideouts better than anyone else, including the places that weren't entirely safe to climb on like the old brick hearth where he was now sitting, along with a bottle of Leland's favorite single-malt Scotch.

There had been one last full bottle of Macallan twenty-five-year-old Scotch in the armoire of the dining room. If that was the bottle he now cradled, he'd put a nice dent in it, though I would have guessed that anyway the moment I laid eyes on him.

"You're drunk," I said.

"And I plan to get drunker still." He smiled the stupid smile of the woefully inebriated and patted a place next to him. "Join me."

The brick floor was uneven and what was left of the chimney didn't look like it could support much weight if I needed to hold on to it while I navigated my way to where he sat. Eli reached out his hand.

"Here. I'll help you. Be careful."

"Why don't we move someplace safer? The mortar between these bricks is practically dust. It could collapse right under us."

"Just like my life."

"Don't."

"Why not? It's true."

"How about letting me drive you back to the house?"

"Thanks, but I'm staying here until this bottle is empty."

"That doesn't sound like a very smart idea."

"Does to me."

"Why?" I gave in and eased myself down next to him.

"Because this is where I took Brandi when I proposed to her."

In the aching silence that followed, I knew my brother had hit rock bottom if he had come back to the place where it all started with Brandi. I closed my eyes and listened, certain I would hear the sound of his heart breaking into pieces.

"Frankie said the two of you spent some time in my office today."

Eli picked up the Scotch and took another swig. "She wants a divorce. There's someone else. Has been for quite a while." He handed me the bottle. "Fabulous stuff. Best in the world."

His eyes slid over mine and I saw his grief.

"I'm so sorry," I said. "I had no idea."

"You and me both. What an ass I was not to see it coming." His mocking laugh echoed against the old bricks. "The husband's always the last to know. You think that's such a crock, but you'd be surprised how easy self-delusion is." He nudged me. "You're not drinking."

"You know I don't like Scotch."

"Am I going to be turned down by two women in one day? Come on, keep me company. Macallan's liquid gold. The old man had first-class taste in booze. You have any idea how much this bottle costs?"

"Nope." I tipped my head and drank. It warmed my

throat and I coughed, but Eli was right. It did taste like liquid gold, making me think of oranges, spices, and a vague vanilla scent. I wiped my mouth with the back of my hand as he reached for the bottle.

The Roman philosopher Seneca said that drunkenness is nothing but voluntary madness. Tonight my brother was crazy with hurt, betrayal, and anger. It scared me to think what he might do in this self-induced state of reckless grief.

"Do you know who it is?" I asked.

"Someone with money."

"He won't have money for long after she gets hold of him," I said.

His laugh was short and crude sounding as he drank more Scotch.

"You can stay at the house as long as you need to, you know," I told him.

He set the bottle down and rubbed his face with his hands. "I appreciate that, Luce, but I've got to find someplace to live. I can't keep mooching off you. Taking your charity."

"It's not charity. You're family. You also don't have to make any decisions right now."

Especially when he was so drunk his breath was flammable.

"I'm going to lose Hope," he said.

I knew he meant his daughter, but the desperation in his voice jangled my nerves like he meant something more.

"You're her father. You're not going to lose her."

"How did Leland and Mom stick it out? He had affairs but he always came back to her."

"They loved each other. I talked to Thelma this afternoon. She told me something."

He slugged some more Scotch and handed me the bottle. "What?"

I drank, too. "She says Leland wasn't the one pursuing

Annabel Chastain. It was the other way around."

Eli's eyes narrowed as he tried to focus on my words. He was already starting to slur his. "So whadda's that mean?"

"It means Annabel lied."

"Any way to prove it?"

"Thelma said Mom told her Annabel wrote letters to Leland. Annabel hung on to Leland's and that was the proof she showed Bobby. But you know Leland. He'd never keep someone else's love letters as a memento."

"So we have nada."

"That's the way it looks." The sky had paled to a silvery gray. "When it's dark out here we're not going to be able to see a thing."

"Relax." He leaned over me and pulled away a brick that I thought was solid in the mortar. "Look what I found."

A couple of fat, partially burned pillar candles and a box of matches.

"Who put those there?" I asked.

"No idea. Not me. Back in the day Brandi and I used it to keep, uh, other things there."

"What other things?"

He eyed me. "You weren't the only one who used the Ruins as a hideout for sex."

"Oh. Those other things."

The matches were still good. He lit the candles and set them between us, a soft pool of flickering light in the darkness. Overhead a pale nearly full moon became visible between banks of clouds.

"Looks like we're going to see a ring around the moon when it gets darker," I said. "Means rain's coming."

"Mom always used to say that."

"I hope the reenactment isn't a washout if that hurricane hangs around through the weekend."

"I talked to Zeke Lee. He said they'll be there come hell or high water. Literally. Said it'd take a monsoon for them to cancel."

"You going to join them?"

"I dunno." He cradled the Scotch like a baby. "Zeke says one of those weekends beats a visit to a shrink. You go back in time so none of your problems happened yet." He gave a drunken chuckle. "Says it's better than free therapy. Anything free looks pretty good from the bottle of the hole I'm in. I mean, bottom."

"Give me that Scotch. Maybe two days of pretend war and shooting at people isn't such a good thing for you to be doing right now."

"Anger management. Sounds terrific." He leered at me and uncorked the bottle again. "Remember when we used to play Civil War here?"

"How could I forget? I always had to be your Union prisoner and you'd stick me in the basement."

"Scared you, huh?"

"I wasn't scared."

"Yeah, you were. Especially the night we told you we saw Mosby's ghost."

"I knew you were joking."

He drank some Scotch and pointed at the moon. "Who says we were? You know he comes out looking for Yankees when there's a full moon."

"He comes out on moonless nights and I'm not falling for that again."

"If you say so. But I feel his presence, moon or no moon. Something's out there."

"Cut it out, Eli."

"You're spooked. I can tell." He chuckled again. "Wonder what happened to all my Civil War stuff?"

He lifted the bottle for another drink. This time I reached over and took it from him. "You've had enough. What Civil War stuff?"

"All the stuff I found out here. Bullets and buttons. You know, stuff. I even found a Condeferate belt buckle."

"You don't say." He seemed oblivious that he'd mangled his syllables. "What'd you do with all of it?"

"Put it in one of Leland's old cigar boxes. It's shumwhere."

"Maybe we can find it and have those things authenticated. Display them at the winery."

"Yeah, sure."

He tried for the Scotch again, but I blocked him with my arm and moved the bottle out of his way.

"Nice try, but it's time to go home."

"I think I'll just stay right here."

"And wait for Mosby?"

His laugh sounded like a pig hunting truffles. "Maybe. He could be along any minute."

"I have a better idea. You come home with me." I blew out the candles and put them back where he'd found them. "The moon's out from behind the clouds. Let's go while we can see our way. I don't want to fall and break my leg."

"The drunk leading the lame or the other way around?" He hiccupped. "Sorry, babe. That was stupid. I didn't mean it."

"Forget it."

It hurt, but he was too drunk and depressed for me to take him seriously right now.

I helped him up and he leaned on me as we staggered to the staircase. It felt like I was dragging an anchor for the *Queen Mary*. By the time we made it back to our cars, I was sweating.

"First one to get back to the house wins." Eli fumbled in his pocket and pulled out his car keys.

I held out my hand. "I'm going to win because you're either walking or riding with me. I suggest the ride, so hand 'em over, sport."

He looked annoyed but at least he didn't protest. Instead he shoved the keys in his pocket and let me help him into the passenger seat of the Mini.

"I wonder who left those matches and candles there." I started the engine and backed onto the main road.

"Mosby."

"I'm serious."

"You 'lose and clock both gates every night?"

"Close and lock? Of course. Quinn takes care of it himself. "

He shrugged. "Maybe you've got people who sneak in shum other way."

Which is what I'd suggested to Bobby and he'd pooh-poohed it. Unless it was someone who was here on a regular basis and didn't need to sneak in. Had Quinn used it for trysts with one of his girlfriends? Chance? Tyler?

I drove back to the house in the quiet darkness, the silence broken only by the waning sound of the cicadas. We couldn't possibly patrol all five hundred acres of this farm, nor keep someone out if he or she really wanted to gain access to the property.

"I'm gonna call Brandi when we get back to the house," Eli said all of a sudden. "Have a lil talk with her."

"I don't think that's such a good idea, Eli."

"Why not? Tell the lil woman she's makin' a huge mishtake. She needs to know."

"Maybe you should sleep on it."

"Who you tellin' what to do? I'm the man of my own housh."

Once when we had to deal with an extremely inebriated

client who'd become hostile during a wine tasting, Tyler had recited something in Latin. I couldn't remember the words, but I did remember the translation: To quarrel with a drunk is to wrong a man who is not even there.

I hoped Eli wouldn't call Brandi. But right now, I was talking to a man who wasn't there. Which was a pity because after tonight's discussion—all teasing about Mosby's ghost aside—I wouldn't have minded the sober comfort of a coherent conversation with my brother to shake off my worries.

Instead I put him to bed and undressed in my own room as the tree branches made skeletal patterns against my windows in the shifting moonlight. Too much talk of ghosts and spirits and hauntings. Mosby, Beau Kinkaid, the restless spirits at Ball's Bluff.

I climbed into bed and lay there, rigid with the irrational fears I knew would seem foolish by morning. I closed my eyes and waited for sleep to come.

Chapter 17

⚜

We spent Wednesday getting the equipment ready so we could bring the Riesling in the next day before Edouard's rains arrived. Quinn's commands were barked orders rather than the usual banter that went on with the cellar rats in the barrel room and the field crew, which only served to further ratchet up tension.

We weren't the only vineyard in the region that decided to pick early, meaning there would be competition to get the experienced pickers. Last spring when we needed extra help for pruning, Chance hired a crew of day laborers from the migrant camp in Winchester. Unfortunately, none of them had ever held a pair of pruning shears before, much less worked in a vineyard. They either cut too much or too little and the result was a disaster.

Around ten o'clock I went over to the barrel room to check on things, arriving just in time to hear Quinn telling Chance not to bring him another inexperienced crew or else.

"You get over to the day laborer place early," he was saying, "and you get me guys who know the difference between the sharp end of a pair of shears and the one with the holes for their fingers."

The two of them faced each other near the row of stainless-steel tanks, Quinn's voice echoing in the large space, reverberating with anger. Off to one side, Javier, Benny, and Tyler looked on. Tyler's eyes were huge behind his glasses and Benny kept folding and unfolding the bill of his baseball cap like a book. Javier saw me come in. He glanced over and shook his head, warning me to stay where I was. The others didn't notice.

"If you don't like the crew I get for you, why don't you take care of it yourself?" Chance replied.

"Because it's your goddamn job, that's why."

"Then back off and let me do it."

"Who are you telling to back off, asshole?"

It was over in seconds. Quinn lunged at Chance as Javier grabbed Quinn's arms, speaking to him in rapid-fire Spanish. Chance looked like he was ready to start shoving Quinn, but Benny stepped in and pinned Chance's hands behind his back. Chance tried to wrestle free.

"Don't, Chance," Tyler said. "Don't do it."

"Stop it, both of you! There will be no fighting here. Is that understood?" I walked toward them.

All of them froze, and Quinn turned toward me first, lowering his arms to his sides. He still looked like he regretted not throwing a punch or two. Chance shrugged off Benny like unwanted clothing and folded his arms across his chest, a hostile expression on his face.

"Everybody out of here except Quinn," I said. "Chance, meet me in the villa in ten minutes. Benny and Javier, maybe you want to go for a smoke. Tyler . . . I don't know. Take a break, okay?"

They filed past me, eyes downcast. The metal door to the

barrel room clanked shut. Quinn looked elsewhere as they left, stoking my anger.

"Are you out of your mind? What was that all about? If Benny and Javier hadn't stepped in, you and Chance would have gone at each other like a couple of street fighters. And you started it."

He held up his hands. "Don't talk to me about who started what. You know what I just found out? Either there are some cases of wine missing or our records are totally screwed up because the numbers don't add up. And I haven't got the goddamn time to deal with it now."

"Are you accusing Chance—?"

"Him. Tyler. Somebody. I don't know. Either way, Chance is a total screwup." He ran a hand through his hair, more weary and at the end of his rope than I'd seen him before. "Dammit, Lucie. I want him out of here."

I pressed my lips together. I didn't need this right now. A squabble between two macho guys with egos, Chance accusing Quinn of abuse; Quinn claiming Chance was incompetent. The timing was lousy, on top of all our other problems.

"I don't want to have this conversation right now," I said. "We have the Riesling to get in tomorrow before the rain gets here. The reenactment's this weekend. Harvest is biting us in the butt. Let's get through the next few days without anyone spilling blood, okay? Back off with Chance and I'll deal with him. I promise I'll sit on him. You just steer clear of him."

Quinn shook his head at the folly of my words. "You're going to be sorry if we don't cut him loose today."

"I'm already plenty sorry about a lot of things, believe me," I said. "But right now we need him."

He stared at me. "Yes, boss."

It was the first time he'd called me that. I ignored his mocking tone and left.

* * *

Chance was in the kitchen drinking coffee when I got back to the villa. I poured myself a cup and gave him the same ultimatum about no fighting.

He nodded. Like Quinn, he avoided looking at me.

"One more thing," I said. "Do you know anything about missing cases of wine or a problem with records that don't tally?"

His eyes hardened. "Is Quinn blaming me for that, too?"

"I don't need your sarcasm and you didn't answer my question."

"It's no."

"You and Quinn need to cool it. And we'll get to the bottom of this other stuff after we get the Riesling in."

"Am I free to go?"

I didn't like his belligerent tone of voice.

"Why don't you take the lugs out to the fields and leave them at the end of the rows so they're ready for tomorrow?"

"Whatever you say."

"By the way," I said, "for the time being, you report to me."

He shot me a look of scorn and left. After I drank my coffee, I went back to the barrel room, but it was like being in a morgue. A mood of gloom and tension had settled over the place like a miasma and no one was talking to anyone.

I hated it.

Frankie called just before noon and asked if I could sign some papers. I fled to the villa, glad to escape the funk. When I got there, she was on the phone.

"It's B.J.," she said. "He's on his way over with that other guy. Ray Vitale. They want to check out the site again. Something about finalizing the script for their battle. Can I just let them do their own thing or do you want to go with them?"

"They can go on their own. Tell B.J. to call me if there's anything else they need."

"Sure."

She showed up in my office a few minutes later.

"I thought I'd run into Middleburg and pick up a sandwich at the deli and a piece of homemade pie from the Upper Crust. My treat for lunch. What can I bring you?"

"A piece of rawhide to chew on."

She grinned. "How about turkey or ham?"

"Sorry. Turkey on a croissant? But I'm paying. I think you bought last time."

Frankie walked over to the small closet in my office and took out her purse. "Forget it. You deserve some pampering after wading through all that testosterone over in the barrel room."

She pulled out her wallet and looked up, a frown creasing her forehead.

"Maybe you'll have to buy, after all. My credit card's missing. Damn."

"Are you sure? Maybe you misplaced it."

"Nope. I'm a creature of habit. I always put it in the slot behind my license."

"Check your purse. Maybe it fell out."

She dumped the contents on the seat of a red-and-white flame-stitched wing chair my mother had recovered when this was her office.

"You were right." She sounded relieved. "Here it is. At the bottom of my purse. Wonder how that happened?"

"Maybe you forgot to put it back the last time you used it. Or Tom used it and forgot to tell you?"

She shook her head. "I doubt it. Tom has his own credit cards."

"Why don't you call the bank and make sure everything's okay? You'll probably feel better."

"Maybe I'll just drop by. It's Blue Ridge Federal, so I pass it on the way to the bakery."

She returned forty-five minutes later with the sandwiches and two glazed white bags from the bakery.

"I brought you a couple of cowpuddles from the Upper Crust. They just finished baking them. Place smelled great," she said. "Sorry it took so long."

She didn't look happy.

"What happened?" I asked.

She pulled up the wing chair and took her sandwich out of the wrapper. "I canceled my credit card. Someone did use it. Today. Can you believe it? Two thousand dollars' worth of stuff at Neiman Marcus."

I set down my croissant. "It wasn't Tom?"

"Tom's allergic to shopping. I buy all his stuff. And I don't spend two grand at Neiman's."

"Maybe it's a mistake and got charged to the wrong account?"

Frankie bit into her sandwich. When she finished chewing she said, "I'm calling them after lunch. Please don't take this the wrong way, but Brandi and Eli were in your office by themselves yesterday. My purse was in your closet like it always is."

"Neiman's is Brandi's favorite store," I said. "Why don't you call them now?"

She called while we ate. Her end of the conversation was a lot of "uh-huhs" and "yups."

"My husband must have ordered that," she said, finally, "and forgot to tell me. I apologize. Umm, would you mind canceling the order, though? Thanks. Sure. I appreciate that. Sorry for the mix-up."

She disconnected and met my eyes.

"What is it?" I asked.

"A couple of designer dresses and a jacket. They were supposed to be delivered to Forty-forty Hunting Horn Lane in Leesburg."

Eli and Brandi's address.

I felt ill. Brandi had told Eli to rob a bank if that's what it took to get money. But there was a difference between being on the brink of homelessness or having nothing to eat and doing something stupid and reckless like stealing a credit card to buy designer clothing from an upscale department store.

"I don't even know how to begin to apologize," I said. "And I don't understand why she'd do something this dumb. I'll get a keyed lock put on that closet so no one but us has access to it from now on."

Frankie was still watching me.

"If you want to press charges," I said, "go ahead. I'm not going to make this difficult or awkward for you."

"Lucie." She picked at a piece of ham. "Brandi was never in your office on her own. Eli was. She joined him and then she left before he did. Even if she used the card, he would have had to know about it." She let the rest of that thought hang in the air between us.

"You're saying Eli used it?" I asked. "Sent Brandi a gift?"

"Maybe. Or at least knew she got the card and copied down the information."

"That doesn't sound like Eli. Desperate, yes. Dishonest, no."

"How else do you explain it?" Frankie asked.

I put my sandwich down and folded the wrapper around it. I had lost my appetite.

"I don't know."

"I'm not going to press charges," she said. "The credit card's canceled so it can't be used again. The stuff wasn't shipped. Tom makes two thousand dollars in a couple of days, so it's not about the money. But I am mad and I want an explanation and an apology. In return, I won't report it to the sheriff."

"Fair enough," I said. "Do you want me to talk to Eli, or do you want to do it?"

"You can do it."

I nodded, feeling heartsick. My father had been called a murderer. Now my brother was branded a thief.

How much worse could it get?

I confronted Eli that night when we were having drinks on the veranda before dinner.

"What are you talking about?" he said. "You actually think I'd steal Frankie's credit card and buy clothes for Brandi?"

"Either you did it or she did it," I said. "Neiman's confirmed the shipping address was your house."

"It must have been Brandi because it wasn't me."

"Frankie said you both were in my office yesterday. She keeps her purse in that closet because we figured it was safer than stashing it under the bar."

"I used the john," he said. "Maybe she did it then."

"Brandi needs to apologize in return for Frankie not reporting this to the sheriff."

He snorted. "She'll probably deny she did it."

"Then the sheriff can ask her about it."

"I'll call her," he said.

He took a long drink from his glass and looked at me like he was about to eat his last meal before the execution. "I'm accusing my soon to be ex-wife of credit card theft. She's gonna love that."

He went inside and made the call out of my earshot. Ten

minutes later he returned. I noticed he had made himself another gin and tonic while he was in the house. Light on the ice.

"Well, that went down just great." He sat down in the glider. "She thinks I'm out of my fricking mind and that it's the beginning of a campaign to prove she's an unfit mother so I can get custody of Hope."

"She said she didn't do it?"

"Nope. Said it's some sick trick of mine."

"You didn't do it, either?"

"I told you already. No."

I reached for my wineglass. "This doesn't make sense."

He set his drink on the glass-topped coffee table and moved it around and around in overlapping circles.

"I love her," he said. "Even now. But she really is flipped out about being broke and on the verge of bankruptcy. I'm sure she's in denial about a lot of stuff."

"You mean denying she stole the card and bought those things?"

"Maybe."

"Well, I guess it's up to Frankie what she's going to do about this," I said.

"I thought you said she wasn't going to report it to the sheriff's office."

"That was before nobody admitted responsibility. She's mad, Eli."

"I'll call her," he said. "Maybe I can persuade her to let this slide. It's not like anything happened since she was able to cancel the order. No harm, no foul. Right?"

He stood up and unclipped his phone from his belt again.

It wasn't right. But he'd already gone back inside to call Frankie. When he came back, he looked relieved as he waved a hand at me.

"All taken care of," he said. "She's cool with it."

I got up to make dinner, but my stomach was churning. What had happened to Eli? He used to know the difference between right and wrong. Getting away with something didn't make it right. It just meant he'd gotten away with it and Frankie was too decent to hold either of them accountable. So now the theft was compounded by lying. What was cool about that?

I didn't recognize any of the workers who showed up with Chance when we picked the Riesling the next morning. Quinn left me on the crush pad to supervise getting the grapes weighed and moved to the refrigerator truck.

"I'm going out in the field with these guys. Wait until I get back before we put the grapes through the destemmer," he said. "I don't have a good feeling about this crew. Some of them look like they never set foot in a vineyard before. Watch 'em all cut themselves with their pruning shears first thing when they start picking. I hope no one takes off a finger."

"What are we going to do?" I asked. "This is who we have. It's them or nobody."

"I told you yesterday what we should have done," he said. "Savannah said she'd be here in an hour, so that's one more person. But I bet we have to sort what these guys pick. Then we're going to have to go back out there and pick anything they missed. What a goddamn mess."

I rubbed my temples. "I hope we can pull this off before it rains."

He glared at me. "The good news is that, since we finally decided to make ice wine, we're not picking everything. Maybe we'll make more than we planned if these rubes leave a lot of fruit on the vines."

"Maybe," I said.

But later in the day as we began sorting the grapes, it began to look like the ice wine project was in jeopardy, too. Quinn set up a sorting table and both of us, along with Benny, Javier, and Tyler, began checking the grapes before putting them in the destemmer.

We worked for about ten minutes and it grew quieter and quieter.

"I don't believe this," Quinn said finally. "They picked everything. Unripe, ripe, overripe. We're screwed. There'll be nothing left to pick in the fall."

"Maybe it's only this batch," I said. "Let's keep going."

But it wasn't just one batch.

We worked outside through the afternoon as the sky grew darker and then the rains began. Benny and Javier moved everything under the overhang so we could keep going. Quinn had already started to press the first batch of grapes. We were barely speaking and I knew if he got his hands on Chance, who had driven the crew back to their camp, this time he'd kill him.

I saw Chance before Quinn did. Frankie called me when she was ready to lock up the villa for the evening and asked if I could drop by. Things had been awkward between us all day. I hoped she hadn't decided to quit.

When I walked in she had two wineglasses set out.

"We need to talk," she said. "Red or white?"

"Either."

She gave me the choose-one look.

"How about white?" I said.

She poured from an opened bottle of Riesling.

"Brandi called me," she said. "She wanted me to know she had nothing to do with those purchases. Says she's pretty sure Eli must have done it because he's so distraught at losing her. She thinks he thought maybe he could win her back that way."

We touched glasses.

"Eli says he didn't do it," I said. "I know he's my brother, but I believe him before I believe her."

"She sounded pretty believable herself."

We drank in silence. Frankie seemed to have made up her mind. I couldn't blame her for believing Brandi. Either way, though, it was an ugly situation involving theft, fraud, and deceit. Tough to put a good spin on that and find anything to salvage.

"I'd like to reimburse you," I said.

Frankie shook her head. "For what? The transaction was canceled. I wanted to tell you that I plan to put this behind me."

I had no doubt she meant it, especially because she was watching me with her usual clear-eyed candor, waiting for me to accept her offer of a truce. But I still felt shamed, like a parent called into the principal's office after some altercation involving a child had been dealt with and cleared up. Punishment and forgiveness had been dispensed, but what was lost—at least to me—were honor and integrity. There would be whispers and doubts the next time something like this happened, and Eli would always be a suspect.

"I'm still so embarrassed—"

She held up her hand. "Forget it. They're both under a lot of strain. I don't want this to come between us, Lucie. I have so much respect and admiration for you and what you've done to turn this vineyard around. You can't take the weight of everyone else's problems on your shoulders. Not even your own family."

"First, Leland. Now Eli. I feel rotten."

She squeezed my arm. "I know you do. That's why you need to promise me we're going to move past this."

"I can't have Eli working here anymore, can I?" I drained my glass.

"I wouldn't put him in a situation where he's handling money right now," she said. "Would you?"

"No."

That was the quid pro quo she wanted and, as usual, she had finessed her request. We couldn't afford another scandal. She was willing to sweep this one under the carpet. But next time . . . ?

"Okay," I said. "I'll handle it. I'll tell Eli we don't need him helping here anymore. He's not stupid. He'll get the message."

We finished our wine.

"Want another glass?" Frankie asked.

"I'd better not. I need to get back to the barrel room. I think we're going to be here all night with the Riesling. I don't know where Chance dug up that crew we had today, but they picked everything. Quinn wants him gone, too."

"I heard," she said. "Look, go on back. I'll close up."

I stood as Frankie began turning off lights. She paused to look out one of the windows.

"Speak of the devil. Chance is just getting out of the pickup."

"Oh, God," I said. "I need to get to him before Quinn does."

We met just inside the courtyard archway. Bruja, who had been following her master, wagged her tail and came to me so I could pet her.

"I ran the crew back to the camp," he said. "You guys done with getting the Riesling in the tanks already?"

"We haven't even started," I said. "Because we have to sort the grapes by hand. All of them."

"What are you talking about?" he asked.

The rain had temporarily let up but the air still felt heavy and damp. I watched Chance and wondered if Quinn was right that he was completely incompetent. How could he not know what he'd done?

"Your crew picked *everything*, Chance. The only thing that could have been worse would be sawing off the vines and dragging those back, too. It's like they'd never worked as pickers before. Of anything. Where'd you get them, anyway?"

"Same place I always get them. The camp in Winchester."

"Where'd you really get them?"

"I told you. The camp in Winchester. Look, remember what I said before?" he asked. "Quinn works those men like dogs. If anyone complains he threatens to sic Homeland Security on them. Word gets around, Lucie. You're lucky I got who I got."

"I've never seen Quinn act like that."

"You're not out in the field every day. How would you know?"

"How come my other manager never told me about it?"

"I didn't know your other manager, but maybe he closed his eyes. Or maybe he didn't think of day laborers as anything other than one step up from a chain gang."

"That's not true!"

"What did you say about a chain gang?"

Quinn's voice, behind me. I turned around. It was just the two of them and me. Quinn moved closer until he was standing about a foot away from Chance. I was not going to be able to stop this fight.

"I'm handling this, Quinn," I said. "Let me settle it."

"Tell this asshole to clear out. He's through here."

"Who're you telling to leave, buddy? You don't run the place."

"I said, clear out."

"That's enough," I said. "Quinn, don't—"

Chance smirked. "Seems the boss doesn't agree with you, Quinn. Go on, Lucie. You're not going to let him bully you like he bullies everyone else—"

Quinn cut him off with a hard blow to his stomach. Chance doubled over and groaned.

"Stop it!" I said. "Quinn! Are you out of your mind? Don't do this."

"Get out of here," he said to Chance. "You're through."

He turned his back on Chance and started to walk away. Chance raised his head, a look of cold fury on his face, and charged after him. I heard Quinn's "ouf" as Chance tackled him and the sound of Quinn's head hitting the ground. He looked dazed, as though the blow had knocked the wind out of him.

"Get up," Chance said. "Get up and fight me, old guy."

"Don't do it! Chance, Quinn!"

"Get out of here, Lucie," Chance said. "Get lost and let us finish this."

As he spoke, Quinn got up. This time Chance was ready. He landed a precise flurry of hooks and jabs before Quinn could raise his fists to defend himself. Quinn staggered backward as blood poured from his nose. Chance went after him, punching him hard in the gut, but when Quinn went down, he managed to take Chance with him. I heard their animal grunts as their fists connected with flesh and bone.

Involuntary manslaughter . . . was that what they called it when someone died in a fight? This had to stop.

I pulled out my phone and called Benny.

"You and Javier, come quick to the courtyard! They're killing each other!"

By the time the two of them pulled Quinn and Chance apart, I wanted to call an ambulance. No one would let me.

"You'll get the sheriff involved." Quinn's words were slurred. "Don't need to do that. Everything's fine."

Tyler showed up then, wild-eyed.

"Get the first aid kit," I said, and he fled.

Quinn had gotten the worst of it, or at least there was more blood on his face and clothes. Benny stood by Chance, who was still doubled over holding his ribs. Quinn lay on the ground as Javier tended to him. I heard him mumble to Javier that he was fine, nothing broken.

"That guy is crazy." Chance straightened up. He was breathing hard as he pointed at Quinn. "And so are you, Lucie, if you let him work here."

Quinn groaned and sat up. One eye was swollen and his face looked like a piece of raw meat.

"Get rid of him," Quinn said and coughed. "He's trouble."

"So what'll it be, Lucie?" Chance's laugh was harsh and challenging. "You can't keep both of us around. You know that."

"No." My voice sounded far away. "I can't."

"You're not thinking . . ." Quinn watched me, incredulous. "Come on, Lucie. He's just messing with your head."

Chance smiled and winked at me. My eyes traveled from him to Quinn. How had it come to this? Was I really contemplating choosing between them? It was Quinn's fault for forcing this showdown, wasn't it? In spite of my feelings for him, I needed to be objective, do what was best for the vineyard, the crew . . .

"You know, Chance, I really like you." My voice wavered.

"Aw, Lucie . . ." Quinn's eyes were anguished. "I don't believe this."

I cleared my throat. "As I was saying, I really like you, Chance. You've charmed our customers and the crew likes you, too."

Chance was grinning now, his eyes holding mine in triumph.

"But I guess I'm just crazy," I continued, "because ever since you joined us, there has never been so much ill will and so many screwups and mistakes as there have been these last few months. And because you laid it down as he goes or I go, I'm firing you. I want you gone now, Chance. Get your stuff and get out of here."

Chapter 18

⁓⁓⁓

Chance's smile didn't fade, but something in his eyes went dead as they flickered down to my cane and my deformed foot, before settling on my face.

"If that's your decision."

"It is."

Quinn got up with Javier's help. "Get out of here. You heard her. You're fired."

"Quinn," I said, "he's going."

"Pretty cruel turning me out on the street like this." Chance stared hard at me. "Especially after your winemaker tried to kill me. That's not your style, Lucie. You've got more class than that, don't you?"

"I'll give you two weeks' severance pay."

"Make it three. And I'll overlook the assault charge."

"Forget it," Quinn said. "Don't do it, Lucie."

Chance shrugged. "Up to you. You know he started it. What I did was only in self-defense."

"Three weeks," I said. "I've got to write a check and the

checkbook's in my office. Chance, you come with me. Everyone else get back to work."

Quinn started to protest but I silenced him with a look.

"I can handle this."

Neither Chance nor I spoke as we walked to the villa. I asked him to wait in the tasting room while I wrote the check. When I came back, he had a bottle of wine in his hand.

"Okay if I take this as a souvenir?"

It was a bottle of Riesling.

"What if I said no?"

"I'd take it anyway."

He flashed a shadow of the heart-stopping smile and I looked away as I handed him the check. He folded it and put it in his pocket without looking at it.

"You're making a mistake," he said, and pulled me into his arms.

Before I could protest his mouth came down hard on mine as he drew me closer in a viselike embrace.

"Chance—"

He loosened his grip on my waist, but it was only to put a finger under my chin and tilt my face to his for another long, bruising kiss. I felt the wine bottle press hard into the small of my back. It hurt. He was making me dizzy, breathless.

"Don't! You can't do this." I put my hands on his chest, gasping, as I tried to push him away.

He laughed and released me. "I just did. I'll be around for a few days. Then I'm probably leaving town. You could change your mind. We could finish this. I've seen the way you look at me, Lucie. I've known for a while that you want me."

He traced his finger down my cheek and my throat. When it moved between my breasts, I caught his hand.

"Stop it, please."

His laugh was low and seductive. He bit my neck and I stifled a cry at the unexpectedness of the sharp little pain.

"I know what you want, too, baby. And I'm good. I'd undress you nice and slow—"

"That's enough!"

He laughed again. Then he walked over to the front door and opened it. I thought he'd look back, but he didn't. I stood there, numb.

How could I have let him do that? Was he right? Had I asked for that kiss?

The door opened again and Benny walked in. How long had I been standing here?

"Jesus, you scared me, Benny!"

"You okay, Lucie? Queen sent me to check on you. Make sure nothing happened."

My face was scarlet. I moved my hand to my neck to the place Chance had bitten me and pretended to rub it. Had he left a mark?

Benny's expression was bland.

"Nothing happened," I said.

He stared at me. "Good."

We both knew that was a lie.

By the time Benny and I got back to the crush pad, Quinn had cleaned up, changing his bloodstained T-shirt to a clean one. His face looked puffy and he was going to have a hell of a shiner. He moved and looked like a dog that had just dragged itself home from a losing fight.

"Maybe you should go back to your place and get some rest," I said. "You look like hell."

"And lose all these grapes? No way." He glanced up at me and went back to sorting fruit. "I'm sorry I took a swing at him. But he was asking for it."

He kept concentrating on the grapes, but I could see his Adam's apple move in his throat. I'd never seen him this uncomfortable before.

"Can I talk to you in private for a minute?" I said.

Benny and Javier glanced up.

"We can take a break, Queen," Javier said, pulling cigarettes out of his pocket. He looked at Benny. "*Vámonos.*"

I picked up a bunch of grapes. "I have to ask you something."

"What is it?"

"Have you ever threatened to turn any of the day laborers over to the Department of Homeland Security if they didn't do something you asked them to do?"

"Have I *what*? What the hell are you talking about? Where'd you get an idea . . . *Chance*?" He looked stunned. "He told you that and you believed him?"

"If I believed him he'd still be working here," I said. "It's not true, is it?"

"Do you even need to ask?"

"Quinn, don't make this difficult for me. Yes or no?"

He shook his finger at me. "I have never, never threatened anyone."

"What would you call that little smackdown, then?"

He shook his head. "Aw, come on. Okay, so I slugged Chance. He had it coming. But you know me. You really think I'd physically abuse the men? Or threaten to turn someone over to DHS? They'd be deported so fast it would make your head spin. Tell me you never took that jerk seriously."

I threw the grapes in the destemmer and avoided his eyes.

"You did believe him." His voice was hard. "Jesus, Lucie. Look, if you want my resignation, too, you can have it."

"Don't be ridiculous. I just needed to ask, is all."

"Why didn't you tell me as soon as he made that accusation? Why did you wait?"

"Because I was afraid you'd do what you did today, that's why. Between Bobby telling me my father is guilty of murder and everything with Eli, I didn't need more heartache. Back off, please, okay?"

He was angry, but that was too damn bad. Some of this was his fault, too.

I picked up more grapes. "Let's get back to work."

"Sure, boss," he said. "Whatever you say."

We barely spoke to each other for the rest of the night. Around midnight, Savannah showed up. Quinn told her he'd walked into the press when she asked about his eye. She looked like she knew she'd been asked to swallow a whopper but didn't bring up the subject again, at least in my presence.

Someone turned on loud rock music and Quinn brought out a couple of cold six-packs. While he and Savannah were busy filling one of the tanks with juice, I asked Benny if we could talk.

"Sure," he said. "Want a beer?"

"No, thanks."

He pulled a bottle out of the cooler for himself and opened it with his knife. We walked into one of the cool, dark bays and stood next to a row of barrels of Pinot Noir. The tangy odor of fermenting wine filled my head.

"Chance told me those guys he hired as pickers today came from the camp in Winchester," I said.

"They aren't from Winchester," he said.

"How do you know?"

"I heard one of them talking. I think they're from Herndon."

"What's in Herndon?"

"A lot of places where ten guys live in two-bedroom apartments. The guys who came today just got here from Salvador." He pronounced the name of the country in his rich accent.

"Meaning what?" I asked.

He shrugged and took a pull on his beer. "They'll do anything. Work *más barato* than guys who've been here awhile. Cheaper."

"I paid the wages of an experienced crew," I said. "The same as we always do."

There was no way, try as we might, that we could find enough workers with green cards who were willing to pick grapes or work in the fields. As a result, we kept a lot of cash on hand because that's how we paid the crews. I didn't always feel good about hiring illegals, but don't-ask-don't-tell was the way it was. And we paid a fair wage—always.

Benny gave me a shrewd look and wiped his mouth with the back of his hand.

"Chance paid the guys. You paid Chance."

A small shock went through me. And the memory of that fierce kiss. "He pocketed some of the money that was supposed to go to the men?"

"People are greedy. I've seen worse. *Ilegales?* Especially new guys. They got no rights. What are they gonna do?" he said.

"That's despicable."

"*¿Cómo?*"

"Awful. Disgusting."

"*Sí.* In Spanish we say something about his mother." He smiled and showed two silver teeth.

"Is there any way you can locate one or two of these men and find out if Chance underpaid them?" I asked. "And let me know?"

"I'll see what I can do," he said. "I could even make Chance sorry about what he did."

"Let's take it one step at a time."

More vigilante violence over labor problems was the last thing I needed.

By the time we finished getting the juice out of the press and into tanks it was three in the morning. Quinn said he planned to sleep in the barrel room to keep an eye on things and Savannah showed no sign of being ready to leave.

Tyler had downed a couple of beers during the evening and I worried about him driving home, even though his parents' bed-and-breakfast was just up the road.

"I'll drive you," I said. "I didn't drink."

"What'll I tell my folks if I don't show up with the car?"

"That you behaved like a responsible adult who turned the keys over to someone else."

It was a five-minute drive to the Fox & Hound on a deserted road. Tyler yawned and moved restlessly in his seat.

"This is hard work," he said. "And these are killer hours."

"Surely you stayed up this late in college?"

"That was for fun stuff."

"Looks like your folks have a full house," I said, pulling into his driveway.

"A lot of people coming for the reenactment."

The sweep of my headlights caught a vanity license plate on a burgundy Mercedes. "CHASTAIN."

"I suppose this is a stupid question, but are Annabel and Sumner Chastain staying here?"

"They showed up a few days ago. Mom says they're sticking around awhile longer because Mr. Chastain wants to look at a horse he might buy."

"Have you met them?"

"Sure. They've had breakfast in the dining room a couple of times when they're not having it in their cottage."

"Which cottage is that?"

"Devon." He eyed me. "You going to talk to them or something?"

"Uh, well, maybe. I didn't realize they were still in town," I said. "Nor that they were staying here."

"It seemed like a good idea not to mention it to you." He sounded wary as he opened the car door. "Thanks for the ride. Can I come in late tomorrow?"

"Of course. Get some sleep."

Tyler got out and I waited so he could see his way to the front door in the wash of my headlights. He swayed a little as he walked and I was glad I'd driven him.

On my way home I thought about calling on the Chastains.

In fact, as soon as possible.

I slept for a few hours and finally got up around eight. My eyes felt like I'd rubbed sandpaper in them. Quinn and I had agreed to finish pressing the last of the Riesling later this morning after yesterday's marathon session. Working around heavy equipment—the forklift, the destemmer, the press—when we were all exhausted was hazardous. I didn't want any more accidents.

I called the Fox & Hound as I stood in front of kitchen windows drinking my morning coffee. The cloud-covered sky gave everything a closed-in melancholy look that suggested a long spell of inclement weather to come. At least it wasn't raining.

Jordy Jordan, Tyler's father, answered the phone. He didn't sound happy when I asked whether the Chastains were in their cottage and if I could speak to them.

He came back on the line a minute later, his voice dry as autumn leaves. "I'll put you through."

Sumner Chastain took my call. "Ms. Montgomery. This is a surprise."

He spoke with the self-assurance of someone who held all the cards and knew it. Though he could have asked Jordy to tell me to get lost, I thought it was interesting he agreed to talk to me. Maybe it wasn't such a surprise that I called, after all. Perhaps he'd been expecting it.

"I was wondering if I might come by to speak with your wife, Mr. Chastain."

A pause, then, "I don't see any purpose in that. Or any value."

"I'm sure you know the Loudoun County Sheriff's Office now considers the murder investigation closed," I said, "largely based on evidence your wife provided to Detective Noland that apparently proved my father murdered Beau Kinkaid. There would be great purpose and value to my family and me if Mrs. Chastain could explain what happened all those years ago. She's the only person who can answer our questions."

"There's no 'apparently' about your father's guilt, Ms. Montgomery. And my wife has already answered—"

"Put yourself in my place," I said. "You'd want to understand what happened, too. You'd want some closure . . . some peace, wouldn't you?"

There was a long silence and I wondered if I hadn't been on a speakerphone all along, so that Annabel had heard everything I'd said.

"One moment, please." Sumner sounded brusque. When he spoke again, I realized I'd been right. He'd turned off the speaker and now it was just the two of us on the line.

"My wife says she will see you," he said. "It would not be my decision, but I respect her wishes. Let me warn you before you get here. I will not tolerate any accusations or threats against her. Do I make myself clear?"

"Yes, sir."

Like many of the buildings in Middleburg and Atoka, the Fox & Hound had been built in the early 1800s. Over the years it had gone through numerous changes, including joining the separate kitchen to the main house and adding double-tiered verandas that overlooked Grace Jordan's lush English gardens, until it evolved into the graceful, rambling estate it was today. The grounds possessed many outbuildings, some of which had been enlarged and converted into guesthouses, which were now the more sought-after lodgings.

Sumner Chastain answered the door to Devon Cottage when I knocked. Taller than I expected, I guessed him to be around six foot two. He wore an open-necked dress shirt, well-cut slacks, and a double-breasted navy blazer, radiating authority and the craggy bonhomie of a good fellow who belonged to all the right clubs and sat on boards of numerous charitable foundations and civic organizations. His eyes lingered on my cane as he looked me over and it seemed to surprise him.

He turned away and called to the bedroom. "Annabel, she's here."

It bothered me that he didn't use my name. I wondered if it was deliberate or if I genuinely didn't register with him as someone of any consequence. After this conversation, we'd have no further reason to speak with each other.

Annabel Chastain—or Annie Kinkaid, as my father knew her—seemed tense and nervous when she walked into the elegant sitting room, which Grace had furnished with fine

English antiques and oil paintings of pastoral settings, mixed in with hunting scenes. Like her husband's attire, Annabel's clothes spoke of understated wealth and good taste. Cream-colored slacks, matching open-toed heels, bottle-green silk tunic, and the same oversized choker pearls I remembered from the Internet photograph.

She examined me with undisguised curiosity and also appeared startled by the cane as her eyes darted between it and my face. I knew then she'd never met my mother. If she had, it would be like seeing my mother's ghost nearly thirty years later. But there was no flicker of recognition when she looked into my eyes.

"A car accident," I said.

She colored faintly. "I apologize for staring. You're just so young . . ." Her voice trailed off.

"Are you all right, darling?" Sumner asked.

"Yes, of course. Won't you sit down, Ms. Montgomery?" she asked.

"No, thank you. I won't take much of your time."

"As you wish." Annabel walked over to a carved button-back chair and sat on the edge as though she were poised for flight.

"Would you like your tea, Annabel?" Sumner asked. "I can bring it from the other room."

"No, thanks, darling. I'm finished." She fluttered a hand.

He came over and stood behind her chair, resting his arms on the rosewood frame as he leaned forward, a tender gesture that made it seem like he was physically shielding his wife. Annabel reached up and stroked the sleeve of his blazer, fidgeting with one of the buttons on his cuff.

"Forgive me for being blunt," I said, "but I understand you and my father were having an affair at the time your ex, rather, Beau Kinkaid, was killed. I wondered how it started."

It didn't appear to be the question she was expecting. Or maybe she was expecting denials or accusations first.

Annabel's eyes grew wide and she briefly tilted her head in Sumner's direction, as though he had an answer for her. For a moment, I thought he was going to be the one to do the talking.

"Beau and . . . your father . . . met each other through a mutual friend," Annabel said finally, her voice breathy and her words rushed. "Some business deal. Sorry, but I don't remember the details. There were so many with Beau, always something. Your father came down to Richmond for a meeting. On his own."

She stroked her husband's sleeve again. "Leland, Beau, and I went out to dinner. Beau's club. A private place with a top-floor restaurant that had a splendid view of the James River."

"That's how you met?"

Annabel shrugged. "Things happen. It was obvious he was attracted to me and I won't deny I was attracted to him. I'll spare you the details, but the next time he came to Richmond, Beau was out of town."

"How long did your relationship go on?"

The litany of questions seemed to pain her. I wouldn't be able to ask many more.

"Six, maybe seven months. Then Beau found out. There was a horrible scene. He threatened to kill your father. Left our house in an awful state and took a gun so I knew that's exactly what he intended to do. I managed to call Leland and warn him." She looked down and stared at her perfect manicure, but her hands were trembling. "For all these years it's haunted me that I might have signed Beau's death warrant, telling your father Beau was on his way."

"Darling, we've been over this. You mustn't blame yourself."

Sumner put his hands on his wife's shoulders and massaged them gently. "You've been through too much."

"Or perhaps you saved Leland's life," I said.

My comment seemed to surprise her. "Perhaps."

"Did you know my mother was pregnant with me that summer?" I asked. "My cousin remembered Beau visiting my father the day she went into labor with me."

Sumner's eyes darkened, but Annabel nodded and said in that breathy voice, "Yes. I did know."

"Why didn't you report him missing?" I asked. "Didn't you speak to my father when Beau didn't return home? I don't understand how you could not have known what happened. Or not cared to find out."

She sat up straight like I'd yanked a puppeteer's string. "You have no right to judge me."

"I'm not judging you. But I don't understand how you know for sure that Leland killed Beau unless my father told you so himself."

"I believe Detective Noland has been over all that with you." Sumner's voice held a warning that I'd crossed a line and his tolerance was wearing thin. "There's nothing further to discuss here."

I asked, anyway.

"Please, Mrs. Chastain. What happened between you and Leland after Beau died?"

Sumner looked like he was ready to come around from behind the chair. I ignored him and focused on Annabel.

"Please," I said to her again. To him I added, "My last question. I promise."

"I didn't want to know what happened." Her voice was still tight with anger. "I was glad Beau didn't come back. You can't possibly understand how it was."

"Show her, Annie," Sumner said. "Then she'll understand."

Annabel slowly raised her hands and tried to unhook her pearls.

"Help me," she said to Sumner.

When he removed them, I saw the large red welt—an enormous slash that girdled her neck—that had been hidden by her jewelry.

"Beau did that," she said. "I nearly died."

"I'm so sorry."

"Let me tell you something." She gripped the arms of the chair and this time I could see the bones of her fingers sharply defined against her thin, taut skin. "I never asked Leland if he did it, but we both knew he did. Afterward your father wouldn't let go of me, and that terrified me. If he could kill Beau, what could he do to me? Especially because I could link him to Beau's murder. Your father called constantly, hounding me until I would no longer answer the phone. One time he drove to Richmond. I left my house by the back door and ran away to spend the night at a friend's place. Then there were the letters. So many letters."

"Some of which you kept as blackmail."

She drew back. "I prefer to think of it as insurance. They were the only proof I had that Leland killed Beau."

"All it proves is that you were having an affair."

"Motive," she said. "It gave him a motive. Leland knew Beau abused me and he probably saved my life by killing him. But I couldn't bring myself to continue the affair, once I knew what he'd done."

"You wrote him letters."

"Asking him to leave me alone." Her eyes swept over me. "You seem like a nice young woman, Ms. Montgomery. Believe it or not, I admire your spunk and your courage in coming here today. It may surprise you, but I hoped your father would return to your mother and his new daughter. You have a brother, too, I believe?"

"And a younger sister," I said. "You said my father was crazy about you. Did you take advantage of that and set him up to kill Beau?"

"This is *over*," Sumner said. "I will not allow my wife to be subjected—"

"No," Annabel's voice cut through his. "No, I did not. At least, I never asked him outright. I told you he was madly in love with me. He would have done anything for me. Anything to have me. Anything to save me. Your father knew if I stayed with Beau, I would end up dead. The beatings were growing more savage."

"How did it end with Leland?"

"Badly. I left him. Finally ran away and hoped I'd never see him again. I moved to Charlottesville and tried to start my life over. Later I married my Sumner. He's given me a wonderful life." She patted Sumner's hand and he smiled. "That part of my old life is over now. Except for one last thing. Something I'd like you to do for me."

I hadn't expected the request. "What is it?"

"I would like to see the place where your father buried Beau."

"Annabel!" Sumner chided her, stroking her shoulders. "My darling, you don't want to do that. Let me send one of the company photographers—"

"I'd be glad to take you there," I said. "But it has to be today. We have a Civil War reenactment on the farm this weekend. There'll be hundreds, perhaps as many as a thousand, people attending."

"What time today?" she asked.

I looked at my watch. "Noon. Meet me in the winery

parking lot. And I suggest changing your clothes, or at least your shoes. We have to walk and it's muddy out there."

After I left, I heard their voices rise and fall behind the closed door. Sumner didn't want her to see the grave site. She wasn't giving in.

I drove back to the vineyard and wondered why Annabel wanted to do it. What if she were lying about not seeing Leland again after Beau was murdered? Suppose she killed Beau and then got Leland to help her bury the body? She seemed like the sort of woman to go over the edge if someone pushed her too far and maybe that's what Beau had done. If Leland were besotted, it wasn't hard to imagine him agreeing to help her out. That made him an accessory to Beau's murder, but not a murderer. Nevertheless, it had made it easy for Annabel to shift the guilt solely to my father, absolving herself. He'd been involved—just not the way she said.

After the brutal beatings Beau had inflicted on Annabel, I couldn't say I blamed her for killing him. Maybe in her shoes, I'd do the same thing—or would I?

But why revisit Beau's grave? Unless she hadn't come along when he was originally buried there, so she'd never seen the site and now merely wanted to satisfy a morbid curiosity. Gloat to herself and to Beau's memory that she'd managed to get away with murder.

Maybe at noon she'd tip her hand and I'd find out. Maybe this was the instance of Locard's principle Officer Mathis had tried to explain to me—that a killer either takes something away or leaves something at the scene of the crime.

Annabel Chastain was finally leaving something behind by visiting Beau's grave nearly thirty years later.

Her guilt.

Chapter 19

When I took over running the vineyard, I stopped believing there are six degrees of separation between people before they find a connection with one another. Maybe it's the Internet and social networking. Maybe it's because everyone travels so much that sooner or later someone bumps into someone whose brother dated a college roommate's sister and that conversation happens to take place at an outdoor café in, say, Salzburg, Austria. I figure we're now down to about four degrees of separation among all of us. In Atoka, however, it shrinks to two.

For that reason I'm not often surprised when two individuals with no apparent connection discover a quirky or circuitous link that moves them inside the same circle. Today was an exception.

Sumner and Annabel Chastain's burgundy Mercedes with its vanity license plates pulled into the parking lot at twelve sharp. Through the villa window I caught sight of Sumner helping Annabel out of the car and hollered to Gina, who was fixing lunch in the kitchen, that I'd be back in half an hour. The Chastains were dressed casually in brightly colored polo shirts and khakis. Both of them wore boots.

Ray Vitale's Honda Accord drove up as I came down the walk to greet the Chastains. Vitale parked next to the Mercedes and Sumner swiveled his head to look. When he turned back to Annabel, I recognized the don't-ding-my-car expression my brother often wore anytime someone with an unworthy clunker parked too close to the Jaguar.

"Hey, you!" Vitale said. "Are you Chastain?"

He was dressed in a full Union officer's uniform: navy wool jacket with gold braid, Dresden blue trousers, blue kepi, and a fringed scarlet sash around his waist.

Sumner turned around again, this time to see who was talking. He looked startled by the uniform.

"I am," he said. "Who are you?"

"Raymond Vitale."

Sumner's expression was suitably bored. "I meet a lot of people."

"And you don't give a damn about most of them or what you build. That's because you employ the shoddiest construction crews and you bribe inspectors to sign off on crap that isn't up to code." Vitale's querulous voice cracked with pent-up anger. "A few years later the problems start. Take my buildings, for instance. Cracks in the foundation. Faulty wiring. Heating systems that don't work. In a nursing home. *Old* people live there with wheelchairs and walkers. Want me to go on?" As Vitale talked, he moved closer to Sumner, who looked askance but showed no sign of being intimidated.

After yesterday's episode with Chance and Quinn, the last thing I wanted was another fistfight. Of the two men, Sumner had the physical advantage. But he didn't have Ray Vitale's scrappiness or his bottled-up fury. Sumner stepped forward until he and Vitale were well inside each other's comfort zones.

"I don't know who you are, but you're out of line." He spoke slowly and deliberately, as if Vitale were mentally challenged. Sumner poked a finger at his chest. "I run one of the best construction companies in the world, sir. We win awards every year for our projects. You make any further unsubstantiated accusations in public and you'll hear from my lawyers."

Vitale laughed. "Your lawyers can't protect you from everything, Chastain. You can't buy everyone off. If you don't believe me, wait and see."

Sumner balled his hands into fists, but before I could move, Annabel caught her husband's arm.

"Don't," she said. "He's just goading you. Probably some construction worker with an axe to grind who's come here for that reenactment."

Vitale looked her up and down, a curious light in his eyes. "The missus, right? I've been reading about you. Your ex-husband's body was found here on this farm. Something shady about that, too. Figures why you'd be hooked up with this fellow."

"Why you son of a—" Sumner began.

"Stop it!" I stepped between the two men as Annabel yanked harder on Sumner's arm. "That's enough."

I always wondered what kind of guts and nerve it took for referees at sporting events to put themselves between two gladiator-sized men who had arms like tree trunks, legs thick as wine barrels, and testosterone-fueled egos. Ray Vitale and Sumner Chastain weren't that big, but they were bigger and stronger than I was. Both of them stared down at me with incredulous expressions, but at least they stopped threatening each other.

"I don't care what beef you have with Mr. Chastain," I said to Vitale. "Take it somewhere else."

"If you lived in one of his buildings, you'd be thanking me," Vitale said. "Chastain Construction was supposed to build five assisted-living homes for my company. They hadn't even finished the second one before the problems started. Once this goes to court, people are going to find out about the corners he cuts and the bribes he pays to get his jobs signed off by the building inspectors."

"I don't know what you're talking about," Sumner said.

"Sumner," Annabel said. "Let it go. He's not worth it."

I was grateful for the distraction of more tires on gravel, particularly when I saw B.J.'s sleek black Lincoln pull in and park next to Vitale's Honda. B.J. climbed out and straightened up, stiff limbed but elegant in a Confederate officer's uniform. I'd heard at reenactments he donned a plumed hat like Colonel Jeb Stuart. Today, though, he was hatless.

"Howdy, folks. What's going on here?" His eyes darted from Vitale to the Chastains to me. He zeroed in on me. "Everything all right, Lucie?"

"Just fine. Let me introduce you to Annabel and Sumner Chastain." I nodded at the Chastains. "B. J. Hunt. He's in charge of the reenactment this weekend. B.J., I'm about to take Mr. and Mrs. Chastain over to visit the grave site. Would you and Mr. Vitale mind waiting at the villa so they can have some privacy? I wasn't expecting you this early, but we'll be back in a few minutes and the site is all yours."

By now B.J. had figured out our little group wasn't Mister Rogers' Neighborhood, but he smiled like we were all friends and nodded at me.

"Of course. You folks take your time. Ray and I've got some paperwork to go over, anyway. Don't we, Ray?"

When Vitale didn't answer, B.J. jostled his elbow. "We'll just get a move on."

They left and I shepherded the Chastains over to the red Mule, which was parked in the lot behind my car. Sumner helped Annabel into the front passenger seat and climbed in back.

"So this Vitale fellow." Sumner's breath was warm near my neck and his voice held quiet anger. "What does he have to do with your reenactment?"

"He's the commander of the Union troops," I said. "I apologize for what happened. I didn't realize he would be here when you arrived."

"It wasn't your fault, but I appreciate that. If he knows what's good for him, he'll steer clear of me. I can make his life miserable."

I had no doubt.

I felt Sumner's weight shift and saw in the rearview mirror that he was now sitting against his seat with his arms spread in a grand manner across the back. The Chastains were silent as I headed out of the parking lot and turned onto the south service road, passing one of our apple orchards. The dull, sallow day seemed to mute all colors and sounds, matching the increasingly gloomy mood of my passengers.

I wondered if Annabel regretted suggesting this expedition. She was fidgeting with the handles of her pretty fabric handbag, twisting them in a knot around her fingers. Sumner, from what I could see in the mirror, looked restless and impatient, and it seemed to feed on Annabel's jangled nerves.

Now that the grave site had been scavenged by Bobby, his deputies, and Savannah Hayden, the place was nothing more than disturbed earth. The tornado's destructive path, however, was still as vivid as a new scar. I parked and everyone got out.

"Where is it?" Annabel asked.

For a second, I hesitated. After all the digging and excavating, the place looked different from the day I'd found the grave. I couldn't let them know I wasn't quite sure.

"It's right over there." Our feet sank in as we squished through the mud.

"It's so isolated." Annabel sounded disappointed. She fumbled in her purse and pulled out a pack of cigarettes. "No wonder he wasn't found for so long."

She shook out a cigarette and put it between her lips, turning to Sumner for a light.

"I thought you wanted to quit, darling," he said.

"Not today." Her voice wasn't strong.

He lit her cigarette and she smoked with stiff, jerky motions, inhaling deeply and closing her eyes as though she were breathing in something heady and intoxicating like incense.

"The only people who come here are hunters," I said. "The Goose Creek Hunt rides through here, and during deer season, I let a few men who used to hunt with my father use my land."

"So how did you find—I mean, what was it that—" Annabel stumbled over the question.

"The, uh, his skull," I said. Had anyone informed her the bones were scattered? That the mandible had been missing?

I didn't want to tell her if she didn't know, nor that what was left of his mouth had reminded me of a scream.

"They said he'd been shot through the temple," she said in a faraway voice. "He probably died right away."

"Come on, Annie." Sumner slipped an arm around her waist. "This isn't doing you any good. You've seen the place now. Let's go back to the cottage so you can rest."

I cleared my throat. "If you'd like to put a marker out here, a cross, maybe? Or something else—"

"No," Sumner said at once. "We wouldn't."

"Thank you, but it won't be necessary," Annabel said. "He didn't die here and he's no longer buried here."

"Do you know where he died?" I asked.

She dropped her cigarette and ground it out under the toe of her boot until it disappeared into the mud. Then she looked up and said in a calm voice, "I do not."

No one spoke until I pulled into the parking lot.

"Thank you very much, Ms. Montgomery. We appreciate what you did." Sumner's smile was tight.

"Lucie." It was the first time Annabel had called me by my first name. "This has been painful for me and I know it has also been difficult for you."

She paused as though she expected me to agree, but I folded my arms and waited for her to continue. They say when you're in a hole, it's time to stop digging. Annabel, it seemed, didn't plan to stop.

"I want you to know this chapter is finally closed for me and I bear Leland no ill will." Her voice had taken on a slight patronizing tone. "You seem like a good person, a decent person, and I'm glad, in the end, your father found his way back to his family where he belonged."

I stared at her. She was *forgiving* Leland? Her whole story hinged on my father's lust for her—a passion so strong it motivated him to commit murder so he could have Annabel to himself. And that's what I couldn't buy. Leland was a love 'em and leave 'em kind of guy. The only constant in his life was my mother. He always came back and she always forgave him.

That was the flaw in Annabel's carefully stitched together story—at least as I saw it—that my father carried a torch for her and never got over her. It was a lie but I couldn't prove it. And I sure as hell didn't need her forgiveness for something my father didn't do.

"I appreciate your compassion," I said, "but there were plenty of women in my father's life. He loved my mother in his way. He just couldn't help getting involved in other relationships."

Annabel drew her head back and I knew then I'd hit a nerve. She hadn't known what a serial womanizer Leland had been and that she had been one of many passing flings rather than the great, unrequited love of his life. No woman, especially a vain one, wanted to discover how easily she had been replaced—and forgotten.

"It's time to go, Annabel." Sumner put his arm around his wife. "We're done here."

He emphasized *done*.

The Mercedes drove off as I walked up the stairs to the villa. A light rain began to fall, as fine as mist. Maybe I had punctured a tiny hole in Annabel's account of what happened between her and Leland and Beau, but it was too little, too late.

I may have won that skirmish, but she had won the war.

B.J. and Ray Vitale stood in front of a hand-drawn map of their battle plans, which they'd unrolled on the oak trestle table at the far end of the tasting room.

"We're finished," I said. "The site's all yours."

"Why'd you take that blowhard and his wife out to see that grave?" Vitale asked. "I wouldn't have given him the time of day."

"Let's go, Ray," B.J. said, rolling up the map.

"Do you think Chastain actually spends time checking out any of the projects he builds?" Vitale persisted.

"You should have read the letters I got from his lawyers—*lawyers*—when I wrote about the foundation cracks in my buildings and the leaks and the shoddy construction practices I found out about later." His voice rose with memory and anger. "Sumner Chastain is a contemptuous, greedy bastard who believes his wealth and power set him above the law."

"Ray, I'm sure Lucie needs to get back to work," B.J. said. "Thanks for letting us spread out here, Lucie."

"No problem. It's starting to rain again," I said. "Call me if you need anything."

B.J. smiled. "They didn't have cell phones in those days, my dear. I'm sure we'll manage. Feel free to stop by anytime."

"Don't worry," I said. "I wouldn't miss this for anything."

Vitale's gaze was hypnotic. "I can't believe you of all people don't agree with me, Ms. Montgomery. Look what he and his wife did to your father. I heard about his publicity goons taking over and controlling what information was parceled out to the press."

"We're out of here," B.J. said, tugging Vitale's arm.

After they left I poured a glass of wine with hands that shook.

Maybe Sumner Chastain was a bully. But Ray Vitale, who seemed obsessed by his hatred for Sumner, was a loose cannon.

Chapter 20

————❦————

Quinn was sitting at the winemaker's table nursing a beer with his feet propped up when I stopped by the barrel room later in the day. I sat down next to him. His eye was less swollen than yesterday, but it still looked spectacular in shades of red and purple. Some of the puffiness in his face had gone down.

"The Riesling's finally chilling in the tanks," he said. "I'll add the yeast tomorrow and get fermentation going."

He delivered the news in a dull, flat voice and took a swig from his bottle. Last night's tension still hung between us like a fog.

"When you're finished adding the yeast, can you help out at the villa?" I matched his tone. "I'll probably be spending most of my time at the reenactment site. Gina will need help in our booth. One person can't handle selling wine tasting tickets to that crowd."

"That depends on what happens with fermentation. That's first priority," he said. "I don't understand why we can't sell wine right there at the site like we do at other festivals."

"Because B.J. and Ray Vitale don't want alcohol around

people who have guns, even if they're shooting blanks," I said. "I had to agree with them."

He tipped his head back and drank more beer. "Your call."

If he wasn't going to bring up last night and what happened with Chance, neither was I.

I traced a pattern on the tabletop with a finger. "What are you doing tonight?"

"Babysitting the Riesling." He set his bottle down. "What'd you expect?"

"Just wondered. Need any help?"

"I got it covered." He swung his feet around and stood up. "Is there anything else?"

"Nothing at all."

"See you in the morning." He walked toward the stainless-steel tanks, which were making quiet gurgling sounds as the glycol coolant circulated between a glass wall and the steel jacket.

I would have preferred an argument to this deep freeze. We'd gotten mad at each other plenty of times, but this was different and I didn't like it.

I finished his beer, which he'd left on the table, and got up to leave. I had no idea if he heard me pull the door shut hard enough that it slammed, or if he even cared.

Either way, it symbolized the current state of our relationship.

I fell asleep in the hammock to the soft sound of a steady rain that invaded my mind like white noise, blocking out all thoughts. Saturday was supposed to be another dishrag day of wet weather, but the daylight that woke me early the next morning held out the surprising promise of clear skies and cool temperatures without the humidity we're so famous for in summer.

I checked my phone. Just past six thirty. I sat up and rubbed at the pattern the rough woven fabric had imprinted on my arm. In the kitchen, I made coffee and toasted pieces of baguette. Eli must have done some grocery shopping because I found a plate of cheese in the refrigerator. He'd bought the usual Brie and Camembert, but also splurged on Pont l'Évêque, Brillat-Savarin, and my favorite, Humboldt Fog. I cut some of each for my bread and left the plate on the counter so the cheese would be room temperature when he finally showed up for breakfast.

After the credit card incident the other day, Eli and I had avoided the subject of whether I needed him to help out today. I hadn't asked and he hadn't offered. He'd also told me he finally decided not to take Zeke Lee up on his offer to be a walk-on reenactor for the weekend, though he still planned to show up as a spectator.

After breakfast I showered, dressed, and drove over to the camp. We had Bush-Hogged the field B.J. wanted to use as a parking lot, but he'd been adamant that the battlefield remain unmowed. As he'd pointed out, nobody cut the grass before the two armies showed up at Ball's Bluff.

I parked on the freshly mowed field at the end closest to the campground. At least fifty vehicles belonging to reenactors who'd arrived last night were parked in ragged rows. In another hour the rest of the participants were due to arrive, so that by ten o'clock all tents would be pitched and the camp in working order when it opened to the public.

I walked past cars and pickups, reading vanity license plates that indicated regiment allegiances or some tie to reenacting. Confederate flags hung across rear windows of pickup trucks along with bumper stickers for the NRA or the Stars and Bars with the slogan "If this flag offends, then study American history."

A breeze carried the scent of wood smoke and a mockingbird sang nearby. I followed a path of newly matted-down grass along the creek bank. Cattails grew by the water, and elsewhere I noticed clumps of daisy fleabane, lacy white yarrow, and pokeweed, bent heavy under the weight of its eggplant-colored berries.

I didn't see the massed clusters of low-slung white tents until I crossed the bridge and turned left at a sign with an arrow and "CS Camp" painted in black. The sign for the Union troops—"US of A Camp"—was farther down the path, indicating a campsite in the woods. The Confederates obviously got the preferred real estate since they were in the open field.

Though it was early, the entire Confederate camp seemed to be awake, caught up in the morning routine of dressing, washing up, and cooking breakfast over campfires that blazed next to open-air dining tents. Everywhere I looked men in patched or tattered jackets and trousers, kepis, and rough-looking shoes seemed purposeful and energized in spite of a night camped out in a downpour. The variety of uniforms was striking, but the impoverished South had been too poor to provide clothing and equipment as the war dragged on, so its troops wore homemade versions of the official uniform in a drab rainbow of colors that ran from gray to butternut brown.

There were fewer women and children than men, but they, too, were dressed in period clothing. The boys wore coarse cotton pants and flannel shirts; the women and girls were graceful and feminine in long hoop-skirted dresses or high-necked white blouses and calico skirts with aprons, hair tucked under bonnets or straw hats with flowing ribbons.

A man in a red flannel shirt, gray trousers, and khaki suspenders directed me to B.J.'s regiment, the 8th Virginia, which had set up their campsite at the far end of the field. I spotted Virginia's deep blue flag, with its warrior woman subjugating a fallen man symbolizing tyranny, next to a faded Confederate flag.

Half a dozen soldiers sat around a pine table under a dining fly talking quietly and drinking coffee.

I greeted them and asked for B.J.

"Behind the tents," someone said. "With his missus."

I found B.J. and his wife, Emma, sitting in a pair of low Adirondack chairs. He was in the middle of reading aloud to Emma from a dog-eared pamphlet as she knit something lacy in pale blue and cream.

Emma saw me first and smiled, setting her knitting in her lap. She wore a brown-and-white sprigged cotton dress and a crocheted hairnet over her white-gold hair.

"Why, Lucie," she said, straightening a lace shawl around her shoulders, "how nice to see you, dear. Come join us. Barnaby, pull up a chair for the child."

I'd forgotten that B.J.'s first name was Barnaby. He caught my eye and grinned. "Glad you could make it."

"How was camping last night?" I sat down in another Adirondack chair.

Emma shook her head. "We're getting too old for this. We brought cots and a porta potty for our tent. No more sleeping on the ground. Or latrines."

"Emma! You're supposed to let her think we're roughing it." B.J. winked at me.

"Why don't you get Lucie a glass of lemonade or a cup of coffee, dear?"

B.J. seemed not to mind being ordered around by his wife. "What'll it be?" he asked. "Lemonade's fresh made from real lemons."

I took the lemonade.

"Are you going to be ready when the gates open?" I asked.

"Don't you worry," he said. "We got all kinds of things planned, besides the usual drilling and some practice on the firing range. I'll be giving a talk at noon on the battle."

"The Black Widow is here," Emma said. "She's always a treat."

"The who?"

B.J. chuckled. "A woman who dresses completely in black. Didn't you see her when you walked through camp? She's got a knock-your-socks-off exhibit on death and mourning during the Civil War. What she doesn't know about burials and grieving a hundred and fifty years ago isn't worth knowing."

"Occupational curiosity for a funeral director?" I drank some lemonade.

He grinned. "You ought to pay her a visit, missy. You might learn a thing or two."

"You should hear her talk about the body watchers," Emma said. "It's like listening to a ghost story."

"The who?"

"People who sat vigil to make sure the dead person had truly passed." B.J. shook his head. "Course it doesn't happen anymore, but those were the days before embalming when they'd put the body on ice. Every so often one of 'em would sit up and scare the bejesus out of folks."

He put his thumb and forefinger together so there was no light between them. "Sometimes they'd come that close to burying someone alive."

"Barnaby," Emma said. "Lucie's gone all pale. Get her some more lemonade, will you?"

B.J. jumped up and took my tin cup. "Didn't mean to upset you, honey."

"It's all right."

"I never should have brought that up with what you've

just been through. I'm sorry, dear. It was thoughtless." Emma picked up her knitting. "How are you coping, by the way? I saw the articles in the paper. One of the tellers at the bank told me the sheriff's department has decided to close the case. I guess that must be a relief."

"Not the way it turned out," I said. "Especially if everyone in town's talking about it."

"Folks are always going to talk, Lucie," Emma said. "But they soon forget and life goes on."

The sound of a fife floated through the air, followed by the martial beat of a drum. Emma cocked her head to listen as B.J. pulled a cigar out of his pocket and lit up.

"I always like the music on these weekends," he said. "Kind of haunts me."

We listened to "When Johnny Comes Marching Home."

When it had finished I said, "I guess I should be going."

The music changed to a sweet, mournful tune I didn't recognize.

"I'll walk with you." B.J. stood up. "I need to check on Tyler. Make sure he's okay."

"What's he doing?" I asked.

"Making his ammunition for tomorrow."

"You make your own ammunition?"

"It's not hard. Can of gunpowder and a brass loader. It's basic math. We're only making blanks, of course. No live ammo."

"How can you be sure it's not live?" I asked.

"We do safety checks. Don't worry. There are hardly ever accidents at these events."

"B.J. says you might be coming by for the dance tonight with that winemaker of yours," Emma said. "I know you can't participate since you won't be in period clothes, but I think you might enjoy the music."

I turned red. That winemaker of mine and I were barely speaking.

"I'll try to come, but I don't know about Quinn. He's, uh, rather busy in the barrel room at the moment."

The music shifted to "The Girl I Left Behind Me." Great timing.

"Nonsense," B.J. said. "Bring him. It'll do him good."

"I hope we'll see you," Emma said. "Don't stay away."

Her eyes were bright, but there was something different in the way she looked at me. Was it curiosity? Or pity? Maybe it was both.

B.J. and Emma knew my parents. I knew what had changed.

Everyone in town thought my father was a murderer.

Quinn called after lunch when I was back at the villa checking on how Frankie and the waitresses from the Goose Creek Inn were coping with the crowds.

"Don't expect to see me there today," he said. "I'm not leaving the barrel room."

Yesterday's chilliness hadn't thawed, but he also sounded ominous.

"What's wrong?"

"I don't know. I've been adding the yeast to the Riesling and racking it into new tanks, but I can't get fermentation to start."

That was bad. Without fermentation, we had tanks of grape juice. No wine. Nothing.

"How many strains of yeast have you added so far?" I asked.

We had agreed to experiment with three different types of yeast now that it was clear there would be no ice wine. Each one would bring out different esters—the flavors people perceived in the wine—and a different bouquet. Blending them after they fermented would result in a more complex, interesting wine. Or so we hoped. If fermentation didn't start, something was wrong.

"Two."

I could tell he was worried.

"Temperature okay?"

The juice, or must, had just spent a couple of days chilling in the refrigerator truck. Maybe it was still too cold. Until the wine warmed up to a certain temperature, which depended on the strain of yeast, nothing would happen.

But Quinn would know all that. It was Winemaking 101.

"I'm going to check again."

"Do you think someone could have dumped the yeast into the tank all at once?"

I racked my brain for all the reasons I could remember why fermentation might not start. Adding the yeast too abruptly was another one. It was like throwing a naked person outside in an arctic snowstorm. The result would be such a bad shock the yeast would die.

He didn't sound happy. "If Chance or Tyler had been here I would have said it was a definite possibility. But I've got Benny and Javier. They know what they're doing."

"Keep me posted," I said.

"When I get a handle on it, you'll be the second to know."

I was glad, at least, he hadn't said "If."

I returned to the battlefield just before two o'clock after Gina called with an SOS that she was swamped at our booth and needed help. A line of cars clogged Atoka Road waiting to get through the south gate, which we had turned into the temporary main entrance for the reenactment. B.J. had arranged for a Scout troop to help manage parking and the sheriff's department had a cruiser sitting at the gate. I didn't recognize the officer leaning against his car eating what looked like a pork barbecue sandwich, but he waved me past the backup once I explained who I was.

Since my last visit, the place had taken on a carnival-like atmosphere. The VFW had set up a canteen-style trailer between the parking lot and the camps, where they sold hot food next to a homemade lemonade and limeade stand run by the Friends of the Loudoun Museum. The business association gave out bottles of water.

It was a sedate, well-mannered crowd that seemed to consist mostly of families with children. Some were dressed in period clothing, but they moved easily and unself-consciously around the booths as though there were nothing special about their attire. Many congregated at the sutlers' tents—merchants who traveled from one reenactment to another selling Civil War goods.

I walked down the alley of large circus-sized tents, peering into open tent flaps at displays of uniforms, tents, cooking utensils, candles, quills, and other old-fashioned items heaped on wooden tables. A lace parasol draped over a tent stay fluttered in the breeze next to a hand-painted sign that read "Virginia Sutlery: Fine Purveyor of All Things Period." Inside, a table lined with oversized mason jars of bright-colored penny candy caught my eye. Gina had a sweet tooth and she'd been working nonstop. I filled a bag with lemon drops, rock candy, and jelly beans, and was getting out money to pay for it when I heard a familiar female voice. Annabel Chastain.

"Oh, look. They've got licorice sticks," she said, as I turned and saw her standing in the doorway with Sumner.

"That's nice." He sounded bored.

What brought them here? I'd thought Sumner had said they were leaving Atoka. Annabel caught sight of me and said something in her husband's ear.

"Look, dear, here's Lucie." Her smile seemed strained.

"I didn't realize you were coming to the reenactment," I said.

"I'll be outside, Annie," Sumner said, without greeting me. "Come find me when you're done shopping."

"We were visiting your next-door neighbor," Annabel said. "We saw all the cars as we were driving back to the Fox & Hound. I thought it might be fun to stop by. I didn't realize it was going to be such a big event."

Neither of my immediate neighbors was at home. The Orlandos were in Hong Kong on business. Mick Dunne, my ex-lover, was home in England visiting his ailing mother.

"Visiting my neighbor?" I said.

"Mick Dunne. Sumner is looking at one of his jumpers," she said. "We're considering purchasing it."

I'd forgotten that Tyler had mentioned something about the Chastains looking at a horse.

"Mick's in London," I said.

"No, he and Selena returned from Cannes about a week ago."

"Really?" Selena? His sister? Did he have a sister?

"Such a beautiful young woman. They make quite a good-looking couple. Seem so happy together." Annabel's eyes narrowed and she gave me a shrewd look. "Oh, dear. Have I said something inappropriate? I didn't realize you and Mick had a history—"

How had she guessed about us?

"We have a business relationship." I cut her off. "He's starting a vineyard and we've been helping him out. I'd better pay for this. Excuse me."

I turned to the cashier. "How much do I—?"

Behind me Annabel gasped as though she'd been stabbed by a sharp pain and cried out.

"You all right, ma'am?" the cashier asked.

"Mrs. Chastain," I said. "Annabel. What is it? A heart attack? I'll get your husband."

"No, no—" She clutched her chest with both hands and her eyes were wide with shock. "Don't."

"She ought to sit down," the cashier said.

"Can you get her to that chair over there while I find her husband?" I asked. "He's probably right outside."

But as I looked through the tent flap at the passersby, the only person I recognized was Eli, who was talking to someone dressed in a Confederate officer's uniform. Sumner had vanished into the crowd.

"Eli! Get in here, will you!" I called.

Behind me, Annabel moaned. "No, please. I don't need help. Thank you all the same. Not him."

"What's going on?" Eli showed up at my elbow.

"This is Annabel Chastain," I said. "She's not well."

"Let's get her to that chair over there."

The cashier transferred Annabel to his stronger arms.

"It's okay, ma'am," he said. "You're going to be fine."

Eli guided her to the wooden chair as the cashier shooed away curious spectators. Annabel still looked pale and she hadn't taken her eyes off Eli.

"You're Leland's son, aren't you?" Her voice was soft.

Eli nodded. "Is there somebody—"

"No, no. Just give me a minute."

As I watched her stare at Eli, I knew now what she'd said a moment ago when she'd cried out. My father's name. She'd seen Eli before I had. He was a double for Leland, just like I resembled my mother.

Not him. The worshipful way Annabel Chastain looked at my brother said it all. Now I knew for sure that Annabel did not spurn my father after Beau's death. It had been the other way around. Leland had rejected her and she had never gotten over it.

Which meant that at least part of her story had been a lie.

Chapter 21

———❦❦❦———

Sumner Chastain appeared at his wife's side and took charge, brushing me away like he was swatting an insect. He bent over Annabel, but not before he fixed me with a frozen look that implied I'd caused whatever was wrong with her. Eli had vanished to fetch a bottle of water, so it was just the three of us.

"You all right, darling?"

"I'm fine." Annabel's voice sounded stronger. "It was nothing. The heat got to me, probably. It's a bit close in here. If we could just leave—"

Sumner helped Annabel to her feet.

"Thanks," he said to me. "I'll take care of this."

I had to hand it to her. Perfect timing—or terrific luck—that Sumner hadn't been there when she first saw Eli. If I could read that anguished look of love and longing on her face, Sumner would have figured it out in a flash. Somehow I didn't think Annabel wanted Sumner to know she still had such strong feelings for my father.

After they left, Eli returned with the water. "Where is she?"

"Her husband whisked her away," I said.

"She didn't look too good."

"That's because she saw you. And you reminded her of Leland."

Eli had been rolling the bottle between his hands. He stopped doing that and looked pained.

"What are you trying to say?"

"She's still in love with Leland. It was written all over her face."

"He's dead and she's married."

"But it means she lied to Bobby."

"So?"

"She didn't dump Leland. He dumped her. Maybe she lied about other things, too. Maybe she killed Beau and got Leland to help her bury his body. Now after all this time, she gets her revenge. Sets up Leland as the killer and walks away from a murder."

Eli twirled his finger next to his temple. "Luce, that woman has bird bones. I could feel them when I helped her to that chair. She'd probably have a tough time squashing a cockroach."

"We're talking about almost thirty years ago. She could have shot him and then persuaded Leland to drive down to Richmond to help her dispose of the body."

"Right. So he goes to Richmond and then drives an hour and a half to Atoka with a dead body in the trunk of his car so he can bury Beau right here in his own backyard instead of dumping him in the James River or some landfill. Come on, babe."

He had a point. Still, if Annabel lied about her relationship with Leland, she could be covering up other things.

"She's a woman scorned, Eli. And now she gets the ultimate revenge. Pinning a murder she committed on her ex-lover."

"Prove it."

"Whose side are you on?"

He sighed. "You know whose side I'm on. But there's no way you're going to get her to admit what she did, if she did it, and Bobby has closed the case. Three strikes and you're out."

Eli handed me the water bottle. "Here. Drink this and cool off. Even if you're right and she is a woman scorned, that means she's mad and dangerous. You can't stop her. Believe me, I ought to know. Brandi plans to clean my clock."

I felt sorry for him, but I was determined to get Annabel to admit she'd lied. Too bad I wasn't sure how to do it. Yet.

I stayed in our booth for the rest of the day, working alongside Gina. She wasn't kidding about business booming, and it looked like we were on track to break last weekend's sales record. Frankie and I went over the receipts in my office at the end of the day. When we were done, she whooped with glee.

"This is amazing." She pounded her fist on my desk, emphasizing each word, and laughed. "You know we're going to completely sell out of our Riesling by tomorrow, don't you? It's flying out the door it's so good."

I sat back in my chair. "I hadn't realized we were that low. Hold back a few cases, will you? We've got problems with this year's wine."

"What problems?" She straightened the receipts and credit card statements into a neat pile.

"It's not fermenting."

"Why not?"

"Quinn doesn't know why not. Or didn't, last time we talked." I glanced at the wall clock. Six fifteen. "He hasn't called since noon. I think I'll head over to the barrel room."

"You two kiss and make up yet after yesterday?"

"I don't know what you're talking about."

She rolled her eyes. "For an intelligent woman, some-times you can be so dense I swear light bends around you."

"You may want to rethink that compliment seeing as I pay your salary."

"Sticks and stones." She picked up the receipts. "Go see him and straighten things out. It's no fun around here when you lovebirds have one of your tiffs."

Quinn was sitting in the same place I'd found him this morning—a chair at the winemaker's table—but now his head was resting on his forearms and he was asleep. He didn't stir when I pulled out a chair and sat next to him, moving the empty beer bottle he clutched in one hand out of his grasp.

His hair was longer than it had been in recent months—maybe a deliberate decision or maybe just too preoccupied with everything going wrong at the winery to get it cut. It curled in long tendrils down the collar of one of his oldest Hawaiian shirts, the one with the burgundy background and acid-green palm fronds. His head was turned so he faced me and, in profile, his sharp, well-chiseled angles reminded me of a relief on a coin. He hadn't shaved in a few days and even the eye without the shiner had dark hollows under it, like another bruise.

"Just how long do you plan to sit there watching me?"

I jumped. "Don't do that! You scared the wits out of me. Don't tell me you've been awake the whole time I was here?"

He opened his good eye. "Yup."

"You could have said something."

He sat up. "It was more fun to watch you."

"You had your eyes closed. Or it looked like you did."

"Not entirely."

"Frankie says it hasn't gone unnoticed that we're not on the best terms."

"Nothing gets past Frankie. A wise and astute woman."

I folded my arms. "Then let's get this settled."

"Sure. If you want to apologize, I'll accept."

"Me? Apologize for *what*?"

"Not trusting me."

"How about you brawling with Chance? You going to apologize for that?"

"He had it coming." He held up his hand. "Wait, wait . . . hold it right there. We wouldn't even be arguing right now if it weren't for him. He set this up, Lucie. He wanted you to doubt me, wonder about me, and you bought it."

"I do trust you," I said. "I think Chance may have skimmed money from our crew. That's why we always got guys with zero experience. Because we weren't paying the going rate. Javier's going to try to find some of the men who picked for us yesterday. See if they'll tell him how much they got paid."

Quinn slammed his hand on the table so hard I jumped again. "If I'd known that yesterday, he wouldn't have walked out of here. They'd be carrying him on a stretcher."

"Don't go there."

"I wish I had. He deserved it," he said. "Apology accepted."

I glared at him.

"And now on a completely different subject," he said, "fermentation has started."

"That's nice."

"Glad you're so excited. It's better than nice, but not by much. It's going slower than it ought to. I need to keep an eye on it, but at least we have ignition."

"That's nice, too."

He glanced at his watch. "You eaten dinner yet?"

"No."

"How about Chinese? We can order in."

"Here? When's the last time you left this place?"

He paused to consider.

"It's Saturday," I said. "I bet you've been here since we picked on Thursday."

"You could be right. All right, let's eat at my place."

"Why don't you go home and take a shower and clean up? I'll order the Chinese. We'll eat at my house."

"One, are you implying that I smell bad? And two, what's wrong with eating at my house?"

"Forgive me, but one, I'd like to use bug spray on you right now, and two, I don't want to eat out of the boxes with my fingers. Do you even own any dishes or silverware? More than one of anything, that is?"

"When I moved here from my cave in California, I did bring a few hollowed-out gourds and some bones and spears."

"See you at my place in, say, forty-five minutes. Any preferences or do you trust me to order?"

"Something that'll set my mouth on fire. Why don't we have dinner at the summerhouse? We could watch the Perseids."

Quinn's interest in astronomy—and the massive amount of information he knew about stars, comets, the galaxy, and everything celestial—still seemed out of character with the rest of his macho rough-and-tumble personality, at least to me. Shortly before Leland died, he'd given Quinn permission to use our summerhouse behind a large rose garden in my backyard as a place to set up his telescope and carry out his stargazing. Perched on a bluff overlooking a valley, the summerhouse had a breathtaking view of the Virginia Piedmont and the Blue Ridge. A few months ago Quinn bought what he told me was the Rolls-Royce of telescopes—a Starmaster. On a clear night when I looked through the lens I felt as though I had a front-row seat on the edge of the galaxy.

I'd learned a few things from him, including what the Perseids were—the galactic residue of a comet that produced a spectacular meteor shower visible every August, primarily in our hemisphere.

"Since you've been holed up here for the past two days," I said, "you probably forgot that Edouard is still hanging around. Today was nice, but a few hours ago the clouds rolled back in. We won't be able to see a thing."

He ran his hands through his unruly hair and rubbed his face like he was trying to wake up.

"Too bad. All right, I'll clean up since you're paying for dinner. It won't take me forty-five minutes. More like half an hour."

"How come I'm paying when you invited me?"

"It's cheaper than paying me for working two days straight. The way I figure it, you get off easy with an order of kung pao chicken and moo shu pork."

He showed up half an hour later in a clean pair of jeans and yet another of his endless collection of Hawaiian shirts, this one red, cream, and yellow with exotic-looking anthurium and birds-of-paradise on it. His hair was still wet but neatly combed. I'd changed, too, into a long cotton dress.

"I like that dress," he said. "Suits you."

He'd brought wine and flowers. A bottle of Gevrey-Chambertin and flowers from a garden—not a florist—wrapped in pages of the *Washington Tribune*.

The garden around his cottage was mostly low-maintenance shrubs. Nothing blooming that I could remember unless he'd done some recent planting. I unwrapped the newspaper and found sprays of lilies, gladiolus, tea roses, and bougainvillea.

"Thank you; they're beautiful," I said.

He heard the unspoken question and looked sheepish.

"I'm better at growing grapes than I am at flowers. Now that no one's living over at Hector and Sera's cottage, the garden has gone wild. I go by every so often to do some weeding. It's a shame to see the place closed up like that. They're Sera's flowers. You probably guessed."

Hector came to work at the vineyard when my parents planted our first grapes, serving as our farm manager until his death a year ago. He and Sera had lived in a cottage at one end of a small cul-de-sac near the winery. Quinn lived at the other end.

Chance had taken Hector's job, but not his place. No one could take care of the vineyard as he'd done, and both Quinn and I hadn't gotten over losing him.

Quinn followed me into the kitchen and uncorked the wine while I found one of my mother's Sèvres vases and began arranging the flowers.

"I miss Sera," I said. "And Hector and Bonita."

He laid the cork on the counter. "I never should have gotten involved with Bonita. It went downhill when she moved in with me."

I arranged a pink gladiolus stem between some peach-colored lilies. "I never should have gotten involved with Mick Dunne. But we did what we did."

"It's really over with Mick?"

"Yup. Annabel Chastain said he came back from Europe with a new girlfriend."

"You mind?"

"Nope."

I nearly asked him about Savannah, but before I could bring it up, he said, "Ever thought about letting Eli live in Hector and Sera's cottage until he gets back on his feet? Shame to have the place empty."

I tucked a spray of pink bougainvillea in the vase. "I don't mind having Eli live here. This house is certainly big enough and it's nice not to be by myself all the time. Besides, now that we have to hire a new farm manager, I figured we'd offer the house to whoever takes the job. Like Hector did."

"It was kind of weird that Chance didn't jump at the offer of a free place to live," Quinn said.

"He said he'd already signed a one-year lease and couldn't get out of it, remember?"

The doorbell rang and Quinn looked hopeful.

"Is that the delivery guy? I'll get it. I could eat a horse."

"My wallet's in my purse in the foyer."

"My treat," he said, and winked at me.

We ate on the veranda. The sky was still heavily clouded and the air had the closed-in feel of being inside a bell jar. Quinn lit all the candles and the torches while I prepared the table.

He poured the wine and sat across from me at the glass-topped dining table. We touched glasses and our eyes met.

"Cheers," he said.

"Cheers."

"How did the reenactment stuff go today?"

"It went all right. We're invited to stop by tonight."

He paused in the middle of scooping a helping of kung pao chicken out of the box.

"That square dance?"

"It's not a square dance." I took the chicken and handed him the rice.

"You really want to go?" he asked. "Sorry, but I still don't get all that playacting stuff. Just seems weird to me, pretending you live in another century and refighting a war that your side lost."

"Then maybe you should come and see what it's all about."

"The extent of my dancing doesn't go beyond the hokey-pokey."

I laughed. "We'd have to be in period clothing to dance . . . whoa! Hold on. I'm not asking you to wear a Confederate uniform and bad shoes."

"You'd better not. Besides, I'd be Union. We'd be on different sides."

"You wouldn't have to do much pretending after all, would you?"

He grinned. "We won."

I took a pancake for my moo shu pork off a Styrofoam plate. "Around here, you're on the wrong side."

"Art imitating life?"

"You'll never guess who I ran into at the reenactment site," I said. "Annabel and Sumner Chastain. Dropped by on their way back from Mick's. They might buy one of his horses."

"Tyler mentioned they were still around. Guess that explains why. Want some plum sauce?"

"Sure. Annabel happened to see Eli. She almost passed out."

"That's the effect your brother has on older women?"

"Real funny. Eli looks just like Leland. Annabel was still in love with my father, Quinn. Leland broke it off with her. Not the other way around."

"Which means what?"

"Which means she lied to Bobby."

"You're still trying to pin it on her that she killed Beau, aren't you?"

He refilled our glasses.

"Lucie." His voice was gentle. "You've got nothing to go on. Her story's going to stick, you know that. Bobby closed the case."

I drank some wine.

"You sound like Eli," I said.

He shrugged.

"Did you ever read *Hamlet*?" I asked.

He squinted. "Who didn't? Required reading in high school."

"Remember when Hamlet talks about catching Claudius for murdering his father when he reenacts the play with that traveling group of actors? When he says, 'The play's the thing wherein I'll catch the conscience of the king'?"

He stared at me. "You going to stage something in that reenactment that will make Annabel reveal she killed Beau? Are you serious? Did she even say she would be there tomorrow?"

"No, but I bet she will. I think something's still eating at her and she can't let go of it."

"What do you have in mind?"

"I'm still working it out."

He looked skeptical. "You'd better watch it."

"Don't worry." I reached for the fortune cookies and held them out. "Choose."

We broke our cookies open at the same time.

" 'Your many hidden talents will become obvious to those around you.' " Quinn grinned. "These things are so true. What's yours say?"

" 'Distant water does not put out a fire.' " I crumpled it up. "How about if we head over to the camp?"

We took his car. On the drive over I thought about what I hoped to pull off with Annabel Chastain. Hamlet had indeed caught Claudius out when he staged his play within a play. But by the time the final curtain went down, nearly everyone in the Danish royal family was dead.

I wanted the truth to be revealed, not more senseless deaths. Little did I know that I would not get my wish. A fire I knew nothing about had ignited and there was no water, distant or otherwise, to put it out. In retrospect, I should have paid more attention to that fortune cookie.

Chapter 22

⠿

The rain had held off for the campground dance, although the air felt so heavy it seemed to wrap itself around Quinn and me like a cloak. We parked on the grassy field and used his flashlight to see our way to the stone bridge and, beyond it, the Confederate camp.

Even Quinn stopped to stare, as I had in the morning, once we crossed the bridge. In the peaceful darkness of a late summer evening, the camp looked serene with its sea of white tents now softly illuminated by candlelight shining from hurricane lanterns and the embers of campfires over which dinners had been cooked. We seemed to have come to a place risen up from the past.

The music of a fiddle and banjo floated through the stillness, accompanied by laughter and voices and the sound of hands clapping in time to the music. I caught the wisps of melody of "Arkansas Traveler."

The dance was held along a wide, flat stretch of road that led to the new fields of grapes and the winery beyond. During the day the road had been off-limits; now the wooden sawhorses with their "Do Not Enter" signs had been pushed out of the way. The Virginia Fiddlers stood on an improvised wooden stage, bathed in the warm glow of candlelight. In front of them, a throng of flashing skirts and uniformed men whirled past us.

B.J. spotted Quinn and me watching on the sidelines and came over to see us.

"Guess we don't blend in too well, huh?" Quinn said in my ear.

"They didn't wear Hawaiian shirts during the Civil War."

B.J. kissed me on the cheek and pulled two cigars out of his pocket, offering one to Quinn.

"You look lovely tonight, my dear," he said to me, then added to Quinn, "If you're sticking around, you'll want that stogie to keep the bugs down. They're pretty fierce tonight." He waved at the dancers. "What do you think?"

"I think it's lovely," I said as the Fiddlers swung into "Dixie."

"I love that song," B.J. said. "Makes me cry every time I hear it. Especially when the Fiddlers sing it with that sweet harmony of theirs."

Emma Hunt emerged from the crowd of dancers and joined us. Her cheeks were flushed pink and her eyes were bright. She had changed since this morning into a teal-colored satin evening dress. Lashed by firelight, it gleamed.

"There you are," she said to B.J. "I've been looking everywhere for you."

She caught his arm, smiling at Quinn and me. "Glad to see you're here with Lucie, Quinn. I was hoping she'd bring you."

"Wouldn't miss it for anything, ma'am."

I resisted the urge to elbow him as Emma gave me a small triumphant smile.

"That's good to know. Will we be seeing more of you this weekend, I hope?" she asked.

Quinn grinned and puffed on his cigar. "I'm not sure. My boss is a real slave driver. I don't get out much."

"What he means," I said, "is that in order to make the quality wine for which we're becoming known, he occasionally puts in long hours just like I do."

"Sure," he said, "that's exactly what I mean."

B.J. and Emma exchanged glances.

"Told you they make a nice couple, didn't I?" Emma said to B.J.

I felt Quinn stir next to me and I blushed.

"I think we should dance, my love." B.J. smiled at me. "You two stick around as long as you like and enjoy the music."

They waited for an opening, then B.J. whirled Emma into the dancers with the fluid ease of lifelong partners. In a moment they were swallowed up, disappearing into the happy, animated crowd.

"Want to find a place to sit and listen?" I asked. "It's nice music, isn't it?"

"Yeah," he said, "it is."

He took my hand and we moved away from the crush of dancers and the crush of spectators that stood around watching them.

"What about that tree stump over there?" Quinn asked. "Might not be too comfortable, but it's better than sitting on the ground. Especially since you've got that pretty dress on."

"Looks okay to me."

He sat down first and surprised me by pulling me onto his lap. I leaned my head on his shoulder as he wrapped his arms around my waist. By now he'd let his cigar go out, but he still smelled of smoke mingled with a masculine scent that reminded me of leather and being outdoors.

I could hear his heart beating in his chest slow and steady and strong. His breath was regular against my ear. Imperceptibly, his arms seemed to tighten around me as mine did around him. We sat there in the semidarkness with its shifting firelight shadows cast by dancers spinning by. I closed my eyes and listened to the music and laughter drift around us. We were kissing. I'm not sure when we started, but after so many miscues in the years we'd known each other, it now felt right and good. His kisses were long and slow, making my head spin. He moved his hands up to my face and moaned softly as he whispered my name.

Someone sneezed.

"What are they doing?"

"Kissing, you idiot. What does it look like?"

We broke apart and Quinn let go of me so abruptly I nearly slid off his lap. Three boys in Civil War–era attire stood in front of us staring with frank, prepubescent curiosity. The oldest couldn't have been more than seven or eight.

I stood and straightened my sundress. Our audience seemed fascinated. Good thing they couldn't see how furiously I was blushing. Good thing I didn't recognize any of them, either.

"Good evening, gentlemen," Quinn said. "Can we help you with something?"

"Nope." The smallest of them scuffed his shoe in the dirt and broke into a toothy grin. "We were just watching you. Hey, Miz Montgomery. That your boyfriend?"

I looked closer at him. Who was he?

"Uh, no. No, not my boyfriend. He's my . . . friend," I said. "Do I know you?"

"Yes, ma'am. My granddad's Seth Hannah. I'm Corey."

Last time I'd seen Corey Hannah I swear he'd been in diapers.

"Well, Corey. What a surprise. I didn't recognize you." I smiled without explaining about the diapers.

"Hey, fellas," Quinn said, "if I gave you a couple of dollars, maybe you could buy something to eat. You know, ice cream. Or candy. They must be selling something here this evening."

"You got Confederate money?" Corey asked. "That's all that works around here."

I looked at Quinn. "I told you that you were on the wrong side."

He grunted.

"I've got a better idea," I said to the boys. "How about if we give you our stump? It's a good place to sit. Actually, we were keeping it for you."

Corey nodded. "Okay."

Quinn stood up and caught my hand.

"Hey, mister?" It was one of the older boys.

"What?"

"You going to kiss her some more?"

Quinn cleared his throat. "I might. Do you think I should?"

"She's real pretty," he said. "I guess so."

"I'll think about it, then," he said.

We left them giggling and whispering.

"I know Corey's mother," I said. "She always gets coffee and a newspaper at the General Store on her way to work."

"She'll tell Thelma."

"No doubt."

"It'll be all over town we were necking like a couple of high school kids just now."

"That'd be my guess."

We reached his car and he helped me in. He got in beside me and ran a finger along my cheekbone.

"Want to give 'em something to really talk about?" he asked.

I caught my breath. "What did you have in mind?"

He started the engine. "Nothing I'd like those kids to watch us doing."

"I think I'd like that."

"Where should we go?" he asked.

His place was as spartan as a monk's cell. Mine was likely to have a chaperone if Eli was there.

"What about the summerhouse?" I knew he had slept there in the past when he stayed out late stargazing.

He seemed surprised, but he said, "Yes. The summer-house."

"Can I ask you something?" I said.

"What?"

"You and Savannah?"

I watched him in profile as he smiled, and my heart stopped beating for a few seconds. Here it was.

"She's a cute kid. You know she's engaged? He's overseas in Afghanistan with the marines."

"No." My voice was faint. "I did not."

"We could use her help, Lucie. She's smart and she's will-ing to work for us. I've been trying to teach her everything I can. It's a pleasure for once to have someone who is as quick a study as she is." He paused and glanced over at me. "You thought there was something going on between us?"

I couldn't con him. He knew me too well. "Yes."

"Nope. Nothing."

He pulled into my driveway. Eli's Jaguar was parked by the old carriage house. Quinn helped me out of the car and then pulled me to him and kissed me.

"I always wondered what your kisses would taste like," he said.

"Me, too." I gasped and grew breathless as he bit my ear

and began moving his hands over my body. "I mean, about your kisses. Oh, God, please don't stop."

We walked to the summerhouse with our arms wrapped around each other, stopping to trade long, slow kisses.

"Wait here," he said when we reached the screen door. "I think I put some candles in the drawer of that old table your mom left out here. I'll get them."

"Where's the flashlight?" I asked.

"The car. I was too busy thinking about ravishing you to remember it. Here they are." He struck a match and lit a fat pillar candle that he set on the table.

"This is nice," I said, as he lit more candles. "I'm up for a little ravishing."

"Or a lot. Come here. I want to see you by candlelight when I undress you."

I caught my breath again. "Quinn—"

He did not let me finish speaking.

After three years of working together, day in and day out, I thought I knew Quinn and there were no surprises left to uncover. I had seen the parade of his girlfriends come and go, even his ex-wife, just as he had watched my erratic relationship with Mick Dunne wax and wane. I did not expect to be swept off my feet by someone as familiar to me as breathing. This was no first love. We were not giddy young kids.

I thought I would find comfort in his arms. Tenderness, maybe. Companionship, surely. What I did not expect was that he would leave me breathless, craving him again each time we finished, and that making love with him would be unlike loving any other man I'd known. When he whispered my name, the eroticism in his voice made me shiver, and he was, by turns, rough and gentle. I closed my eyes and wrapped my legs around him, terrified and awed by what was happening between us. The feeling spread like warmth through my veins, as seductive and addictive as drugs, and I knew there would be no going back to the way it had been between us before tonight.

We dozed intermittently, between lovemaking. Once, when he was sleeping and I was still awake, I turned on my side and studied him, wondering how he could still be such an enigma. Then, I think he felt the weight of my gaze. He opened his eyes and pulled me to him, crushing his mouth down on mine. I clutched him closer as though I could somehow imprint my body on his, leave my mark so he would not forget me.

I don't remember the last time I fell asleep, but when I woke up he was gone. I felt a small stab of pain in my chest. When did he leave and why didn't he wake me to kiss me good-bye? No note, no nothing.

I found my phone in the pile of clothes near the sleeping bag we'd lain on. Twenty before seven. I sat up and clutched the blankets around me. It probably wasn't that cool, except that I was naked.

I dressed quickly. The rains would come today for sure. I smelled coffee as soon as I walked in the house. His note was there, propped up by the coffeemaker.

Didn't want to wake you. Went to the barrel room. Call me.

A man of few words. I poured a cup that looked like sludge and tasted like rocket fuel. He must have used the entire bag of coffee I just bought.

I slurped some coffee and called him. He answered on the second ring.

"Just wake up, sleepyhead?"

"Thanks for making the coffee. Why'd you leave so early?"

"You're welcome. I didn't want to make it too strong since I know you don't like it."

I smiled. "That was considerate."

"Can you get over here?" He was back to all business.

"Sure. What's wrong?"

"I don't know. The Riesling again. It's stopped fermenting. I don't want to lose it all, but it's bad."

"Give me a few minutes. I need a shower."

In the shower the steam brought Quinn's scent back to me all over again. I watched the water sluice off my breasts and shuddered, remembering what we had done.

He was standing next to one of the stainless-steel tanks when I walked into the barrel room twenty minutes later. Like me, he'd managed to shower and change into desert camouflage pants and a T-shirt with our logo on it. He turned around when he heard me, and our eyes met.

What passed between us was like a jolt of electricity, but I managed to say in a calm voice, "What's going on?"

He picked up a Dixie cup and turned the lever handle of a small faucet a few inches under the label that listed Riesling and the strain of yeast we'd used. An opaque brownish green liquid spewed out into the cup.

"Smell this."

He didn't tell me to taste it, which wasn't good. Even before I brought it to my nose, the funky odor of wine going bad hit me. Something like rotten eggs. A chemistry class nightmare.

"What happened? Can you save it?" Stunned, I sniffed the wine again. The smell was revolting.

"I guess we'll find out."

Not the answer I'd been hoping for.

"Want me to stay here and help you?"

"Thanks, but I've got to wrap my head around this. I'm better off working by myself. Besides, we've got the reenactment today. The place is going to be a madhouse. You need to be there."

"Will you at least keep in touch and let me know how it's going?"

He wrapped an arm around my waist and pulled me to him for a bruising kiss. When he was done, we were both breathing hard.

His voice was rough against my hair. "What are we going to do about this?"

I closed my eyes. "This" being "us." Did he have regrets? Morning-after jitters?

I didn't want to know. Right now he was focused on trying to figure out what had gone so wrong with one of our signature wines. It was not the time to ask if last night had been only about physical pleasure, or whether it had meant something more.

"We could just take it a day at a time," I said.

"You're okay with that?" He stroked my cheek with the back of his finger.

I nodded. "Absolutely."

It was hard not to read too much into the relief in his smile.

"Good. That's great. Thanks."

I broke the awkward silence. "Guess I'd better go set things up at the villa. Frankie and Gina and the girls ought to be arriving anytime now. You know we're going to close the winery when they actually do the reenactment of the battle," I said. "I want to be sure everyone has a chance to watch it."

"Good. Great."

He wasn't listening. "You think you might be able to break away and come see it?"

"Nah, I'd better sit tight."

"Sure. Well, see you later."

"Hey—"

"Yes?"

I turned to face him and prayed I didn't sound too hopeful or like I was wearing my heart on my sleeve. There's nothing worse for some men than a needy woman. I wasn't going to do that, be like that. I didn't want to drive him away.

"You're not still thinking of trying to trip up Annabel Chastain with something today, are you?" He crumpled the Dixie cup into a tight ball. "If she shows up."

"I'll be fine. I know what I'm doing."

He shook his head. "What'd they say in *Hamlet*? 'The lady doth protest too much, methinks.'"

I smiled. "So you did read it."

He looked aggrieved. "Yes, but only the comic book version. That's all we had in California."

"Boy, are you thin-skinned."

"As a Riesling grape." He grinned. "'To be, or not to be. That is the question. Whether 'tis nobler—'"

"Okay, okay. You've made your point. I apologize."

We were back on our old footing. He threw the Dixie cup at me and I ducked.

"'Whether 'tis nobler in the mind to suffer the slings and arrows of outrageous fortune, or take arms against a sea of troubles—'" He paused. "You got a sea of troubles, buttercup. Be careful."

It started to rain lightly as I walked over to the villa.

He was right.

I did have a sea of troubles.

Chapter 23

⎯⎯◦⎯⎯

The dark, swollen clouds that guaranteed heavy rains later in the day lowered the sky as though a dome enclosed the camp and the battlefield. The setting took on the surreal atmosphere of a movie soundstage. With the battle only hours away, anticipation of what was to come rippled through the place with a feverish energy that seemed contagious.

Frankie and the waitresses from the Goose Creek Inn joined Gina and me by the sutlers' tents just after eleven. With the camps closing to the public in an hour, we decided to walk over and watch the last-minute preparations. We split up after crossing the bridge since Cheryl and Sandy, the waitresses, had boyfriends in the Union camp.

"Poor guys. They both get bumped off as soon as the fighting starts," Frankie said. "The girls wanted to cheer them up since they're going to lose so badly. Plus they wanted to decide on a restaurant for dinner tonight."

"I wonder how they figure out who's going to die," Gina said. "It's kind of creepy."

"Actually, it's kind of random," Frankie said. "Cheryl said

they either hand out cards that tell you what to do or the men count off and everyone with a certain number is supposed to fall down like he's been killed or wounded."

"Unless you're somebody important," I said. "Then they follow what happened in the real battle. B.J. and Ray Vitale, the Union commander, have been working on their plans for weeks."

"I know it's only acting," Gina said, "but right now it feels sort of real."

"It does, doesn't it?" Frankie said. "Which is strange because you know it's not."

At the Confederate camp, a somber mood of preparation had replaced yesterday's easy camaraderie. All around us soldiers tended to guns or lined up in formation to receive final orders from their commanding officers. We heard gunfire from beyond a stand of trees on the far side of the campground. Gina jumped.

"Have they started already?" Frankie asked. "How come they're shooting?"

"Relax. Those are probably the safety checks," I said, as a drum took up a steady martial cadence. "To make sure no one's got live ammunition."

"I don't feel good," Gina said. "I think this war stuff is getting to me."

A gray-haired woman dressed like a Halloween witch came out of a large tent as Gina laid her hand on her forehead.

"Is she all right?" The woman pulled a vial out of the folds of black fabric and waved it under Gina's nose. "Smelling salts, dearie. They should help."

Gina jerked her head back as I caught a whiff of ammonia. "Who are you?"

"Phyllis Katz." The woman smiled. "But around here

everyone calls me the Black Widow. Come, there are chairs inside my tent and it's starting to rain. You need to sit down until you get some color back."

I saw the astonished look on Gina's face as the Widow had slipped her arm around her waist.

"It's all right," she said. "I don't bite."

She and Gina disappeared through the tent flap.

"Is she for real?" Frankie asked. "Come into my parlor?"

"B.J. told me about her yesterday," I said. "Apparently she's got an educational display of—"

"Coffins," Frankie said, as we stepped inside. "She collects coffins."

Rows of them flanked by dressmaker forms draped with mourning attire filled every corner of the tent. Shelves and display cabinets held letters, dishes, crystal vials, and more death mementos than I had ever seen in one place.

Gina looked even paler than she had outside as the Widow led her to a small rocking chair and waved the vial under her nose again. She opened a black lace fan, fluttering it in front of Gina.

"Please," the Widow said to Frankie and me, "have a look around. It's taken me years to put together this collection. You won't see another like it. The Victorians placed great significance on memorializing the dead, you know."

Savannah had said the same thing about the Egyptians. What was it about certain cultures that they had this macabre fascination with death? But Frankie was already making a slow tour around the tent, hands clasped behind her back as she examined everything.

"What are the little bottles for?" Frankie asked. "More smelling salts?"

"To catch the tears of sorrow a woman shed for her dead husband," the Widow said. "She placed a cork to seal them for one year and on the first anniversary of the death of her loved one, she sprinkled them on his grave."

Gina caught my eye behind the Widow's back and pointed to the exit, drawing a slash across her throat.

"I'm feeling better now." She stood up. "We ought to be going."

"Your exhibit is very interesting." Frankie was polite. "Thank you for your hospitality."

Something danced in the Widow's eyes as she smiled at us. "You girls run along now."

When we were back outside, Gina said, "That was weird."

"I thought it was fascinating," Frankie said. "I wonder how you get your tears in that bottle. I can't quite work that out. Can you, Lucie? Hey . . . Lucie?"

"Pardon? Look, isn't that B.J.'s regiment?"

A column of men marched toward us, two by two, rifles on shoulders and eyes straight ahead. A drummer bringing up the rear beat time as a young boy with a fife played "Glory, Glory Hallelujah."

"It is," Gina said. "There's Tyler."

He glanced at the three of us, serious and sober eyed, a flicker of acknowledgment on his face. His jacket looked too short and his pants were patched at the knees. His red curls stuck out from his kepi and he'd exchanged his wire-rimmed glasses for an old-fashioned pair that gave him an owl-like look.

"My God, he looks like he's really leaving for war." Frankie fished in her pocket for a tissue and wiped her eyes. "Sorry. I cry at movies all the time."

"Do you think they were scared when they marched off to the real thing?" Gina asked.

It had begun to rain lightly, softening the hard edges of the scene.

"I'd be terrified." Frankie wadded her tissue and shoved it in her pocket.

"We ought to be going," I said.

"I left my umbrella in my car," Frankie said. "I need to go back to the parking lot and get it."

"Mine's with yours," Gina said. "I'll come, too. What about you, Lucie?"

"Mine's at home. I wasn't thinking when I left this morning." Or maybe I was thinking about other things. My thoughts drifted to Quinn.

"We'll share," Frankie said. "Why don't you go over to the spectator field and stake out a spot? We'll meet you there."

They drifted off to the parking lot after we crossed the bridge. I joined the steady stream of spectators carrying umbrellas, camping chairs, cameras, and binoculars as they moved toward the roped-off viewing area. Despite the crowd, I spotted Annabel and Sumner Chastain right away; Sumner carried an oversized red umbrella with his company's logo on it and their bright yellow rain jackets shone through the dull drizzle like a pair of beacons. Sumner had binoculars slung over one shoulder.

The jaunty-sounding refrain of "Southern Soldier" sung by the Virginia Fiddlers floated through the portable sound system B.J. had set up. I listened to the grim lyrics and threaded my way through the crowd until I caught up with the Chastains. Annabel turned when I called her name.

"Have you recovered from yesterday?" I asked.

"Pardon?" Her eyes flickered. Today they looked dull and I wondered if she was on medication. Tranquilizers, maybe? "Oh, yes. Yes, I'm fine."

"Well, I hope you enjoy yourselves. Will you be staying for the whole thing?"

The chitchat was going to last only so long with Sumner.

I needed to get them someplace private where we could talk.

Sumner gave me an irritated dumb-question look and answered me with exaggerated patience. "Yes, that's what we plan to do."

Unlike Annabel, he seemed tense and edgy.

"I'd like to talk to both of you," I said. "In private. It'll only take a few minutes."

"If this is about your father and Kinkaid," Sumner said, keeping his voice low, "I think we've exhausted the subject."

He put his arm around his wife.

"Leland kept letters, too," I said. "I found them last night."

Sumner froze and Annabel's hand moved to her throat.

"You're lying." Her voice dropped to a whisper.

"I'm afraid not," I said. "I found them by accident. My brother happened to mention the other day that he had a collection of Civil War artifacts he'd found on the farm. I went looking for them yesterday because I thought it'd be nice to display them in the winery." I shrugged. "Imagine my surprise when I opened an old cigar box expecting to find bullets and a Confederate belt buckle and instead it was full of love letters."

I kept my expression bland, hoping they'd believe me as Sumner grabbed my arm. "Do we have to have this conversation right here?"

"How about behind the Virginia Sutler?" I shrugged out of his grasp.

We walked over to the tent in silence. Quinn liked to joke that every time I tell a lie my nose grows. Could I plant enough doubt in Annabel's mind—persuade her I really did have her letters to Leland—that maybe she'd finally admit she lied about her relationship with my father?

Annabel's voice was cold as she faced me, but she looked panicked. "You don't have any letters. You're bluffing."

"After Beau died," I said, "you claimed you were the one who tried to put a stop to the affair. But that's not true, is it? Leland ended it and you couldn't stand it. So you kept writing him, begging him to take you back."

"No. That's not true."

"You were in love with him, Annabel. My father spurned you, not the other way around," I said. "What I don't understand is how he was involved in Beau's murder. Because Leland didn't kill Beau. I think you did. Then you got him to help you bury Beau. I don't think you came with him because you really were surprised to see his grave site. But you somehow persuaded Leland to bury Beau here on Highland Farm."

"That's not true—"

"What are you saying?" Sumner's voice cracked. It took a couple of beats before I realized he wasn't talking to me. "Annie, that's not true, is it? You didn't go back to him after—"

"After what?" I asked. "After she killed Beau?"

"Sumner," Annabel was pleading. "It's not what you're thinking."

"These letters," Sumner said. "Where are they?"

"Oh, they're someplace safe," I said. In my head. "You two knew each other when Beau was alive? Did you know my father, Sumner?"

"You don't have to tell her anything," Annabel rasped at him. "She doesn't know what she's talking about."

She turned on me. "I'll pay you for the goddamn letters. Is that what this is about? Blackmail?"

I felt like I'd been slapped. "No. My God, of course not. I don't want your money. I just want to know what happened. Leland didn't kill Beau. You did. Maybe it was self-defense, but you killed him. Please, Annabel. I just want to know the truth. Don't make this my father's legacy. It's not right."

It will be a long time before I forget the agonizing look that passed between Annabel and Sumner just then.

"You did it?" I stared at Sumner. "You killed him?"

"Don't—" Annabel's face was still tormented.

"Why?" I persisted. "To protect her?"

But the dam was broken, the damage done. He practically spat the words at me.

"I have nothing to say to you except that your letters don't prove a goddamn thing. We're leaving."

"Don't we have to—" Annabel started to cry.

"That's enough! You've said enough." Sumner took her by the arm—for once, not so lovingly—and they left. I held on to one of the tent stays as though the wind had been knocked out of me.

The letters were a bluff and Sumner was right: I still had no proof of anything. Not even the brand-new revelation that he'd killed Beau—hadn't he?

It made sense, if that's what happened. All this time Annabel had been protecting Sumner, not herself. She'd almost gotten away with it until Sumner found out about her betrayal, or what I'd tricked her into admitting. Sumner hadn't known—until right now—that his wife was still in love with Leland. That she'd gone back to my father after he killed Beau for her. Sumner had been in love with Annabel, but she couldn't get my father out of her mind, couldn't let go of him.

What I didn't know was what happened after that. Who buried Beau? Sumner? Sumner and Leland? Did my father even know about the grave? I probably would never know the answers to any of these questions. The Chastains would admit nothing; they would slam the door to the fortress of Chastain Construction, with its phalanx of lawyers and media spinners who would shield them behind an impenetrable wall.

The truth would be the truth they fabricated. End of story.

I was still holding on to the tent stay when Kit Eastman called my name. We had not spoken since that awful day in her office. She walked toward me carrying a green-and-yellow plaid umbrella.

"You all right?" she asked. "What are you doing standing out here in the rain? You look terrible."

"I'm okay."

"Sure you are." She held her umbrella over my head. "Want to talk about it?"

"Some other time."

We started walking.

"The reenactment's that way," she said. "This is the wrong direction."

"I thought maybe I'd skip it," I said. "You go on ahead."

She gave me a curious look. "I don't know what happened to you, but you're not skipping anything."

She hooked her arm through mine as the rain changed to the steady downpour we'd been expecting all day.

"Shake a leg, will you?" she said. "I don't want to miss the battle."

She was the only one who could crack jokes about my infirmity. It was our way of dealing with the accident—the "afterlife," as I called it, where my world had been turned upside down, but hers remained the same. She'd carried around a weird kind of survivor's guilt for a long time because she was supposed to be in the car that night, too, until her date fell through. But we'd finally worked through it and it hadn't destroyed our friendship. The rift of the past few weeks wouldn't break us apart, either.

"How've you been?" she asked.

"I've been better."

"I know it's been rough for you." She draped an arm around my shoulder. "We could always share a bottle of wine down at the old Goose Creek Bridge one of these days. Talk about every little thing. Bury the hatchet. Stuff like that."

"I'd like that," I said. "I'd especially like to bury the hatchet."

"About your father," she said. "I'm sorry, Luce. You know I never meant to hurt you. Never would deliberately hurt you—"

"Leland didn't kill Beau Kinkaid, Kit. I know that for a fact."

She stopped walking and turned to face me. "What are you talking about?"

"I know he didn't do it. But I can't prove who did."

"You want to tell me?"

I shook my head. "Not right now."

I heard B.J.'s voice over the loudspeaker warming up the crowd and announcing that the battle was about to begin.

"Let's go," I said. "It's starting."

If there was any doubt that the spectators were rooting for the South, the cheering that erupted when the Confederate soldiers came into view made it clear who the good guys were. I saw Frankie and Gina making their way toward us and waved to them.

B.J.'s voice boomed over the loudspeaker. "As we all know, the Battle of Ball's Bluff was the result of faulty intelligence and misguided decisions. It began with the Union falsely believing the Confederates had pulled out of Leesburg and an unfortunate decision by a rookie scouting party of Federals who thought a grove of trees in the moonlight was an abandoned Confederate camp."

The first battlefield skirmish between a small group of Confederates and Union troops reminded me of rival groups of kids on a playground, daring each other to come closer. Then one of the commanders roared, "Fire," and the shooting began in earnest. At first it seemed orderly as rows of soldiers fired their guns, then knelt to reload while the rank behind them took their turn.

"My God, look at them," Frankie said. "They're just walking toward each other with their guns pointed. They have to know the ones in the front row are going to be mowed down."

"I thought they were arriving in boats." Frankie waved her hand in front of her face like she was fanning herself. "Can you smell that gunpowder?"

"They came by boat in the real battle, but B.J. said they're only going to use the canoes in the last event where Senator Baker arrives and gets killed," I said.

By now the rows of soldiers had disintegrated and the gunfire became a barrage. Smoke clouded the field in a rainy haze like we were watching something out of a dream.

"How can they see anything through that smoke?" Kit said.

"Unfortunately for the Confederates," B.J. hollered above the din, "the brave boys of the Eighteenth Mississippi charged into an open area where two wings of Federals waited for them in the woods."

As he spoke, a group of Confederate soldiers wheeled toward a group of Union soldiers. Gunfire erupted from the woods, along with a cannon blast. More smoke filled the battlefield and above the uproar came the primitive, inhuman sound of the rebel yell.

I heard B.J.'s voice over the loudspeaker again, but this time it was impossible to make out what he was saying.

"What's going on?" Gina asked.

I pointed to the creek. "I think he's saying Baker just arrived. See the guy in the red sash?"

A group of Union soldiers pulled a canoe up the creek bank as Ray Vitale, playing the role of Edward Baker, climbed out and made his way to the battlefield.

In the distance, I saw the silver flash of his sword as Vitale raised his arm above his head, gesturing for his troops to advance. There was an explosion of shots, followed by another cannon blast. Vitale dropped his sword and clutched his chest as he fell to the ground. Men in gray and blue uniforms ran toward him as the gunfire continued.

"My God," Frankie said, "it's so authentic. My heart's pounding"

Kit shaded her eyes against the rain and squinted at the battlefield. "Something's going on."

"Hold your fire!" B.J. shouted. "Hold your fire!"

We heard more shouting and the pop of sporadic gunfire as the dense smoke now enveloped the battlefield like a shroud.

"Is this how it really happened?" Frankie asked. "Everybody running like that?"

"I don't think so," I said.

B.J. spoke again. This time his voice sounded anguished and urgent.

"Ladies and gentlemen, there's been an incident on the battlefield. We will not be continuing with our planned activities."

"What happened?" Frankie asked. "What is he talking about?"

"I'm not sure, but I have a feeling someone just shot Ray Vitale," I said. "With real ammunition."

Chapter 24

───∞∞∞───

B.J.'s announcement sent the crowd, especially families with children, into a panicked exodus toward the parking lot as word spread that someone had been shot.

"This is crazy," I said. "There were safety checks. How did someone get on the field with real bullets?"

"No one should leave," Kit said, as people pushed past us. "It's a crime scene. We've got to try to secure the place until the sheriff's department arrives. That's the first thing Bobby would do."

"Forget it. You are not going to be able to keep a crowd this size here against their will," I said. "Especially since no one knows who the shooter was and whether someone's still out there with more live ammunition. Maybe it was an accident, maybe not. Let's get out of the way before we get stampeded. Frankie, Gina, come on!"

"I'm calling Bobby." Kit reached for her cell phone as we pushed closer to the yellow "Do Not Cross" tape that had been strung up to keep spectators off the battlefield. With the crowd surging in the other direction, we now had a front-row view as hundreds of soldiers in blue and gray streamed away from the fighting toward the campgrounds.

"Call 911 and have them get word to that cruiser by the gate," I said to Kit. "He may just think people are leaving because it's over. Plus tell the dispatcher to send an ambulance. Maybe even the medevac helicopter. There's enough room for it to land on the field. I'm going to get to B.J.'s sound system and see if we've got any doctors here. Or anyone with medical training."

"What about Gina and me?" Frankie asked.

"Try to get to the south gate and ask that deputy what you can do to help."

"Someone's probably called 911 already from out on the battlefield," Kit said.

"I wouldn't bet on it. They didn't have cell phones in the 1860s. They only way these men could send a message is by smoke signal," I said.

By now we'd abandoned Kit's umbrella since it was slowing us down. I could hear her shouting into her cell phone.

"The dispatcher told me they're sending backup," Kit said as we made our way to the open-air tent where B.J. had been broadcasting only a few moments ago. "They can't send the helicopter. Too much rain and wind. They've got an ambulance coming."

B.J.'s microphone was still live, but the tent was empty. He'd probably gone to be with Ray Vitale.

I picked up the mike. "If there are any doctors or anyone with EMT experience here this afternoon, could you please come immediately to the tent with the sound system?"

Kit climbed up on a folding chair and scanned the crowd. "No one's heading this way," she said. "Ask 'em again."

I made two more announcements and then my phone rang. Frankie's number flashed on the display.

"The parking lot's insane," she said. "Once people found out they can't leave by the gate because the cruiser's blocking the exit, anyone with four-wheel drive is getting out any way they can. Someone dismantled part of the split-rail fence on the property line."

"You can't stop them," I said. "We'll deal with the damage later. If you run into a doctor, can you please beg him or her to consider returning? I don't know how long it's going to take the ambulance to get here."

"I'll try. The officer here told us to take names and license numbers," she said. "And ask if anyone saw anything. People have been taking pictures. Maybe someone caught something with their camera."

"Good luck," I said, and disconnected.

"Thank God," Kit said. "Here comes Marty."

Dr. Martin Gamble, dressed in running clothes and a hooded rain jacket, sprinted toward us.

"Hey, ladies." Marty stepped into the shelter of the tent and took off his hood. "Tina was here with the kids when it happened. She called my cell. Lucky I was nearby. Sorry it took so long to get here, but I came on foot. I'm training for the Marine Corps Marathon."

Marty worked at the Catoctin Free Clinic in Leesburg. We hadn't seen each other much in the past year since I'd inadvertently discovered he'd been carrying on an affair while I was trying to help one of his colleagues who was also a friend of mine. The revelation, which had stayed a private matter between us, had nevertheless made things awkward when we ran into each other.

"You really are hardcore to be running in a downpour," Kit said.

His smile was thin as he stared at me. "Takes my mind off things I'd rather forget. Let's get going. Where's the victim?"

"On the other side of the creek. We can either hike to the bridge and come all the way back to the battlefield. Or"—I pointed to Goose Creek—"it'd be faster to cross the creek right here."

"You want to swim across?" Kit sounded incredulous.

"She's talking about taking one of the canoes," Marty said. "Aren't you?"

"If someone will get one of them over to our side first."

"Are you serious?" Kit asked.

"It's not the Potomac. They did it at Ball's Bluff."

"Piece of cake," Marty said. "Let's do it."

The three canoes, turned over to keep from filling with rain, had been pulled well up onto land on the opposite bank of Goose Creek. Marty, Kit, and I yelled and waved until a teenager in a Union uniform saw us.

"We've got a doctor here," I shouted. "Can you get us over there?"

He cupped his hands around his mouth. "I don't know. The current's pretty strong."

"Please," I said, "the ambulance won't be here for a while. Please try."

The wind had picked up, bending tree limbs and sending leaves sailing through the air like tiny parachutes. All three of us were now soaked through our rain gear, our clothes sticking to us like they'd been glued on. The soldier gestured for someone to help him launch the canoe and a boy in a Confederate uniform joined him.

"Come on, come on," Marty muttered next to me. "You guys can do it."

The boys flipped one of the canoes and pushed it into the creek. The Union soldier climbed in and picked up a paddle.

"Damn," Marty said. "The rain and the current are pushing him downstream."

"At least he's making his way across," Kit said. "We can catch him when he gets in range. Let's go."

The canoe bobbed closer.

"Throw us your line," Marty called. "We'll pull you in."

As the boy fumbled for the bowline, the canoe caught a current that buffeted him, shooting the craft farther downstream. Marty waded into the water as the boy tossed the rope and missed. The second time it struck Marty's shoulder. He grabbed it and began pulling.

"Ladies first," he said. "I'll steady it for you."

Kit climbed in and the canoe rocked crazily.

"Sit down," he told her, "or you'll capsize us."

I went next, using my cane to steady me and moved crablike until I could sit on the seat in front of Kit's. Marty knelt in the stern, taking a paddle the Union soldier handed him. Rain and creek water that had sloshed over the gunwale filled the hull with about an inch of water. It seeped through the seams of my work boots until my feet felt like two blocks of ice. Kit's white-blond hair was plastered to her head. I glanced back at her as I brushed my own dripping hair off my face. Her eyes were closed and she seemed to be praying.

The battlefield was still shrouded in mist and smoke as rain ricocheted off the water like more gunfire. The Confederate teenager, who had waited for us on the opposite bank, now waded into the water and pulled us to shore. Marty jumped out as we reached the creek bank and sprinted over to the knot of men tending Ray Vitale.

"Lucie!"

I looked up as B.J. strode toward Kit and me. By now the battlefield was nearly empty.

"I watched you two with Marty and that canoe," he said.

"Good thinking. We really needed a doctor. An EMT from the Eighteenth Mississippi did what he could, but Ray's in bad shape."

"They can't send a helicopter," I said. "An ambulance is coming. Where was he shot?"

"Looks like somewhere in the abdomen, " he said. "He's unconscious and he's lost a lot of blood. The EMT's got his hand inside his gut."

I swallowed. "You think he'll make it?"

"I don't know," he said. "Whoever shot him knew where to aim."

After the ambulance had come and gone, Kit and I walked back to the Confederate camp, where the Black Widow's tent had been turned into a field office for the sheriff's department. For the rest of the afternoon and into the evening deputies took names and questioned all the reenactors, who were told to produce their rifles and ammunition boxes. Kit and I sat at a table under a nearby dining tent, wrapped in blankets the Widow had lent us.

At dusk the rain let up. Someone found dry firewood and started a campfire. We moved our chairs next to it, trying to dry out and warm up. As it grew dark, a few modern amenities appeared, including battery-powered lanterns and thermoses of coffee. Several whiskey flasks, which I'd thought were strictly forbidden, also showed up. Kit borrowed paper and a pencil from the Widow and began making notes by lantern light. Around us, people struck tents and packed up supplies. Gradually the campground emptied out.

I pulled my phone out of the pocket of my jeans. The battery was nearly empty. I called Quinn, who answered on the first ring.

"I've been trying to reach you," he said. "I drove over there but some deputy told me it's restricted access."

"My phone's about to die," I said. "And they're still questioning reenactors."

"Frankie and Gina are back here. The winery was a madhouse. Everybody wanted a drink. Eli's there, too."

"Tell them they can go home."

"Sure. Call me when they cut you loose," he said. "I'll be in the barrel room."

"Everything all right there?"

"You don't want to know," he said as my phone went dead.

Kit looked up from her paper. "Hey, that's Grace and Jordy Jordan next to the Widow's tent. They must be looking for Tyler."

She waved as they caught sight of us. Grace's snow-white hair, usually pulled into a neat chignon, hung wild and disordered around her shoulders. She looked like she'd been crying. Jordy's face was ashen.

"Do you know where they're holding Tyler?" Grace asked. "I hope they haven't taken him away yet."

"Where who's holding him? Taken him where?" I asked.

"Is he in trouble?" Kit asked.

"B.J. called us. They found live ammunition in Tyler's cartridge box." Jordy put his arm around Grace as she slumped against him. He sounded incredulous. "B.J. says Tyler claims someone else must have put it there by accident. There's no way he would deliberately—"

Grace interrupted. "He couldn't see well with those Civil War glasses he had on. I don't know why he didn't wear his own."

"They think *Tyler* shot Ray Vitale?" I asked. "That's crazy. He wouldn't—"

Jordy nodded, his face bleak. Tyler was their eldest child. Their only son.

"The safety check doesn't include the cartridge boxes," he said. "He's just a kid, even if he is over eighteen. He probably got all excited and reached for the wrong bullet in the heat of the battle."

"Then it's an accident," I said. "They can't hold him responsible—"

"He's responsible for bringing live ammunition to an event like this." Jordy's shoulders sagged. "We already called Sam Constantine. Tyler's going to need a lawyer."

"Is there anything I can do to help?" I asked.

Grace nodded and started to cry again.

"Pray," she said.

It was midnight when Kit and I finally left the campgrounds and returned to our cars in the deserted parking area. Our shoes sank into the tire-rutted mud.

"You going home?" I asked.

"Only to change clothes. Then back to work. I need to write this up. It's too late for tomorrow's paper, but it'll be on the website. Sorry, kiddo. It's big news."

I kept my voice light. "Well, I wouldn't want the *Washington Tribune* to run out of things to write about and go out of business. I do what I can to keep your circulation up."

"We appreciate it." Her smile was rueful. "Be my maid of honor?"

"If I make it through this, sure I will."

She blew me a kiss and got into her Jeep. I followed her down Atoka Road. As I signaled to turn into the main gate to the winery, she pulled alongside me and tooted her horn.

"I'll phone you," she called through her open window. "Drink. Goose Creek Bridge. Soon."

Then she waved and sped into the darkness.

The lights still blazed in the villa as I drove by. Frankie's car was parked next to Eli's Jaguar, the only two cars in the lot. What were they doing here together so late? I drove home, got a drink, and called the winery.

Frankie answered.

"I saw your car," I said. "And Eli's. Everything all right?"

"The news at eleven said Ray Vitale is in critical but stable condition," she said.

"The sheriff's department thinks they've got a suspect," I replied.

"Who?"

"I hope you're sitting down. It's Tyler. They found live ammunition in his cartridge box."

I expected her stunned silence. Finally she stammered, "Tyler? Oh, my God, Lucie. Tyler would never shoot anyone. There must be a mistake."

"Grace and Jordy hired Sam Constantine."

More silence on her end. Then she said, "I guess it's serious."

"Seems so. I'd better call Quinn and tell him. Have you talked to him lately?"

"He packed it in an hour ago. He's getting a few hours' sleep in the barrel room. More problems with the Riesling."

"Maybe I should go over there."

"You get some sleep, too," she said. "He's got Benny and Javier with him. They'll get a handle on it. You can deal with it in the morning. Don't give Quinn any more bad news tonight."

I hung up and slowly climbed the spiral staircase to my bedroom. Had Tyler really shot Ray Vitale by accident? I knew enough about guns to know there was a difference between shooting blanks and live ammunition. In the confusion and roar of noise on the battlefield, though, maybe no one had been able to hear the live shot that felled Vitale. But wouldn't the shooter have known what he did?

I undressed and took a long, hot shower that left my skin bright pink.

Was Tyler lying because he was scared and didn't want to get blamed for this, or was he just too inexperienced and caught up in the moment to realize what he'd done?

The third possibility was that he was telling the truth.

Which meant there was another shooter out there— someone who'd gotten away with it—and Tyler had been set up to take the fall for something he didn't do.

Chapter 25

—∞∞∞—

Sunday's rainstorm cleared the air so that when I woke on Monday all traces of Edouard had vanished and we were back to crystalline sunshine and sharp shadows. The sky was a limitless hard-lacquered shade of blue. Plants, trees, and my lawn—after the deluge of rain—had turned the vivid artificial green of Astroturf. The mountains, finally visible after being masked by days of low-hanging clouds, were the dusky color of Scottish heather.

Kit called while I was in the kitchen drinking coffee.

"The story's on the *Trib*'s website," she said. "I wanted to tell you myself."

"Thanks. You all right? You sound beat."

"I am beat," she said. "I got about two hours' sleep."

"Go home and go to bed."

"I wish I could, but I've got a problem. Someone's been using my credit card. I just found out. I'm driving over to Blue Ridge Federal to talk to Seth."

I set my mug on the table and rested my forehead on my hand. First Frankie, now Kit.

"Since when?"

"The past two days. They bought stuff online, dammit. That card never left my purse, I swear. Maybe someone swiped it at some restaurant. I eat out every damn meal these days. You never know, do you?"

My thoughts raced.

"What are you going to do?" I asked.

"Bobby wants me to talk to the detective in charge of financial crimes. Plus I canceled the card, of course. What a pain."

I closed my eyes. Eli? Brandi? Would either one of them be so stupid as to copy down credit card numbers and rack up charges on accounts of people we knew?

"I need to talk to you," I said.

"About what?"

"Can we do it in person?"

"How about the end of the day? I'll come by for a drink."

"Sure. Fine."

"What's wrong, Luce?"

"I don't know," I said. "But maybe I'll have an answer when I see you. Say, six?"

"Six o'clock. I'll be there."

My next phone call was from Frankie.

"You need to get over here," she said. "Annabel Chastain's here and she's loaded for bear. She's looking for you. I'm going to do my best to keep her calmed down so she doesn't drive over to your house, but you need to come here now. She's either on drugs or she's been drinking or both. But she's hysterical."

It took me ten minutes to finish getting dressed and drive to the villa.

"She's on the terrace," Frankie said when I walked in. "Good luck."

Annabel stood at the railing with her back to me. She swung around as soon as I stepped outside. Today she wore no makeup and it looked like she hadn't slept. She'd aged years since yesterday.

"How much do you want for those letters?" she asked. "I'll give you whatever you want. I know your vineyard just sustained a huge financial loss after that tornado. So name your price. You don't have to beat around the bush, either. Let's just get this over with."

"Did Sumner send you to do this?" I asked.

"Sumner is being questioned by some deputy because he feuded publicly with that horrid Vitale man." She sounded bitter. "Did *you* set them on him? Is this your idea of revenge?"

"No, I didn't. My guess is the sheriff's department heard about that argument from B.J. No one asked me anything. As for revenge, I don't believe in an eye for an eye." I paused. "Unlike you."

Her voice was low and guttural. "How dare you?"

"There is no price," I said. "There are no letters. You said so yourself yesterday. It was a bluff and you were right about that. But now I know the truth. Sumner killed Beau, not my father."

She hissed like a snake. "You have no proof."

"That's right," I said. "I don't. Which means he's going to get away with murder and you're abetting that crime. Even now, when you have a chance to clear the name of an innocent man."

"Beau deserved to die," she said. "He was a despicable man."

"We're a society of laws," I said, "not vigilantes. If everyone took the law into his own hands, we'd have anarchy."

She looked like she'd been slapped.

"Did Sumner have anything to do with Ray Vitale's shooting?" I asked.

"I won't dignify that with an answer," she said. "You really are Leland's daughter, you know? Tricking us the way you did."

She left and I spent a long time staring at the mountains.

Quinn finally called me after lunch.

"Damned if I can figure out why the Riesling stopped fermenting," he said. "The only thing that makes sense is if the grapes were sprayed with pesticide or sulfur or they got treated with something right before harvest. That would do it."

"You know what? I'm going to drive by Chance's place and ask him. I've got an errand in Middleburg, anyway."

"I wouldn't do that, Lucie. Besides, you think he'd tell you if he was the one who did it?"

I closed my eyes and thought about how Chance had kissed me the other night and that offer to finish what we'd started.

"I might be able to persuade him."

"I'm coming with you."

"After that brawl the last time you two were together? You can get more with honey than vinegar." Or a honeypot. I swallowed. "Stay with the wine. I won't be long. I'll come by as soon as I get back."

"I don't trust him."

"I know you don't. But I might be able to persuade him to tell me the truth. He's got nothing to lose now."

"What are you going to do?"

"Charm him," I said.

Chance lived in a small house that belonged to a series of cottages that were part of a larger estate just off Sam Fred

Road. When I got there it had the quiet air of no one at home. I rang his doorbell and listened to the silence for a few minutes before I started looking through windows. The living room contained a sofa, flat-screen television, and cheap-looking coffee table. A rug remnant covered part of the floor.

Maybe he was out job hunting. I walked around to the back of the house. A blackened industrial-sized trash can sat in the middle of the weedy backyard. I peered into it. He'd burned something.

I touched the side of the can. Cold. Why set a fire out here when I'd seen a fireplace in the living room? It looked like he'd burned clothing.

I tried to knock the can on its side, but it was heavier than it looked. By the time I succeeded, my hands were soot covered. I wiped them on the grass and spotted a garden rake propped against the garage. Nice of him to leave it there. I fetched it and used it to drag the blackened lump in the bottom of the barrel out of the can.

Along with the cloth, pieces of plastic the size of small playing cards had melted and fused together in the tarry mess. Nothing on any of them, except a black stripe running across the width of the card.

I swallowed. Like the stripe that contained someone's personal information on the back of a credit card. One of our customers? Had Chance been swiping credit cards at the winery? How many names could he have collected? I could think of one, probably two. Frankie, and maybe Kit.

I raked through the rest of the ashes. Something dull gleamed and I fished it out.

A button with CSA stamped on it. Confederate States of America.

"You make a habit of going through other people's trash?"

I stood and palmed the button. Did Chance have a twin

brother? The man who stood there had jet-black hair and dark eyebrows. Same voice, though.

"Chance?"

"What are you doing here, Lucie?"

He wasn't stupid, but maybe he believed I was.

"I stopped by to take you up on your offer." I smiled. "Finish what we started the other night."

He smiled his heartthrob smile, but this time it was tinged with regret.

"You might be a little late, sweetheart."

"It's never too late, Chance."

He walked over to me and I stepped back, banging into the overturned trash can and momentarily losing my balance. He grabbed my arm and I dropped the button. It hit the ground and rolled where he could see it. His grip tightened.

"Why'd you have to come here?" He picked up the button and shoved it in his pocket.

"I told you why."

He started to laugh. The dusky blue eyes grew cold. "Wish you hadn't done this. I'm on my way out of town. Looks like you're going to have to keep me company. Let's go."

"Where?"

"You'll know when we get there."

He pulled out a gun from under his jacket.

"Get moving," he said.

Chapter 26

$\iff$

We took my car. I drove. He kept the gun on his lap where I could see it. At the end of Sam Fred Road, he told me to turn east on Mosby's Highway. The Blue Ridge was behind us.

"Where's Bruja?"

"With my girlfriend."

I'd never heard anything about a girlfriend.

"She know about all this?"

"All what?"

"The credit card scam. Shooting Ray Vitale. That was you, wasn't it? You must have shown up as a walk-on after you dyed your hair. Somehow you planted live ammunition in Tyler's cartridge box."

He leaned against the passenger door, facing me.

"I don't know what you're talking about. And slow down. I don't want to get pulled over for speeding."

We crawled through the village of Aldie doing twenty-five. If we kept going east on this road, we'd eventually end up in Washington, D.C. But when we got to the light at Gilbert's

Corner, he said, "Get in the left lane and put on your turn signal. We're taking Fifteen."

Route 15 went north to Leesburg and on to Maryland.

The music of a heavy-metal song startled me. He pulled his phone out of his pocket and smiled as he glanced at the display.

"Hi, baby. Miss you so much."

I could hear a woman's voice through the phone. The girlfriend, probably.

"Naw. Change of plans. I got a passenger." He stroked his gun as he listened. The voice on the other end of the phone screeched. It sounded like Baby thought three was a crowd.

"Aw, come on. It'll be fine . . . hey, have I ever let you down?"

We had come to the bypass around Leesburg. Chance pointed to the sign, indicating that was the road I should take.

"Yeah, sure, okay, baby. I can handle it. Don't worry . . . all right, all right . . . yeah, it's cool. See you soon."

He disconnected as we drove past the outlet mall.

"Where's your phone?" he said.

"In my purse. On the floor in the back."

He reached around and got my purse, rummaging through it until he found the phone.

"Can't have you making any calls, can I?" He turned it off and took aim, throwing it out the window as we passed a meadow. I watched it hit the grass. Then he pulled out my wallet. "And for good measure, I'll take these."

He helped himself to my credit cards, stuffing them in his jeans pocket.

"At the next light, turn right," he said.

It was the road that led to Ball's Bluff.

"Why are we going here?" My voice shook. "Meeting your girlfriend?"

He laughed. "Not hardly. She doesn't want to meet you."

It sounded like his girlfriend called the shots. "What does that mean?"

"It means I'll be going on by myself."

He was going to shoot me here in the park.

"Why are you doing this? Please, Chance. You won't get away with two murders."

That seemed to surprise him. "What are you talking about?"

"Ray Vitale." I licked my parched lips. "And me."

"The news said Vitale's going to make it," he said. "And I'm not going to kill you. Just slow you down for a while. It's a big park, but someone will find you eventually. By then I'll be gone where no one can find me. As for Vitale, he deserved what he got. The guy paid his employees slave wages. He was a mean-spirited bastard and everybody who worked for him hated him."

"You said once you'd worked at a nursing home. It was one of his, wasn't it?"

"Don't you have a good memory." It wasn't a compliment. "For a while, I did. Finally I took what he owed me and left."

"Did those day laborers you hired the other day deserve slave wages?"

"Those guys were illegal. Every one of them. What they got was more than what they earn at home. They should be grateful I hired them. If they don't like it, let them go back to their villages and their mud huts."

"You have some ugly prejudices, Chance."

"I'm a patriotic American. America is for Americans."

"How much did Sumner Chastain pay you to shoot Ray Vitale?"

"I don't know what you're talking about," he repeated.

"You must have known Vitale was going to sue Sumner, so Sumner would be happy to have someone get rid of him. Were you working for Ray when he had those problems with Chastain Construction?"

"Ask Sumner."

I pulled into the gravel parking lot and my heart sank. Today there wasn't a single car here.

"Give me your keys. And get out," he said.

"I need my cane."

"Then get it and let's go."

I knew he'd take the route to the river, but I wasn't going to make it easy for him. Quinn knew where I was going. Kit expected to have a drink with me tonight. How long before someone put two and two together and started looking for me?

He kept his hand on my arm as we made our way through the park. When we reached the river route, there was no choice but to go single file.

"You first," he said. "And don't try anything. I've got the gun."

Yesterday's rain had turned the path into a slippery slope of mud. I tripped over a root and fell, landing on a stone out-cropping. A pain shot up my back.

"Get up."

"I can't!" I was breathing hard. "Give me a minute."

"Stop stalling." He jerked my arm and yanked me up. "Get moving."

My cane skidded off into the underbrush. "I can't without my cane."

"Yes you can. I've seen you."

He hung on to my arm, forcing me to keep going. We had nearly reached the floodplain when I tripped over another tree root. This time I took him with me. We both tumbled into the brush and he seemed to go headfirst.

He swore as he got raked by brambles with thorns. A moment later he called my name and I held my breath, waiting.

"Dammit, Lucie. Answer me."

I crawled back to the path. The river was only about ten yards away. I slid down to the floodplain like I was on a playground slide.

Would he come after me, or wait to see if I survived the current? Why wasn't he shooting at me? Maybe he lost his gun in the bushes when we fell.

I kicked off my shoes and waded into the water. After my accident, I'd had daily sessions of hydrotherapy to strengthen my bad leg. Afterward I moved to my mother's home in the south of France, where I swam almost daily. I was a good, strong swimmer. If I could keep up with the current, Harrison Island was probably, at most, fifteen or twenty minutes away. Even if the river took me downstream—as it probably would—I reckoned I could make it to the opposite shore before I ran out of land.

He called my name again and now something whizzed past my head. He'd found the gun, after all. I dove underwater and propelled myself off the river bottom. If he planned to follow, at least I had a head start. Before my accident I'd been on the track team and ran cross-country. The coach drummed into me that looking back to see who was chasing my tail could cost the race. I kept swimming and didn't look back until my feet touched the river bottom once more. When I finally turned around, I didn't recognize the scenery back on the Virginia side of the river. How far downstream had I drifted?

Wherever I was, Chance was gone.

Tyler had said Harrison Island was privately owned, a place for hunters. Deserted most of the time. I made my way through the underbrush and reached a flat, treeless place that looked like someone had plowed an enormous field that now lay fallow. On the horizon were several low buildings. A pickup truck was parked next to one of them.

A path wide enough for a vehicle skirted the perimeter of the field. I began walking toward the house but someone saw me before I got there.

The pickup began moving toward me, bouncing on the mud-rutted road.

I waved my arms in the air and waited as a memory of Chance driving across the field to find me the day the tornado ripped open Beau Kinkaid's grave flashed through my head. How long had it been? Two weeks?

Now I knew the truth about who killed Beau, but I'd never be able to prove it. Chance was probably on his way out of town in my car. If he'd made a deal with Sumner to kill Ray Vitale, I reckoned it wouldn't be long before one of them would rat out the other.

Annabel thought I wanted revenge for what she did to Leland, but she was wrong. I wanted justice. What I got—by default—was retribution. Annabel and Sumner might never be punished in this life for Beau's murder, but they had to live with the burden of their guilt, now heavier for accusing my father, who was innocent, of their crime and corrupted from within by the revelation of Annabel's infidelity.

Maybe it was cold comfort, but it was better than believing my father was a murderer. Even if my friends and neighbors thought differently, the talk would quiet down. Emma Hunt was right.

The acts of this life are the destiny of the next. Though

Leland's acts had ended up changing the destiny of my life, we had just written the last chapter. It was over, finished.

The pickup pulled alongside me. A girl who reminded me of Savannah Hayden sat behind the wheel.

"You lost?" she asked.

"Not anymore," I said.

Chapter 27

⎯⎯⎯⎯⎯⎯⎯⎯⎯

The police found my car in Pennsylvania two days later. Chance and his girlfriend had vanished, but by now Bobby had told me that Chancellor Miller was one of many names he'd gone by over the past five years. The FBI was brought in because of the stolen credit cards and I cooperated fully, turning over as much information as I could provide so they could contact anyone whose credit cards might have been compromised.

Benny finally tracked down a couple of the laborers who had picked our Riesling, confirming what Chance had admitted about skimming their pay.

"We're going to have a hell of a lot of fence mending to do to clean up our reputation," Quinn said.

"I know," I told him. "But we'll clean it up. Speaking of which, Seth Hannah called. The Romeos would like to reschedule that barrel tasting."

Quinn nodded. "I think that can be arranged."

Within the week Tyler was cleared in the shooting of Ray Vitale once it was established that he'd been shot with a

.44-caliber ball which couldn't have come from Tyler's Enfield rifle.

Annabel and Sumner returned to Charlottesville. I had no idea if they bought Mick's horse, though sooner or later word would get around to the Romeos or Thelma and I'd find out one day at the General Store.

I told Bobby what I suspected about Sumner paying Chance to shoot Ray. He shook his head and told me so far they had turned up nothing to connect them.

"But don't worry," he said. "We're looking. And when we get Miller, I'm sure he'll roll on Chastain."

We talked about it one evening when he and Kit came by the vineyard after work for a drink with Quinn and me.

We were sitting on the terrace, watching another spectacular sunset behind the Blue Ridge. Quinn looked weary after working flat out to salvage the Riesling, even though we'd never figured out what, if anything, Chance had done to sabotage it.

We were back on the subject of Chance, Sumner, and Ray Vitale.

"Chance, or whoever he is, had enough motive on his own to shoot Ray Vitale," Bobby said. "He worked for Vitale a few years back. He's the one who wrecked Vitale's credit and ran up tens of thousands of dollars of bills."

"Ray was going to sue Sumner," I said. "B.J. and I were there when they argued in my parking lot."

"We've been all over that," Bobby said. "It's a leap to say Chastain ordered a hit on Vitale and hired Chance to carry it out."

"I think it's the other way around. Chance went to Sumner with a proposition," I said.

"You know, I understand how Chance swiped my card," Kit said. "But who made those charges at Neiman Marcus with Frankie's card?"

"I think I figured that out," I said. "The day Brandi came by to see Eli, she threw her purse down on the bar stool. I found the store catalog on the floor after she left and stuck it behind the bar. When Chance helped out pouring wine, he probably took it. Lucky for him it had her address on it, too. Made it easier to cast suspicion on Eli or Brandi."

Kit shook her head. "Go figure. What about Sumner killing Beau?" she asked.

"Sumner never admitted it," I said. "But I know he did it to protect Annabel."

Bobby finished his wine and covered Kit's hand with his.

"It's an imperfect world," he said. "We do the best we can and we go on to fight another day. I've learned to live with that or I'd go crazy."

After they left, Quinn and I stayed on the terrace until it grew dark.

"Got any interest in seeing the Pleiades tonight?" he asked.

"I might."

He looked sideways at me. "You don't sound too excited."

"Throw in dinner and I might be excited."

"What about dessert?" He raised an eyebrow.

"Dessert would be nice, too."

"You're easy," he said. "A real pushover."

"Not as much of a pushover as you think. I'm going home to shower and change. Pick me up in an hour? I'm sure Dominique will give us a good table at the Inn."

"What are you talking about? You mean dinner, like dinner?" He looked wounded.

I smiled. "And dessert, like dessert."

"What about the Pleiades?"

"One thing at a time," I said.

The Battle of Ball's Bluff

❧

Ball's Bluff Battlefield Regional Park is located at the end of a street in a quiet subdivision near a sprawling outlet shopping mall a few miles from Leesburg, Virginia. But once inside the 223-acre park, the noise and bustle of the twenty-first century recede, and a visitor, out to exercise the dog or take a walk with friends or family, is soon enveloped in silence in the sun-dappled woods. Well-marked paths, Civil War monuments, and the third smallest military cemetery in the United States, where the remains of fifty-four Union soldiers lie in twenty-five graves, make it impossible to forget that a bloody battle occurred here—and some will swear that the park is haunted.

The Battle of Ball's Bluff took place on October 21, 1861, three months after the Union army lost the First Battle of Bull Run, the first great land battle of the Civil War. Ball's Bluff was, plain and simply, an accident that evolved as a result of a mistake by an inexperienced Union officer. In a few years' time, it would be considered of relatively minor importance when compared to other battles such as Gettysburg, Antietam, or Chancellorsville, but its significance on the remainder of the Civil War is indisputable: Congress, eager for a scapegoat after the death of one of their own, Senator Edward Baker, a Union commander responsible for much of the bungling, decided to form the Joint Committee on the Conduct of the War. Shocked by Baker's death and the sight of so many bodies in blue floating down the Potomac River past Washington, the committee oversaw the strategy and battle plans of Union commanders, who chafed under this authority for the remainder of the war.

James A. Morgan III, author of *A Little Short of Boats: The Fights at Ball's Bluff and Edwards Ferry* (Ironclad Publishing, 2004), describes the bluffs as a six-hundred-yard-long stretch of heavily wooded shale and sandstone cliff on the Virginia side of the Potomac River. A floodplain lies between the water and the cliffs, which rise about 110 feet above the river. Harrison Island, a long, narrow island that bisects the Potomac at the bluffs, played a significant role in the battle as the place from which Union soldiers launched their boats. The geography of Ball's Bluff then, as now, is unforgiving.

In the fall of 1861, under orders of Major General George McClellan, Union troops were keeping an eye on the area around Leesburg. Because all Potomac bridges between Harpers Ferry and above the Chain Bridge near Washington, D.C., had been burned, the ferry crossings above and below Leesburg were of strategic importance to both armies. Whoever controlled the area controlled invasion routes leading north and south.

For several weeks in October, Confederate commander Nathan "Shanks" Evans watched uneasily as a growing number of Union troops amassed in the area. Worried that he might be cut off without nearby reinforcements, Evans withdrew from Leesburg on October 16 without getting permission from his commanding officers.

Union troops monitoring Evans's departure assumed

Leesburg had been left unprotected. What they did not know was that Evans's commander, General P.G.T. Beauregard, had ordered him to return to the town, which he did on October 19. The following day, Union soldiers, under orders of Brigadier General Charles P. Stone, staged a small show of force to see what, if anything, the Confederates would do. That night a small Union patrol crossed the Potomac River to investigate the impact their demonstration had had on the Confederates. Unfortunately, in the moonlight their inexperienced leader mistook a row of trees for an enemy camp and reported this to Stone, who ordered a raid the next day.

But early on the morning of October 21, the raiding party was discovered by a company of Confederate soldiers who engaged them in fighting—ironically just as General Stone was being told there was no camp. Stone handed off what he believed was an expanded reconnaissance mission to Baker who, without evaluating the situation, immediately began sending more troops across the river.

Ball's Bluff was not so much a single battle as a series of smaller skirmishes that gradually escalated over the course of the day as both armies sent more troops. Though each side had almost the same number of men, Baker's troops—relatively inexperienced compared to the Confederates, some of whom had fought at Bull's Run—were eventually trapped at the end of a long, punishing day of fighting at one end of the battlefield with their backs to the bluff. Overwhelmed and panicking after a seesaw battle that cost Baker his life, Union soldiers fled and were injured or killed attempting to escape down the steeply sloped cliffs of Ball's Bluff. Those who made it to the floodplain found only three small boats to take them back to Harrison Island. Some tried to swim and either drowned or were shot. Many surrendered.

Though Balls Bluff would later be overshadowed by larger, bloodier battles, it was significant as a stunning early success for the South. According to Jim Morgan, neither side was expecting the Civil War to drag on as it did, nor to turn into a bloodbath. But the South would always remember their surprising victory, practically in the backyard of the Northern capital. For the North, however, the name Ball's Bluff became a curse.

More About Riesling

Riesling (REES-ling), one of the *vitis vinifera* or "noble" grapes of Europe, is a versatile white grape with the unique ability to produce wines that vary from light to full-bodied and span the spectrum of styles from dry to sweet to sparkling. A hardy late-ripening grape that thrives in cool climates and poor soils, Riesling is currently enjoying a renaissance in the wine world because of its crisp, refreshing taste and ability to pair with so many different foods. Together with Chardonnay, it is considered to have the most distinctive character of all white wine grapes.

The first historical mention of Riesling in 1435 traces the grape to the Rheingau area of Germany; it remains the most widely planted grape in that country. In the seventeenth century its prestige and prominence grew after Alsace was ceded to France at the end of the Thirty Years' War and the region was extensively replanted with Riesling.

Today Germany and Alsace remain the two premier Riesling-producing regions in the world, but the grape is also grown in Austria, Luxembourg, northern Italy, Australia,

New Zealand, Canada, South Africa, China, Ukraine, and the United States. It is not widely planted in Virginia because of the unsuitable climate, though a handful of vineyards do produce Riesling.

More than almost any other grape variety, Riesling takes on the characteristics of the *terroir*, or locality, where it's grown, which is reflected in its wines. It is generally not blended with other varietals and seldom aged in oak, which would overwhelm its delicate flavor. Because it is such a pure wine, Riesling shows cork taint more readily than any other varietal, with the result that German, U.S., and Australian Rieslings are now often bottled using screwcaps.

Many Rieslings are drunk young when they make a fruity, aromatic wine that evokes flavors of orchard fruits such as green apples, peaches, and apricots, or tropical scents of lychees and guava. Aged Rieslings tend to acquire an aromatic note of petroleum associated with kerosene or diesel. Though this gasoline—or "petrol"—aroma is sought after by those who know it indicates a high-quality mature wine, too much can be detracting or even a turn-off.

Although most people associate long aging potential with red wine, Riesling is one of the rare white wines that ages extremely well. Some dessert-style Rieslings—which have a high sugar content—have the longest ageability of any wine, reaching up to 100 years.

German Rieslings—the world's best known—are categorized by the grape's ripeness at harvest and style (dry or sweet). While German wine labels can seem daunting or tough to decipher, here are a few basic rules for declassifying what is what:

1. Ripeness classification—how early or late the grape was picked—is ranked from least to most ripe as follows: *Kabinett, Spätlese, Auslese,*

Beerenauslese (BA), and *Trockenbeerenauslese (TBA)*. *Kabinett* are the youngest, lightest wines while *Trockenbeerenauslese* are the ultra-sweet, highly concentrated late-harvest dessert wines made from individually selected grapes that have been left on the vine so long they have become as withered as raisins. For that reason, TBA is the most complex Riesling produced and among the world's most expensive wines. Keep in mind that, except for TBA, all of these wines can be dry or sweet. Two other basic categories—*QbA* and *QmP*—refer to "quality wine" and "quality wine with distinction."

2. Style of wine—sweet or dry: *Trocken* is dry; *Halbtrocken* is half-dry; *Fruchtsüß* is fruity sweetness; *Feinherb* is roughly translated as fine-bitter.

When it comes to food, Riesling can stand up to the most challenging flavors and spices. These range from the lightest seafood and salads to rich meat dishes and sauces, including spicy Asian, Mexican, or Moroccan foods. Rieslings also pair well with sweet desserts.

Acknowledgments

As usual, I owe thanks to many people who took time out of their busy schedules to let me pester them with questions or hang around and watch them at work. If it's right, they said it; if not, blame me. Thanks to Rick Tagg, winemaker at Barrel Oak Winery in Delaplane, Virginia, for taking my calls at all hours, whether he was driving a tractor, operating a forklift, or crushing grapes. Cheryl Kosmann of Swedenburg Estate Vineyard in Middleburg, Virginia, answered a multitude of questions about the business of selling wine.

I'm especially indebted to Karen Quanbeck, Rick Etter, and Pam Stewart of the Loudoun Museum in Leesburg, Virginia, for their generous time and valuable assistance in explaining Civil War reenacting and directing my attention to the small but important Battle of Ball's Bluff. Without their help, I would still be wandering in the wilderness.

Jim Morgan, who spent years researching the Battle of Ball's Bluff and is widely considered the authority on the subject, kindly took the time to review my own essay on the battle and answer numerous questions. Two volunteer guides at the park, Mike Wolford and Max Gutierrez, gave me my first tour of the battlefield. Special thanks to Max Gutierrez who invited me back for a more in-depth tour and took me down to the Potomac River floodplain one steamy summer day—much like the day Lucie visited Ball's Bluff—and patiently answered my many follow-up questions, e-mails, and phone calls.

On the subject of Civil War reenacting, I'm grateful to Doug Becktel, who spent considerable time with me at the 145th anniversary of the Battle of Chancellorsville, and also to Tom Dunn and Michael Schaffner. Allison Willcox made time to answer questions on forensic anthropology and the process of identifying human remains, as did Dr. Diane France. Dr. Andrew Thompson and Dr. Doug Arendt helped with medical questions; John French talked to me about crime scene investigation. Lieutenant Ed O'Carroll, Officer Ron Miller, and Detective Dave Smith of the Fairfax County, Virginia, Police Department responded to queries about law enforcement as did author and former homicide detective John Lamb. Terry Jones helped me with firearms matters.

Thanks, as always, to the RLI gang who are the first to read what I've written and put me right: Donna Andrews, Carla Coupe, Laura Durham, Peggy Hanson, Val Patterson, Noreen Wald Smith, and Sandi Wilson. I'm grateful to André de Nesnera, Catherine Kennedy, and Martina Norelli, who read and commented on later drafts of this book. Elizabeth Arrott, who by day uses her blue pencil as a senior editor at an international news organization, gave up her nights to go over this book not once, but twice. Tom Snyder gave me more help than I deserved and drummed into me *Elmore Leonard's Ten Rules of Writing*, especially rule 10 about leaving out the stuff that readers tend to skip. I tried to do that, and it's not his fault if I didn't.

As always, it takes a village—or a first-rate publisher—to

make a book. At Scribner, I owe thanks to many people, but especially to Anna deVries, Christina Mamangakis, and Heidi Richter, as well as to Micki Nuding, Danielle Poiesz, Maggie Crawford, and Melissa Gramstad at Pocket. Last, but by no means least, I wouldn't be writing any of this if Dominick Abel, my agent, hadn't made it all possible.

Turn the page for a sneak peek at the next

Wine Country Mystery

THE VIOGNIER VENDETTA

from award-winning author

Ellen Crosby

Coming soon in hardcover from Scribner

I spent an hour walking the paths of the Reflecting Pool before I went back to the Vietnam Veterans Memorial. My D.C. reunion with Rebecca had been odd, almost as though she had staged it with me as her spectator. She'd changed since I knew her at school; there was a harder edge to her now.

A flock of geese honked noisily overhead in an untidy V. I stopped in front of the roses Rebecca had left at the memorial and did the math. Rebecca's newly announced father, Richard Boyle IV, would have been among the last to die—in 1975—based on Rebecca's age. I put my hand on the Wall and stared at my reflection in the polished stone, letting the heat from the hot granite warm me. Why didn't she want to find him? Saying she was late to pick up a package in Georgetown sounded like a made-up excuse.

I scanned the names of the dead and missing from 1975 and 1974. Any earlier and the numbers really didn't add up. More than 58,000 names were engraved here, commemorating decades of sorrow and loss for an unpopular war. Wherever Richard Boyle IV's name was, I didn't find it. Maybe

Rebecca knew more than she told me and that's why she asked me to say nothing about our visit to the memorial.

The sun slipped behind a wall of clouds and the breeze grew sharper. I turned up my jacket collar and decided to return to our hotel—the Willard. On my way back to Ohio Drive, I passed others who, like me, knew Vietnam only from history books. For us, this place was a tourist attraction, the same as the Eternal Flame at Arlington or the other monuments scattered throughout the city honoring dead heroes. But for some, like the woman who'd left some letters, it had to be like visiting a grave at a cemetery.

On the cab ride to the hotel, I couldn't get Rebecca's face out of my mind.

They were still serving lunch at the Occidental Grill when I got back from my trip downtown. Another Washington landmark, it was located next door to the Willard. A man in a dark suit seated me in a booth where I could study the rows of black-and-white head shots of unsmiling political celebrities from an earlier era that covered every wall. I ate a club sandwich and drank a glass of unsweetened ice tea before walking back to the hotel.

The lobby was noisier and more animated than when I had checked in. Underneath the sound of laughter, chatter, and the clink of glasses from the bar around the corner, a pianist played "The Way You Look Tonight." Most of the couches and chairs were now occupied. I wondered how many of the people were hotel guests and how many were well-dressed people-watchers. I walked down an opulent corridor called Peacock Alley, passing a few people taking tea, and peeking into ballrooms and salons set up for some upcoming event. One of them looked like someone's wedding reception. Finally, I rode the elevator to the seventh floor.

More Beaux Arts elegance in our suite, which was decorated in regal shades of scarlet and gold. Someone had placed my suitcase on a small mahogany bench with a red-and-gold striped satin cushion. Rebecca's suitcase occupied the matching bench next to it. A floor-length, one-shoulder black evening gown hung in the closet next to my garment bag. In the bathroom her makeup—mostly Chanel and La Prairie—spilled out of a Vera Bradley cosmetic bag on the marble countertop. Among the blush, lip gloss, and eye shadow was a package of birth control pills. I wondered if there was a new man in her life?

She'd left her red leather planner, closed and bristling with papers, in the middle of the desk in the sitting room. Next to it, bound in green cloth with gilt-edged pages, was a very old copy of *The Poetical Works of Alexander Pope*. I opened the cover and saw that she had inscribed the flyleaf to me:

> For Little.
>
> May you come to know these poems and treasure them as much as I do.
>
> Big.

I brought the book over to the gold damask sofa and sat down to look at it. The second dedication—to her—was on the title page and had been crossed out, though I could still read what had been written:

> For my darling Rebecca,
>
> Where'er you walk, cool gales shall fan the glade;
> Trees, where you sit, shall crowd into shade;
> Where'er you tread, the blushing flow'rs shall rise,
> And all things flourish where you turn your eyes.
>
> With all my love, Connor

Underneath, Rebecca had written her own message:

> Our passions are like convulsion fits, which, though they make us stronger for a time, leave us the weaker ever after.

Presumably the words were originally written by Alexander Pope—Professor Connor's declaration of love and Rebecca's bitter recrimination. But there, in a nutshell, was their affair and the breakup. I closed the book feeling as if I'd violated her privacy, though obviously she meant for me to see it if she were giving it to me as a present. I put it back on the desk as someone knocked on the door to the suite.

A woman about my age wearing a businesslike white oxford blouse and a slim navy skirt stood there, long tapered fingers playing with her cell phone. Heart-shaped face, delicate winged eyebrows, English-rose complexion, light brown hair pulled up in a chignon, she wore almost no makeup except for lipstick in Madonna red.

When she saw me, she frowned. "Lucie Montgomery?"

She had to be hotel staff since no one else knew I was here. Maybe they needed a credit card on file after all.

"Yes. You're with the Willard?"

She looked taken aback. "Good Lord, no. I'm Olivia Tarrant. Sir Thomas Asher's personal assistant. I work with Rebecca for him."

Tommy Asher seemed to surround himself with beautiful young women. Somehow I expected that his personal assistant would be a man—someone older who'd been with him for years. A private secretary or a faithful butler.

"What can I do for you?" I asked.

"I'm looking for Rebecca."

"She had an errand in George—"

Olivia Tarrant cut me off. "I know that. She should have been back here two hours ago. I can't reach her anywhere and she's not answering her phone. I spoke to Dr. Shelby. He told me she kept her taxi waiting while she picked up a package for Sir Thomas and Lady Asher. Rebecca didn't spend ten minutes there."

I opened the door wider and gestured to the room. "I don't know what to tell you, but she's not here, either."

"May I?" Olivia sailed past me before I could answer.

She walked over to one of the two windows overlooking Pennsylvania Avenue and pulled the sheer privacy curtain aside as though she expected to find Rebecca hiding there. I wondered if she planned to look under the bed as well.

"You were with her before she left for Georgetown?" She didn't turn around.

"Yes."

"When was that?" She released the curtains and faced me.

"I met her at one o'clock at the Lincoln Memorial. We did some sightseeing."

"What time did she leave?"

"I don't know. Probably around two, maybe a little before. I didn't check the time."

"Did she say anything else, about where she might go?"

In a moment, I figured Olivia Tarrant would read me my rights. "No."

She fiddled with her phone some more, turning it over and over. "I don't know what I'm going to tell Lady Asher."

"Maybe Rebecca met someone for coffee or a drink afterward."

The winged eyebrows arched in annoyance. "First of all, she was supposed to return directly here. Second, if that's what she did then she shouldn't have turned off her phone."

"Hey," I said. "I'm not Rebecca or Lady Asher. Go tell them."

Her mouth dropped open, then she said, "I'm sorry. I shouldn't have snapped at you. But you have no idea how valuable that package she retrieved is."

I don't have a good poker face. Everyone tells me that. I tried, anyway, to look like I had no idea what she was talking about.

"Rebecca is very responsible. I'm sure everything's fine and she'll show up any minute."

Olivia Tarrant crossed her arms, sizing me up. "How well do you know her?"

Right now I could have told her I wasn't so sure anymore and that would be the truth. Instead I said, "Do you always ask so many questions?"

For the second time she looked taken aback. "I suppose I do. It's part of my job. You can't imagine how many people want my boss's time and attention . . . and money. It's my responsibility to know who he's dealing with."

She seemed to relish the power of her position as gatekeeper and all-roads-pass-through-me. Sir Thomas may have made the *Forbes* list of billionaires every year for the past decade and was well known for his philanthropy, but he still put his pants on one leg at a time just like every other man I knew. I wasn't as impressed with him as she was.

"I don't want any of those things, and I'm an old friend of Rebecca's. She invited me to be her guest for the weekend."

"You're in investment banking as well?"

"I own a vineyard."

She did a double take and said, "So you flew in from the West Coast?"

I hate it when people think the only place anyone makes wine in America is California.

"I drove here from Atoka, Virginia. It took me about an hour," I said.

"Atoka," she repeated. "Is that near Middleburg or Upperville?"

"It's in between. Why do you ask?"

"Sir Thomas's brother just bought an estate there. Upperville, I think it was."

"He's moving to Virginia?"

"No." Her smile was tolerant. "It'll be a weekend place when he's not at one of his other homes."

Her phone rang before I could reply.

"Yes, sir?" Olivia turned away from me and walked back to the window. "No, I'm sorry. She's not in her suite, either. Yes, sir. Right away."

She tapped her phone and I heard the *click* of a disconnected call.

"I have to go," she said.

"That was Sir Thomas?"

She ignored the question and walked to the desk, bending over to write something on a hotel notepad. She tore off the page and handed it to me.

"My number. Please call me if you hear from Rebecca. And for God's sake, tell her to call me and get the hell back here," she said. "I'll see myself out."

I folded the paper and threw it on the desk. Somehow I didn't think I'd be calling Olivia Tarrant.

I spent the rest of the afternoon reading a book on canopy management—pruning, spraying, and how often to do it— and trying not to glance up at the door to the suite every five minutes as though I expected Rebecca to waltz in with some breezy tale of a drink with another friend in Georgetown.

Where was she?

The book wasn't a page-turner, but I forced myself to concentrate because it was a subject I needed to know more about. A lot of people think owning a vineyard means living a glamorous life spent wandering among the grapevines, sipping champagne and admiring God's handiwork. The reality is that it's backbreaking, mind-numbing, tedious work, often in withering heat or the damp chill of a wine cellar. During harvest, we put in eighteen-hour days for weeks on end. Tempers are short because no one gets much sleep and we're usually racing against the clock and the weather. A good day is when only a few things go wrong. As for glamour, I wouldn't like to say how much scrubbing it took to get most of the dirt out from under my fingernails before I showed up here today. Dark red nail polish did the rest. Luckily my clothes concealed the Technicolor bruise on my thigh from banging into a metal rack when one of the five-hundred-gallon wine barrels slipped in the middle of turning it. That said, I love what I do.

By six o'clock Rebecca still hadn't turned up. I tried her number one more time and it again went to voice mail. No point leaving a third message. Next I called Quinn Santori, my winemaker, to see how things had gone at the vineyard today. This time of year we were gearing up for spring, which meant the beginning of weeding and planting new vines. For a few more weeks, though, it would still be relatively quiet in the winery until we began bottling in May. Lately we'd been doing wine trials—blending wine in varying ratios from different barrels and stainless-steel tanks to decide how we'd make the wine we would eventually bottle.

Quinn and I didn't see eye-to-eye on this—in fact, lately, we didn't seem to agree on much of anything. Eight months ago, we broke a long-established rule of not mixing personal and professional relationships and had gone to bed together. Foolishly, I thought we could handle what happened the next morning and the mornings and days after that.

He was a passionate and exciting lover, and reliving that first night and the handful of others that followed still made my face go hot. Then in December his mother passed away in California. As far as I knew, she was the only family Quinn had left, since he kept a monastic vow of silence about his life before he came to work at Montgomery Estate Vineyard, which was three years ago. My father had hired him shortly before his death without doing much of a background check, and Quinn never bothered to fill in any of the blanks.

He remained in San Jose for a month after his mother's funeral, leaving Antonio, our new farm manager, and me to run the place. When he returned from California, something was different. He was different. Not quite distant, but remote, I guess. Or restless maybe. By unspoken mutual agreement, he stopped showing up at my house at night. We never discussed the reason, but the fallout was that we didn't spend much time in each other's company during the day, either, unless it was business. Personally, I was miserable. I had no idea how he felt.

His phone, like Rebecca's, went to voice mail.

"Hi, it's me," I said, after his message. "Just checking in. No need to return the call unless something's come up. See you tomorrow."

Then I took a long shower and got ready for the gala.

At 6:45 Olivia Tarrant knocked on my door again. She'd gone from buttoned-up to siren, glamorous in a red satin gown with a plunging neckline. A black cashmere evening coat and a black sequined purse were draped over one arm. This time she wore plenty of makeup—theatrical, smoky eyes, rouged cheeks, and that Madonna-red lipstick that made her look like some doll on the cover of a '50s pulp novel—except for the phone that she still clutched in one hand and the vexed expression on her face.

"I guess you haven't heard from Rebecca," I said, "or you wouldn't be here. You look very nice."

She looked me over and seemed surprised by what she saw. My own dress came from an upscale consignment shop called Nu-2-You where I occasionally bought clothes since I always needed something for one of the many formal parties and charity events we hosted at the vineyard. This dress was my favorite—silk, with a black-and-gray large floral print, low, square-cut neckline, beaded shoulder straps, and a deeply pleated skirt that swirled gracefully when I moved.

"That dress," Olivia said, "is absolutely stunning. And no, we haven't heard from her. We're contacting cab companies in D.C. to see if we can find out who picked her up and where they dropped her off."

"Why didn't you ask that professor what cab company she used?"

She pursed her lips. "Are you kidding? He couldn't even remember the color. Said he didn't really pay attention."

"What about contacting the D.C. police?"

"Sir Thomas has his own security people looking into this. He isn't ready to involve the police yet. Rebecca's actually more AWOL than missing. So far."

"What about the fact that she picked up something quite valuable?" I asked. "She's nearly four hours late now. Maybe someone followed her and robbed her. I know Rebecca. She'd put up a fight."

Olivia didn't look happy that I appeared to have some knowledge of why Rebecca had gone to Georgetown. I had a feeling she was dying to ask me how much I knew. Instead, she changed the subject.

"Our people are checking all the hospitals. If she's anywhere, we'll find her." She pulled on her evening coat. "I have a car waiting downstairs to take me to the National Building Museum. You're welcome to join me if you like."

Under the circumstances I didn't feel much like going to the gala, but Olivia and Sir Thomas would be the first to hear if their security people found Rebecca, and that's where they'd be. It was a quick ride from the Willard to the Building Museum—though I still thought of it by its former name, the Pension Building—but Olivia, who never seemed to tire of asking questions, continued to quiz me about Rebecca.

"How did you two meet?"

"In college."

"What was she like back then?"

"Smart, ambitious. Like she is now."

"She never talks about her family, but I have a feeling she didn't come from money." Her tone of voice implied that this was a major character flaw.

"Oh, really?" I'd had enough of being grilled and Rebecca's private life was none of her business. "You know, the only person we haven't talked about since we met is you. How'd you get this job, if you don't mind my asking?"

"I . . . well." She sat up straighter. "I've known Sir Thomas all my life. My father manages several private investment funds and he and Sir Thomas do business together. When my predecessor moved to our London office five years ago, he asked Daddy if I'd be interested in the position."

I'd never called my father anything but "Leland," which is what he wanted me to call him. He wasn't a Daddy kind of dad.

"Thomas Asher Investments is a family business," Olivia went on, emphasizing the word *family*.

"Sir Thomas and Lady Asher take care of us like we're their children. As a result we're a pretty tight-knit group—we party together, take vacations together, that sort of thing. That's why we're so well run and successful. Everyone's incredibly loyal to them. Outsiders just don't get that. Sir Thomas watched me grow up and he knew I'd understand the world he lives in. Knew I'd understand what would be involved in working as closely with him as I do."

She was starting to sound like an infomercial . . . or a cult member.

"Rebecca is part of the family, too?"

Olivia hesitated. "Of course she is. She, ah . . . well, yes."

Maybe only because Rebecca was Tommy Asher's protégée. It didn't sound like much love lost there. Perhaps Olivia was jealous.

Her phone rang and she turned away to answer it. I heard a series of "uh-huhs" as our driver pulled up in front of the redbrick Pension Building. Though it was a full city block long, the curbs were choked with limousines, taxis, and cars with official or diplomatic license plates. Police directed traffic as men with wires in their ears scanned the crowd.

Then Olivia said, sounding grim, "Sure, I'll tell him."

She disconnected.

"What's wrong?" I asked.

"Rebecca's cab dropped her off in front of some restaurant in Georgetown after she retrieved Sir Thomas's package," she said. "Near the corner of Wisconsin Avenue and P Street, wherever that is. The cabbie said she stood there as though she were waiting for someone to pick her up."

I thought about Rebecca and her trysts at school with Connor. Both of them had managed to keep their affair off the radar for more than a year until someone spotted her slipping into a motel room and recognized his car in the parking lot with its faculty parking sticker.

"What time?" I asked.

"Around three." She checked the clock on her phone. "That was four hours ago."

"Perhaps she's still with her friend."

Olivia's eyes flashed as she flounced out of the car. "Then she's got a hell of a lot of explaining to do. A few of us are ready to kill her."

She sounded like she meant it literally. I wondered who else at Thomas Asher Investments was on the list of people who did not like Rebecca . . . and where she was and with whom on a cold, dark evening when she was supposed to be at her boss's star-studded gala. The sleek black dress hanging in the closet in the Willard; her invitation to me to be her guest . . . Rebecca meant to be here.

If she wasn't, it was because she had been detained by something or someone. And I didn't think it was willingly, either.